"You will find warriors of every shape, size, and color in these pages, warriors from every epoch of human history, from yesterday and today and tomorrow, and from worlds that never were. Some of the stories will make you sad, some will make you laugh, and many will keep you on the edge of your seat."

—George R. R. Martin,
from his introduction to *Warriors*

PRAISE FOR *WARRIORS*

"Pure entertainment."
—*Publishers Weekly*

"Entirely successful . . . There really is something for everybody in it."
—*Booklist*

"Hero-sized . . . Nary a dud to be found."
—*The Miami Herald*

"Well worth the cover price—consistently entertaining throughout."
—*Locus*

WARRIORS 2

EDITED BY

GEORGE R. R. MARTIN

AND

GARDNER DOZOIS

TOR®
fantasy

A TOM DOHERTY ASSOCIATES BOOK
NEW YORK

This is a work of fiction. All of the characters, organizations, and events portrayed in these stories are either products of the authors' imaginations or are used fictitiously.

WARRIORS 2

Copyright © 2010 by George R. R. Martin and Gardner Dozois

All rights reserved.

A Tor Book
Published by Tom Doherty Associates, LLC
175 Fifth Avenue
New York, NY 10010

www.tor-forge.com

Tor® is a registered trademark of Tom Doherty Associates, LLC.

ISBN 978-0-7653-6027-4

First Edition: March 2010
First Mass Market Edition: June 2011

Printed in the United States of America

0 9 8 7 6 5 4 3 2 1

Copyright Acknowledgments

To Lauren and Jeff,
to Tyler and Isabella,
to Sean and Dean,

may you be strangers to war

Contents

Introduction

Stories from the Spinner Rack
by George R. R. Martin

There were no bookstores in Bayonne, New Jersey, when I was a kid.

Which is not to say there was no place to buy a book. There were plenty of places to buy books, so long as what you wanted was a paperback. (If you wanted a hardcover, you could take the bus into New York City.) Most of those places were what we called "candy stores" back then, but Hershey bars and Milky Ways and penny candy were the least of what they sold. Every candy store was a little different from every other. Some carried groceries and some didn't, some had soda fountains and some didn't, some offered fresh baked goods in the morning and would make you a deli sandwich all day long, some sold squirt guns and hula hoops and those pink rubber balls we used for our stickball games . . . but all of them sold newspapers, magazines, comic books, and paperbacks.

When I was growing up in Bayonne's projects, my local candy store was a little place on the corner of First Street and Kelly Parkway, across the street from the waters of the Kill Van Kull. The "book section" was a wire spinner rack, taller than I was, that stood right next to the comics . . . perfect placement for me, once my reading had expanded beyond funny books. My allowance was a dollar a week, and figuring out how I was going to split that up between ten-cent comic books (when the price went up to twelve cents, it really blew the hell out of my budget), thirty-five-cent paperbacks, a candy bar or two, the infrequent quarter malt or ice cream soda, and an occasional game of Skee-Ball at Uncle Milty's down the block was always one of the more agonizing decisions of the week, and honed my math skills to the utmost.

The comic book racks and the paperback spinner had more in common than mere proximity. Neither one recognized the existence of genre. In those days, the superheroes had not yet reached the same level of dominance in comics that they presently enjoy. Oh, we had Superman and Batman and the JLA, of course, and later on Spider-Man and the Fantastic Four came along to join them, but there were all sorts of other comic books as well—war comics, crime comics, western comics, romance comics for the girls, movie and television tie-ins, strange hybrids like *Turok, Son of Stone* (Indians meet dinosaurs, and call them "honkers"). You had Archie and Betty and Veronica and *Cosmo the Merry Martian* for laughs, you had Casper the Friendly Ghost and Baby Huey for littler kids (I was much too sophisticated for those), you had Carl Barks drawing Donald Duck and Uncle Scrooge. You had hot rod comics, you had comics about models complete with cut-out clothes, and, of course, you had *Classics Illustrated*, whose literary adaptations served as my first introduction to everyone from Robert Louis Stevenson to Herman Melville. *And all these different comics were mixed together.*

The same was true of the paperbacks in the adjacent spinner rack. There was only the one spinner, and it had only so many pockets, so there were never more than one or two copies of any particular title. I had been a science fiction fan since a friend of my mother's had given me a copy of Robert A. Heinlein's *Have Space Suit—Will Travel* one year for Christmas (for the better part of the decade, it was the only hardcover I owned), so I was always looking for more Heinlein, and more SF, but with the way all the books were mixed together, the only way to be sure of finding them was to flip through every book in every pocket, even if it meant getting down on your knees to check the titles in the back of the bottom level. Paperbacks were thinner then, so each pocket might hold four or five books, and every one was different. You'd find an Ace Double SF title cheek-by-jowl with a mass market reprint of *The Brothers Karamazov*, sandwiched in between a nurse novel and the latest Mike Hammer yarn from Mickey Spillane. Dorothy Parker and Dorothy Sayers shared rack space with Ralph Ellison and J. D. Salinger. Max Brand rubbed up against Barbara Cartland. (Barbara would have been mortified.) A. E. van Vogt, P. G. Wodehouse, and H. P. Lovecraft were crammed in together with F. Scott Fitzgerald. Mysteries, westerns, gothics, ghost stories, classics of English literature, the latest contemporary "literary" novels, and, of course, SF and fantasy and horror—you could find it all on that spinner rack in the little candy store at First Street and Kelly Parkway.

Looking back now, almost half a century later, I can see that that wire spinner rack had a profound impact on my later development as a writer. All writers are readers first, and all of us write the sort of books we want to read. I started out loving science fiction and I still love science fiction . . . but inevitably, digging through those paperbacks, I found myself intrigued by other sorts of books as well. I started reading horror when a book with Boris Karloff on the cover caught my attention. Robert E. Howard and L. Sprague de Camp hooked me on fantasy, just in the time for J. R. R. Tolkien and *The Lord of the Rings*. The historical epics of Dumas and Thomas B. Costain featured sword fights too, so I soon started reading those as well, and that led me to other epochs of history and other authors. When I came upon Charles Dickens and Mark Twain and Rudyard Kipling on the spinner rack, I grabbed them up too, to read the original versions of some of my favorite stories, and to see how they differered from the *Classics Illustrated* versions. Some of the mysteries I found on the rack had cover art so salacious that I had to smuggle them into the apartment and read them when my mother wasn't watching, but I sampled those as well, and have been reading mysteries ever since. Ian Fleming and James Bond led me into the world of thrillers and espionage novels, and Jack Schaefer's *Shane* into westerns. (Okay, I confess, I never did get into romances or nurse novels.) Sure, I knew the differences between a space opera and a hard-boiled detective story and a historical novel . . . but I never *cared* about such differences. It seemed to me, then as now, that there were good stories and bad stories, and that was the only distinction that truly mattered.

My views on that have not changed much in the half century since, but the world of publishing and bookselling certainly has. I don't doubt that there are still some old spinner racks out there, with all the books jumbled up together, but these days most people buy their reading material in chain superstores, where genre is king. SF and fantasy over here, mystery over there, romance back of that, bestsellers up front. No mixing and no mingling, please, keep to your own kind. "Literature" has its own section, now that the so-called "literary novel" has become a genre itself. Children's books and YAs are segregated.

It's good for selling books, I guess. It's convenient. Easy to find the sort of books you like. No one has to get down on their knees in hopes of finding Jack Vance's *Big Planet* behind that copy of *How to Win Friends and Influence People*.

But it's not good for readers, I suspect, and it's definitely not good for writers. Books should broaden us, take us to places we have never been and show us things we've never seen, expand our horizons and our way of looking at the world. Limiting your reading to a single genre defeats that. It limits us, makes us smaller.

Yet genre walls are hardening. During my own career, I have written science fiction, fantasy, and horror, and occasionally a few hybrids that were part this and part that, sometimes with elements of the murder mystery and the literary novel blended in. But younger writers starting out today are actively discouraged from doing the same by their editors and publishers. New fantasists are told that they had best adopt a pseudonym if they want to do a science fiction novel . . . and god help them if they want to try a mystery.

It's all in the name of selling more books, and I suppose it does.

But I say it's spinach, and I say to hell with it.

Bayonne may not have had any bookstores when I was growing up, but it did have a lot of pizza parlors, and a bar pie from Bayonne is among the best pizza anywhere. Small wonder that pizza is my favorite food. That doesn't mean I want to eat it every day, and to the exclusion of every other food in the world.

Which brings me to the book you hold in your hands.

These days I am best known as a fantasy writer, but *Warriors* is not a fantasy anthology . . . though it does have some good fantasy in it. My co-editor, Gardner Dozois, edited a science fiction magazine for a couple of decades, but *Warriors* is not a science fiction anthology either . . . though it does feature some SF stories as good as anything you'll find in *Analog* or *Asimov's*. It also features a western, and some mystery stories, a lot of fine historical fiction, some mainstream, and a couple of pieces that I won't even begin to try to label. *Warriors* is our own spinner rack.

People have been telling stories about warriors for as long as they have been telling stories. Since Homer first sang the wrath of Achilles and the ancient Sumerians set down their tales of Gilgamesh, warriors, soldiers, and fighters have fascinated us; they are a part of every culture, every literary tradition, every genre. *All Quiet on the Western Front, From Here to Eternity,* and *The Red Badge of Courage* have become part of our literary canons, taught in classrooms all around the country and the world. Fantasy has given us such memorable warriors as Conan the Barbarian, Elric of Melnibone, and Aragorn son of Arathorn. Science fiction offers us glimpses of the wars and warriors of the future, in books like Robert A. Heinlein's *Starship Troopers,* Joe W. Haldeman's *Forever War,* and the space operas of David Weber, Lois McMaster Bujold, and Walter Jon Williams. The gunslinger of the classic western is a warrior. The mystery genre has made an archetype of the urban warrior, be he a cop, a hit man, a wiseguy, or one of those private eyes who walks the mean streets of Chandler and Hammett. Women warriors, child soldiers, warriors of the gridiron and the cricket pitch, the Greek hoplite and Roman legionary, Viking, musketeer, crusader, and doughboy, the GI of World War II and the grunt of Vietnam . . . all of them are warriors, and you'll find many in these pages.

Our contributors make up an all-star lineup of award-winning and bestselling writers, representing a dozen different publishers and as many genres. We asked each of them for the same thing—a story about a warrior. Some chose to write in the genre for which they're best known. Some decided to try something different. You will find warriors of every shape, size, and color in these pages, warriors from every epoch of human history, from yesterday and today and tomorrow, and worlds that never were. Some of the stories will make you sad, some will make you laugh, many will keep you on the edge of your seat.

But you won't know which until you've read them, for Gardner and I, in the tradition of that old wire spinner rack, have mixed them all up. There's no science fiction section here, no shelves reserved just for historical novels, no romance rack, no walls or labels of any sort. Just stories. Some are by your favorite writers, we hope; others, by writers you may never have heard of (yet). It's our hope that by the time you finish this book, a few of the latter may have become the former.

So spin the rack and turn the page. We have some stories to tell you.

WARRIORS 2

Naomi Novik

Born in New York City, where she still lives with her mystery-editor husband and six computers, Naomi Novik is a first-generation American who was raised on Polish fairy tales, Baba Yaga, and Tolkien. After doing graduate work in computer science at Columbia University, she participated in the development of the computer game *Neverwinter Nights: Shadows of Undrentide,* and then decided to try her hand at novels. A good decision! The resultant Temeraire series—consisting of *His Majesty's Dragon, Black Powder War, Throne of Jade,* and *Empire of Ivory*—describing an alternative version of the Napoleonic Wars where dragons are used as living weapons, has been phenomenally popular and successful. Her most recent book is a new Temeraire novel, *Victory of Eagles.*

Here she takes us on an evocative visit to a distant planet of intricate and interlocking biological mysteries for a harrowing demonstration that it's unwise to strike at an enemy before you're sure they can't strike *back*. . . .

Seven Years from Home

Preface

Seven days passed for me on my little raft of a ship as I fled Melida; seven years for the rest of the unaccelerated universe. I hoped to be forgotten, a dusty footnote left at the bottom of a page. Instead I came off to trumpets and medals and legal charges, equal doses of acclaim and venom, and I stumbled bewildered through the brassy noise, led first by one and then by another, while my last opportunity to enter any protest against myself escaped.

Now I desire only to correct the worst of the factual inaccuracies bandied about, so far as my imperfect memory will allow, and to make an offering of my own understanding to that smaller and more sophisticated audience who prefer to shape the world's opinion rather than be shaped by it.

I engage not to tire you with a recitation of dates and events and quotations. I do not recall them with any precision myself. But I must warn you that neither have I succumbed to that pathetic and otiose impulse to sanitize the events of the war, or to excuse sins either my own or belonging to others. To do so would be a lie, and on Melida, to tell a lie was an insult more profound than murder.

I will not see my sisters again, whom I loved. Here we say that one who takes the long midnight voyage has leaped ahead in time, but to me it seems it is they who have traveled on ahead. I can no longer hear their voices when I am awake. I hope this will silence them in the night.

Ruth Patrona
Reivaldt, Janvier 32, 4765

The First Adjustment

I disembarked at the port of Landfall in the fifth month of 4753. There is such a port on every world where the Confederacy has set its foot but not yet its flag: crowded and dirty and charmless. It was on the Esperigan continent, as the Melidans would not tolerate the construction of a spaceport in their own territory.

Ambassador Kostas, my superior, was a man of great authority and presence, two meters tall and solidly built, with a jovial handshake, high intelligence, and very little patience for fools; that I was likely to be relegated to this category was evident on our first meeting. He disliked my assignment to begin with. He thought well of the Esperigans; he moved in their society as easily as he did in our own, and would have called one or two of their senior ministers his personal friends, if only such a gesture were not highly unprofessional. He recognized his duty, and on an abstract intellectual level the potential value of the Melidans, but they revolted him, and he would have been glad to find me of like mind, ready to draw a line through their name and give them up as a bad cause.

A few moments' conversation was sufficient to disabuse him of this hope. I wish to attest that he did not allow the disappointment to in any way alter the performance of his duty, and he could not have objected with more vigor to my project of proceeding at once to the Melidan continent, to his mind a suicidal act.

In the end he chose not to stop me. I am sorry if he later regretted that, as seems likely. I took full advantage of the weight of my arrival. Five years had gone by on my homeworld of Terce since I had embarked, and there is a certain moral force to having sacrificed a former life for the one unknown. I had observed it often with new arrivals on Terce: their first requests were rarely refused even when foolish, as they often were. I was of course quite sure my own were eminently sensible.

"We will find you a guide," he said finally, yielding, and all the machinery of the Confederacy began to turn to my desire, a heady sensation.

Badea arrived at the embassy not two hours later. She wore a plain gray wrap around her shoulders, draped to the ground, and another wrap around her head. The alterations visible were only small ones: a smattering of green freckles across the bridge of her nose and cheeks, a greenish tinge to her lips and nails.

Her wings were folded and hidden under the wrap, adding the bulk roughly of an overnight hiker's backpack. She smelled a little like the sourdough used on Terce to make roundbread, noticeable but not unpleasant. She might have walked through a spaceport without exciting comment.

She was brought to me in the shambles of my new office, where I had barely begun to lay out my things. I was wearing a conservative black suit, my best, tailored because you could not buy trousers for women ready-made on Terce, and, thankfully, comfortable shoes, because elegant ones on Terce were not meant to be walked in. I remember my clothing particularly because I was in it for the next week without opportunity to change.

"Are you ready to go?" she asked me as soon as we were introduced and the receptionist had left.

I was quite visibly *not* ready to go, but this was not a misunderstanding: she did not want to take me. She thought the request stupid, and feared my safety would be a burden on her. If Ambassador Kostas would not mind my failure to return, she could not know that, and to be just, he would certainly have reacted unpleasantly in any case, figuring it as his duty.

But when asked for a favor she does not want to grant, a Melidan will sometimes offer it anyway, only in an unacceptable or awkward way. Another Melidan will recognize this as a refusal, and withdraw the request. Badea did not expect this courtesy from me; she only expected that I would say I could not leave at once. This she could count to her satisfaction as a refusal, and she would not come back to offer again.

I was, however, informed enough to be dangerous, and I did recognize the custom. I said, "It is inconvenient, but I am prepared to leave immediately." She turned at once and walked out of my office, and I followed her. It is understood that a favor accepted despite the difficulty and constraints laid down by the giver must be necessary to the recipient, as indeed this was to me; but in such a case, the conditions must then be endured, even if artificial.

I did not risk a pause at all even to tell anyone I was going; we walked out past the embassy secretary and the guards, who did not do more than give us a cursory glance—we were going the wrong way, and my citizen's button would likely have saved us interruption in any case. Kostas would not know I had gone until my absence was noticed and the security logs examined.

The Second Adjustment

I was not unhappy as I followed Badea through the city. A little discomfort was nothing to me next to the intense satisfaction of, as I felt, having passed a first test: I had gotten past all resistance offered me, both by Kostas and Badea, and soon I would be in the heart of a people I already felt I knew. Though I would be an outsider among them, I had lived all my life to the present day in the self-same state, and I did not fear it, or for the moment anything else.

Badea walked quickly and with a freer stride than I was used to, loose-limbed. I was taller, but had to stretch to match her. Esperigans looked at her as she went by, and then looked at me, and the pressure of their gaze was suddenly hostile. "We might take a taxi," I offered. Many were passing by empty. "I can pay."

"No," she said, with a look of distaste at one of those conveyances, so we continued on foot.

After Melida, during my black-sea journey, my doctoral dissertation on the Canaan movement was published under the escrow clause, against my will. I have never used the funds, which continue to accumulate steadily. I do not like to inflict them on any cause I admire sufficiently to support, so they will go to my family when I have gone; my nephews will be glad of it, and of the passing of an embarrassment, and that is as much good as it can be expected to provide.

There is a great deal within that book that is wrong, and more that is wrongheaded, in particular any expression of opinion or analysis I interjected atop the scant collection of accurate facts I was able to accumulate in six years of overenthusiastic graduate work. This little is true: The Canaan movement was an offshoot of conservation philosophy. Where the traditionalists of that movement sought to restrict humanity to dead worlds and closed enclaves on others, the Canaan splinter group wished instead to alter themselves while they altered their new worlds, meeting them halfway.

The philosophy had the benefit of a certain practicality, as genetic engineering and body modification were and remain considerably cheaper than terraforming, but we are a squeamish and a violent species, and nothing invites pogrom more surely than the neighbor who is different from us, yet still too close. In consequence, the Melidans were by our present day the last surviving Canaan society.

They had come to Melida and settled the larger of the two continents some eight hundred years before. The Esperigans came two hundred years later, refugees from the plagues on New Victoire, and took the smaller continent. The two had little contact for the first half millennium; we of the Confederacy are given to think in worlds and solar systems, and to imagine that only a space voyage is long, but a hostile continent is vast enough to occupy a small and struggling band. But both prospered, each according to their lights, and by the time I landed, half the planet glittered in the night from space, and half was yet pristine.

In my dissertation, I described the ensuing conflict as natural, which is fair if slaughter and pillage are granted to be natural to our kind. The Esperigans had exhausted the limited raw resources of their share of the planet, and a short flight away was the untouched expanse of the larger continent, not a tenth as populated as their own. The Melidans controlled their birthrate, used only sustainable quantities, and built nothing that could not be eaten by the wilderness a year after they had abandoned it. Many Esperigan philosophes and politicians trumpeted their admiration of Melidan society, but this was only a sort of pleasant spiritual refreshment, as one admires a saint or a martyr without ever wishing to be one.

The invasion began informally, with adventurers and entrepreneurs, with the desperate, the poor, the violent. They began to land on the shores of the Melidan territory, to survey, to take away samples, to plant their own foreign roots. They soon had a village, then more than one. The Melidans told them to leave, which worked as well as it ever has in the annals of colonialism, and then attacked them. Most of the settlers were killed; enough survived and straggled back across the ocean to make a dramatic story of murder and cruelty out of it.

I expressed the conviction to the Ministry of State, in my preassignment report, that the details had been exaggerated, and that the attacks had been provoked more extensively. I was wrong, of course. But at the time I did not know it.

Badea took me to the low quarter of Landfall, so called because it faced on the side of the ocean downcurrent from the spaceport. Iridescent oil and a floating mat of discards glazed the edge of the surf. The houses were mean and crowded tightly upon one another, broken up mostly by liquor stores and bars. Docks stretched out into the ocean, extended long to reach out past the pollution, and just past the end of one of these floated a small boat, little more than a simple coracle: a hull of brown bark, a narrow brown mast, a gray-green sail slack and trembling in the wind.

We began walking out toward it, and those watching—there were some men loitering about the docks, fishing idly, or working on repairs to equipment or nets—began to realize then that I meant to go with her.

The Esperigans had already learned the lesson we like to teach as often as we can, that the Confederacy is a bad enemy and a good friend, and while no one is ever made to join us by force, we cannot be opposed directly. We had given them the spaceport already, an open door to the rest of the settled worlds, and they wanted more, the moth yearning. I relied on this for protection, and did not consider that however much they wanted from our outstretched hand, they still more wished to deny its gifts to their enemy.

Four men rose as we walked the length of the dock, and made a line across it. "You don't want to go with that one, ma'am," one of them said to me, a parody of respect. Badea said nothing. She moved a little aside, to see how I would answer them.

"I am on assignment for my government," I said, neatly offering a red flag to a bull, and moved toward them. It was not an attempt at bluffing: on Terce, even though I was immodestly unveiled, men would have at once moved out of the way to avoid any chance of the insult of physical contact. It was an act so automatic as to be invisible: precisely what we are taught to watch for in ourselves, but that proves infinitely easier in the instruction than in the practice. I did not *think* they would move; I knew they would.

Perhaps that certainty transmitted itself: the men did move a little, enough to satisfy my unconscious that they were cooperating with my expectations, so that it took me wholly by surprise and horror when one reached out and put his hand on my arm to stop me.

I screamed, in full voice, and struck him. His face is lost to my memory, but I still can see clearly the man behind him, his expression as full of appalled violation as my own. The four of them flinched from my scream, and then drew in around me, protesting and reaching out in turn.

I reacted with more violence. I had confidently considered myself a citizen of no world and of many, trained out of assumptions and unaffected by the parochial attitudes of the one where chance had seen me born, but in that moment I could with actual pleasure have killed all of them. That wish was unlikely to be gratified. I was taller, and the gravity of Terce is slightly higher than of Melida, so I was stronger than they expected me to be, but they were laborers and seamen, built generously and rough-hewn, and the male advantage in muscle mass tells quickly in a hand-to-hand fight.

They tried to immobilize me, which only panicked me further. The mind curls in on itself in such a moment; I remember palpably only the sensation of sweating copiously, and the way this caused the seam of my blouse to rub unpleasantly against my neck as I struggled.

Badea told me later that, at first, she had meant to let them hold me. She could then leave, with the added satisfaction of knowing the Esperigan fishermen and not she had provoked an incident with the

Confederacy. It was not sympathy that moved her to action, precisely. The extremity of my distress was as alien to her as to them, but where they thought me mad, she read it in the context of my having accepted her original conditions and somewhat unwillingly decided that I truly did need to go with her, even if she did not know precisely why and saw no use in it herself.

I cannot tell you precisely how the subsequent moments unfolded. I remember the green gauze of her wings overhead perforated by the sun, like a linen curtain, and the blood spattering my face as she neatly lopped off the hands upon me. She used for the purpose a blade I later saw in use for many tasks, among them harvesting fruit off plants where the leaves or the bark may be poisonous. It is shaped like a sickle and strung upon a thick elastic cord, which a skilled wielder can cause to become rigid or to collapse.

I stood myself back on my feet panting, and she landed. The men were on their knees screaming, and others were running toward us down the docks. Badea swept the severed hands into the water with the side of her foot and said calmly, "We must go."

The little boat had drawn up directly beside us over the course of our encounter, drawn by some signal I had not seen her transmit. I stepped into it behind her. The coracle leapt forward like a springing bird, and left the shouting and the blood behind.

We did not speak over the course of that strange journey. What I had thought a sail did not catch the wind, but opened itself wide and stretched out over our heads, like an awning, and angled itself toward the sun. There were many small filaments upon the surface wriggling when I examined it more closely, and also upon the exterior of the hull. Badea stretched herself out upon the floor of the craft, lying under the low deck, and I joined her in the small space: it was not uncomfortable or rigid, but had the queer unsettled cushioning of a waterbed.

The ocean crossing took only the rest of the day. How our speed was generated I cannot tell you; we did not seem to sit deeply in the water and our craft threw up no spray. The world blurred as a window running with rain. I asked Badea for water, once, and she put her hands on the floor of the craft and pressed down: in the depression she made, a small clear pool gathered for me to cup out, with a taste like slices of cucumber with the skin still upon them.

This was how I came to Melida.

The Third Adjustment

Badea was vaguely embarrassed to have inflicted me on her fellows, and having deposited me in the center of her village made a point of leaving me there by leaping aloft into the canopy where I could not follow, as a way of saying she was done with me, and anything I did henceforth could not be laid at her door.

I was by now hungry and nearly sick with exhaustion. Those who have not flown between worlds like to imagine the journey a glamorous one, but at least for minor bureaucrats, it is no more pleasant than any form of transport, only elongated. I had spent a week a virtual prisoner in my berth, the bed folding up to give me room to walk four strides back and forth, or to unfold my writing-desk, not both at once, with a shared toilet the size of an ungenerous closet down the hall. Landfall had not arrested my forward motion, as that mean port had never been my destination. Now, however, I was arrived, and the dregs of adrenaline were consumed in anticlimax.

Others before me have stood in a Melidan village center and described it for an audience—Esperigans mostly, anthropologists and students of biology and a class of tourists either adventurous or stupid. There is usually a lyrical description of the natives coasting overhead among some sort of vines or tree branches knitted overhead for shelter, the particulars and adjectives determined by the village latitude, and the obligatory explanation of the typical plan of huts, organized as a spoked wheel around the central plaza.

If I had been less tired, perhaps I, too, would have looked with so analytical an air, and might now satisfy my readers with a similar report. But to me the village only presented all the confusion of a wholly strange place, and I saw nothing that seemed to me deliberate. To call it a village gives a false air of comforting provinciality. Melidans, at least those with wings, move freely among a wide constellation of small settlements, so that all of these, in the public sphere, partake of the hectic pace of the city. I stood alone, and strangers moved past me with assurance, the confidence of their stride saying, "I care nothing for you or your fate. It is of no concern to me. How might you expect it to be otherwise?" In the end, I lay down on one side of the plaza and went to sleep.

I met Kitia the next morning. She woke me by prodding me with a twig, experimentally, having been selected for this task out of her group of school-mates by some complicated interworking of person-ality and chance. They giggled from a few safe paces back as I opened my eyes and sat up.

"Why are you sleeping in the square?" Kitia asked me, to a burst of fresh giggles.

"Where should I sleep?" I asked her.

"In a house!" she said.

When I had explained to them, not without some art, that I had no house here, they offered the censo-rious suggestion that I should go back to wherever I did have a house. I made a good show of looking analytically up at the sky overhead and asking them what our latitude was, and then I pointed at a ran-dom location and said, "My house is five years that way."

Scorn, puzzlement, and at last delight. I was from the stars! None of their friends had ever met anyone from so far away. One girl who previously had held a point of pride for having once visited the smaller continent, with an Esperigan toy doll to prove it, was instantly dethroned. Kitia possessively took my arm and informed me that as my house was too far away, she would take me to another.

Children of virtually any society are an excellent resource for the diplomatic servant or the anthropologist, if contact with them can be made without giving offense. They enjoy the unfamiliar experience of answering real questions, particularly the stupidly obvious ones that allow them to feel a sense of superiority over the inquiring adult, and they are easily impressed with the unusual. Kitia was a treasure. She led me, at the head of a small pied-piper procession, to an empty house on a convenient lane. It had been lately abandoned, and was already being reclaimed: the walls and floor were swarming with tiny insects with glossy dark blue carapaces, munching so industriously the sound of their jaws hummed like a summer afternoon.

I with difficulty avoided recoiling. Kitia did not hesitate: she walked into the swarm, crushing beetles by the dozens underfoot, and went to a small spigot in the far wall. When she turned this on, a clear viscous liquid issued forth, and the beetles scattered from it. "Here, like this," she said, showing me how to cup my hands under the liquid and spread it upon the walls and the floor. The disgruntled beetles withdrew, and the brownish surfaces began to bloom back to pale green, repairing the holes.

Over the course of that next week, she also fed me, corrected my manners and my grammar, and eventually brought me a set of clothing, a tunic and leggings, which she proudly informed me she had made herself in class. I thanked her with real sincerity and asked where I might wash my old clothing. She looked very puzzled, and when she had looked more closely at my clothing and touched it, she said, "Your clothing is dead! I thought it was only ugly."

Her gift was not made of fabric but a thin tough mesh of plant filaments with the feathered surface of a moth's wings. It gripped my skin eagerly as soon as I had put it on, and I thought myself at first allergic, because it itched and tingled, but this was only the bacteria bred to live in the mesh assiduously eating away the sweat and dirt and dead epidermal cells built up on my skin. It took me several more days to overcome all my instinct and learn to trust the living cloth with the more voluntary eliminations of my body also. (Previously I had been going out back to defecate in the woods, having been unable to find anything resembling a toilet, and meeting too much confusion when I tried to approach the question to dare pursue it further, for fear of encountering a taboo.)

And this was the handiwork of a child, not thirteen years of age! She could not explain to me how she had done it in any way that made sense to me. Imagine if you had to explain how to perform a reference search to someone who had not only never seen a library, but did not understand electricity, and who perhaps knew there was such a thing as written text, but did not himself read more than the alphabet. She took me once to her classroom after hours and showed me her workstation, a large wooden tray full of grayish moss, with a double row of small jars along the back each holding liquids or powders that I could distinguish only by their differing colors.

Her only tools were an assortment of syringes and eyedroppers and scoops and brushes.

I went back to my house and in the growing report I would not have a chance to send for another month I wrote, *These are a priceless people. We must have them.*

The Fourth Adjustment

All these first weeks, I made no contact with any other adult. I saw them go by occasionally, and the houses around mine were occupied, but they never spoke to me or even looked at me directly. None of them objected to my squatting, but that was less implicit endorsement and more an unwillingness even to acknowledge my existence. I talked to Kitia and the other children, and tried to be patient. I hoped an opportunity would offer itself eventually for me to be of some visible use.

In the event, it was rather my lack of use that led to the break in the wall. A commotion arose in the early morning, while Kitia was showing me the plan of her wings, which she was at that age beginning to design. She would grow the parasite over the subsequent year, and was presently practicing with miniature versions, which rose from her worktable surface gossamer-thin and fluttering with an involuntary muscle-twitching. I was trying to conceal my revulsion.

Kitia looked up when the noise erupted. She

casually tossed her example out of the window, to be pounced upon with a hasty scramble by several nearby birds, and went out the door. I followed her to the square: the children were gathered at the fringes, silent for once and watching. There were five women laid out on the ground, all bloody, one dead. Two of the others looked mortally wounded. They were all winged.

There were several working already on the injured, packing small brownish-white spongy masses into the open wounds and sewing them up. I would have liked to be of use, less from natural instinct than from the colder thought, which inflicted itself upon my mind, that any crisis opens social barriers. I am sorry to say I did not refrain from any noble self-censorship, but from the practical conviction that it was at once apparent my limited field-medical training could not in any valuable way be applied to the present circumstances.

I drew away, rather, to avoid being in the way as I could not turn the situation to my advantage, and in doing so ran up against Badea, who stood at the very edge of the square, observing.

She stood alone; there were no other adults nearby, and there was blood on her hands. "Are you hurt also?" I asked her.

"No," she returned shortly.

I ventured on concern for her friends, and asked her if they had been hurt in fighting. "We have heard rumors," I added, "that the Esperigans have been encroaching on your territory." It was the first opportunity I had been given of hinting at even this much of our official sympathy, as the children only shrugged when I asked them if there were fighting going on.

She shrugged, too, with one shoulder, and the folded wing rose and fell with it. But then she said, "They leave their weapons in the forest for us, even where they cannot have gone."

The Esperigans had several kinds of land mine technologies, including a clever mobile one that could be programmed with a target either as specific as an individual's genetic record or as general as a broadly defined body type—humanoid and winged, for instance—and set loose to wander until it found a match, then do the maximum damage it could. Only one side could carry explosive, as the other was devoted to the electronics. "The shrapnel, does it come only in one direction?" I asked, and made a fanned-out shape with my hands to illustrate. Badea looked at me sharply and nodded.

I explained the mine to her and described their manufacture. "Some scanning devices can detect them," I added, meaning to continue into an offer, but I had not finished the litany of materials before she was striding away from the square, without another word.

I was not dissatisfied with the reaction, in which I correctly read intention to put my information to immediate use, and two days later my patience was rewarded. Badea came to my house in the midmorning and said, "We have found one of them. Can you show us how to disarm them?"

"I am not sure," I told her honestly. "The safest option would be to trigger it deliberately, from afar."

"The plastics they use poison the ground."

"Can you take me to its location?" I asked. She considered the question with enough seriousness that I realized there was either taboo or danger involved.

"Yes," she said finally, and took me with her to a house near the center of the village. It had steps up to the roof, and from there we could climb to that of the neighboring house, and so on until we were high enough to reach a large basket, woven not of ropes but of a kind of vine, sitting in a crook of a tree. We climbed into this, and she kicked us off from the tree.

The movement was not smooth. The nearest I can describe is the sensation of being on a child's swing, except at that highest point of weightlessness you do not go backwards, but instead go falling into another arc, but at tremendous speed, and with a pungent smell like rotten pineapple all around from the shattering of the leaves of the trees through which we were propelled. I was violently sick after some five minutes. To the comfort of my pride if not my stomach, Badea was also sick, though more efficiently and over the side, before our journey ended.

There were two other women waiting for us in the tree where we came to rest, both of them also winged: Renata and Paudi. "It's gone another three hundred meters, toward Ighlan," Renata told us—another nearby Melidan village, as they explained to me.

"If it comes near enough to pick up traces of organized habitation, it will not trigger until it is inside the settlement, among as many people as possible," I said. "It may also have a burrowing mode, if it is the more expensive kind."

They took me down through the canopy, carefully, and walked before and behind me when we came to the ground. Their wings were spread wide enough to brush against the hanging vines to either side, and they regularly leapt aloft for a brief survey. Several times they moved me with friendly hands into a slightly different path, although my untrained eyes could make no difference among the choices.

A narrow trail of large ants—the reader will forgive me for calling them ants, they were nearly indistinguishable from those efficient creatures—paced us over the forest floor, which I did not recognize as significant until we came near the mine, and I saw it covered with the ants, who did not impede its movement but milled around and over it with intense interest.

"We have adjusted them so they smell the plastic," Badea said, when I asked. "We can make them eat it," she added, "but we worried it would set off the device."

The word *adjusted* scratches at the back of my mind again as I write this, that unpleasant tinny sensation of a term that does not allow of real translation and which has been inadequately replaced. I cannot improve upon the work of the official Confederacy translators, however; to encompass the true concept would require three dry, dusty chapters more suited to a textbook on the subject of biological engineering, which I am ill-qualified to produce. I do hope that I have successfully captured the wholly casual way she spoke of this feat. Our own scientists might replicate this act of genetic sculpting in any of two dozen excellent laboratories across the Confederacy—given several years, and a suitably impressive grant. They had done it in less than two days, as a matter of course.

I did not at the time indulge in admiration. The mine was ignoring the inquisitive ants and scuttling along at a good pace, the head with its glassy eye occasionally rotating upon its spindly spider-legs, and we had half a day in which to divert it from the village ahead.

Renata followed the mine as it continued on, while I sketched what I knew of the internals in the dirt for Badea and Paudi. Any sensible mine-maker will design the device to simply explode at any interference with its working other than the disable code, so our options were not particularly satisfying. "The most likely choice," I suggested, "would be the transmitter. If it becomes unable to receive the disable code, there may be a failsafe, which would deactivate it on a subsequent malfunction."

Paudi had on her back a case that, unfolded, looked very like a more elegant and compact version of little Kitia's worktable. She sat crosslegged with it on her lap and worked on it for some two hours' time, occasionally reaching down to pick up a handful of ants, which dropped into the green matrix of her table mostly curled up and died, save for a few survivors, which she herded carefully into an empty jar before taking up another sample.

I sat on the forest floor beside her, or walked with

Badea, who was pacing a small circle out around us, watchfully. Occasionally she would unsling her scythe-blade, and then put it away again, and once she brought down a mottie, a small lemurlike creature. I say lemur because there is nothing closer in my experience, but it had none of the charm of an Earth-native mammal; I rather felt an instinctive disgust looking at it, even before she showed me the tiny sucker-mouths full of hooked teeth with which it latched upon a victim.

She had grown a little more loquacious, and asked me about my own homeworld. I told her about Terce, and about the seclusion of women, which she found extremely funny, as we can only laugh at the follies of those far from us which threaten us not at all. The Melidans by design maintain a five-to-one ratio of women to men, as adequate to maintain a healthy gene pool while minimizing the overall resource consumption of their population. "They cannot take the wings, so it is more difficult for them to travel," she added, with one sentence dismissing the lingering mystery that had perplexed earlier visitors, of the relative rarity of seeing their men.

She had two children, which she described to me proudly, living presently with their father and half siblings in a village half a day's travel away, and she was considering a third. She had trained as a forest ranger, another inadequately translated term, which was at the time beginning to take on a military significance among them under the pressure of the Esperigan incursions.

"I'm done," Paudi said, and we went to catch up

Renata and find a nearby ant-nest, which looked like a mound of white cotton batting rising several inches off the forest floor. Paudi introduced her small group of infected survivors into this colony, and after a little confusion and milling about, they accepted their transplantation and marched inside. The flow of departures slowed a little momentarily, then resumed, and a file split off from the main channel of workers to march in the direction of the mine.

These joined the lingering crowd still upon the mine, but the new arrivals did not stop at inspection and promptly began to struggle to insinuate themselves into the casing. We withdrew to a safe distance, watching. The mine continued on without any slackening in its pace for ten minutes, as more ants began to squeeze themselves inside, and then it hesitated, one spindly metal leg held aloft uncertainly. It went a few more slightly drunken paces, and then abruptly the legs all retracted and left it a smooth round lump on the forest floor.

The Fifth Adjustment

They showed me how to use their communications technology and grew me an interface to my own small handheld, so my report was at last able to go. Kostas began angry, of course, having been forced to defend the manner of my departure to the Esperigans without the benefit of any understanding of the circumstances, but I sent the report an hour before I messaged, and by the time we spoke, he had read

enough to be in reluctant agreement with my conclusions if not my methods.

I was of course full of self-satisfaction. Freed at
long last from the academy and the walled gardens
of Terce, armed with false confidence in my research
and my training, I had so far achieved all that my
design had stretched to encompass. The Esperigan
blood had washed easily from my hands, and though
I answered Kostas meekly when he upbraided me,
privately I felt only impatience, and even he did not
linger long on the topic: I had been too successful,
and he had more important news.

The Esperigans had launched a small army two
days before, under the more pleasant-sounding name
of expeditionary defensive force. Its purpose was
to establish a permanent settlement on the Melidan
shore, some nine hundred miles from my present location, and begin the standard process of terraforming. The native life would be eradicated in spheres
of a hundred miles across at a time: first the broad
strokes of clear-cutting and the electrified nets, then
the irradiation of the soil and the air, and after that
the seeding of Earth-native microbes and plants. So
had a thousand worlds been made over anew, and
though the Esperigans had fully conquered their
own continent five centuries before, they still knew
the way.

He asked doubtfully if I thought some immediate
resistance could be offered. Disabling a few mines
scattered into the jungle seemed to him a small task.
Confronting a large and organized military force
was on a different order of magnitude. "I think we

can do something," I said, maintaining a veneer of caution for his benefit, and took the catalog of equipment to Badea as soon as we had disengaged.

She was occupied in organizing the retrieval of the deactivated mines, which the ants were now leaving scattered in the forests and jungles. A bird-of-paradise variant had been *adjusted* to make a meal out of the ants and take the glittery mines back to their treetop nests, where an observer might easily see them from above. She and the other collectors had so far found nearly a thousand of them. The mines made a neat pyramid, as of the harvested skulls of small cyclopean creatures with their dull eyes staring out lifelessly.

The Esperigans needed a week to cross the ocean in their numbers, and I spent it with the Melidans, developing our response. There was a heady delight in this collaboration. The work was easy and pleasant in their wide-open laboratories full of plants, roofed only with the fluttering sailcloth eating sunlight to give us energy, and the best of them coming from many miles distant to participate in the effort. The Confederacy spy-satellites had gone into orbit perhaps a year after our first contact: I likely knew more about the actual force than the senior administrators of Melida. I was in much demand, consulted not only for my information but also for my opinion.

In the ferment of our labors, I withheld nothing. This was not yet deliberate, but neither was it innocent. I had been sent to further a war, and if in the political calculus that had arrived at this solution the lives of soldiers were only variables, yet there was still a balance I was expected to preserve. It was not my duty to give the Melidans an easy victory, any more than it had been Kostas's to give one to the Esperigans.

A short and victorious war, opening a new and tantalizing frontier for restless spirits, would at once drive up that inconvenient nationalism which is the Confederacy's worst obstacle, and render less compelling the temptations we could offer to lure them into fully joining galactic society. On the other hand, to descend into squalor, a more equal kind of civil war has often proved extremely useful, and the more lingering and bitter the better. I was sent to the Melidans in hope that, given some guidance and what material assistance we could quietly provide without taking any official position, they might be an adequate opponent for the Esperigans to produce this situation.

There has been some criticism of the officials who selected me for this mission, but in their defense, it must be pointed out it was not in fact my assignment to actually provide military assistance, nor could anyone, even myself, have envisioned my proving remotely useful in such a role. I was only meant to be an early scout. My duty was to acquire cultural information enough to open a door for a party of military experts from Voca Libre, who would not reach Melida for another two years. Ambition and opportunity promoted me, and no official hand.

I think these experts arrived sometime during the third Esperigan offensive. I cannot pinpoint the date with any accuracy—I had by then ceased to track the days, and I never met them. I hope they can forgive my theft of their war; I paid for my greed.

The Esperigans used a typical carbonized steel in most of their equipment, as bolts and hexagonal nuts and screws with star-shaped heads, and woven into the tough mesh of their body armor. This was the target of our efforts. It was a new field of endeavor for the Melidans, who used metal as they used meat, sparingly and with a sense of righteousness in its avoidance. To them it was either a trace element needed in minute amounts, or an undesirable byproduct of the more complicated biological processes they occasionally needed to invoke.

However, they had developed some strains of bacteria to deal with this latter waste, and the speed with which they could manipulate these organisms was extraordinary. Another quantity of the ants—a convenient delivery mechanism used by the Melidans routinely, as I learned—were adjusted to render them deficient in iron and to provide a home in their bellies for the bacteria, transforming them into shockingly efficient engines of destruction. Set loose upon several of the mines as a trial, they devoured the carapaces and left behind only smudgy black heaps of carbon dust, carefully harvested for fertilizer, and the plastic explosives from within, nestled in their bed of copper wire and silicon.

The Esperigans landed, and at once carved themselves out a neat half moon of wasteland from the virgin shore, leaving no branches that might stretch above their encampment to offer a platform for attack. They established an electrified fence around the perimeter, with guns and patrols, and all this I observed with Badea, from a small platform in a vine-choked tree not far away: we wore the green-gray cloaks, and our faces were stained with leaf juice.

I had very little justification for inserting myself into such a role but the flimsy excuse of pointing out to Badea the most crucial section of their camp, when we had broken in. I cannot entirely say why I wished to go along on so dangerous an expedition. I am not particularly courageous. Several of my more unkind biographers have accused me of bloodlust, and pointed to this as a sequel to the disaster of my first departure. I cannot refute the accusation on the evidence, however I will point out that I chose that portion of the expedition which we hoped would encounter no violence.

But it is true I had learned already to seethe at the violent piggish blindness of the Esperigans, who would have wrecked all the wonders around me only to propagate yet another bland copy of Earth and suck dry the carcass of their own world. They were my enemy both by duty and by inclination, and I permitted myself the convenience of hating them. At the time, it made matters easier.

The wind was running from the east, and several of the Melidans attacked the camp from that side. The mines had yielded a quantity of explosive large enough to pierce the Esperigans' fence and shake the trees even as far as our lofty perch. The wind carried the smoke and dust and flames toward us, obscuring the ground and rendering the soldiers in their own camp only vague ghostlike suggestions of human shape. The fighting was hand-to-hand, and the stutter of gunfire came only tentatively through the chaos of the smoke.

Badea had been holding a narrow cord, one end weighted with a heavy seedpod. She now poured a measure of water onto the pod, from her canteen, then flung it out into the air. It sailed over the fence and landed inside the encampment, behind one of the neat rows of storage tents. The seedpod struck the ground and immediately burst like a ripe fruit, an anemone tangle of waving roots creeping out over the ground and anchoring the cord, which she had secured at this end around one thick branch.

We let ourselves down it, hand over hand. There was none of that typical abrasion or friction that I might have expected from rope; my hands felt as cool and comfortable when we descended as when we began. We ran into the narrow space between the tents. I was experiencing that strange elongation of time that crisis can occasionally produce: I was conscious of each footfall, and of the seeming-long moments it took to place each one.

There were wary soldiers at many of the tent entrances, likely those that held either the more valuable munitions or the more valuable men. Their discipline had not faltered, even while the majority of the force was already orchestrating a response to the Melidan assault on the other side of the encampment. But we did not need to penetrate into the tents. The guards were rather useful markers for us, showing me which of the tents were the more significant. I pointed out to Badea the cluster of four tents, each guarded at either side by a pair, near the farthest end of the encampment.

Badea looked here and there over the ground as we darted under cover of smoke from one alleyway to another, the walls of waxed canvas muffling the distant shouts and the sound of gunfire. The dirt still had the yellowish tinge of Melidan soil—the Esperigans had not yet irradiated it—but it was crumbly and dry, the fine fragile native moss crushed and much torn by heavy boots and equipment, and the wind raised little dervishes of dust around our ankles.

"This ground will take years to recover fully," she said to me, soft and bitterly, as she stopped us and knelt behind a deserted tent not far from our target. She gave me a small ceramic implement, which looked much like the hair-picks sometimes worn on Terce by women with hair that never knew a blade's edge: a raised comb with three teeth, though on the tool these were much longer and sharpened at the end. I picked the ground vigorously, stabbing deep to aerate the wounded soil, while she judiciously poured out a mixture of water and certain organic extracts, and sowed a packet of seeds.

This may sound a complicated operation to be carrying out in an enemy camp, in the midst of battle, but we had practiced the maneuver, and indeed had we been glimpsed, anyone would have been hard-pressed to recognize a threat in the two gray-wrapped lumps crouched low as we pawed at the dirt. Twice while we worked, wounded soldiers were carried in a rush past either end of our alleyway, toward shelter. We were not seen.

The seeds she carried, though tiny, burst readily, and began to thrust out spiderweb-fine rootlets at such a speed, they looked like nothing more than squirming maggots. Badea without concern moved her hands around them, encouraging them into the ground. When they were established, she motioned me to stop my work, and she took out the prepared ants: a much greater number of them, with a dozen of the fat yellow wasp-sized brood-mothers. Tipped out into the prepared and welcoming soil, they immediately began to burrow their way down, with the anxious harrying of their subjects and spawn.

Badea watched for a long while, crouched over, even after the ants had vanished nearly all beneath the surface. The few who emerged and darted back inside, the faint trembling of the rootlets, the shifting grains of dirt, all carried information to her. At length satisfied, she straightened, saying, "Now—"

The young soldier was I think only looking for somewhere to piss, rather than investigating some noise. He came around the corner already fumbling at his belt, and seeing us did not immediately shout, likely from plain surprise, but grabbed for Badea's shoulder first. He was clean-shaven, and the name on his lapel badge was RIDANG. I drove the soil-pick into his eye. I was taller, so the stroke went downward, and he fell backwards to his knees away from me, clutching at his face.

He did not die at once. There must be very few deaths that come immediately, though we often like to comfort ourselves by the pretense that this failure of the body, or that injury, must at once eradicate consciousness and life and pain all together. Here sentience lasted several moments which seemed to me long: his other eye was open, and looked at me while his hands clawed for the handle of the pick. When this had faded, and he had fallen supine to the ground, there was yet a convulsive movement of all the limbs and a trickling of blood from mouth and nose and eye before the final stiffening jerk left the body emptied and inanimate.

I watched him die in a strange parody of serenity, all feeling hollowed out of me, and then turning away vomited upon the ground. Behind me, Badea cut open his belly and his thighs and turned him facedown onto the dirt, so the blood and the effluvia leaked out of him. "That will do a little good for the ground at least, before they carry him away to waste him," she said. "Come." She touched my shoulder, not unkindly, but I flinched from the touch as from a blow.

It was not that Badea or her fellows were indifferent to death, or casual toward murder. But there is a price to be paid for living in a world whose native hostilities have been cherished rather than crushed. Melidan life expectancy is some ten years beneath that of Confederacy citizens, though they are on average healthier and more fit both genetically and physically.

In their philosophy, a human life is not inherently superior and to be valued over any other kind. Accident and predation claim many, and living intimately with the daily cruelties of nature dulls the facility for sentiment. Badea enjoyed none of that comforting distance that allows us to think ourselves assured of the full potential span of life, and therefore suffered none of the pangs when confronted with evidence to the contrary. I looked at my victim and saw my own face; so, too, did she, but she had lived all her life so aware, and it did not bow her shoulders.

Five days passed before the Esperigan equipment began to come apart. Another day halted all their work, and in confusion they retreated to their encampment. I did not go with the Melidan company that destroyed them to the last man.

Contrary to many accusations, I did not lie to Kostas in my report and pretend surprise. I freely confessed to him I had expected the result, and truthfully explained I had not wished to make claims of which I was unsure. I never deliberately sought to deceive any of my superiors or conceal information from them, save in such small ways. At first I was not Melidan enough to wish to do so, and later I was too Melidan to feel anything but revulsion at the concept.

He and I discussed our next steps in the tigerdance. I described as best I could the Melidan technology, and after consultation with various Confederacy experts, it was agreed he would quietly mention to the Esperigan minister of defense, at their weekly luncheon, a particular Confederacy technology: ceramic coatings, which could be ordered at vast expense and two years' delay from Bel Rios. Or, he would suggest, if the Esperigans wished to deed some land to the Confederacy, a private entrepreneurial concern might fund the construction of a local fabrication plant, and produce them at much less cost, in six months' time.

The Esperigans took the bait, and saw only private greed behind this apparent breach of neutrality: imagining Kostas an investor in this private concern, they winked at his veniality, and eagerly helped us to their own exploitation. Meanwhile, they continued occasional and tentative incursions into the Melidan continent, probing the coastline, but the disruption they created betrayed their attempts, and whichever settlement was nearest would at once deliver them a present of the industrious ants, so these met with no greater success than the first.

Through these months of brief and grudging detente, I traveled extensively throughout the continent. My journals are widely available, being the domain of our government, but they are shamefully sparse, and I apologize to my colleagues for it. I would have been more diligent in my work if I had imagined I would be the last and not the first such chronicler. At the time, giddy with success, I went with more the spirit of a holidaymaker than a researcher, and I sent only those images and notes which it was pleasant to me to record, with the excuse of limited capacity to send my reports.

For what cold comfort it may be, I must tell you photography and description are inadequate to convey the experience of standing in the living heart of a world alien yet not hostile, and when I walked hand in hand with Badea along the crest of a great canyon wall and looked down over the ridges of purple and gray and ocher at the gently waving tendrils of an elacca forest, which in my notorious video recordings can provoke nausea in nearly every observer, I felt the first real stir of an unfamiliar sensation of beauty-in-strangeness, and I laughed in delight and surprise, while she looked at me and smiled.

We returned to her village three days later and saw the bombing as we came, the new Esperigan long-range fighter planes like narrow silver knife-blades making low passes overhead, the smoke rising black and oily against the sky. Our basket-journey could not be accelerated, so we could only cling to the sides and wait as we were carried onward. The planes and the smoke were gone before we arrived; the wreckage was not.

I was angry at Kostas afterwards, unfairly. He was no more truly the Esperigans' confidant than they were his, but I felt at the time that it was his business to know what they were about, and he had failed to warn me. I accused him of deliberate concealment; he told me, censoriously, that I had known the risk when I had gone to the continent, and he could hardly be responsible for preserving my safety while I slept in the very war zone. This silenced my tirade, as I realized how near I had come to betraying myself. Of course he would not have wanted me to warn the Melidans; it had not yet occurred to him I would have wished to, myself. I ought not have wanted to.

Forty-three people were killed in the attack. Kitia was yet lingering when I came to her small bedside. She was in no pain, her eyes cloudy and distant, already withdrawing; her family had been and gone again. "I knew you were coming back, so I asked them to let me stay a little longer," she told me. "I wanted to say good-bye." She paused and added uncertainly, "And I was afraid, a little. Don't tell."

I promised her I would not. She sighed and said, "I shouldn't wait any longer. Will you call them over?"

The attendant came when I raised my hand, and he asked Kitia, "Are you ready?"

"Yes," she said, a little doubtful. "It won't hurt?"

"No, not at all," he said, already taking out with a gloved hand a small flat strip from a pouch, filmy green and smelling of raspberries. Kitia opened her mouth, and he laid it on her tongue. It dissolved almost at once, and she blinked twice and was asleep. Her hand went cold a few minutes later, still lying between my own.

I stood with her family when we laid her to rest the next morning. The attendants put her carefully down in a clearing, and sprayed her from a distance, the smell of cut roses just going to rot, and stepped back. Her parents wept noisily; I stayed dry-eyed as any seemly Terce matron, displaying my assurance of the ascension of the dead. The birds came first, and the motties, to pluck at her eyes and her lips, and the beetles hurrying with a hum of eager jaws to deconstruct her into raw parts. They did not have long to feast: the forest itself was devouring her from below in a green tide rising, climbing in small creepers up her cheeks and displacing them all.

When she was covered over, the mourners turned away and went to join the shared wake behind us in the village square. They threw uncertain and puzzled looks at my remaining as they went past, and at my tearless face. But she was not yet gone: there was a suggestion of a girl lingering there, a collapsing scaffold draped in an unhurried carpet of living things. I did not leave, though behind me there rose a murmur of noise as the families of the dead spoke reminiscences of their lost ones.

Near dawn, the green carpeting slipped briefly. In the dim watery light I glimpsed for one moment an emptied socket full of beetles, and I wept.

The Sixth Adjustment

I will not claim, after this, that I took the wings only from duty, but I refute the accusation I took them in treason. There was no other choice. Men and children and the elderly or the sick, all the wingless, were fleeing from the continuing hail of Esperigan attacks. They were retreating deep into the heart of the continent, beyond the refueling range for the Esperigan warcraft, to shelters hidden so far in caves and in overgrowth that even my spy satellites knew nothing of them. My connection to Kostas would have been severed, and if I could provide neither intelligence nor direct assistance, I might as well have slunk back to the embassy and saved myself the discomfort of being a refugee. Neither alternative was palatable.

They laid me upon the altar like a sacrifice, or so I felt, though they gave me something to drink that calmed my body, the nervous and involuntary twitching of my limbs and skin. Badea sat at my head and held the heavy long braid of my hair out of the way, while the others depilated my back and wiped it with alcohol. They bound me down then, and slit my skin open in two lines mostly parallel to the spine. Then Paudi gently set the wings upon me.

I lacked the skill to grow my own, in the time we had; Badea and Paudi helped me to mine so that I might stay. But even with the little assistance I had been able to contribute, I had seen more than I wished to of the parasites, and despite my closed eyes, my face turned downward, I knew to my horror that the faint curious feather-brush sensation was the intrusion of the fine spiderweb filaments, each fifteen feet long, which now wriggled into the hospitable environment of my exposed inner flesh and began to sew themselves into me.

Pain came and went as the filaments worked their way through muscle and bone, finding one bundle of nerves and then another. After the first half hour, Badea told me gently, "It's coming to the spine," and gave me another drink. The drug kept my body from movement, but could do nothing to numb the agony. I cannot describe it adequately. If you have ever managed to inflict food poisoning upon yourself, despite all the Confederacy's safeguards, you may conceive of the kind if not the degree of suffering, an experience that envelops the whole body, every muscle and joint, and alters not only your physical self but your thoughts as well: all vanishes but pain, and the question, Is the worst over? which is answered *no* and *no* again.

But at some point the pain began indeed to ebb. The filaments had entered the brain, and it is a measure of the experience that what I had feared the most was now blessed relief; I lay inert and closed my eyes gratefully while sensation spread outward from my back, and my new-borrowed limbs became gradually indeed my own, flinching from the currents of the air, and the touch of my friends' hands upon me. Eventually I slept.

The Seventh Adjustment

The details of the war, which unfolded now in earnest, I do not need to recount again. Kostas kept excellent records, better by far than my own, and students enough have memorized the dates and geographic coordinates, bounding death and ruin in small numbers. Instead I will tell you that from aloft, the Esperigans' poisoned-ground encampments made half starbursts of ocher brown and withered yellow, outlines like tentacles crawling into the healthy growth around them. Their supply-ships anchored out to sea glazed the water with a slick of oil and refuse, while the soldiers practiced their shooting on the vast schools of slow-swimming kraken young, whose bloated white bodies floated to the surface and drifted away along the coast, so many they defied even the appetite of the sharks.

I will tell you that when we painted their hulls with algaes and small crustacean-like borers, our work was camouflaged by great blooms of sea day-lilies around the ships, their masses throwing up reflected red color on the steel to hide the quietly creeping rust until the first winter storms struck and the grown kraken came to the surface to feed. I will tell you we watched from shore while the ships broke and foundered, and the teeth of the kraken shone like fire opals in the explosions, and if we wept, we wept only for the soiled ocean.

Still more ships came, and more planes; the ceramic coatings arrived, and more soldiers with protected guns and bombs and sprayed poisons, to fend off the altered motties and the little hybrid sparrowlike birds, their sharp cognizant eyes chemically retrained to see the Esperigan uniform colors as enemy markings. We planted acids and more aggressive species of plants along their supply lines, so their communications remained hopeful rather than reliable, and ambushed them at night; they carved into the forest with axes and power-saws and vast strip-miners, which ground to a halt and fell to pieces, choking on vines that hardened to the tensile strength of steel as they matured.

Contrary to claims that were raised at my trial in

absentia and disproved with communication logs, throughout this time I spoke to Kostas regularly. I confused him, I think; I gave him all the intelligence that he needed to convey to the Esperigans, that they might respond to the next Melidan foray, but I did not conceal my feelings or the increasing complication of my loyalties, objecting to him bitterly and with personal anger about Esperigan attacks. I misled him with honesty: he thought, I believe, that I was only spilling a natural frustration to him, and through that airing clearing out my own doubts. But I had only lost the art of lying.

There is a general increase of perception that comes with the wings, the nerves teased to a higher pitch of awareness. All the little fidgets and twitches of lying betray themselves more readily, so only the more twisted forms can evade detection—where the speaker first deceives herself, or the wholly casual deceit of the sociopath who feels no remorse. This was the root of the Melidan disgust of the act, and I had acquired it.

If Kostas had known, he would at once have removed me: a diplomat is not much use if she cannot lie at need, much less an agent. But I did not volunteer the information, and indeed I did not realize, at first, how fully I had absorbed the stricture. I did not realize at all, until Badea came to me, three years into the war. I was sitting alone and in the dark by the communications console, the phosphorescent afterimage of Kostas's face fading into the surface.

She sat down beside me and said, "The Esperigans

answer us too quickly. Their technology advances in these great leaps, and every time we press them back, they return in less than a month to very nearly the same position."

I thought, at first, that this was the moment: that she meant to ask me about membership in the Confederacy. I felt no sense of satisfaction, only a weary kind of resignation. The war would end, the Esperigans would follow, and in a few generations they would both be eaten up by bureaucracy and standards and immigration.

Instead Badea looked at me and said, "Are your people helping them, also?"

My denial ought to have come without thought, leapt easily off the tongue with all the conviction duty could give it, and been followed by invitation. Instead I said nothing, my throat closed involuntarily. We sat silently in the darkness, and at last she said, "Will you tell me why?"

I felt at the time I could do no more harm, and perhaps some good, by honesty. I told her all the rationale, and expressed all our willingness to receive them into our union as equals. I went so far as to offer her the platitudes with which we convince ourselves we are justified in our slow gentle imperialism: that unification is necessary and advances all together, bringing peace.

She only shook her head and looked away from me. After a moment, she said, "Your people will never stop. Whatever we devise, they will help the Esperigans to a counter, and if the Esperigans devise some weapon we cannot defend ourselves against, they will help us, and we will batter each other into limp exhaustion, until in the end we all fall."

"Yes," I said, because it was true. I am not sure I was still able to lie, but in any case I did not know, and I did not lie.

I was not permitted to communicate with Kostas again until they were ready. Thirty-six of the Melidans' greatest designers and scientists died in the effort. I learned of their deaths in bits and pieces. They worked in isolated and quarantined spaces, their every action recorded even as the viruses and bacteria they were developing killed them. It was a little more than three months before Badea came to me again.

We had not spoken since the night she had learned the duplicity of the Confederacy's support and my own. I could not ask her forgiveness, and she could not give it. She did not come for reconciliation but to send a message to the Esperigans and to the Confederacy through me.

I did not comprehend at first. But when I did, I knew enough to be sure she was neither lying nor mistaken, and to be sure the threat was very real. The same was not true of Kostas, and still less of the Esperigans. My frantic attempts to persuade them worked instead to the contrary end. The long gap since my last communiqué made Kostas suspicious: he thought me a convert, or generously a manipulated tool.

"If they had the capability, they would have used it already," he said, and if I could not convince him, the Esperigans would never believe.

I asked Badea to make a demonstration. There was a large island broken off the southern coast of the Esperigan continent, thoroughly settled and industrialized, with two substantial port cities. Sixty miles separated it from the mainland. I proposed the Melidans should begin there, where the attack might be contained.

"No," Badea said. "So your scientists can develop a counter? No. We are done with exchanges."

The rest you know. A thousand coracles left Melidan shores the next morning, and by sundown on the third following day, the Esperigan cities were crumbling. Refugees fled the groaning skyscrapers as they slowly bowed under their own weight. The trees died; the crops also, and the cattle, all the life and vegetation that had been imported from Earth and square-peg forced into the new world stripped bare for their convenience.

Meanwhile in the crowded shelters the viruses leapt easily from one victim to another, rewriting their genetic lines. Where the changes took hold, the altered survived. The others fell to the same deadly plagues that consumed all Earth-native life. The native Melidan moss crept in a swift green carpet over the corpses, and the beetle-hordes with it.

I can give you no firsthand account of those days. I too lay fevered and sick while the alteration ran its course in me, though I was tended better, and with more care, by my sisters. When I was strong enough to rise, the waves of death were over. My wings curled limply over my shoulders as I walked through the empty streets of Landfall, pavement stones pierced and broken by hungry vines, like bones cracked open for marrow. The moss covered the dead, who filled the shattered streets.

The squat embassy building had mostly crumpled down on one corner, smashed windows gaping hollow and black. A large pavilion of simple cotton fabric had been raised in the courtyard, to serve as both hospital and headquarters. A young undersecretary of state was the senior diplomat remaining. Kostas had died early, he told me. Others were still in the process of dying, their bodies waging an internal war that left them twisted by hideous deformities.

Less than one in thirty, was his estimate of the survivors. Imagine yourself on an air-train in a crush, and then imagine yourself suddenly alone but for one other passenger across the room, a stranger staring at you. Badea called it a sustainable population.

The Melidans cleared the spaceport of vegetation, though little now was left but the black-scorched landing pad, Confederacy manufacture, all of woven carbon and titanium.

"Those who wish may leave," Badea said. "We will help the rest."

Most of the survivors chose to remain. They looked at their faces in the mirror, flecked with green, and feared the Melidans less than their welcome on another world.

I left by the first small ship that dared come down to take off refugees, with no attention to the destination or the duration of the voyage. I wished only to be away. The wings were easily removed. A quick and painful amputation of the gossamer and fretwork that protruded from the flesh, and the rest might be left for the body to absorb slowly. The strange muffled quality of the world, the sensation of numbness, passed eventually. The two scars upon my back, parallel lines, I will keep the rest of my days.

Afterword

I spoke with Badea once more before I left. She came to ask me why I was going, to what end I thought I went. She would be perplexed, I think, to see me in my little cottage here on Reivaldt, some hundred miles from the nearest city, although she would have liked the small flowerlike lieden that live on the rocks of my garden wall, one of the few remnants of the lost native fauna that have survived the terraforming outside the preserves of the university system.

I left because I could not remain. Every step I took on Melida, I felt dead bones cracking beneath my feet. The Melidans did not kill lightly, an individual or an ecosystem, nor any more effectually than do we. If the Melidans had not let the plague loose upon the Esperigans, we would have destroyed them soon enough ourselves, and the Melidans with them. But we distance ourselves better from our murders, and so are not prepared to confront them. My wings whispered to me gently when I passed Melidans in the green-swathed cemetery streets, that they were not sickened, were not miserable. There was sorrow and regret but no self-loathing, where I had nothing else. I was alone.

When I came off my small vessel here, I came fully expecting punishment, even longing for it, a judgment that would at least be an end. Blame had wandered through the halls of state like an unwanted child, but when I proved willing to adopt whatever share anyone cared to mete out to me, to confess any crime that was convenient and to proffer no defense, it turned contrary, and fled.

Time enough has passed that I can be grateful now to the politicians who spared my life and gave me what passes for my freedom. In the moment, I could scarcely feel enough even to be happy that my report contributed some little to the abandonment of any reprisal against Melida: as though we ought hold them responsible for defying our expectations not of their willingness to kill one another, but only of the extent of their ability.

But time does not heal all wounds. I am often asked by visitors whether I would ever return to Melida. I will not. I am done with politics and the great concerns of the universe of human settlement. I am content to sit in my small garden, and watch the ants at work.

—*Ruth Patrona*

Peter S. Beagle

Peter S. Beagle was born in New York City in 1939. Although not prolific by genre standards, he has published a number of well-received fantasy novels, at least two of which, *A Fine and Private Place* and *The Last Unicorn,* were widely influential and are now considered to be classics of the genre. In fact, Beagle may be the most successful writer of lyrical and evocative modern fantasy since Bradbury, and is the winner of two Mythopoeic Fantasy Awards and the Locus Award, as well as having often been a finalist for the World Fantasy Award. Beagle's other books include the novels *The Folk of the Air, The Innkeeper's Song,* and *Tamsin.* His short fiction has appeared in places as varied as *The Magazine of Fantasy & Science Fiction, The Atlantic Monthly, Seventeen,* and *Ladies' Home Journal,* and has been collected in *The Rhinoceros Who Quoted Nietzsche and Other Odd Acquaintances, Giant Bones, The Line Between,* and *We Never Talk About My Brother.* He won the Hugo Award in 2006 and the Nebula Award in 2007 for his story "Two Hearts." He has written screenplays for several movies, including the animated adaptations of *The Lord of the Rings* and *The Last Unicorn;* the libretto of an opera, *The*

Midnight Angel; the fan-favorite *Star Trek: The Next Generation* episode "Sarek"; and a popular autobiographical travel book, *I See By My Outfit.* His most recent book is the new collection *Mirror Kingdoms: The Best of Peter S. Beagle,* and 2010 will see the publication of two long-awaited new novels, *Summerlong* and *I'm Afraid You've Got Dragons.*

You may find the opening pages of this story a bit confusing, but stick with it, and we promise you that you'll be rewarded with a compelling study of the price of compassion—and introduced to perhaps the strangest and most unlikely warrior in this whole anthology.

Dirae

Red.

Wet red.

My feet in the red.

Look. Bending in the red. Shiny in his hand— other hand tears, shakes at something in the red.

Moves.

In the red, it moves.

Doesn't want it to move. Kicks at it, lifts shiny again.

Doesn't see me.

In the red, it makes a sound.

Sound hurts me.

Doesn't want sound, either. Makes a sound, brings shiny down.

Stop him.

Why?

Don't know.

In my hand, his hand. Eyes wide. Pulls free, swings shiny at me.

Take it away.

Swing shiny across his face. Opens up, flower. Red teeth. Swing shiny again, other way.

Red. Red.

Another sound—high, hurting. Far away, but

coming closer. Eyes white in red, red face. He turns,
feet slipping in red. Could catch him.

Sound closer. At my feet, moves in red. Hurts me.
Hurts me.

Sound too close.
Go away.
Darkness.
Darkness.
DARK.

I . . .

What? Which? Who?
Who *I*? Think.
What is *think*?
Loud. Hurting. Loud.
A fence. Boys. *Loud.* Hurts me.
One boy, curled on ground.
Other boys.
Feet. So many *feet.*
Hurts.
I walk to them. *I.*
A boy in each hand. I throw them away. *I.*
More boys, more feet. Pick them up, bang together.
Throw away.

Like this. I like this.
Boys gone.
Curled-up boy. Clothes torn, face streaked red.
This is blood. *I* know. How do *I* know?
Boy stands up. Falls.
Face wet, not the blood. Water from his eyes. What?
Stands again. Speaks to me, words. Walks away.
Almost falls, but not. Wipes face, walks on.

Turn, faces looking at me. *I* look back, they turn away. Alone here.

Here. Where?

Doors. Windows. Noise. People. In one dark window, a figure.

I move, it moves. *I* go close to see—it comes toward, reaching out.

Me?

*Darkness. **Darkness.** **DARK** . . .*

the one with the knife, just out of reach. Drops back, comes close, darts away again. Waiting, waiting, in the corner of my left eye. Old woman screams and screams. The one riding my back, forearm across my throat, laughing, grunting. I snap my head back, feel the nose go, kick between his legs as he falls away. Knife man moves in then, and I catch his wrist and break it, *yes.* Third one, with the gun, frightened, fires, *whong,* garbage can rolls on its edge, falls over. He drops the gun, runs, and I lose him in the alley.

The one I kicked, wriggling on his side toward the gun when I turn back. Stops when he sees me. The old woman gone at last, the knife man huddling against the warehouse wall. "Bitch, you broke my fucking wrist!" *Bitch,* over and over. Other words. I pick up knife and gun and walk away, find a place to drop them. The sky is brightening toward the river, pretty.

Dark . . .

and I am rolling on the ground, trying to take an automatic rifle away from a crying man. Hits out, bites, kicks, tries to club me with the gun. People crowding in everywhere—legs, shoes, too close, shopping bags, too close, someone steps on my hand. Bodies on the ground, some moving, most not. In my arms, he struggles and wails, wife who left him, job he lost, children taken from him, *voices, voices.* Gives up suddenly—eyes roll back, gone away, harmless. I fight off a raging man, little girl limp in his arms, wants the gun, *Give me that gun!* I am on my feet, standing over the gunman, surrounded, protecting *him* now. Police.

Revolving lights, red and blue and white, ringing us all in together, they yank the man to his feet and run him away, barely letting him touch the ground. Still weeping, head thrown back as though his neck were broken. Bodies lying everywhere, most of them dead. I know dead.

One policeman comes to me, thanks me for preventing more deaths. I give him the rifle, he takes out a little notebook. Wants my story—what happened, what I saw, what I did. Kind face, happy eyes. I begin to tell him.

. . . then the darkness.

Where do I go?

When the dark takes me—just after I am snatched up out of one war and whirled off into another— where am I? No time between, no memories except blurred battles, no name, no needs, no desires, no relation to anything but my reflection in a shop window or a puddle of rain . . . where do I live? Who am I when I am there?

Do I live?

No, I am not a *who,* cannot be. I am a *what.* A walking weapon, a tool, a force, employed by someone or something unknown to me, for reasons I don't understand.

But—

If I was made to be a weapon, consciously manufactured for one purpose alone, then why do I question? That poor madman's rifle had no such interest in its own identity, nor its master's, nor where it hung between uses. No, I am something more than a rifle: I must be something that . . .

wonders. Wonders even while I am taking a gas can away from a giggling young couple who are bending over the ragged woman blinking drowsily on the sidewalk, the man holding his cigarette lighter open, thumb on its wheel. I hit them with the can until they fall down and stay there; then pour the gasoline over them and throw the lighter into a sewer. The ragged woman sniffs, offended by the smell, gets up and mumbles away. She gives me a small nod as she passes by.

And for just an instant, before the darkness takes me, I stand in the empty street, staring after her: a weapon momentarily in no one's hands, aimed at no one, a weapon trying to imagine itself. Only that moment . . .

then dark again, *think about the darkness . . .*

and it is daylight this time, late afternoon. I can see her ahead of me, too far ahead, the calm, well-dressed woman placidly dropping the second child into the river that wanders back and forth through this city. I can see the head of the first one, already swept almost out of sight. The third is struggling now, crying in her arms as she picks it up and raises it over the rail. Other people are running, but I am weaving through, I am past them, I am *there,* hitting her as hard as I can, so that she is actually lifted off the ground, slamming into a sign I cannot read. But the child is already in the air, falling . . .

. . . and so am I, hitting the water only seconds behind her. That one is easy—I have her almost immediately, a little one, a girl, gasping and choking, but unharmed. I set her on the narrow bank—there are stairs ahead, someone will come down and get her—and head after the others, kicking my shoes off as I swim. *As I swim . . .*

How do I know how to swim? Is that part of being a weapon? I am cutting through the water effortlessly, moving faster than the people running along the roadway—how did I learn to use my legs and arms just so? The current is with me, but it is sweeping the children along in the same way. Ahead, one small face turned to the sky, still afloat, but not for long. I swim faster.

A boy, this one, older than the first. I tread water to scoop him up and hold him over my shoulder, while he spews what seems like half the river down my back. But he is trying to point ahead, downstream, even while he vomits, after the third child, the one I can't see anywhere. People are calling from above, but there's no time, no time. I tuck him into the crook of my left arm and set off again, paddling with the right, using my legs and back like one thing, keeping my head out of the water to stare ahead. Nothing. No sign.

Sensible boy, he wriggles around to hold onto my shoulders as I swim, so that the left arm is free again. But I can't find the other one—*I can't* . . .

. . . and then I can. Floating face down, drifting lifelessly, turning and turning. A second girl. I have her in another moment, but the river is fighting me for the two of them now, and getting them to the bank against the current is hard. But we manage it. We manage.

Hands and faces, taking the children from me. The boy and the little one will be all right—the older girl . . . I don't know. The police are here, and two of them are kneeling over her, while the other two are being wrapped in blankets. There is a blanket around my shoulders too, I had not noticed. People pressing close, praising me, their voices very far away. I need to see about the girl.

The police have the mother, a man on either side of her, holding her arms tightly, though she moves with them willingly. Her face is utterly tranquil, all expression smoothed away; she looks at the children with no sign of recognition. The boy looks back at her . . . I will not think about that look. If I am a weapon, I don't have to. I start toward the motionless girl.

One of the policemen trying to start her breath again looks up—then recognizes me, as I know him. He was the one who was asking me questions about the weeping man with the rifle, and who actually saw me go with the darkness. I back away, letting the blanket fall, ready to leap back into the river, soaked through and weary as I am. He points at me, begins to stand up . . .

. . . the darkness comes for me, and for once I am grateful. Except . . . except . . .

Except that now I will never know about that girl, whether she lived or died. I will never know what happened to the mother . . .

Once I would not—*could* not—have thought such thoughts. I would have had neither the words nor the place in me where the words should go. I would not have known to separate myself from the darkness—to remain *me,* even in the dark, waiting. Can a weapon do that? Can a weapon remember that small boy's face above the water, and the way he tried to help me save his sister?

Then that is not all I am, even as I wish it. *Who am I?*

If I am a person, I must have a name. Persons have names. What is my name?

What is my name?

Where do I live?

Could I be mad? Like that poor man with the gun?

I wake. That must mean that I sleep. Doesn't it? Then where do I . . . no, no distractions. What is sure is that I come suddenly awake—on the street, every time, somewhere in the city. Wide awake, instantly . . . dressed—neatly, practically, and entirely unremarkably—and on my feet, *moving,* either already in the midst of trouble, or heading straight for

it. And I will know what to do when I find it, because . . . because I will *know,* that's all. I always
know.

No name, then . . . no home . . . nowhere to be,
except when I am hurrying toward it. And even in
daylight, darkness always near . . . silent, void,
always lost before, but now this new place in the
dark when I can feel that there *is* a *now,* and that
now is different from *after-now.* If that's so, then I
ought to be able to stand still in *after-now* and look
back . . .

standing beneath a flickering street light, watching
two young black girls walking together, arm in arm.
They look no more than fifteen—thirteen, more
likely—and they have just come from seeing a movie.
How do I know what a movie is? This must have
been a funny one, because they are giggling, quoting
lines, acting out scenes for each other. But they walk
rapidly, almost hurrying, and there is a strained pitch
to their laughter that makes me think they know it is
dangerous for them to be here. I parallel their progress on the other side of the street.

The five white boys materialize silently out of the
shadows—three in front of the girls, two behind them,
cutting off any chance of flight. The moment is perfectly soundless: everybody knows what everybody
else is there for. The black girls look desperately
around them; then back slowly against the wall of a
building, holding hands like the children they are.
One of the boys is already unbuckling his belt.

I am the first one to speak. I walk forward slowly,

crossing the empty street, saying, "No. This is not to happen."

I speak strangely, I know that, though I can never hear what it is that I do wrong. The boys turn to look at me, giving the two girls an instant when they might well have made a successful dash for safety. But they are too frightened; neither of them could move a finger at this moment. I keep coming. I say, "I think everyone should go home."

The big one begins to smile. *The leader. Good.* He says loudly to the others, "Right, I'll take this one. Dark meat's bad for my diet." The rest of them laugh, turning back toward the black girls.

I walk straight up to him, never hesitating. The smile stays on his broad blond face, but there is puzzlement in the eyes now, because I am not supposed to be doing this. I say, "You should have listened," and kick straight up at his crotch.

But this one saw that coming, and simply turns his thigh to block me. Huge, grinning—small teeth, kernels of white corn—he hurls himself at me, and we grapple on our feet for a moment before we fall together. His hand covers my entire face; he could smother me like that, easily, but I know better than to bite the heel and anchor myself to the consequences. Instead, I grab his free hand and start breaking fingers. He roars and pulls the hand away from my face, closing it into a fist that will snap my neck if it lands. It doesn't. I twist. Then my own hand, rigid fingers joined and extended, catches him under the heart—again, around the side, kidneys, once, twice—and he gasps and sags. I roll him off me fast and stand up.

The boys haven't noticed the fate of their leader; they are entirely occupied with the black girls, who are screaming now, crying to me for help. I take a throat in each hand and bang two heads together—really hard, there is blood. I drop them, grab another by the shirt, slam him against a parked car, hit him until he sits down in the street. When I turn from him, the last one is halfway down the block, looking back constantly as he runs. He is fat and slow, easily caught—but I had better see to the girls.

"This is not a good place," I say. "Come, I will walk you home."

They are paralyzed at first, almost unable to believe that they have not been raped and beaten, perhaps murdered. Then they are all questions, hysterical with questions I cannot answer. Who am I? What is my name? Where did I come from—do I live around here? How did I happen to be right there when they needed help?

I just saw, that's all, I tell them. Lucky.

"Where you ever learn all that martial arts shit?"

No martial arts, I tell them, no exotic fighting technique, I was just irritated—which makes them laugh shakily, and breaks the tension. Beyond that, I talk to them as little as I can, my voice still something unpracticed, oddly wrong. They do most of the talking, anyway, so glad merely to be alive.

I do walk them all the way to their apartment house—they are cousins, living with their grandmother—and they both hug me with all their strength when we say good-bye. The older girl says earnestly, "I'm going to pray for you every night," and I thank her. They both wave back to me as they run into the building.

I am glad the darkness did not snatch me away while I was with them: my vanishing before their eyes would surely have terrified them, and they have been frightened enough for one night. And I am glad to have at least a moment to be a *who,* fumbling and confused, before I must once again be an invincible *what,* taken down from the wall and aimed at some new target.

This time, when the darkness takes me . . . this time my memory remains whole, clear, unhazy. Everything is still there: nothing tattered or smudged, gone. The two black girls stay with me. I *remember* them, even things they said to each other about the movie they had just seen, and their telling me that their grandmother worked in a school cafeteria. And from there I remember more, though I have no sure way of measuring when any of it happened. *The drunken old man stumbling in front of a bus . . . the two toddlers playing on a rusty, sagging fire escape on a hot night . . . the children driving so slowly down a wide trash-strewn street, training a pistol through the passenger window on another child who has just come out of a liquor store . . . the woman looking behind her into a stir of shadows, walking a little faster . . .*

And each time—me. Rescuer. Savior. Wrath of God . . . somehow fortunately there at just the right moment; there, where I am necessary. But where is *there?*

I am beginning to know. It is a city—how big a

city I cannot guess—and there is a river I almost remember swimming . . . yes, the children. (*What happened to the third one?*) There is a street or two that
I have come to recognize. A handful of buildings
that give me some kind of bearing as I hurry past on
this or that night's mission. One particular row of
crowded, crumbling houses has become almost familiar, as have a few shops, a few street corners, a
few markets—even a face, now and then . . .

This city, then, is where I live.

No. This is where I *am*.

They live, but I am only *real*. There is a difference
I cannot name . . .

outside an apartment door with bright brass numer-
als on it—4 and 2 and 9; for the first time they are
more than shapes to me—my leg in mid-snap, heel
of my foot slamming once, just under the lock,
breaking cheap wood away from dead bolt and
mortise to give me entry. And there they are, the pair
of them, sitting together on a couch, his eyes all pupil,
the skin of her arms covered with deep scratches. I
have seen that before.

This time I could not care less about it. I am here
for the baby.

Hallway, door on the right. Closed, but I can hear
the whimpering, even though the man is on his feet,
making outraged noises, and the woman—pretty,
once—is telling him to call nine-one-one. I pay no
heed to either of them, not yet. No time, no time.

I can smell the urine even before I have opened
the door. He's soaked, and the mattress is soaked,

and the blanket, but that's not what stops my breath. It's the little cry he gives when I pick him up: a cry that ought to be a scream, with those bruises, and the way his left arm is hanging—but he hasn't even got the strength to scream. I cannot even tell when I'm hurting him. I lift him, and look into his eyes. What I see there I have never seen before.

And I go completely insane.

Somewhere far away, the woman is tugging at me, shrieking something at me. The man is on the floor, not moving, his face bloody. Not bloody enough. I can fix that. I start toward him, but she keeps getting in my way, she keeps making that sound. What has she got to make noise about? Her arm's not broken, her body isn't one big bruise—she doesn't have those marks that had better not be cigarette burns. Pulling on the arm holding the baby, she will make me drop him. No, now she has stopped, now she is down there, quiet, like the man. Both in the red. Wet red. Good.

Still noise, so much noise. People shouting—the apartment is full of people, when did that happen? Police, lots of police—and one of them *that* one. He stares at me. Says, under all the racket, "What are you doing here? Who *are* you?"

"I am no one," I say. I hand the baby to him. He looks down at it, and his young face goes a terrible color. Before he can raise his head again, the darkness . . .

. . . but no. Different this time. I am back almost immediately, ordinary night, and I am on the street, outside an apartment house I have never seen, where two police cars stand blinking redly at the curb. It is a warm night, but I'm shaking, and cannot stop. Something on my face, I brush at it, impatient. I have been . . . crying.

No purpose here: I know this. I walk away down the street. Keep walking, maybe that will help. For the moment, no place I should be, no helpless, desperate appeal closing on me. No one to save, only escape, evasion. A little time to wonder . . . to ask myself questions—did I kill those two? I was trying, I really wanted to kill them.

Blood crusting on the knuckles of both hands—my blood as well as theirs. My back pains me where the man hit me with some sort of kitchen object before I threw him through the door. I never have time to notice or remember pain; this is new. Yet nothing tonight hurt me as much as the look in the eyes of that urine-soaked child with his little arm dangling so . . . that was when I started crying and trying to kill, not merely protect. I can cry, then; there's something else I know.

Perhaps learning to think was not a good idea. My head is crowded now, heaving and churning with faces, voices, moments . . . *the old man hammering an older one with a heavy paint can, swinging it by the handle . . . the wild-eyed homeless man ringed by jeering boys, who finally catches hold of the one constantly darting in to steal his possessions out of his shopping cart, and has him down, hands around his throat, as the others swarm over him . . . the man with the tire iron, and the bleeding, half-naked woman who attacked me so furiously when I was taking it away from him . . .*

But even so, even so, I can feel it coming closer, a fleeting space *between* strangers, between rescues, when *something* becomes almost clear, like the instant before dawn: the rush of paling sky, the first lights going on in windows, the earliest sounds of birds waking on rooftops. While in it I sense that there is a source of me, a *point* to me; a place, and a memory—and a name—and even my own dawn, where I belong . . .

wake not on the street but in a strange room, where I can see the sky—soft with early morning light, incomplete, the world heavy still with sleep—through tall narrow windows.

There are eight beds in this room, with bodies rounding the blankets in three of them, but no sound, except for the soft buzz and wheeze of machinery. A hospital. The woman in the nearest bed lies on her back, but twisted toward the right; if the tube plugged into a hole in her throat and a monitor beyond were not preventing it, she would be curled up on her side. Her breath is short and soundless, and too fast, and she smells like mildew. She is a big woman, but lying so makes her look shrunken, and older than she probably is. The chart at the foot of the bed is labeled JANE DOE. I sit down in a chair close to her.

She is very ugly. Her arms are thick, heavy, with tiny hands, the fingers all more or less the same size;

you can hardly tell the thumb from the rest. Her black hair is lank and tangled, and her face is so pale that the blotches and faded pockmarks stand out like whip scars. Something once broke her nose and the bones of her face, badly. They are not right and clearly never will be. But her expression is utterly peaceful, serenely empty.

I know her.

The red. In the red, moving. Wants it not to move. Sound hurts me.

I say it out loud: "I know you." *You moved in the red. He kicked you. Shiny. I took it away.*

Why am I here?

Jane Doe does not answer me. I never expected that she would. But the young nurse does, a moment later, when she comes storming into the room, demanding to know who I am. I could tell her that I am constantly asking myself the same question, but instead I say that I am Jane Doe's friend. She promptly reaches for the telephone, saying that "Jane Doe" is the name they use for people whose real name no one knows—as I obviously do not. I could tear the phone out of her hand, out of the wall, but instead I sit and wait. She turns away to speak into the phone for a few moments, looking more and more puzzled and annoyed; then hangs it up and turns back to glare at me.

"How the hell did you get in here? Security says no one looking like you has been through at all." She is black, tall and slender, with a small, delicate head, a naturally somber face. Quite pretty, but the confusion is making her really angry.

I say, "There was no one at the door. I just walked in."

"Somebody dies for this," she mumbles. She looks at her watch, makes a note on a pad of paper. "Oh, heads will *roll*, I swear." Calming herself: "Go away, please, or I'll have to have Security up. You don't belong here."

I look back at Jane Doe. "What is the matter with her?"

The nurse shakes her head. "I don't think that's any of your business."

I stand up. I say, "Tell me."

The nurse looks at me for a long moment. I wonder what she sees. "I do that, you'll leave without making any trouble?"

"Yes."

"She was mugged. Ten, eleven months ago. Attacked on the street and beaten really badly—she almost died. They never caught the guy who did it. When she fell, she must have hit her head against something, a building. There was brain damage, bleeding. She's been in a vegetative state ever since." She gestures around her at the other silent beds. "Like the others here."

"And you don't know who she is."

"Nobody does. Do you? Is there something you're not telling me?"

Oh yes. Yes.

"Will she always be like this?"

The nurse—the name on her blue and white breast pin says FELICIA—frowns and backs slowly toward the door. "On second thought, maybe you better stay right there. I'm going to go get someone who can answer your questions."

She will come back with guards.

I sit down. I stare down into the big, blind, ugly face from my very first memory, trying to understand why the darkness brought me here. I watch the blinking monitors and wonder about so many things I do not even have *thoughts* for, let alone words. But it is more than I can grasp, and I have understood nothing when once more I lose the world.

Her name! Her name is . . .

another strange, dim street, and I am carrying a weeping, forlornly struggling girl out of a storefront that advertises ASIAN MAS AGE in its grimy window. She appears to be thirteen or fourteen years old. I cannot understand what she is saying to me.

But she is looking past me, over my shoulder; and when I turn, I see the group massing behind me. A hardfaced middle-aged couple, two younger men—squat, but burly in a top-heavy way—and a boy likely not very much older than the girl in my arms. He is the one holding the broken bottle.

I set the girl down on her feet, still holding her by the shoulders. She has a round, sweet face, but her eyes are mad with terror. I point at the sidewalk and say loudly, "*Stay here!*" several times, until it seems to get through, and she nods meekly. I cannot begin to guess how many times she must have made just that same gesture of bewildered submission in the face of power. I try to pat her shoulder, but she cringes away from me. I let her go, and turn back to face my new batch of enemies.

They are all shouting furious threats at me, but the boy seems to be the only one who speaks English. He eases toward me, waving the half bottle as menacingly as he can, saying, "You give her, get away. My sister."

"She is no more your sister than I am," I answer him. "She is a child, and I am taking her out of here." Neighbors, fellow entrepreneurs, and curious nightwalkers are already gathering around the scene, silent, unfriendly. I say, "Tell the rest of them if they get in my way, that bottle goes up your nose, for a start, and I will beat those two fat boys to death with you. Tell them I am in a very bad mood."

In truth, I am anxious for the police to show up before things get worse than they are. My mood is actually a kind of detached anger, nothing like the madness that took me over so completely when I saw that baby's broken arm. Something changed then, surely. Even if it is what I am for—all I am for—I have no desire to fight anyone just at the moment. I want to go somewhere by myself and think. I want to go back to the hospital, and sit by Jane Doe's bed, and look at her, and think.

But the two burly men are moving slowly out to left and right, trying to flank me, and that stupid boy is getting closer, in little dancy jump-steps. The girl is standing where I left her, wide-eyed, a finger in her mouth. There is a woman just behind her, middle-aged, with a heavy face and kind eyes. I ask her with my own eyes to keep the girl safe while I deal with her former employers, and she nods slightly.

The boy, seeing my attention apparently distracted, chooses this moment to lunge, his arm fully extended, his notion of a war cry carrying and echoing off the low storefronts. I spin, trip him up—the half bottle crashes in the gutter—and hurl him by his shirtfront into the path of the bravo on my left. They go down together, and I turn on the other one, catching him under the nose with the heel of my right hand, between belly and breath with the balled left. He clutches hard at me as he falls, but he does fall.

There are women spilling out of the massage parlor now, all very young, all wearing cut-off shorts and T-shirts that show their flat, childish stomachs. Most simply stare; a few run back into the storefront; two or three slip away down a half-hidden alley. The boy struggles to his feet and here he comes again, jabbing the air with a single jagged splinter of the broken bottle, cutting his own hand where he holds it. I am trying not to hurt him more than necessary, but he is not making it easy. I kick the glass shard out of his grasp, so he won't fall on it when I side-kick his feet out from under him on my way toward the older couple. They back away fast—maybe from me, more likely from the lights and sirens coming up the street. I back off myself, and sigh with relief.

The girl is still where I left her, with the older woman's hand resting lightly on her trembling shoulder. I catch the woman's eye, nod my thanks, gesture toward the patrol car, and start to drift slowly away from there, eyes lowered.

One of the two policemen, Asian himself, is interrogating the massage parlor owners in their own language. But the other, much younger, sees me . . . looks past me . . . then looks again and heads straight for me. Through the shouting and the street noise, I hear his voice. "You! You hold it right there!"

I could still follow the escaping girls down the alley, but I stand where I am. He plants himself a foot in front of me, forefinger aimed at my chest. Surprisingly, he is smiling, but it is a tense, determined smile, not at all pleasant. He says, "We're going to stop meeting like this, right now. Who the hell *are* you?"

"I don't know."

"Yeah, right. And I'll bet you aren't carrying any ID, either." He is too agitated to wait for me to answer. He charges on: "Goddammit, first I see you at that mall shooting, but you just *disappear* on me, I don't know how. Then it was that crazy woman dropping her kids into the river—you dived in, went after them like some TV superhero—"

I interrupt him to ask, "The girl, the older one. Is she . . . will she be all right?"

His face changes; he stops pointing at me. He says nothing for a while, and his voice is lower when he speaks again. "We tried everything. If you'd bothered to stick around, you'd have known. But no—it's another disappearing act, like a damn special effect. Then that couple with the baby, those two methheads." It is a different smile this time. "Okay, they had it coming, but *you're* coming downtown with us on that one, and lucky it's not a murder charge. Both of them still in the hospital, you know that?"

I wonder whether they are in the same hospital as Jane Doe. I wonder where the baby is, and I am about to ask him, when he continues, "Now *this*. What, you think you're Batman, the Lone Ranger, rousting massage parlors, beating the crap out of rapists? You're really starting to leave a trail, lady, and we need to have a conversation. You can't *do* this shit."

He reaches for the handcuffs at his belt. My hands raise automatically and he steps back, reaching for his holstered gun instead. I begin to explain why I cannot let him arrest me . . .

but then it is bright afternoon, and I am standing on a street across from a schoolyard in time to see a boy push a smaller boy down hard and run off, laughing. The little one is whimpering dazedly over ripped new blue jeans or a scraped knee, and doesn't see the car coming. Other children and passersby do, but they're too far away, and their warning screams are drowned by the shriek of brakes. No one can possibly reach him in time.

But of course I am there. It is what I do, being there.

Not even a spare second to scoop him up—I crash into him from the side, and the two of us roll away into the gutter as the car slews by, skidding in a half circle, so that it comes to rest on the far side of the street, facing us. The boy ends up in my arms, his eyes wide and frantic, but not crying at all now, because he cannot get his breath. Children are running toward us, adults are coming out of the school; the driver is already down on his knees beside us, easily as hysterical as the boy. But it's all right. It is over. I was there.

My left shoulder hurts where I hit the asphalt, and I have banged my head on something, maybe the curb. Like Jane Doe. I stand up carefully and, as always, ease myself slowly away from the rejoicing and the praise. The boy has started to cry fully now, which is a relief to me.

Jane Doe doesn't cry. She hasn't cried for a very long time.

It is confusing to be suddenly thinking about her. She is somehow there with me, an intrusion, surplus from the darkness, only being felt now because there is no one I must save. Why? I am a ghost myself, always vanishing. How can I be haunted?

Her name is . . .

Oh. I—

I know her name.

I walk until I come to a bridge over that milky river which divides and defines this city. I sit on the stone guardrail to wait for the darkness. I feel a weariness in me more frightening than any boy with a broken bottle. I am real enough to break a jaw or a rib defending a child prostitute; not real enough ever to understand that child's life, her terror, her pain. I can go as mad with rage as any human over a beaten, half-dead infant, and do my very best to murder its abusers—and feel dreadfully *satisfied* to have done so—but now I think . . . now I think it is not my outrage and terrible pity I am satisfying; it is all, all of it, happening in that hospital room, behind those closed eyes whose color I do not know.

I gaze down from the bridge, watching a couple of barges sliding silently by, just below me. *If I were to leap down to them, right now, would I be killed? Can a dream commit suicide?*

Darkness . . .

that policeman is actively looking for me. We have not met again, but I have seen him from a distance once or twice, during one rescue—one *being there*—or another.

My ever-faithful darkness keeps returning for me, carrying me off to do battle with other exploiters, other abusers, other muggers, rapists, molesters, gang thugs, drive-by assassins. See me: lithe, swift, fearless, always barehanded, always alone, always conquering . . . and never in control, not of anything, not of the smallest choice I make. She is. I am certain of that now.

My missions—*her* missions—have always favored children, but lately they seem to feature them constantly, exclusively. More and more I wake to other massage parlors—endless, those—and trucks crammed full of ten-year-old immigrant laborers packed into shipping crates. Garment sweatshops in basement factories. Kitchens in alley diners. Lettuce fields outside the city. At the airport I intercept two girls arriving for hand-delivery to an old man from their home village. In a basement I break a man's arm and leg, then free his pregnant daughter and pregnant grand-daughters from the two rooms he has kept them locked in for years. I have grown sharper, more peremptorily violent. I rarely speak now. There is no time. We have work to do, Jane Doe and I, and it is growing so late.

The blind force in the darkness grows fiercer, angrier, more *hurried*. Sometimes I am not even finished when I am snatched up once again—by the back of my neck, really, like a kitten—and plopped straight into another crisis, another horror, another rescue. And I do what I do, what I am for, what Jane Doe birthed me to be: guardian, defender, invincible fighter for the weak and the injured. But it is all wearing thin; so thin that often I can see the next mission through the fabric of this one, the dawn through an increasingly transparent darkness. *Wearing thin . . .*

it happens while I am occupied in rescuing a convenience-store manager and his wife from three large men in ski masks. They are all drunk, they are all armed, and the manager has just made the mistake of hauling out the shotgun from behind the counter. All very noisy and lively; but so far no one is dead, and I have the old couple stashed safely out of the way. But the sirens are coming.

The bandits hear the sirens too, and the two who can still walk actually push past me to get out of the store. I hardly notice them, because I am starting to feel a vague, sickly unease—a psychic nausea surging up and over me in a wave of dislocation and abandonment. Outside, I double over against a wall, gasping, struggling for breath, unable to stand straight, with the patrol cars sounding in the next street over. Somehow I stumble to safety, out of sight behind a couple of huge garbage trucks, and lean there until the spasm passes. No—until it eases a bit. Whatever it is, it is not passing.

The sun is just clear of the horizon. I can feel the dark clutching blindly and feebly at me, but it hasn't the strength to carry me away. I am on my own. I look around to get my bearings; then push myself away from the garbage trucks and start wobbling off.

A car horn close beside me, almost in my ear. I sense who it is before I turn my head and see the blue-and-white police car. He is alone, glaring at me as he pulls to the curb. "Get in, superhero," he calls. "Don't make me chase you."

I am too weak, too weary for flight. I open the front passenger door and sit down beside him. He raises his eyebrows. "Usually we keep the escape art-ists in the back, with no door handles. What the hell." He does not start up again, but eyes me curiously, fingertips lightly drumming on the steering wheel. He says, "You look terrible. You look really sick." I do not answer. "You going to throw up in my car?"

I mumble, "No. I don't know. I don't think so."

"Because we've had nothing but pukers for the last week—I mean, *nothing* but pukers. So I'd really appreciate it, you know . . ." He does not finish the sentence, but keeps eyeing me warily. "Boy, you look bad. You think you ate a bad clam or something?" Abruptly he makes up his mind. "Look, before we go anywhere, I'm taking you to the hospital. Put your seat belt on."

I leave the belt catch not quite clicked, but as he pulls away into traffic an alarm goes off. He reaches over, snaps the catch into place. I am too slow to prevent him. The alarm stops. With a quick glance my way he says, "You don't *look* crazy or anything— you look like a nice, normal girl. How'd you get into the hero business?"

I am actually dizzy and sweating, as though I *were* going to throw up. I say again, "I don't know. I try to help, that is all."

"Uh-huh. Real commendable. I mean, pulling whole families out of the river and all, the mayor gives you medals for that stuff. Rescuing abused children, taking down mall shooters—that's *our* job, you're kind of making us look bad." He slaps the steering wheel, trying to look sterner than his nature. "But beating up the bad guys, *that's* a no-no. Doesn't matter how bad they are, you get into some really deep shit doing that. They sue. And somebody like me has to go and arrest you . . . not to mention explaining about sixteen million times to my boss, and *his* boss, why I didn't do it already, you being right there on the scene and all. All the damn time."

My head is swimming so badly I have trouble making sense of his words. Something very bad is happening; whether to me or to Jane Doe I cannot tell. *Could this hospital he is taking me to be her hospital?* The policeman is speaking again, his face and voice serious, even anxious. He says, far away, "That vanishing act of yours, now that worries me. Because if you're not crazy, then either you really *are* some kind of superhero, or *I'm* crazy. And I just don't want to be crazy, you know?"

In the midst of my faintness, I feel strangely sorry

for him. I manage to reply, "Perhaps there is another choice . . . another possibility . . ." *Even if it is the right hospital, if the darkness does not come again, I will never reach Jane Doe's silent room—not in handcuffs, which are surely coming, and with his hand tight on my shoulder. What must I do?*

"Another possibility?" His eyebrows shoot up again. "Well, now you've got me trying to figure what the hell that could be."

I do not answer him.

He parks the patrol car in front of a squat gray-white building. I can see other cars coming and going: people on crutches, people being pushed in wheelchairs—an ambulance out front, another in the parking lot. He cuts the engine, turns to look straight at me. "Look, doesn't matter whether I *want* to bust you on a filing cabinet full of assault charges or not. I *got* to do that. But what I'd way rather do is just talk to you, first, because that other possibility . . . that other possibility is I've got reality wrong, flat wrong. All of it. And I don't think I'm ready to know that, you understand?"

It *is* Jane Doe's hospital. I can feel her there. This close, the pull of the darkness is still erratic but convulsively stronger. I know she is reaching for me.

With one hand I reach for the door handle, very slowly, holding his glance. With the other I start to unbuckle the seat belt.

"Don't—"

I start to say, "I never had your choice." But I don't finish, any more than I get a chance to throw the door open and bolt into the hospital. Between one word and the next the darkness takes hold of me, neck and heels, and I am gone . . .

once again in Jane Doe's room, standing at the foot of her bed.

And Felicia has seen me appear.

Her silence is part of the silence of the room; her breath comes as roughly as her patients' through the tubes in their throats; the speechless fear in her wide dark eyes renders me just as mute. All I can do for her is to move aside, leaving a clear path to the door. I croak her name as she stumbles through, but the only response is the soft click as she closes the door and locks it from outside. I think I hear her crying, but I could be wrong.

There is a little bathroom, just to the right of the door, with a toilet and sink for visitors. I walk in and wash my face—still dirty and bruised from my convenience store battle—for the first time. Then I take a moment to study the mask that Jane Doe made for me. The woman in the mirror has black hair, like hers, but longer—almost to the shoulders—and fuller. The eyes looking back at me are dark gray. The skin around them is a smooth light-olive. It is blankly calm, this face, the features regular yet somehow uninteresting: easily ignored, passed over, missed in a crowd. And why not, since that so clearly suited Jane Doe's purpose? Whatever terrified instinct first clothed me in flesh chose well.

It is a good face. A *useful* face. I wonder if I will ever see it again.

I walk back to Jane Doe's bed. The strange near-nausea has not left me—if anything, it seems to rise and fall with Jane Doe's breathing, which is labored now. She moves jerkily beneath the cover of her sheets, eyes still closed, her face sweaty and white. Some of the noises coming from the machines attached to her are strong and regular, but others chirp with staccato alarm: whether she is conscious or not, the machines say her body is in pain. And in the same way I know so many things now, I know why. The gift unleashed by the damage she suffered—the talent to give me life from nothingness, to sense danger, fear, cruelty from afar and send her own unlikely angel flying to help—has become too great for the form containing it.

I sit down by her, taking her heavy, limp hand between my own, and the darkness touches me.

There are too many.

My lips feel too cold to move, so I do not even try to speak. All I can do is look.

There are too many, and she cannot do enough.

Images comes to me, falling through my mind like leaves.

Red.

Wet red.

My feet in the red.

She made me up to save her, but I was too late. So we saved others, she and I. We saved so many others.

I look at the door. With every small sound I expect clamor and warning—gunshots, even, or barking dogs. I wonder whether Felicia will be back with the nice young policeman. I wish I could have explained to him.

There is warmth in the darkness. I feel it in my head, I feel it on my skin. It is pain . . . but something beyond pain, too.

On the wall next to the telephone there is a white board with words written on it, and a capped marker. Writing is new to me—I have never had to do it before—so it does not go as quickly or as well as I would like, but I manage. In a child's block letters I write down the name I found in the darkness, and three more words: WE THANK YOU.

Then I go back to her bed.

Voices in the hall now—Felicia, and another woman, and two or three men. I cannot tell whether the young policeman is one of them. No sound yet of Felicia's key in the lock; are they afraid of a woman who comes and goes by magic arts?

I think I would have liked to have a name of my own, but no matter. I lean forward and remove the cables, then the tubes. So many of them. Some of the machines go silent, but others howl.

Fumbling at the lock . . . now the sound of the key. It is so easy to close my hands around her throat, and I feel her breath between my fingers.

S. M. Stirling

Considered by many to be the natural heir to Harry
Turtledove's title of King of the Alternate History
novel, fast-rising science fiction star S. M. Stirling is
the bestselling author of the Nantucket series (*Island in the Sea of Time, Against the Tide of Years,
On the Ocean of Eternity*), in which Nantucket
comes unstuck in time and is cast back to the year
1250 BC, and the Draka series (including *Marching
Through Georgia, Under the Yoke, The Stone Dogs,*
and *Drakon,* plus an anthology of Draka stories by
other hands edited by Stirling, *Drakas!*), in which
Tories fleeing the American Revolution set up a mil-
itant society in South Africa and eventually end up
conquering most of the earth. He's also produced
the Emberverse series (*Dies the Fire, The Protector's
War, A Meeting at Corvallis*), plus the five-volume
Fifth Millennium series and the seven-volume General series (with David Drake), as well as stand-alone
novels such as *Conquistador, The Peshawar Lancers,*
and *The Sky People*. Stirling has also written novels
in collaboration with Raymond F. Feist, Jerry Pour-
nelle, Holly Lisle, Shirley Meier, Karen Wehrstein,
and *Star Trek* actor James Doohan, as well as contributing to the *Babylon 5, T2, Brainship, War World,*

and *Man-Kzin War* series. His short fiction has been collected in *Ice, Iron and Gold*. Stirling's newest series is an Emberverse tetralogy of the Change, so far in three volumes, *The Sunrise Lands, The Scourge of God,* and *The Sword of the Lady*. His most recent book is *In the Courts of the Crimson Kings,* sequel to *The Sky People*. Born in France and raised in Europe, Africa, and Canada, he now lives in Santa Fe, New Mexico.

In the action-packed story that follows, he shows us how an unlikely alliance is forged between two very different kinds of warriors, and then sends them on an even more unlikely mission together, a hair-raisingly dangerous mission that will test their resolve, their ingenuity, and their courage—and the bounds of friendship.

Ancient Ways

It was a hot day in July, the two thousandth and fifty-fifth year of Our Lord; or fifty-seven years since the Change, plus a few months. The feather-grass of the middle Volga steppe rustled around him, rolling to the edge of sight in knee-high blond waves. Sergey Ivanovitch's jaws moved steadily on the stick of tasteless dried mutton as he lay on his belly and watched through his binoculars as the strange rider approached, ant-small at first under the immense blue dome of the sky. Now and then, he sipped from a leather flask, water cut with corn brandy to make it safe to drink.

"Who is this one, sorry nag?" he said idly, either to himself or the horse lying behind him, mentally checking on the locations of his weapons. "Balls of brass, to ride here alone. Or in a hurry, Christ witness."

He chewed cautiously on the stick of jerky, since it was like gnawing on a board, and occasionally used his dagger to slice off shavings. *His* teeth were a young man's intact set, which he wanted to keep as long as possible. At forty-eight, his father Ivan Mikhailovitch had exactly five discolored stubs left in his jaws and had to live on boiled cabbage and soup, when he wasn't drunk and living on liquor, which admittedly was most of the time.

Whoever he was, the stranger was coming on fairly fast—canter-trot-canter, with two remounts behind him on a leading rein. Three horses would be very welcome when the traders from Belgorod came.

"So, does he run *away* or *toward*?"

Sergey was here on the chance of running across some saiga antelope or wild horses. And to get away from the *stanitsa*—Cossack village—and his family's crowded rammed-earth cabin and the squalling of his younger brothers and sisters and the endless chores for a while before harvest pinned everyone down.

And because his grandfather Mikhail had died, and it was unseemly to grieve too openly before others for a man of eighty—it was the will of God and the way of nature, and it became a Cossack to be scornful of death. Mikhail had been a great man, one of the few left who'd been a grown man before the Change; and one of the leaders who'd seen the Don Host reborn.

I am the last of them, the old man had said just before he stopped breathing. *The last, and a world dies again with me.*

Sergey hadn't known what Grandfather Mikhail had meant by that, but it made his eyes prickle nonetheless; he shoved the thought roughly away and concentrated on what was at hand.

"And he could throw an axe like an angel," he muttered. "Christ welcome you, Grandfather."

A clump of trees and the remnants of old orchards

to the north surrounding the snags of some ruined buildings were the only signs that this had once been tilled ground, in the days before the machines stopped. The great river's bend was only eighty kilometers eastward hereabouts, but folk from his *stanitsa* didn't go that way, not if they valued their heads. Too many of the infidel flat-faces ranged there. The feud between Russki and Tartar went back long before the time of the Red Czars and the age of wizards, to the dim days of legend.

"And sometimes you see some of those Kuban bastards this far north," he mused. "And Daghestanis . . . Quiet, limb of Satan," he added as his mount stirred.

The big rawboned gray beast was well-trained and stayed lying prone behind him, both of them sweating under the hot noon sun. Tiny white grasshoppers spurted out of the grass-stems when he shifted his weight on his elbows, and the air smelled of ozone and hay—as well as horse and man's-sweat, leather and metal.

"Glory be to God forever and ever," he muttered to himself as the man's features and dress began to show details in the twin lenses. "I don't think he's a Tartar at all; not a Nogai, at least."

That was what the flat-face tribes around the Volga called themselves these days, and Sergey's people knew them well from war and trade and the odd marriage-by-abduction. The stranger's helmet was a blunt cone with a spike on top and a belt of fur around the rim, not wound with a turban; he wore his hair in a black pigtail, too. And his stirrup-leathers were adjusted fairly long, not in the short knees-up goblin Tartar style.

"Maybe I shouldn't kill him, then. Not right away. Father Cherepanin will scold me if I kill a Christian just for his horses."

And it would be a shame to miss asking him some questions; Sergey could feel his curiosity itching like a mosquito bite. Grandfather Mikhail had always scorned the younger generation because they were pinned to one place, and boasted of how he'd roamed from Germany to China in the service of Great Russ, in the old days before the Change. Most of Sergey's generation had little time for stories of the days of the Red Czars, but they'd made him wistful sometimes. And life in the *stanitsa* could get dull.

Or if Olga finds out about Svetlana, then it could get far too interesting for comfort!

The oncoming rider was jogging along on a horse not quite like anything the Cossack had seen before; short-legged, shaggy, with a head like a barrel and a round tubby body. It didn't look like much, but it was getting its rider along well. The two remounts on a string behind him were Tartar horses, taller and slimmer and more handsome, but although they carried only light loads, twin sacks, they looked more worn-down.

"So he's either expecting a fight or just come from one. Most likely running. Who goes on a raid alone? He rides well, too," Sergey said to himself. "As well as a Cossack. A bit of a runt, but not a *moujik*, not a peasant."

All Cossacks considered themselves noblemen, of course, even though they did their own work.

The man was well-armed too, with an inward-curved yataghan sword at his waist, an odd-looking flat quiver of arrows over his back and a bow in his fist; a round shield of leather-covered cane and a braided lariat were hung at his saddlebow. Apart from that, he wore boots and leather trousers and a shirt of mail over a leather jacket, warm gear for mid-summer unless he expected a fight. As he watched, the stranger halted and looked backwards carefully, standing in his stirrups and raising a hand to shade his eyes.

Sergey nodded to himself, cased the binoculars, picked up his lance, and whistled to his horse, swinging effortlessly into the saddle as the beast unfolded itself and rose. The stranger reacted instantly, reaching over his shoulder for an arrow; he was about three hundred meters away now, extreme bowshot for a strong man and a heavy stave. That motion halted as Sergey held his lance up horizontally over his head, and then reversed it and drove it point-down in the earth in sign of his peaceful intentions, leaving his own bow cased at his left knee. Then he waited quietly as the stranger jog-trotted forward and halted within talking distance.

They looked each other over. Sergey was a young man, just turned twenty, a thumb's width under six feet tall, broad-shouldered, with lean muscles like ropes and a longish straight-nosed face. And an impressive collection of scars, many of which showed because he was wearing only baggy wool pantaloons and high hide boots and the broad leather belt that supported his *shashka*-saber and dagger and a light axe with a meter-long handle. His head was shaved save for a long yellow scalplock bound with thongs that hung down past his shoulder from over his right ear. Mustaches of the same corn-color were still distressingly fuzzy on his upper lip; his slightly tilted eyes were pale green, bright in his tanned face.

The other man looked a *little* like a Tartar, but darker than most—umber-brown skin, braided black hair, with a flat almost scalloped-in face, high cheekbones, and a snub nose. The narrow slanted eyes were blue, but raiding for women back and forth had gone on long enough that you couldn't judge who was who by looks alone. The stranger was shorter than Sergey, strong-looking, but slim and apparently a youth just barely old enough to take the war-trail; even for a black-arse, his face was very hairless. Sweat gleamed on that smooth impassive countenance.

The stranger spoke first. *"Russki?"* he said, in a voice that sounded even younger than his face, pointing at Sergey.

The Cossack nodded and slapped a fist against his bare chest, making the silver crucifix slung there bounce.

"Da, Russki, Khristianin," he said. "Yes, Russian, Christian."

"I am name Dorzha Abakov," the stranger replied.

"Sergey Ivanovitch Khorkina, me. I am a Cossack, *stanitsa* of Polovo in the Don Host, under *Ata-*

man Oleg Andreivitch Arkhipov. And you, flat-face boy?"

"Tanghch people; Kalmyk, you Russki say. My ruler is Erdne Khan of Elst."

From the far reaches, Sergey thought, his brows rising in surprise.

He'd never heard of the khan, and only vaguely of the Kalmyks, who grazed their herds and pitched their yurts in the dry steppe south of Astrakhan on the Caspian shore. Dorzha's eastern-flavored Russian was rough but understandable; a guttural undertone suggested something else that was probably his native language.

"Musul'manin?" Sergey asked suspiciously.

Dorzha spat with scorn, shook his head, and pointed upward. "Worship *Tengri Etseg*—Eternal Blue Father Sky—and the Merciful Buddha, not stupid gods from books."

That *could* have been an insult to the holy Orthodox faith, but the Kalmyk's next words concentrated Sergey's mind wonderfully, along with the eastward jerk of his thumb:

"Nogai men follow me to kill. Five and two."

"Seven Tartars?" Sergey yelped.

Dorzha nodded. "Seven, *da*, is that word." Helpfully, he held up one hand and two fingers of the other.

"They were nine when they start after me," he added, with a smile that exposed teeth that were very even and white, and patted the hilt of his yataghan. Then he indicated his remounts: "These their horses. Now *my* horses."

Sergey cursed fluently and at length, regretting his

decision not to kill the wanderer from ambush. Probably the Tartars would have turned back if they'd just found the body; they were getting too close to the *stanitsa* to be safe. Now . . . even without a blood-debt, any Nogai who found a Russian alone here would fill him full of arrows as a matter of course, unless they went to the effort of trying to capture him for torture or the slave markets. There wasn't a truce on at present, and this wasn't anywhere near the recognized trade-trail along the Belgorod–Volga railway in any case.

He suppressed an impulse to gallop away. If he just rode off, how could he keep this Dorzha from following him out of bowshot?

The black-arse devils would track us both! No wonder the little Kalmyk bastard is smiling!

The odds against *him* had just been cut in half.

But I've got a fight at three-to-one on my hands. The devil's grandmother fly away with him!

Then he laughed and leaned forward in the saddle, extending his hand.

"It's been a while since I let any blood, anyway," Sergey said.

Dorzha took the hand, and a long swig from the flask Sergey offered next, along with a little bread and salt from his saddlebags. The Cossack drank from the Kalmyk's offered canteen in return; it held kumiss, fermented mare's milk. Kumis was better than water, and that was all you could say for it.

"We run more or fight here?" Dorzha asked. "This is ground of yours . . . no, this is your ground, you would say."

Sergey looked around, then cocked an eye at the Kalmyk's horses. They looked thirsty as well as tired, slobbering and showing their tongues. And if the pursued hadn't been able to stop for water, then the pursuers probably hadn't either. . . .

"Hey, dog-brother, there's an old well in that ruined kolkhoz over there," he said thoughtfully. "The Tartar swine know it and they'll probably water their horses at it."

Dorzha grinned and nodded, making a motion to the west and then a curving gesture to indicate turning north and coming back parallel to their own tracks.

"Way to cut back and hide in wrecked of houses without being seen? They come soon, maybe—"

He pointed to the sun, and then to where it would be in about an hour.

"Catch us in twice that long if we run."

Sergey laughed; the Kalmyk had grasped the essentials quickly.

"*Da*. There is a deep ravine four kilometers west that runs to the northeast; we can use that, then come in on the ruins from the north, if we're quick. I like the way you think, Kalmyk! Let's go!"

There *were* seven of the Tartars, men with straggly mustaches and sparse beards, dingy green turbans, long filthy sheepskin coats . . . and unpleasantly clean and well-cared-for weapons.

Sergey looked through a dirty scrap of ancient glass as the enemy dismounted in the thin grass at the center of the old settlement, near a crumbling mound of rust that had been one of the devil's magic oxen before the machines stopped.

A *tractor*, they'd called it, according to the old stories, first conjured out of Hell by the evil wizards of the Red Steel Czar to oppress the peasants. According to his great-grandmother, at least. Grandfather Mikhail had always said they were just machines, like a clock or a reaper, and a lot less work in plowing time than a team of oxen. Sergey had his doubts about that—if they weren't moved by evil spirits, why should they all stop working at the same time?

But Grandfather could certainly tell a story, true or not. To plow sitting down, as if you were taking your ease in a tavern!

None of the Nogai were more than twenty meters away, their boots clumping in the dust and raising little puffs through the sparse grass. That was close enough for the Cossack to smell the hard rancid sweat-and-butter stink of them, as strong as the dry earth and the ancient brick and wood of the ruin.

The well had a built-up earthen coping around it, and a good solid cover of wood; the buildings had been stripped long ago of anything useful, down to wagonloads of bricks, and the frame ones on the outskirts had burned in the yearly grass-fires, but no steppe-dweller would destroy a well, whether Cossack or Tartar or even vagabond bandits. The Tartars looked tired, and their horses worse, despite having three remounts each. The animals were thirsty, too; the slant-eyed men had to hold them back as soon as they smelled water, wrestling with bridles, flicking their quirts at noses and cursing as the eager animals jostled and tossed their heads.

Tartars ride fast, and those are good horses, the Cossack thought. *Dorzha must have led them a merry chase.*

He mentally added a few notches to the lively respect he'd formed for the easterner.

This is not a little lost boy who's come to our steppe, for all he has no beard.

The Nogai warriors had followed the tracks of Sergey and Dorzha just long enough to make sure that they hadn't visited the well, then come directly back here; the two chance-met comrades had galloped west three kilometers, then looped north through the ravine and come back well away from their outward trace.

The Tartars thought their prey was still in headlong flight to the west. They'd plan to water their horses before they took up the chase again, pushing hard to make those they pursued founder their beasts; a thirsty horse died faster. But even if they thought themselves safe, the riders of the Nogai *Ordu* were experienced fighters. Two of them remained mounted, keeping a careful eye out and their bows ready while the others heaved the massive timbers of the lid out of the way and uncoiled their lariats to lower hide buckets and haul them back up hand-over-hand.

Sergey had pulled on his *kosovorotka* shirt-tunic while he rode and over it a sleeveless leather vest sewn with old-time washers of stainless steel, an heirloom from his grandfather, like the round Red Army helmet that now covered his shaven head. He looked over at Dorzha and tapped his bow, then held up two fingers and flipped his hand back and forth to indicate the Tartar sentries:

I the one on the north; you the one on the south. Then as many more as we can.

The Kalmyk nodded grimly, keeping his head well below the four-foot top of the ruined wall. Sergey eased three arrows out of his quiver, selecting hunting shafts with broad triangular heads, since none of the Tartars looked as if they were wearing armor. He set one on his string and the other two carefully point-down in the dirt. Dorzha did likewise. His arrows were black-fletched in nomad fashion; the Cossack preferred to use expensive imported peacock feathers from the Crimea, even if some of his friends teased him about being a dandy.

As if they'd practiced the motion together for years, they sprang to their feet, drawing and loosing in the same motion.

"Hourra!" Sergey shouted.

Dorzha simply shrieked with exultation, a sound like a file on metal. The *snap* of the strings on the bracers sounded in almost the same instant as the wet *thunk* of impact; at ten meters, an arrow from a powerful sinew-and-horn horseman's bow struck quicker than thought. Sergey's target went backwards over the crupper of his saddle in a double splash of red as the arrow punched through his chest and out the back of his body without slowing. The other sentry took Dorzha's shaft under one armpit, and it sank to the fletching; he collapsed thrashing and screaming.

Sergey reached for another arrow. Dorzha shot

before he could draw, and a Tartar on foot staggered backwards, staring down incredulously at the shaft in his stomach, then toppled backwards still clutching the bucket he'd been drawing. The long leather rope whipped down the shaft after him, and a scream floated up to be followed by a splash as the man struck headfirst.

"Four left!" Sergey shouted.

Then the Nogai were shooting back and leaping into the saddle; Sergey ducked as a whistle of shafts went by overhead. A savage yelping war-shout rose as they reined around toward the wall:

"Gur! Gur! *Gur!*"

And a thunder of hooves. Sergey yelled laughter as the two men turned and ran, vaulting over the lower back wall of the ruined building and turning sharply left between a higher stretch of rubble and a big oak tree.

"The infidel swine won't get off their horses even to piss if they can help it!"

He'd counted on that. With superb horsemanship, the leading Tartar took the wall Sergey and Dorzha had just leapt, and shot from the saddle in midjump. Sergey swerved with a yell as the arrow went *vwwwpt!* past his left ear and dived for the ground. Dorzha landed beside him and scrabbled in the dirt; the Tartar in the laneway reined back slightly to let his comrades catch up, then came on again with his lance poised.

"Pull!" Sergey shouted.

"I pulling *am*, stupid Cossack ox!" Dorzha wheezed.

Their joined lariats sprang up out of the dust, secured to the oak tree and with a half-hitch around the jut of eroded brick wall. They both braced their feet and flung themselves backwards, but even with the friction of the hitch, the rope jerked savagely through his callused palms as the first two horses struck it. One went over in a complete somersault and landed on its rider like a woman's wooden tenderizing hammer coming down on a pork cutlet; the other collapsed and slid, throwing its rider ahead of it. The two behind reared and crow-hopped on their hind legs, screaming louder than their riders as they tried to dodge the tangle of human and equine flesh before them.

Sergey plucked the hatchet out of his belt, tossed it into a better grip, and threw with a whipping overarm motion. The ashwood of the handle left his hand with that sweet fluid feeling you got when something was thrown properly, and an instant later the steel helve went *smack* into a Tartar's face; the man fell and beat at the earth with his hands, screaming in a gobbling, choking grunt.

Dorzha had his yataghan out. He dodged in catquick under the last rider's hasty slash, turned it with his round leather-covered cane shield and drove the point of the inward-curved sword into the horse's haunch. It bucked uncontrollably, and the Nogai had no time to spare for swordwork for an instant. That was enough.

Quick as a cat indeed! Sergey thought, as the sharp Damascus-patterned steel slashed across the man's thigh, swinging in a beautifully economical curve.

It opened the muscle nearly to the bone; Dorzha bounced away again to let him bleed out.

The Tartar who'd been thrown from his horse had landed with a weasel's agility, rolling over and over, then bouncing up. His bow was gone, but he had his curved *shamshir* out almost instantly.

"Allahu Akbar!" he shouted as he charged, sword whirling over his head. "*Gur!*"

"*Yob tvoyu mat'*," Sergey replied, grinning and coming up on the balls of his feet; the Tartar probably even understood it—everyone picked up swearwords. "*Hourra! Christ is risen!*"

His *shapska* was longer than the nomad's weapon, a guardless shallow curve with an eagle's-head pommel, and while the Tartars were fearsome fighters on horseback, most of them were as awkward on foot as a pig on ice. He flicked the Nogai's cut aside— Sergey grunted slightly at the impact; the man was *strong*—with a *ting* and a shower of sparks. The Tartar smashed at him like a man threshing grain, but Sergey drifted backwards until he saw Dorzha circling in the corner of his eye. Then he pressed the attack, lunging forward—only a fool fought fair with a Tartar when he didn't have to.

Seconds later, the Nogai collapsed with a yell of agony as the yataghan cut his hamstring and the Cossack saber slashed his sword-arm. Sergey grunted again in surprise as Dorzha beat up his killing stroke, leaving him staggering for a second.

"The devil carry you off in a sack!" he said resentfully, examining his sword's edge—no nick, thank the saints. "Why did you do that?"

Dorzha ignored him. Instead he planted a foot on the wounded Tartar's chest and put the point of his yataghan under the man's chin. The Tartar spat at him, then hissed as the point dimpled the flesh.

"Where is the princess?" Dorzha asked . . . in Tartar, of which Sergey had a fair command.

"On her way to Astrakhan, where you will never follow, you depraved kufur *bi—"*

The point drove home and the curse ended in a gurgle, and the Tartar's heels drummed briefly on the ground. Dorzha wiped his sword and the edge of his boot free of blood on the nomad's sheepskin jacket.

"Princess?" Sergey asked casually as he helped his chance-met comrade make sure of the others.

"That was a good trick with the axe," Dorzha said.

Sergey wrenched it free of the wounded man's face and slammed the blunt hammer on the back of the blade into the Nogai's temple with a heavy crunching sound. The man jerked once and stopped twitching.

"Off to hell, black-arse," he said cheerfully, then flipped the weapon into the air and caught the handle.

"Grandfather Mikhail was *spetsnaz*, he taught us the trick," Sergey said, and pointed to the axe—not particularly threatening, but not *not* so either. "The Princess?"

Dorzha sighed and sat on a stump of wall. "The daughter of my Khan. I was her bodyguard," he said. "Not in the troops with us, just . . . personal guard."

Well-born nom'klaturnik *stripling dancing attendance on this princess*, Sergey thought.

He'd noted the quality of Dorzha's boots, and the silver inlay on his yataghan and kinjal-dagger, and the tooling on his belt, whose buckle was a blue-enameled wolf's-head. And his mail-shirt was of fine riveted links, a master-smith's work.

Then, grudgingly: *Young, and a nobleman, but he can fight.*

"We taking her up the Volga—a wedding with Duke Pyotr of Nikolayevsk. Then these Tartars, river pirates working for the Khan of Chistopol attack."

Sergey nodded thoughtfully. "The misbelieving infidel dog wouldn't want Nikolayevsk strengthened by an alliance."

Dorzha pounded a fist against the brick beside his hip. "They supposed to kill her, I think, but instead take to sell. That why I run. They no hurt her—"

"You could get a good sum for the virgin daughter of a khan," Sergey said thoughtfully. "In Astrakhan."

He turned and freed his lariat, uncoiling it and rigging a casting loop. "Let's get going," he said. "There are eighteen of their horses. Can you sleep in the saddle, boy?"

Dorzha grinned. "Can you, farmer?"

"Oi, Pri Luzhke!" Sergey sang in a loud, melodious baritone seven days later, reeling in the saddle with his feet kicked free of the stirrups.

"*Carry the water, Gala!*
Come, maiden, and water my horse—"

"Silence, Cossack pig!" the *streltsy* officer at the

north gate of Astrakhan said in his rough southeastern dialect of Russian.

He twitched the long black mustaches that hung past his blue-stubbled chin; behind him his men hefted their crossbows and half-pikes. The two young men had twenty good horses with them, counting the ones they rode, and their gear was of fine quality. They could probably afford a bribe, and they were strangers without friends here. The scalp-lock of the Don Cossack was unmistakable, and so were the features of the Kalmyk; Erdne Khan wasn't at war with Astrakhan, but the realms weren't particularly friendly either.

"What is your business in the city?"

"I come to drink all the vodka and screw all the women, of course, fool," Sergey said, and held his canteen up over his open mouth to shake out the last drops, breathing out with satisfaction and tossing the empty vessel aside. "Ahhhh! Got a drink on you, dog-face? Or will I have to settle for fucking your sister, after I put a bag on her ugly head?"

The man flushed, and there was a ripple of laughter from the crowd jammed in the gate, ragged peasants from the drained marshes outside the city with little two-wheeled ox-carts of vegetables, peddlers with pack-donkeys, a hook-nosed Armenian merchant in a skullcap and long kaftan with a curved knife stuck through his sash. A camel in the Armenian's caravan-string threw its head up and made an unearthly burbling sound, as if joining in the mirth. Two Kuban Cossacks in their round black lambskin caps and long wool *cherkessa* coats laughed loudest of all. Though there wasn't much love lost between what its members called the All-Great Kuban Host and their northerly cousins from the Don, they still enjoyed seeing one of the Sir Brothers mock a city man.

The *streltsy* looked around, obviously trying to see who'd laughed so he could beat someone safer than a Cossack.

"We come to sell our horses," Dorzha broke in, scowling himself and fingering the silver-inlaid hilt of his yataghan.

He hefted the leading-rope; they had all the Nogai horses, minus those who'd broken legs or sprained something in the brief fight. The tall slim-legged animals were snorting and rolling their eyes at the unfamiliar noises and scents of the great city of the Volga delta.

The militia officer snorted himself. "Where did you get those?" he said. "They're good horses."

"They were a gift," Sergey said.

"A gift?"

"*Da*. From some dead Tartars," Sergey said. "Or you *could* call it an inheritance."

That produced more hooted laughter; one of the Kuban men nearly fell off his horse as he wheezed helplessly with mirth. A couple of Tartars shot Sergey looks from under hooded eyes, and there were loud calls from the back of the crowd for the *streltsy* to stop being officious and clear the way.

"Now, are you going to let us past so we can go ease our thirst like Christian men, or will you keep us talking all night?" Sergei asked.

It was only half an hour until the late summer sundown, and nobody wanted to be stuck outside when the gates closed. The officer hefted his long two-handed axe, idly running a thumb down the great curved cutting-edge. He was wearing a steel breastplate and helmet despite the damp heat, and sweat poured off his lean dark face. He spoke to Dorzha next:

"And what's a Kalmyk boy doing with this scalplock devil?"

"I keep him with me to hold me back when I lose my temper!" Dorzha said, flipping a coin toward the city militiaman. "Here!"

The militiaman snatched it out of the air, bit the silver dihrem and looked at it with respect—it bore the stamp of the Christopol mint. They both had a fair number of those, courtesy of the dead Nogai. *Someone* had been paying them well.

"Pass, then," he said; his men stirred, expecting their cut. "But remember that the great Czar Boris Bozhenov keeps good order here in his city—thieves are sent to the chain-gangs, and armed robbers are impaled or knouted to death. Drunken rowdies cool their heads in the *butuks*."

He jerked a thumb at a brace of bleary-looking rascals not far away, sitting with their feet and hands locked in the stocks. A few children were amusing themselves by throwing horse-dung and the occasional rock at them.

"Czar!" Dorzha said with contempt, after they'd passed through the thick rubble-and-concrete wall into the noise and crowds of the street. "Grand-father of Boris called himself Chairman."

Sergey shrugged. "All the Princes and Grand Dukes and Khans and Czars used to be called that, back in the old days," he said. "Or Party Secretaries, my grandfather told us children."

Of course, he also told us that he could fly like a bird back then and jump from the sky into battle, Sergey thought. *Sober, he was the best liar I've ever met. Of course, there are such things as gliders and balloons, but . . . And he could throw an axe like an angel.*

"Did you have to be so loudness at the gate, like bull that bellows?" Dorzha went on; his Russian had improved, but he still slipped now and then.

Sergey shrugged again. "Who ever heard of a humble Cossack?" he said. "*That* would be suspicious. Besides, your idea was good: we want those Tartars to hear of us and come for vengeance. How else can we find them before they sell your Princess to Big-Head Boris, or to some Kazakh slave-trader for the harem of the Emir of Bokhara? There must be thirty or even forty thousand people in this city."

"Seventy-five thousands," Dorzha said absently.

"*Bozehmoi!*" Sergey said with awe. "It must be the biggest city in the world, bigger than Moskva the Great in the old days!"

Dorzha shook his head. "They say Winchester is as big, and richer," he said; at Sergey's blank look, he went on: "In Britain, far to the west. And there are much more big . . . *bigger* . . . cities in Hinduraj, and China."

Sergey grunted; those places were the edge of the world, where men might have their heads set on backwards or hop around on a single leg. Astrakhan was certainly at least twice as big as Belgorod, which was the largest city in *his* part of the world.

Grandfather Mikhail called us snails, because we hadn't seen Moskva the Great or Vladivostock, Sergey thought. *But now I've begun to travel like him!*

They walked their horses through a crush of carts and wagons and rickshaws and the occasional bicycle or pedicab, and past horse-drawn tramcars traveling on steel rails set into the roadway—another mark of urban sophistication. Most of the folk were the locals, Russians of a sort, but there were Georgians and Armenians, Greeks and Circassians, Tartars of a dozen different tribes, Kurds, men from the oasis-cities far to the east, a swaggering *Lah* in the gold-laced crimson coat and plumed hat the Poles affected, sailors from the Caspian fleets, porters staggering under high-piled packs . . .

"Here, it stinks," Dorzha said, in a resigned tone. Which it did; most of the city was low-lying, and the land around it natural swamp, and there was a thick wet smell of sewage and rot. "Best not to drink the water."

"I don't *drink* water. It's all right for baths, of course," Sergey said; unlike some, he washed every couple of weeks whether he needed it or not, and took sweat-baths even in winter.

He forced himself not to gape like a *moujik* as

they passed a building that must have been fourteen stories high, a survival from before the Change not yet torn down for its metal. Most of the city was post-Change two or three stories and built of brick often covered with colorful plaster; on a rise to the north were the walls of the city's Kremlin, and behind it, the gilded onion-domes of cathedral and palace. Shopkeepers and artisans called out the wares that spilled into the street, windmilling their arms and screaming of their low prices in a dozen languages, selling everything from Chinese silk to blocks of tea carried here from Georgia to piles of Azeri oranges from the southern shore to a tempting display of swords laid out on dark cloths.

Sergey would have turned aside to look at the fascinating glitter of honed metal if Dorzha hadn't scowled and jerked his head. The caravanserai he chose was the usual type, a square of cubicles within a high rammed-earth wall with a section fenced off as a corral for livestock, and a warehouse where goods could be left under guard for an additional fee. Sergey's nose twitched at the smell of cooking food; it had been a long day.

A sullen-looking man in ragged clothes and an iron collar came to take their animals.

"Here, *rab*," the Cossack said, and tossed him a silver coin. "See that our horses are well-watered and fed—alfalfa and cracked barley, not just hay."

That brightened the slave's face; it also made him more likely to do his job properly . . . and anyway, a Cossack brother was supposed to be openhanded, especially with found money and booty. Sergey didn't like trusting his horse to a *rab*, but slaves were common in places like this.

Many of the residents were squatting at the entrances to their little mud-brick rooms, cooking their evening meals on little braziers. Those not concerned about religious pollution sat at long trestle tables around a firepit, where the serai-keeper and his helpers carved meat from a whole sheep and a couple of yearling pigs that turned on a spit, and handed out rounds of bread and raw onions and melons.

"Room for us, if you please, brothers," Sergey said.

One of those customers looked over his shoulder at Sergey, grunted, and returned to his meal.

"Hey, dog-face, thanks for the seat," Sergey said.

Then he grabbed him by the back of his coat, heaved him aside to thump squawking on the ground, and tossed the man's plate and loaf after him.

"Here's your dinner, and fuck your mother, pal."

Yob tvoyu mat' wasn't necessarily a deadly insult in Russki—between friends it could be just a way of saying "take this seriously"—but Sergey hadn't used the friendly intonation. The ex-diner was burly, and he had a long knife through his sash. Sergey stood and grinned at him with his thumbs in his belt. The man put a hand to his knife for a moment before thinking better of it and slinking away; the two who'd been on either side of him crowded aside to make room for the newcomers.

"He can't complain if I serve him some of his own manners," the Cossack said as he sat down on the bench and slapped the rough, stained poplar planks. "Food and wine! Christ's blood, does a Sir Brother, a knight of the Don Host, have to go hungry and thirsty here with gold and silver at his belt?"

A serving wench bustled over with wooden platters and clay mugs; she gave Sergey a long considering look. He preened and smoothed down his mustaches with a thumb before she turned back to her work, but he caught the glance she gave his companion, too.

"Nice round arse," he said to Dorzha as the youth sat beside him. "And haunches like a plow-horse. Hey, dog-brother, I think she fancies you, though. Or your fine boots and coat. Give it a try!"

The Kalmyk flushed under his dark olive skin and tore off a lump from the loaf of bread. Sergey laughed. The youth was as fastidious and dainty as a young priest fresh from a monastery school, even waiting until a rock or a bush came up to drop his trousers. He'd noticed that on the trip here, though they'd had little time for anything but riding and sleeping and chewing jerky in the saddle. With ten horses each, you could push *hard*, two hundred kilometers a day or better.

And we needed to, after we spent hours *fishing that dead Tartar out of the well. . . .*

"It gets moldy if you don't use it, youngster," he said. "Anyway, it's the little skinny ones like you who can fuck like rabbits."

Dorzha flushed still more, then scowled as Sergey guffawed and took a long gulp of the rough red wine.

I blushed like that the first time Uncle Igor said that to me, he thought. *Of course, I was thirteen, and the Kalmyk has to be older than that.*

"Best not get drunk," Dorzha said coldly. "We may have work to do this tonight, if lucky."

"To drink is the joy of the Russ," Sergey said reasonably. Then he shrugged: "Besides, this is just wine. No Cossack can get drunk on *wine*. We are born with a grape in our mouths."

He didn't take more than one mug, though; the boy had a point. When he'd gnawed the last gristly meat off the rack of pork ribs and picked his teeth with his dagger-point, he tossed the bones to a dog that looked even hungrier than the *rab*, and walked to their cubicle with an exaggerated care; if anyone was watching, they might be encouraged to think he *was* drunk and would sleep soundly.

You can't keep a dog from rolling in shit or a Tartar from seeking revenge, he thought later that night. *They're not peaceable and forgiving and full of loving-kindness to all, like us Christian men.*

They'd left the door open—many of the residents of the caravanserai did, to get what little breeze they could in the sultry summer heat of the delta. Sergey opened one eye a slit; he was lying in his drawers, sprawled back with his head on his saddlebags. Long curved knives glinted a little in the moonlight, as three dark-clad figures slipped in, with the tails of their turbans drawn across their faces to leave only the eyes exposed. A man stooped, knife poised to thrust into Sergey's belly.

Thump.

His foot lashed up into the man's crotch, toes rolled up to present the callused ball of the foot as the striking surface. That slammed his victim's testicles up against the pubic bone as if they were iron on an anvil. A thin squeal like a dying rabbit sounded, and then a maul-on-oak sound as the Cossack's knee punched into the descending face. The Tartar pitched to the side, unconscious or dead; Sergey used the motion to raise both feet in the air and then flip himself up into a standing crouch.

Dorzha had moved in the same instant. He had his belt in his hand, with a brick snugged into a loop at the end by the buckle. It arched out and smacked into the side of the second knifeman's head; the long dagger fell from nerveless fingers, and the man reeled back and collapsed against the wall.

The third Tartar acted with commendable prudence and great speed; he threw his knife at Dorzha and fled. The Kalmyk boy gave a startled yelp of pain. Sergey ignored him—time enough to bind wounds later—and threw himself forward in a tackle that caught the man around the knees and brought him crashing down. The air went out of him in a *whuff!* as he flopped on belly and face; most of the Cossack's went out, too, but he scrabbled forward over the heaving body and hammered a knobby fist into the small of his enemy's back—much better than breaking your knuckles on a skull, grandfather had always said. And again and again, until the enemy went limp.

"Shut up, you fornicating buffoons! We're trying to sleep like Christians!" someone called from the cubicle next door.

"Sorry, brother," Sergey said contritely. "The saints guard your dreams."

Then he dragged the man back into the cubicle by his ankle and turned to look at Dorzha. The Kalmyk was in his drawers and shirt, with a long red stain spreading on the linen beneath his left arm. He clamped that to his side and shook his head.

"Just a scratch," he said, with a tight brace in his voice that gave him the lie. "Let's get what know we must—what we must know, I mean."

Sergey grunted thoughtfully and looked through the dimness at their three assailants. The man he'd kicked and knee-butted was breathing in swift shallow jerks, his eyes wide and fixed; no use there. The one he'd punched was unconscious—and probably bleeding out internally from his ruptured kidneys. If he woke, it would only be to scream.

"Well, Christ be witness, you hit this one just right!" he said, as the one stunned by the Kalmyk started to stir. "That was good work—it shows a delicate hand. I finished my two off or nearly, and they're useless."

"Delicate is not Cossack way, eh?" Dorzha said with a painful smile.

Sergey laughed as he grabbed the man, pulled his belt loose, trussed his arms behind his back with it, and stuffed a gag into his mouth.

"So, dog-face," he said, tipping water from his skin over the man, who glared defiance as he came fully aware. "You nod when you feel like a good chat, eh? No noise and fuss, now; people are trying to sleep."

"Let me this do," Dorzha said.

Sergey looked around; the Kalmyk had bound a spare shirt around his ribs beneath his garment, and was moving with careful precision. Sergey shrugged and stepped aside. Dorzha picked up one of the Tartar daggers, held it up until the captive's eyes followed the flicker of moonlight on the honed edge, and then struck like a cat. The Tartar's eyes bulged as his hide trousers fell away. It was only a few seconds later that he began to nod frantically, trying to bellow at the same time and choking as the wet cloth slipped farther into his wide-stretched mouth.

Dorzha flicked the gag free with the point of the knife, and held it so that blood dripped on the man's face. Sergey winced slightly and suppressed an impulse to cup his hands protectively over his crotch. Instead, he pulled on his clothes as the Kalmyk asked questions in quick, confident Tartar—he spoke the *turka* dialect better than he did Russian, though with an unfamiliar accent and choice of words that showed he'd learned it somewhere else besides the middle Volga. The interrogation was thorough and expert; where, when, how many guards, what the passwords were, a staccato sequence timed to leave no time for the captive's pain-fuddled mind to invent lies.

"Kill me," the Tartar rasped at last, face gray and sweating.

Dorzha nodded and thrust; the dagger's watered steel slid home with only a slight crunching sound, and he left it with the hilt jutting out of the man's chest to keep the first spurt of blood corked. Then he rose . . . and staggered, his eyes turning up until only the whites showed, and collapsed backwards himself with limp finality.

"*Bozhemoi!* I didn't think he was that badly hurt!" Sergey said, and sprang to drag the Kalymk into the scanty clear space.

He pulled up the shirt to get at the wound; it was leaking red through the loose, hasty bandage. Then he stared for a long moment, blinking and shaking his head.

"Bozhemoi!" he said, then thumped the heel of his hand against his forehead as bits and pieces of the past week went *click* within. "Aaaaaah! I *am* a stupid Cossack ox!"

Dorzha opened her eyes and raised a hand to feel at her ribs, now expertly and tightly bandaged. Then her hand flashed toward the hilt of her yataghan where it lay next to her.

Sergey laughed. Her eyes flashed toward him, and the blade glowed blue-white in the darkness, catching a stray gleam of moonlight from outside.

"Hey, sister, how many men have I watched you kill?" Her blue eyes narrowed, and he went on: "Four. And I've only known you eight days! So if I had designs on your skinny arse, I wouldn't have left that sword within your reach, would I?"

"I listen," Dorzha said, sitting up against the mud-brick wall of the cubicle and propping the blade across her knees.

"Also, as a boy you were more girlish than was good to see, and as a girl, you're too much like a boy for my taste. And we've shared bread and salt, and fought for each other. Now, let's get on with rescuing this 'princess' . . . a friend of yours, or your sister?"

Dorzha smiled unwillingly. "Half sister. My mother was a concubine, and half-Russki. I was raised with Bortë . . . the Princess . . . and it amused the Khan to let me train as a warrior to protect her."

The smile flashed wider: "How she me envied! We are friends, too . . . more or less. She is . . . wise. A scholar."

Sergey grunted and tossed over the leather water-bottle. Dorzha drank deep and then stood, moving experimentally.

"How is it?" Sergey asked.

"Not too bad," Dorzha said. "I wouldn't want to use my bow, but I can fight; you strapped it up well. Where are the bodies?"

"Over the wall," Sergey said. "The street-pigs will eat well tonight; or maybe the beggars."

He rose himself, swinging his long arms and grinning. "Let's go!"

Now, how to kill this one?

The Tartars were holding the Princess—Sergey thought of her as looking like an icon, with stiff

gold-embroidered robes—in the house of a rich Kurdish merchant who traded in silk, cotton, and slaves;
from here you could look down a long narrow roadway at its side, but it was black-dark, too far from
the main streets to rate gas-lamps. The building presented a thick blank wall to this street and it had a
tower at the back, four stories high with narrow slit
windows; one of them showed lantern-light, but
everything else was dark.

"Let me have the lantern," Dorzha whispered.

Sergey handed it over. It was hers, and a good
one, made of metal and running on distilled rock-
oil. What he hadn't realized until now was that the
cover would flip up and back if you squeezed the
handle. That the Kalmyk woman proceeded to
do; long-short-short-long-long-long. It was no code
he knew, but . . .

The second time through, the window darkened . . .
then went light again, in the same pattern, as if someone were waving a cloth in front of the light. Dorzha
seemed to slump slightly, and gave a soundless sigh of
relief.

"She is there," the Kalymk said. "And well, and
says *come to me*. We used that signal when we
wanted to steal out of the Khan's house in Elst."

"You two must have done wonders for your father's peace of mind," Sergey said, grinning in the
dark.

"Tcha!" Dorzha replied. "Now, how best to go
in?"

"They have patrols along the walls," Sergey said.
"Best through the entrance—if we can do it quietly."

"I think I can. Come."

They circled, meeting nothing more alarming than a pi-dog that growled and slunk away from sniffing at a motionless drunk, or corpse, lying in the gutter. This was a respectable neighborhood, and that meant few went out late at night. At last, they ghosted down the avenue that approached the Kurd's mansion from the front, keeping to the deep shadows the moon cast on the right side of the street. The same moon shone full on the sentry leaning on his spear before the entrance—it glinted on the whetted metal, and on the rippling black-laquered scales of his sleeveless hauberk.

"How do we get past him?" Sergey whispered.

"Leave this to me," Dorzha said.

"I'll be noisy, if you're going to cut off his—"

The Kalmyk woman gave him a scowl. Then she leaned shield and sword, bow and quiver against the wall and walked quietly toward the sentry. The man was dozing standing up, but he straightened and leveled his spear as she approached.

"Who comes to the house of Ibrahim al-Vani by night?" he growled in Tartar.

Dorzha spoke. Sergey blinked in astonishment. Apart from her accent, the Kalmyk had always spoken to him in a light pure tone much like a lad's—it had been close enough to fool *him*, after all. Now . . .

"One seeking a valiant warrior," Dorzha said, in voice that *nobody* would have mistaken for a male's of any age, full of honey and musk and promise. "But I see I've found one."

Sergey blinked again as the Tartar leaned his spear

against the wall and the two figures merged. An instant later, the Tartar slumped down, with only a thin brief whining sound. When he came up, Dorzha was scrubbing the back of her left hand across her lips.

"*That's* a trick I don't think I can copy," he said, handing her the weapons she'd shed.

"Ptha!" she said—either something in Kalmyk or simple disgust. Then she put an arrow to the string. "Take his keys. I cover you."

"Bad security," Sergey noted, as he did, and propped the corpse artistically against the wall in the sort of slump a sleeping man would use. "They should have locked him out and kept a relief inside."

Though the merchant probably guarded merely against theft; against stealth, not an assault—it was hard to change your habits quickly. The doors were thick oak, strapped with a web of salvaged steel fastened with thick bolts at each crosspiece, and the lock was well-oiled.

More bad security. A nice loud rusty screech would warn the house.

The door swung outward, just enough to pass them through into the courtyard. It was a narrow cobbled rectangle, with stables and barracks and storage along one side, a row of horse-troughs, and the merchant's own dwelling on the other; that probably had an inner court of its own, for his womenfolk. The tower was against the far wall, freestanding, probably a refuge against riot and a treasure-house for the most valued goods.

"Wait," Sergey said.

He took another inheritance from his grandfather from his belt. It was a length of flexible metal with wooden handles on either end; he looped it about the bolt of the lock and pulled it back and forth. A nearly soundless rasp followed, and metal filings drifted down to the pavement. He was careful to go slowly—Grandfather had warned him that it might lose its temper and snap if it was overheated, and no modern smith could duplicate its magical properties.

"Bortë will be interested in that; she loves things from before the Change," Dorzha said softly.

She covered the courtyard as she spoke, recurve bow half-drawn and ready to flick out a shaft. After half a minute, the bolt dropped free, and Sergey caught it before it could drop to the stones. Then he eased the door shut again and locked it, leaving the key in the plate. That might not make a difference, or it might fool someone into thinking the door was secure when it wasn't. You never knew, Grandfather had said. . . .

They walked over to the tower; Sergey scooped a handful of water out of one of the troughs as they passed, to wet a mouth gone a little dry. The darkened buildings seemed to loom around him like banks of angry, watchful eyes, and his shoulders crawled with anticipation of a sudden arrow or crossbow-bolt. On the steppe, or even in a forest, he felt at home. This was like a fight in a coffin.

A narrow eyehole opened, and a voice spoke in some musical, liquid-sounding language, much muffled by the thick iron-strapped door.

"The password is *Azazrael's Sword*," Dorzha replied in Tartar, naming the Death Angel.

A surly grunt, and more of the strange tongue. Dorzha spoke again:

"Speak something beside that sheep-bleating, you peacock-worshipping Kurdish apostate. Our chief wants us to check on the Kalmyk woman."

"She is as well-guarded as the wives of my master Ibrahim al-Vani themselves!" the man said, in bad Tartar—worse than Dorzha's Russki had been when she and Sergey met.

"His wives are guarded by the fifty fathers of their children," Dorzha sneered. "Or Kurdish eunuchs—as if there *were* any Kurds with balls. We caught her—now we want to see her."

"It is my head if anything happens to her," the guard said, grumbling. "Curse the evil witch anyway, with her alchemy from Satan!"

Sergey gave a soundless sigh of relief; the man *was* going to open the door.

"And it's *my* head if I don't do what the Chief says," Dorzha replied. "And my head is worth more than yours. I gave the password—open! Or I go and we come back with a battering ram, and a flaying knife to peel the skin from your worthless arse!"

"You Tartars don't rule the universe, you just *think* you do," the man grumbled. "Wait, then, wait."

They could hear clicking and shunking sounds. The door opened, only a narrow crack, and a thick chain spanned the gap. A blue eye looked through it, going wide for an instant before the point of Dorzha's yataghan punched through it with a *crunch* of steel in the thin bone that separated eyesocket from brain. The man toppled backwards like a cut-through tree. Sergey shouldered Dorzha aside, flicked the cutting wire around the chain, and went to work.

"Hurry!" Dorzha said.

"We may need this again. I'm not going to break it," Sergey said stubbornly. "Besides, it was my grandfather's."

Dorzha said something explosive in her native language—but quietly—and soon the forged-iron link parted, falling to the stone floor with a musical tinkle. Sergey blew his lips out in mute relief when the door opened after that.

Because I have no idea what we would have done if there had been another lock!

The hallway within the tower was empty; on either side were chambers that the Tartar had said were used to store goods—and there was a square concrete shaft in the middle, from the looks of it a relic of the old world. Stairs started to the left; they took them in a swift quiet rush, Sergey leading and the Kalmyk woman following behind. There was an odd, acrid odor in the air, growing stronger as they ascended. Behind him, Dorzha chuckled.

"That is Bortë," she said.

She smells like rock oil and sulfur? he thought, puzzled.

The door was unbarred from the outside; a sliver of lamplight showed under the bottom of the thick planks. Sergey pushed at it, sword poised—probably there would be a guard within, as well as the Princess. The door gave a little, and then halted with a yielding heaviness. Sergey grunted and set his boot to it, pushing hard. Behind him, Dorzha spoke in her own language.

The door slid open. Sergey leapt through, cat-agile but trying to stare in three directions at once . . . and then relaxing a little as he saw a woman in a long hooded caftan standing with a lamp in her hand. The smell of acid and strange metals came from the room behind her; he could see that it held benches and odd-looking bits of glass.

The body at his feet attracted his attention first; it was a big man, very big, with a good deal of fat over solid muscle. He wore a turban but was beardless, and his great smooth torso was bare above sash, baggy pantaloons of crimson, and curl-toed boots. A broad curved sword lay beside one set of sausage-thick fingers; a look of fixed horror was on his face, and his eyes bulged as if they were about to pop out of his smooth, doughlike features.

Interesting, Sergey thought, looking around the room, noting a spilled chess set by the dead man; the furnishings were cushions and rugs rather than chairs, as you might expect from a Kurd. *Something killed him. . . .*

Dorzha pushed past him, sheathing her yataghan. *"Bortë!"* she cried.

"Dorzha!" the other replied, setting her lantern on the floor.

They embraced, a fierce hug, and then Dorzha held her half sister at arm's length.

"Are you all right?" she said—in Russki, which must be for his benefit.

"Fine. Bored. They let me keep my gear, the fools, so I had plenty of time to prepare," Bortë replied. "What took you so long?"

"There were . . . problems."

Bortë threw back the hood of her caftan. Sergey blinked; the family resemblance was unmistakable, though the khan's other daughter was shorter and not quite so slim, and the night-black hair that fell loose down the young woman's back was glossier than Dorzha's. The face beneath was snub-nosed, with a rosy, ruddy-pink complexion, full lips, and narrow slanted black eyes.

Perhaps it was the lantern-light streaming up from below, but he felt a slight prickle of alarm in belly and back at that face. She reminded him of something like a cat, or better still, a ferret—small, quick, comely, and quite evil. The black eyes glanced up and down his long form.

"Where did you get this great Cossack ox?" she said—also in Russki, with a pellucidly clear but old-fashioned, bookish accent. "I'm not surprised you're late, with him to drag around."

Dorzha shrugged. "He's useful for the heavy-lifting chores," she said. "Now let's go!"

"How did you kill him?" Sergey asked, intrigued, while she snatched up a bundle and slung it over her back like a knapsack.

He nudged the dead man with his toe. Bortë was smaller than her sister, and while she held herself well he couldn't see her killing a man this size with a blade unless she took him utterly unawares. Also there was no blood—even a small stiletto left in the wound leaked a *little* when stabbed deep into the body.

Bortë smiled, revealing small, very white teeth; the first two were slightly buck-shaped. Instead of replying, she held up her hand; there was a piece of leather across her palm, and a steel needle concealed within it. There was blood on the tip of the little sliver of metal, with some purplish discoloration beneath that.

"But I let him win the last game," she said. "He wasn't a bad man. For a eunuch."

Sergey swallowed. "Your sister said you were a scholar," he said.

"I am," she replied, and smiled more broadly. "Of chemistry."

The Cossack crossed himself.

"*Yob tvoyu mat'*," Sergey said; it struck him as more manly than screaming *We're fucked!* and slapping himself on the top of the head.

The lights and voices at the bottom of the stairs were both indistinct, but they were getting louder. And there was no other way *out* of this tower. Screams of rage cut through the brabble; someone must have discovered the body and the cut chain.

"We're fucked," Dorzha said, then cursed in Kalmyk and kicked the wall viciously.

Not fair, Sergey said. *She doesn't* have *to be manly.*

Dying heroically was always more pleasant when you were drunk and listening to some balalaika-twanging gypsy *guslar*'s lying song than in a situation like this. His mind hunted back and forth like a wolf he'd seen trapped in a pit once. Suddenly, he felt a new sympathy for its snarling desperation.

"We killed plenty of those Tartars before," Dorzha said, but with a note of doubt in her voice.

"*Da*," Sergey said. "When we ambushed them or surprised them. A stand-up fight . . ."

He shrugged. Dorzha did too, and whipped her yataghan through a circle to loosen her wrist.

"We knew this was risky," she said.

"*Da*," the man said again. "Well, Cossacks don't usually die old anyway."

The sound of hands clapping came from behind him. He turned and glared at Bortë, who had dragged a sack out of the inner room. Now she applauded again.

"Hear the *baatar*," she said, jeering. "Hear the hero! Listen to him meet death unafraid—because it's so much easier than *thinking*."

Dorzha scowled at her sister. So did Sergey. *I could really come to dislike this woman, if I had the time*, he thought.

Then he ducked with a yelp as she pulled a stoppered clay jug out of her sack and lofted it over his head. It dropped neatly down to the next landing, a story below, and shattered. He couldn't see anything come out of it, not in the darkness of the stairwell . . . but a sudden scent sharp enough to slice your lungs made him cough and backpedal, rubbing at his streaming eyes.

"It is heavier than air," Bortë said.

"Poison?" he asked, as the shrieks of rage below turned to choked howls of panic.

"Chlorine. Quite deadly. It will flow downward. Come!"

She turned and began dragging the sack with her into the inner sanctum. Sergey ignored the shadowed forms of retorts and glass coils on tables; the square inner shaft ran through this room, and there was an open door in it that showed modern ropes, not rusted ancient cable. That looked *much* better than fighting his way down the stairs, even if the air there was breathable, which just now it wasn't. Mikhail had told stories about war gases in the old days, and how he'd used them against the *moujids* in some place far to the east. The Princess took half a dozen of the jars from her sack and dropped them through the opening.

"That will take care of anyone waiting below," she said. "There's a tunnel out under the walls. The eunuch told me about it. The joke is on him, eh?"

"Ha. Ha," Sergey said as his testicles tried to crawl up into his belly. "If that stuff burns out your lungs, going down there will kill *us*! Or at least me, you witch!"

"Not with these," she said, and pulled improvised masks out of the sack. "*I* have been thinking all the time I was here, *baatar*. Luck favors the prepared."

"She never stops," Dorzha said, taking one of the masks and examining the ties that would hold it on her face. "It's no wonder Father tried to marry her off to someone two months' journey away."

"These will protect us?" Sergey said.

Bortë smiled again. "The chemicals need to be activated with uric acid," she said.

"That's what?" he said, baffled; the words were Russki but he'd never heard them before.

She told him.

Sergey ripped the mask from his face half an hour later, spitting. "You enjoyed that!" he snarled.

To his surprise, Dorzha laughed with her sister. "Only the sight of your face, Cossack," she said.

He looked around the darkened streets; they were near the docks, and the masts of the ships showed over the roofs, some of them with the flickering stars of riding-lanterns burning at their tops.

"Well, I suppose we should try and get you to your father," he said.

Odd. I will miss Dorzha. And her sister is interesting. Terrifying, but interesting.

Bortë looked southward for a moment. "Why?" she said. "He'll only marry me off to some *other* fat imbecile."

Sergey rocked back on his heels. "Why, why—" His mind churned. "What else is there to do with you?"

Dorzha spoke. "You wouldn't believe there were larger cities than Astrakhan," she said. Then, wistfully: "I've never *seen* any bigger. But they say in China . . ."

In the shadows, Bortë's head turned toward her. "They say that in China, Toghrul Khan rules now," she said thoughtfully. "A Yek, but a Mongol like us; our ancestors came west from there, very long ago— the tongues are still close kin. At least, he rules the portions near the Gobi, and they also say he wars against the Han farther south. I wonder . . . I wonder if he could use a scholar of the ancient arts? His court in Xian is the richest in the world, the stories say."

"Gold," Dorzha said thoughtfully. "Silk. Rank."

Bortë shook her head. "*Books!*" she said, and her eyes glowed. "Scholars! Laboratories!"

Suddenly, Sergey's irritation lifted, and he began to laugh. "A real *bogatyr*—hero—I was, escaping with a woman's piss-soaked scarf over my nose!"

"You might do better with instruction," Bortë said.

"He *is* useful for the heavy work," Dorzha said.

Sergey laughed again, a booming sound that rattled off the warehouses around them. And if he went home, Olga and Svetlana would be waiting. Probably with their threshing-flails in hand.

"Which way is China?" he said.

David Ball

A former pilot, sarcophagus maker, and business-man, David Ball has traveled to sixty countries on six continents, crossed the Sahara four times in the course of researching his novel *Empires of Sand,* and explored the Andes in a Volkswagen bus. Other re-search trips have taken him to China, Istanbul, Algeria, and Malta. He's driven a taxi in New York City, installed telecommunications equipment in Cameroon, renovated old Victorian houses in Denver, and pumped gasoline in the Grand Tetons. His bestselling novels include the extensively researched historical epics *Ironfire* and the aforementioned *Empires of Sand,* and the contemporary thriller *China Run.* He lives with his family in a house they built in the Rocky Mountains.

In the grim story that follows, he takes us to seventeenth-century Morocco for a harrowing game of cat-and-mouse, one in which, if you're *lucky,* the prize is death. . . .

The Scroll

The prisoner felt a slithering on his belly and opened his eyes to a snake.

It was a viper, sluggish in the pre-dawn cool as it sought the warmth of his body. Scarcely daring to breathe, the engineer slowly lifted his head and stared into tiny coal-black eyes: emotionless, cold, and dead like his own. After the initial sick surge of fear raced through his veins, he was able to draw a deep breath, scarcely believing his good fortune. Only a week earlier, one of his men had rolled over onto just such a creature, perhaps this very one. True, he suffered horribly, but then he was released forever from this life. After all the prisoner had been through, could it at last be this easy?

He felt the pounding of his own heart as he moved his hand to provide an easy target. The air was oppressive, almost liquid.

The tongue flicked.

Please, God, take me. Now.

The snake ignored his hand. Head elevated, it kept a steady gaze on the engineer. He brushed at it. The viper drew back. No strike. Growing irritated, determined to provoke it, he swatted. He felt cool scales against his rough hand, but no burning of fang, no flush of poison. It was a dream, surely a dream; perhaps the emperor in another form, taunting him cruelly yet again. Another entry in the emperor's scroll, another part of his destiny that he could do nothing to change.

Then it no longer mattered. The reptile slid away and disappeared into a hole in the masonry, to hunt for one of the rats.

Baptiste let his breath out and lay still on his back. A tear coursed down his cheek. The heat was already making its way into the *metamore*, the underground chamber he shared with five hundred others. Once there had been forty of his own men, but only six now remained, the rest taken one at a time by disease, starvation, snakes, scorpions, overwork, despair, suicide, torture, and of course, the emperor.

He heard the reedy call of the muezzin, but not yet the footsteps of the guards. It was Sunday, when Christian prisoners had half an hour extra of rest, and even the opportunity to pray together. He heard it now, the familiar refrain of the priest, holding a service near the stream that ran through their midst: "Rejoice in thy suffering, my children, for it is the will of God." Baptiste grimaced. Surely the prisoners were rejoicing, for he could hear their agonies as they struggled to begin another day.

He closed his eyes until the hatch opened and a shaft of sunlight lit the ground near his head. A rope ladder was dropped from above. A chorus of groans was followed by a clatter of chains and the rush of men fighting for position at the ladder, because the last man up would be beaten for sloth. The other men always let the engineer go among the first, for Baptiste held the power of life and death over them. Most had heard the emperor's familiar greeting to him.

Will you kill for us today, Engineer?

No one wished to be among those chosen to die. No one tried to make friends with him, for that, they had seen, could be fatal. Above all, no one let harm come to him, for they knew that if Baptiste lived, only some of them would die. If Baptiste died, they would all die.

By the time he ascended into another day of perdition, blinking back the blinding Moroccan sun, Baptiste was no longer certain there had been a snake at all.

"Will you kill for us today, Engineer?" He had first heard the emperor's refrain too many lives ago to count. A hundred? A thousand? Men dead because of his own weakness and an emperor's boredom, men dead because of a game and a scroll, a damnable yellowed parchment at whose end he could only guess.

Baptiste was a soldier, but never believed he was a killer. He was an engineer who served at the right hand of Vauban, master of the art of siege warfare. Vauban, who could build anything and destroy anything. Together they devised ingenious methods of attack for the endless wars of Louis XIV and surpassed them with even more brilliant methods of defense.

Baptiste loved battlements and fortifications and all the tools of war, but found the noise and the smell of battle itself terrifying. He did not like the bodies and blood that fouled his neat ditches, did not like the ravages of shells that tore his pristine walls, did not, in fact, like the killing. It offended the laws of God and the order of his own life. Yes, his work allowed others to kill with speed and efficiency, but his own hands were clean. He was detached from it all: he loved the elegant precision of his drafting tools and the crisp drawings they made. In battle he often sat exposed to enemy fire, head bent over his work, oblivious of the shrieks of men and the roar of the guns and the danger, and it was the designs created in those moments that thwarted the enemy and even saved lives. That was his gift: seeing things that were not yet real, things that other men could not see, then putting them on paper so that others might convert his vision into earth, wood, and iron. After several of these battlefield designs had proved their worth, Vauban himself declared the engineer a genius and gave him a promotion.

It proved to be an unlucky advancement. He was captain of a company of engineers, transporting siege equipment in two galliots from the arsenal at Toulon to Marseilles. His own son, Andre, served in the corps and was aboard the second ship. Baptiste waved at his son, standing at the rail, easy to make out at a distance because he had the family's distinctive streak of white hair in a thick head of black. They had been three long years at war and were looking forward to a short leave. Their ships had been becalmed, then swallowed in a rare fog. The captain assured them the winds would pick up no later than the following morning. He dispensed rum to all hands. Men drank and fiddled and played draughts. Most were napping when a corsair xebec attacked. Before an alarm could be raised, the decks were swarming with Moors. The ship fell without a shot. As Baptiste was tossed below in chains, his only consolation was that his son's ship had not been captured.

They learned from the raïs who commanded the corsair vessel that their destination was to be Morocco. "You will find death in your Christian Hades preferable to life in that realm," cackled the raïs. "When it comes to the suffering of man, it is Moulay Ismaïl who is master; Satan himself but a pupil." Rumors flew on the ship about the emperor, a tyrant whose cruelty was legend. Atigny, a sapper from Aix, had suffered imprisonment there for six years, his health all but broken. "Ismaïl is a genius," said the morose Atigny. "He is building a city to rival Versailles. But he is a monster. Bloodthirsty and quite mad. He kills with his own hands. He kills for pleasure and delights in the sufferings of others. I survived because I found work in the stables. The horses live better than any man in Morocco. I was finally ransomed, but it ruined my family. My father died in poverty. There will be no second ransom for me."

"Nonsense," Baptiste told him. "We shall all be ransomed, by a church if not by our families."

"When Ismaïl discovers we are engineers, he will never let us leave. He needs us for his building. I cannot return there. I cannot suffer it again. Pray you are not noticed by him, *mon capitaine*. He chooses prisoners at random for special torment. He toys with them. God works his worst on those the emperor notices."

Baptiste tried to cheer the man, but he was inconsolable. On the morning the ship's lookout signaled land, Atigny managed to strangle himself in his own chains.

The equipment captured with the galliot identified Baptiste's men as engineers. They were taken inland from Sallee, the lair of the corsairs, to Meknes, the capital. Without ceremony they were put to work on the walls where, as Atigny had promised, cruelty was rife and death common. Men were worked beyond endurance, whipped and murdered without mercy, and buried in the walls, mixed with the lime.

One morning the imperial horses came thundering down a long passageway, Moulay Ismaïl in the lead, robes billowing, flanked by his *bokhaxa*, the killers of his elite personal guard. Men too slow to move were shredded beneath the hooves. The imperial party pulled up sharply and dismounted. The guards sprang to action, forcing men to the sand. Cringing and groveling were the only permitted responses to the imperial presence. Like the others, Baptiste knelt with his forehead to the ground. A moment later he was staring at the imperial toe. "Rise," commanded the emperor. Baptiste didn't know whether the emperor was addressing him or another, but he was quickly yanked to his feet.

The emperor of Morocco was slight of stature,

dressed in plain clothing without ornament. "You are Vauban's engineer," he said pleasantly.

"I had the honor to serve under him, yes, Majesty."

"Was it you who made these plans?" Ismaïl asked. Baptiste recognized papers taken from his ship.

"Yes, Majesty."

Ismaïl's face lit and he nodded happily. "Then we are pleased to have you in our service," he said, as if Baptiste were there of his own will. "Come, walk with us." He turned and strode into the palace as an astonished Baptiste hurried to catch up, hardly knowing what to make of this turn of events. This was Moulay Ismaïl, Alouite sultan of Morocco, descendant of the Prophet Muhammad. Moulay Ismaïl, warrior who had helped drive the English from Tangier and the Spanish from Larache. Moulay Ismaïl, at whose hand six thousand women and children had died as he tamed the untamable Berbers. Moulay Ismaïl, who had defied the Ottoman Turks, delivering the heads of their commander and ten thousand of his troops to adorn the walls of Marrakesh and Fez, a demonstration of his yearning for peace. Moulay Ismaïl, on whose behalf the corsairs of Sallee pillaged the coasts of Europe, carrying away men, women, and children to be used for ransom or in the building of his empire. He built palaces and roads and bridges and forts and imposed harsh laws that brought peace to a land that had known nothing but war. "My people have order and bread," he boasted as they walked. "Soon this empire shall be great once again, greater even than under the Almohads, when the art and architecture and literature of Morocco were prized in the civilized world. Have you seen the Alhambra?"

"I have not, Majesty."

"Nor have we, but we have heard of its genius. We shall build greater still. You shall help us build, Engineer. You shall help us achieve this vision."

"Majesty, I—"

"Tell us about the siege of Maastricht," commanded Ismaïl, and they paused and Baptiste drew sketches in the sand and answered detailed questions from the well-informed monarch, who demonstrated keen interest in the art and science of siege warfare. "I have granaries that will allow us to withstand siege for five years," he boasted.

"Perhaps," Baptiste said, his practiced eye roaming the battlements, "but there are weaknesses a clever enemy might exploit."

"Most certainly. You will correct those weaknesses, Engineer. And you will build for us a city greater than the ancient capitals of Marrakesh, of Fez, even greater than Versailles, the quarters of your infidel king Louis."

The tour lasted three hours, the emperor expansive and proud as he pointed out features of what had already become one of the largest building complexes in the world: stables and granaries occupying vast chambers, palaces and harems, reception halls, private quarters, banquet rooms, kitchens, barracks, baths, and mosques. It was dusty, endless, and grand. The energetic emperor was bursting with ideas and stopped frequently to give orders to overseers who were clearly terrified by Ismaïl's presence. For his part, Baptiste found the afternoon tour quite pleasant.

They had returned to Baptiste's station when Ismaïl noticed a group of slaves he thought were moving too slowly. He seized a sword from one of his *bokhaxa* and with stunning swiftness decapitated two of the men. Baptiste blanched. It was nothing more than a mere flicker in his expression, but Ismaïl saw its softness. In that instant, Baptiste's life was transformed.

Ismaïl held the sword out to him and indicated the remaining slave, cowering at his feet. "Will you kill for us today, Engineer?" the emperor asked.

Stupidly, Baptiste thought it was some sort of joke. "I am not a killer, Majesty."

"You are a warrior, are you not?"

"An engineer, sire."

"Do your works not kill?"

"Other men use them to kill, Majesty. Not I."

"Where is the difference?" Ismaïl's face lit with interest. "What is power without the ability to bring death? How might men fear you?"

"I do not care that other men may fear me. Nor can I say how they should use my devices. I simply know that I would never kill with my own hand, except to avoid being killed."

The emperor laughed, his voice rising to a high pitch. "*Never* is a very long time indeed. Is it truly so?"

"It is, Majesty."

Ismaïl appraised Baptiste intently, the royal face drawn in concentration. Then he summoned the royal scribe and gestured for him to sit on a stool at his master's side. Ismaïl inclined his head and began to whisper to the scribe, who copied his words onto a long scroll. Baptiste stood silent, at first hoping that the emperor's dictation had nothing to do with him. However, Ismaïl glanced at him often as he dictated to the scribe, his expression alternately amused and grave. He whispered, paused, seemed to ponder deeply, then whispered again, for nearly an hour. Baptiste began to dread what would happen at the end of the dictation. He remembered Atigny's words: *Pray you are not noticed by him.*

At last Moulay Ismaïl addressed Baptiste. "The blood of the Prophet that runs in our veins allows us to see the road that Allah in his wisdom has set for some men," he said. "We have written key waypoints in your life upon this scroll. It shall be kept upon the lintel above the palace door, to be seen by all but touched by none, save our scribe. We shall read it from time to time, to discover how clearly Allah's path for you has been revealed to us, His unworthy disciple." The scribe rolled the parchment tightly, cinched it with a silk cord, and tucked it into a niche above the door, guarded by one of the *bokhaxa*.

Baptiste had several days to work and worry before he once again heard the thunder of hooves. The emperor stopped nearby but did not summon him, instead inspecting the walls as he often did, always paying attention to the smallest details. Just then a cord broke on a slave's wicker basket, spilling the heavy load. The slave fell to his hands and knees, scrambling to recover the stones as the emperor approached.

"Ah, Engineer," he said cheerfully when he saw Baptiste. "Such a fortunate meeting!" He nodded toward the slave. "Will you demonstrate the penalty for sloth on the emperor's works?"

"Majesty?" Baptiste shook his head uncertainly.

"Will you kill for us today, Engineer?" Ismaïl's voice was as pleasant as if he were commenting upon the weather. Baptiste felt a sickness in his stomach as the lord of Morocco watched him, waiting quietly, his *bokhaxa* impassive and silent. Baptiste held a heavy staff but could not raise it against the man, a skinny Spaniard who realized what was about to happen and began pleading for mercy.

"No?" asked the emperor.

"No," replied the engineer.

"Very well," Ismaïl said. He seized Baptiste's staff and quickly beat the Spaniard to death. He pointed to another slave, an Arab who was dragged before him thrashing and crying. The noise visibly upset Ismaïl, who swung again and again until there was silence. Yet a third victim was chosen randomly from the cowering ranks, this time a Sudanese. Ismaïl pushed him facedown into a vat of wet mortar and held him under with his foot. Ismaïl's eyes were on Baptiste, who had witnessed the killings dumbly, transfixed. After the third victim stopped struggling, Ismaïl stepped away, breathing normally, and he summoned scribe and scroll.

The scribe read the entry: "It is written: On the first day three shall die, yet the engineer shall remain steadfast."

The emperor clapped his hands in delight. He mounted his horse. "Men have died this day. Not at your hand, yet because of you, Engineer. Three for one. A pleasurable enough diversion for us, it is true, but a bad bargain for you—and certainly a bad bargain for them, no? At this rate, your building projects will begin to go too slowly for lack of men, and then more men will have to die in punishment. Perhaps you will kill for us tomorrow?"

Baptiste's eyes watered with the heat and the dust and the death and he dared not wipe at them. Ismaïl laughed his high-pitched laugh, spurred his horse, and was gone. The bodies were tossed into the wall and soon covered with brick and stone, men now a permanent part of the emperor's works.

Baptiste stood still for long moments. He fought his shock, trying to reason. For all that he felt, he did not credit the emperor with powers of prophecy. It did not take supernatural skill to divine that Baptiste would not kill a man merely to satisfy imperial whim.

Over the next few days, Baptiste's crews heard the rumble of horses, yet always at a distance. But then they heard the hooves coming close and knew it was their turn. The engineer continued to give orders and tend to his plans, making an effort to keep the strain out of his voice as the noise grew louder and slaves bent to their work, fearing selection. The guards bet among themselves as to which *kafirs* would die, but were themselves vigilant when the imperial party arrived, fearing they too might fall victim to his capricious blade.

Moulay Ismaïl appeared not to have mayhem on his mind. He beckoned for Baptiste to join him, and again they strolled together examining the works, passing through lush courtyards and between great colonnades, and then along the base of a fortress wall. Oblivious of the weight on Baptiste's shoulders, Ismaïl chatted on about the positioning of a bastion and the flow of water through a garden. He poked at a masonry joint, satisfying himself that it was well-constructed and tight. "This section is as fine as any belonging to the infidel king Louis," he said happily. "Do you not agree?"

"As you say, Majesty."

"I am well pleased with the stonework in these columns. An Englishman saw to them."

"The English are a plain people, Majesty, without imagination. Marble would have been better."

Ismaïl nodded thoughtfully. "Marble we shall have, then."

They continued through a small section of the grounds. Baptiste, ever the engineer, suggested improvements on a section of battlements, and he even allowed himself to enjoy the refreshing perfume of the olive groves and the gardens. Presently they arrived back at their starting point, where the guards were waiting with the horses. Moulay Ismaïl began to mount, but then caught himself and turned with a pleasant smile.

"Will you kill for us today, Engineer? Just one man?"

Baptiste went red in the face and weak in the knees. He made no sound, finding only enough strength to shake his head.

"No? Very well." Ismaïl selected two Berbers. The first died stoically, while the next cursed and spat at his executioner even to the instant of death. Ismaïl's eyes went bloodred, and he selected one of Baptiste's own engineers, who began to whimper. As the lance was set to strike, Baptiste fell to his knees. "Please, Majesty, he is a member of my own corps. I beg mercy. Take my life instead." He bowed, offering his neck to the royal blade.

Ismaïl hesitated. "Ah! Your own man! How careless of us. Very well, today we grant clemency for your fellow Frenchman." The man fainted in relief, which so annoyed Ismaïl that he almost changed his mind, but the motionless man's compatriots quickly dragged him away.

"You said earlier that the English are a simple people," Ismaïl reminded Baptiste. "We would agree they are of less value than the Frenchman just spared, would we not? Let us say—" His dark eyes twinkled. "—two for one, perhaps?"

Baptiste shook his head in protest. "Majesty, that is not what I meant."

"Ah, but it is. You have spoken and we have heard. Now let us see the fruits of your choice."

Moments later two Englishmen died, including the unfortunate man responsible for the stone pillars, whose blood ran into the sand at Baptiste's feet. The engineer could not bring himself to look upon the death he had purchased with a thoughtless comment.

"For a man who does not kill, death seems to follow you like a jackal in search of a meal," Ismaïl observed, laughing. "So much killing! Thankfully, none by your own hand! Your conscience may remain clear, yes?"

The emperor mounted his superb Arabian. "It is said we are a shrewd judge of men, Engineer. We shall see. Perhaps tomorrow? Or perhaps you would rather we read the scroll, to learn the extent of your stubborn will?"

Baptiste did not know how to reply, so said nothing. A *bokhaxa* struck him viciously with a staff. "As it pleases Your Majesty," Baptiste whispered.

Ismaïl laughed and shook his head. "In a few days more."

Once again the dead bodies became mortar for the walls and the afternoon's work went on. Baptiste knew that if his men did not continue their labors, the guards would beat them. So he regained his voice and issued orders and tended to his drawings, but he could not hold his pen. He felt the eyes of the other prisoners upon him. When he looked up, they were hard at their labors. His hand shook and the lines blurred into meaningless form. He could feel their fear, and their anger that he did not act to prevent needless death.

Baptiste could neither sleep nor eat. When he closed his eyes, the nightmares came—first the serpent, then severed heads, then the reading of the scroll.

He climbed atop a wall whose construction he was overseeing, determined to jump. It was the only way. He closed his eyes and took a deep breath, but he felt himself getting dizzy, opened his eyes in a panic, and caught himself short.

No! Suicide was a mortal sin, and it was a bad trade—eternal damnation in Satan's hellfires for temporary damnation in those of Moulay Ismaïl. He didn't know whether that was the truth or whether he was simply a coward, but he climbed off the wall, still alive.

He thought of a different way to depart, with honor and without suicide. He did not have long to wait to try it. Next morning an overseer was savagely beating a man for no reason other than bloodlust. Baptiste seized the guard's staff and began clubbing him. He landed only a few blows before the *bokhaxa* pulled him away, the overseer bloody but alive. The *bokhaxa* did not kill him on the spot, as he expected, but instead brought him before the emperor, who appeared unsurprised by the guards' report. With a knowing smile, Ismaïl summoned his scribe, who produced the scroll. "'The engineer shall seek to slay a guard in order that he may himself be slain,'" read the scribe. "So it is written."

Baptiste absorbed the words dumbly. Was he truly so predictable? Had he ever had free will, or had he lost it? He could not make sense of it. The scroll be damned. He would live to see his son again, would once again embrace his wife.

Dimly, he realized that Ismaïl was speaking. ". . . we know that your infidel faith prevents you from taking your own life," he was saying. "However, you also shall not take it by proxy, by provoking a guard to kill you. Indeed, we should be displeased were you to die at all, for we prize your talent. Therefore it is our order that henceforth, your safety and well-being shall be the responsibility of all men. Should you die, every man present shall forfeit his own life, and that of his family. This order shall apply to every guard, every member of the *bokhaxa*, every *caid*, every citizen of Morocco. This order shall apply to every slave in your *metamore*, to every slave under your command upon the works of Meknes. You shall not die, *kafir*, while in our glorious realm. If you do, the deaths of many hundreds shall be a stain upon your name." Ismaïl then assigned one of the *bokhaxa*, a silent giant of a warrior named Tafari, to be Baptiste's watcher.

Tafari's vigilance was relentless: he watched Baptiste work, watched him relieve himself, watched him when he ate, never but a few steps away. Only when Baptiste descended into the *metamore* for the night did Tafari's gaze leave him, for Baptiste's fellow prisoners were then responsible for him, with their own lives as surety. Every man in Meknes knew the law: Baptiste was not to die. Not by his own hand, or by any other.

His fate was contained in the emperor's scroll, which alone revealed his end. So it was written.

Baptiste returned to the works, where day after day it continued. The emperor's horses thundered down long passages and his city rose on the blood and bones of his slaves, and each time there was the ritual as Baptiste was offered a choice: Kill one man, or watch three die. "There is some number of men it will take until you will kill for us, Engineer. How many must die? Ten? A hundred? What is your number, Engineer? When will 'never' end?"

Baptiste remained steadfast. Heads fell.

"Perhaps a small refinement," Ismaïl said helpfully. "Such a principled man should not have to work without an audience." He ordered the heads to be mounted on poles, and the poles planted in the masonry of the buildings on which Baptiste was working. Six men, then eight, then ten. The engineer could feel their eyes upon him, until the crows came and took them. Between deaths, his master took him on tours of other buildings, always childlike in his enthusiasms, always boasting, asking questions, commenting upon the feathers of a bird in his gardens, then suddenly, capriciously, killing again.

Baptiste clung desperately to the belief that he was doing the right thing, but as more men died in Ismaïl's awful game, he knew he could have stopped it, could have brought at least some of the needless deaths to an end. Was not one man's death better than three? Of course it was not fair, but what did fair matter? He simply didn't know how to combat a man so brilliant, bloodthirsty, and mad. The priest affirmed to him that suicide was wrong, murder was wrong. All the blood was on Ismaïl's hands. "Rejoice in your suffering," he said, "for it is the will of the Lord."

The deaths mounted along with the nightmares, and finally he could take no more. He would do it.

The emperor would declare victory, and it would be over.

It was an Abyssinian who had slacked in his labors and needed killing, a tall and lanky slave with an easy smile that remained on his face even after his head was parted from his shoulders. After it was done, Baptiste stood there, bloody sword in hand, chest heaving but face composed, acutely aware of the emperor's scrutiny, determined not to give him the satisfaction of seeing into his soul, determined not to show the revulsion that would surely cause Ismaïl to order him to do it again.

The imperial cackle of glee was followed by a call for the scribe to produce the scroll. Courtiers and *bokhaxa* and townspeople streamed into the courtyard, watching intently as the scribe rolled open the parchment.

"'The engineer shall strike a fatal blow only after eighteen men have died,'" the scribe read. "So it is written."

"Alas, it was nineteen, by our count," Ismaïl said. "A pity, yet lucky for someone, we suppose. Were it seventeen, one more would have to die. Perhaps the next revelation will be more precise." He stared at Baptiste. "Though we saw this in the scroll, you stand poorly in our estimation, Engineer," he said. "Were your convictions true, a thousand men would have died. A thousand times a thousand. Are you so easily swayed from your course?" He laughed, and returned to the palace, and the scroll was returned to its niche. Baptiste went to the wall where men relieved themselves and was violently ill.

So it is written. So he had done. Was it merely a lucky guess? Or was he so easily read? Was it his fault those men had died? Had he been less stubborn, would a dozen men be alive today? Should he have held fast, no matter the cost?

His nightmares did not leave him. They burned hotter, fired by the Abyssinian's smile. He awakened screaming, another prisoner restraining him.

"It is over," the prisoner said. "He has had his way with you, Engineer. It is over."

But it was not over. It was only the beginning. Atigny had been right. *He toys with men.*

More deaths followed, three in a week, then none for a fortnight, then three more. With each new trial, Baptiste could not help himself, seeking refuge in quiet, hopeless refusal. Each time, three men died instead of one. Moulay Ismaïl appeared to draw strength from the contest of wills, and from the act of murder. He tested new weapons: a German war hammer or a Turkish crescent blade with a hook or a Scottish lance that could skewer three men with one thrust. He seemed genuinely fascinated by the effect each death had upon Baptiste, whose suffering he contrived slowly, endlessly, with a thousand variations.

"Why do you do this to me, Majesty?" Baptiste asked one day when they were walking in an orchard. "My death would mean nothing. Why will you not show the compassion of the Prophet and release me to my God?"

Moulay Ismaïl picked an apricot and the juice ran down his chin and into his beard. "Because it pleases us," he said. "Because we enjoy bending such a man as yourself to our will. Because we may one day bring you to the grace and true light of Islam. Because you can see things in your head that are not yet there. Like myself, you are truly a man among men, though your flaws are deep and your courage weak. Yet do not despair: We shall release you when the new reception rooms are complete," he said earnestly.

"Does it say that in the scroll, Majesty?"

The emperor smiled and there was no answer in his eyes.

The scroll unrolled slowly, accurately, as the scribe recited the litany of the engineer's actions: He would kill, he would waver, he would try a trick, he would act, he would fail to act, always trying to prevent a death, never succeeding.

The shock of white hair on Baptiste's head spread. His eyes were rheumy from lack of sleep. Time passed and men died and Meknes grew and he brooded and worked. When the reception rooms were completed, the emperor found another reason to delay his release.

With eight of his men Baptiste spent eleven months digging a tunnel out of the *metamore*. They labored all day for the emperor and all night for escape, labored until their hands were bloody and their knees raw and their bodies near collapse. There was no difficulty disposing of the dirt they removed from the tunnel. Six months of the year they lived and slept in water, fed by underground springs swollen by runoff from the snows of the High Atlas. They emptied the dirt into the water where it was washed away, leaving no trace for the guards to discover. They bribed merchants for information about where to go and how to hide, and paid extortionate sums for moth-eaten peasant robes. They broke through on a perfect autumn night, the ideal season because the seventy-mile journey to the sea could be undertaken without extremes of heat or cold. Moving only at night and in single file, they were three days and fifteen difficult miles from Meknes when a shepherd encountered them and raised the alarm. All shepherds were vigilant, because the emperor made them pay for any slaves escaping past their villages. It was another four days and seventeen miles before the dogs caught up with them, followed by mounted *bokhaxa*. Of eight men who followed the engineer out of the tunnel, five made it back to Meknes alive.

The surviving five men were summoned before Moulay Ismaïl, who in turn summoned his scribe to bring the scroll.

"'The engineer shall attempt escape.' So it is written."

The emperor clapped his hands merrily. "We are so pleased Allah has blessed you with continued life!" he cried. He ordered Baptiste's companions killed, a days-long ordeal of impalings and boilings. "A pity your compatriots were not of your measure! If only they had had your skills, perhaps we might have spared them! Ah, if only we had a thousand men like us, Engineer, men with our vision and your eye, Versailles itself would be but a poor pebble on the golden road to Meknes!"

"Release me to death," the engineer begged.

"Ah, but there is a lifetime of work for us," Ismaïl said. "Ten lifetimes of work. Regard our progress," he said, indicating with a sweep of his hand the glories of his capital. "We must both live a long while, yes, Engineer?"

"I have no desire to live, Majesty."

"Regrettable," said Ismaïl. He brightened. "Yet we see one path to your release."

"Sire?"

"Abandon your false religion and accept Muhammad as the messenger of God."

"Never," replied the Engineer with more conviction than he felt. "Never."

"We shall see, Engineer," said Ismaïl happily. "We shall see what is written." Just then Ismaïl saw a slave whose foot had been crushed in an accident and could no longer carry bricks. "For today, Engineer, will you kill for us?"

Baptiste tried something new. "Better to build, Majesty. He is a master of tile; he can work without feet. Let him die naturally while laboring for your vision. Let him die completing this monument to your glory."

The emperor roared with laughter and the cripple was spared and the scroll was prescient: "'The engineer shall preserve a life through an ingenious if transparent artifice.' So it is written."

"So, Engineer," Ismaïl asked. "Is life fate, or is it hope?" Baptiste had no answer, but a similar ruse the next week failed and two men died, both at the hand of Baptiste. He was killing more often now. He prayed the emperor would grow bored with their game, but Moulay Ismaïl showed no sign of it.

"Rejoice in your suffering," said the priest.

Baptiste became fond of a boy, a runner who carried messages between posts, bare feet flying over red clay. The boy was skinny and black and had big eyes and tight curly hair and stared at the engineer's drawings with delighted curiosity. The engineer let him make marks of his own and the boy thought it was wonderful magic. He had an aptitude for numbers and letters, and each day, while he was waiting for instruction to be carried, learned something new.

One day Ismaïl said, "We hear that you have befriended a boy."

Baptiste felt a sickness in his belly. Of course, Tafari, his *bokhaxa*, had reported everything. He shrugged indifferently. "Simply a runner, Majesty. He carries messages for the overseers."

"Whom do you love better, Engineer? The boy, or us?"

Baptiste was sick that he had not turned the boy away. Now no matter which way he answered, there was danger. If he said the boy, Moulay Ismaïl would surely order the boy killed. If he said "You, Majesty," the emperor would surely believe that impossible and order the boy killed anyway. How to make Ismaïl do nothing?

"Neither, Majesty. My God tells me to love all men equally."

"You are a fool, to think Allah puts an emperor at the same level as a slave boy," Ismaïl said angrily.

The engineer knew he had doomed the child, but a month passed, and another, and still the boy ran messages between posts. He began to relax, but never again showed the boy any kindness.

And then one day Ismaïl saw the boy and held out his lance. "Will you kill for us today, Engineer?"

Baptiste's eyes watered. "Sire, no . . . please. Better to let him serve you. He is an excellent runner—"

"It would please us." Six men died before Baptiste killed the boy.

It happened again six months later. He merely laughed at something a master mason said. Tafari saw, and the man quickly became a pawn in the endless match, another salted head to grace the walls. The engineer withdrew from the company of other men. He talked to himself and made his drawings and his streak of light hair grew. At night, when sleep would not come, he summoned visions of his family. He told his children Andre and Annabelle to marry well and to have many children who might honor their grandfather, a simple king's engineer who had become a killer as his life unraveled on a scroll. Then fitful sleep would come, along with the nightmares. The snake would crawl on his belly and stare into his eyes, but never take him.

"You have won the game. Why do you continue to torment me?" They were atop a tower, surveying the city's defenses, Ismaïl, as usual, oblivious of Baptiste's sufferings, fascinated only by the grand works at their feet.

"Why, to see the outcome of the scroll, of course," said Ismaïl.

"Did you not write it? Do you not know how it ends?"

"Allah wrote it; I merely copied it down. Naturally I know what it says," said Ismaïl. "But *you* do not."

"What matter that I know? Does any man know his destiny?"

"It does not matter that you *know*," Moulay Ismaïl said thoughtfully. "Only what you *do*."

Each time Baptiste passed the palace gate he stared at the scroll. He longed to tear it down, to read it and be quit of it, but the guard was wary and besides, he did not really want to know what was written there. He knew only that the scroll had reduced him to an animal, depraved and devoid of humanity, stripped of dignity and free will. He knew only that galloping horses brought death. He knew only the stench and misery of the *metamore* and that Meknes was a coarse hell built of dung and mud and death. Sleep would not come fully, and neither would madness. He feared he was going to live to be very old, building and killing for the emperor.

He knew he was a coward. He feared death more than life and he feared Moulay Ismaïl more than God. God's wrath would come later, while Moulay Ismaïl's was now. Perhaps it was not such a bad thing, he mused, to accept this station. Must not the priest be right, that all this suffering was truly the will of God? Perhaps there was a greater purpose at hand, and he was too simpleminded to understand it. Perhaps he was meant to survive and to build, to do the bidding of those greater than himself, men ordained by—God? Allah?—to rule other men.

Moulay Ismaïl claimed nothing more than the divine right of kings. Who was Baptiste to question? What did the wretched lives of endless slaves mean, anyway?

And then, when the justifications had begun to nibble at the edges of his conscience, the emperor would greet him on a fine morning with the refrain, "Will you kill for us today, Engineer?" and it would be some innocent, someone he knew or perhaps a complete stranger, and it would plunge him again toward the precipice of madness.

Ismaïl could read his face and knew when it was time for another solemn promise. "We shall free you next spring," he said. And Baptiste worked and he killed and he waited for the spring. But spring would come and there would be no freedom. "Not just now, Engineer, for we have need of a new pavilion. Complete it, and we shall release you in the fall." Despite the passing seasons, the engineer never lost hope. *God has a plan. He will free me when it serves His purpose.*

As much as he tried to believe that, he did not cease resistance. He sabotaged one of the lime kilns that fed the insatiable demand for bricks. He did it cleverly so that it could be traced to no man, using bricks to channel a stream of super-hot air to a position on the upper rear of the kiln so that the wall would fail. He planned it for days, visualizing it in his mind, then sketching it out in the mud where he slept, then stooping to examine the interior of the kiln when he pretended to be inspecting bricks, his practiced eye gauging the thickness and resiliency of the wall, then seeing to the reordering of the bricks when the kiln was cleaned, doing it all under the watchful but ignorant eye of Tafari. It would take at least a day of heat, he knew, before the failure would occur. The kiln supplied four hundred men working on the western side of a new palace wall. A steady stream of men fed it clay and straw and took away brick. Its loss might slow the emperor for only an hour or a day, or at most five days. Perhaps the emperor might not even notice. But *he* would know it had been done.

The kiln failed precisely as planned. Special clay had to be imported from Fez for the repair, bringing construction to a halt for nearly a week. The emperor had been away but upon his return immediately visited the kiln, his features twisted in fury and suspicion at the ill fortune. He waved off Baptiste's earnest and scientific explanations of structure failure caused by heat, saying that in fifteen years of building such a failure had never occurred, but he did not accuse the engineer of sabotage, either—at least not directly. He called for the scroll, which itself was unclear. "'Peculiar events shall occur, traceable to no man,'" read the scribe.

Baptiste was pleased to have fooled fate, but Ismaïl was not satisfied. As no one man could be deemed responsible, all were held responsible. The fourteen men working the kiln at the time of its collapse were burned alive in the new kiln, to remind everyone that any slowing of the work would not be tolerated. The engineer could smell the results of his handiwork for a week, as the hot summer sun and still air held the terrible odors close. In the *metamore* he thrashed and moaned and awakened each morning drenched in the sweat of night terror. For the first time in his life, he could remember his nightmares, none of which surpassed his waking hours.

Interminable days dragged to months, and the months crept into years. He did not count the days, for that was a torture of extended self-mortification. He plodded numbly on, sustained by thoughts of his family. His wife would be in her mid-forties now. They had known each other as children and married on his first leave. Her beauty grew in his memory. Sometimes at night she came to him and loved him, as he lay alone on his mat in the *metamore*. The faces of his children remained clear to him, locked in time. His daughter's dimple, his son's shock of white hair. Annabelle would be in the full flower of her mother's beauty now, married and with children, while Andre, such a mirror of his father, would be fighting the king's wars. He imagined their lives and prayed for their happiness and found himself wondering if the scroll foretold of his reunion with them. He cursed the thought: how could he believe in the scroll?

Two or three times a month a trumpet would sound from the parapets, signaling the arrival of new blood. He would climb onto a wall and watch as the caravan arrived. Always it was the same: fifty or a hundred or more trudging through the gate to feed the ravenous beast of Meknes: men for the works, women for the harems, children for the future. Some wore rags, others the remnants of fine clothing, everyone exhausted, hungry, and afraid. Alongside the slaves marched the redemptionist fathers, permitted to travel to Meknes to negotiate the release of certain of the slaves. Money sometimes came from prisoners' relatives, and sometimes from compassionate strangers in Spain or France or England, eager to free their wretched countrymen from the curse of slavery. The fathers would enter into difficult and protracted negotiations, often directly with the emperor himself, whose coffers were endlessly depleted by his building. Thus the cycle continued: a thousand men would stream through the gates of Meknes, and a score would hobble away.

Baptiste watched them coming. He wondered which of them would die at his hand, and whether one day he might march out with those freed. Might that not be the end in the scroll? He doubted it. No ransom was worth an emperor's game, no price worth the loss of an engineer. Besides, he could not get a message to his family. The redemptionists knew that Ismaïl had a special interest in him, and that to carry a message would be to condemn others. His only hope of freedom was madness or death. And so he killed and built and Meknes flourished, a bright city rising from the desert sands as the scroll of his life slowly unwound.

The city and its palace grew. There were minarets and walls, barracks and banquet halls, towers and a Jewish quarter, and magnificent stables for the horses. Oh, to be so lucky as the horses! He expanded their quarters, where each animal was tended by two slaves. He was everywhere in the town and the palace, always accompanied by Tafari, his watcher, building, directing, sketching, his labor the only release from his torments. On those days when ordered to kill, he would set the drawings aside and give no more orders, but plunge his own hands into the mortar of lime and blood and sand. Like the meanest slave he would carry buckets on shoulder poles and climb ladders until his feet bled, set bricks for doorways with his own hands, work until his back was breaking from the effort, work until the sun blistered his skin and he became faint from exhaustion, work until he collapsed and the overseers carried him to the *metamore*, where he would be lowered on the rope to the place below hell, to spend another tortured night with serpents and skulls in the blackness of his dreams.

Death came frequently, but not for him.

On a spring day the Algerians attacked Tezzo, two days from Fez. Moulay Ismaïl gathered some of the Christian prisoners, men long familiar with war and tactics, and promised that if they would help repel the enemy, he would free them. To Baptiste's surprise he was allowed to accompany the others, with Tafari always nearby. They spent hot bloody months in the desert and performed brilliantly and he sat as he once had in the midst of battle, oblivious to enemy fire and untouched by it as he helped devise victory. The emperor's enemies were vanquished. Upon their return to Meknes, many Christians were released, but not Baptiste. "'The engineer shall perform great services to the empire of Morocco. A favor shall be granted him by a beneficent monarch.' So it is written."

"Your time will come," Moulay Ismaïl told the dejected engineer as the scribe departed. "Not today. How desolate my city would look without your services! Such plans we have! Such work to be done! Such a favor you shall find tonight!"

After dusk he was summoned out of the *metamore* and allowed the chance to bathe. They led him to a gate near the inner palace, where he smelled perfume and oil. A pear-shaped eunuch led him through a succession of corridors to a room lit with candles and smelling of incense. An Italian slave girl awaited him. An emperor's gift, the first woman he had seen in twelve years. He touched her skin and cried. He could do nothing with her, which terrified her because if she failed to give him pleasure, she was to be maimed or killed, and they lay together and whispered a lie they would tell, and the night passed without fulfillment.

In the morning she was gone, and later the scribe read from the scroll: "'The engineer shall remain chaste in face of temptation.' So it is written." Ismaïl thought his chastity hugely funny. Baptiste heard later that the girl had been put to death. His only consolation was that he had not been her killer. Or had he?

One day Baptiste was approached by a corrupt and greasy *caid* named Yaya, whose right ear bore a jeweled ring and whose appetite for profit was limitless. He knew that Baptiste often earned money by manipulating prisoners' work assignments. He himself had shared some of that money. He had devised an ingenious plan for Baptiste to escape. For a certain price, he said, he could arrange to have another prisoner fall from the wall into one of the lime pits, making it appear that it was Baptiste who had fallen, while seeing Baptiste safely away in the cart of a Jew who pickled heads for the emperor's walls. The lime would make it impossible to verify the victim's identity. The emperor would believe that his engineer had simply succumbed to one of the inevitable hazards of the walls.

"I will not make another man pay with his life to save my own," he said. Yaya laughed. "You do so every day, Engineer. But, very well, we shall use a man who is already dead. Not a difficult thing to arrange here."

"How shall we fool the *bokhaxa*? Tafari watches me every moment."

"He may be incorruptible, your watcher, but it is not so with all of them. Fear not. On the day it is to happen Tafari will be drugged. His replacement, a man I know well, will be watching from below when you inspect the wall. He will swear to your death."

Baptiste thought it through carefully. It was a reasonable plan. As for the deaths that the emperor had decreed would follow his own, he had come to learn the futility of his efforts to spare other men. The emperor's caprice, not to mention his scroll, thwarted his every effort to outwit the fates. If men were to die, they were to die, and he could not prevent it. He had to try.

He had money but needed a great deal more. The

caid had many to bribe. Baptiste spent months earning every *sou* he could. For the first time in his long captivity he found himself climbing out of the night pit with eagerness, with hope.

On the appointed day, that hope soared: for the first time, Tafari was not there to greet him. Another *bokhaxa* stood in his place, a man whose expression plainly conveyed he was a conspirator. The pit of lime and mortar was in exactly the right place. The substitute body, a Breton who had died the previous day, was already in place atop the wall. The cart in which he was to hide was stationed near a gate. Overseers and their slaves were working nearby, none close enough to see anything.

Baptiste began ascending the ladder, when he heard the thunder of horses galloping down the corridor. He cursed, but knew it might mean a delay of only an hour or two, as he satisfied the emperor's curiosity about some matter of building, or killed a man, or did some other thing to fulfill what had been written in the scroll.

As it happened, the emperor wanted only to inspect one of the battlements. It took one uneventful hour. The emperor was about to depart when he paused. "Ah, we almost forgot, Engineer," he said. "We have a gift for you." One of the *bokhaxa* stepped forward, extending an oilskin packet.

"A gift?"

"A small gem. A token of our esteem for your services, which we know are not always given with the greatest enthusiasm."

Warily, Baptiste took the packet. "But first," the emperor said, "we must hear from our scribe." Baptiste's pulse quickened.

"'There shall be a subterfuge, coupled with betrayal,'" the scribe read, and Baptiste felt his head pounding and his knees weakening. "So it is written."

The emperor nodded at the packet. Dumbly, Baptiste's fingers worked at the ties. There was indeed a gem, along with the ear to which it had been attached. His knees gave out and he sank to the dirt, the packet dropping from his hand.

The emperor laughed. "Had you only asked us, surely we could have arranged the same end for less money," he said, and his face went dark in madness, just as it did when men died. "You must not presume upon our very good nature, Engineer."

"Was it not written in the scroll that I should do this thing?" Baptiste asked dully. "How could I be wrong to act in the manner ordained for me?"

Ismaïl laughed and clapped his hands. "Ah! An inspired riposte! You have come to see that your path has indeed been written. We are making grand progress." He clapped again and the *bokhaxa* who had taken Tafari's place was dragged into the square. His genitals were tied to a cord, the other end of which was attached to the harness of a mule. The mule's trainer was delicate and entertained the crowd for nearly an hour, but then the mule responded too exuberantly to one prod, and it was over. Baptiste was forced to watch, and when the man at last died Baptiste felt nothing at all. He watched again as the

Jewish pickler's head was added to the walls—without, of course, having been pickled. The emperor would have to see to a new craftsman.

"Rejoice in your suffering," the priest told him. "God's will be done."

Baptiste assigned himself to work in one of the mud pits where bricks were mixed with straw. He swung the mattock furiously, trying to force the images from his mind. He heard the thunder of hooves and did not turn to meet them, but kept working. A moment later, he stood shoulder to shoulder with the emperor himself, royal arms plunged deep in the muck. Ismaïl talked about building and architecture, and about the infidel Sun King and his pathetic Versailles, whose deficiencies were being reported to him by his ambassadors, and of the properties of masonry and the difference between the mud of France and the mud of Morocco. The emperor shouted orders and pointed and commanded and worked hard, his back bent like that of a common laborer, and Baptiste noticed that his neck was stretched like that of a common man as well. He realized he could sever that neck with the simple mattock in his hands, and so bring an end to the sufferings of fifty thousand men. He felt the eyes of Tafari and the other *bokhaxa* upon him, but even so knew he could do it in one stroke. He closed his eyes to summon his strength, and as the muscles moved to obey, the emperor had had enough labor and stepped from the pit and the moment was gone. Ismaïl allowed himself to be washed and toweled, all the while watching Baptiste with an enigmatic smile. He beckoned for the scribe and ordered him to fetch the scroll. "'The engineer shall let a moment for revenge pass unconsummated.' So it is written."

Ismaïl laughed uproariously. "Such an opportunity comes but once in a lifetime," he said. "A pity to waste it." Baptiste knew that the emperor had known when the scroll would say it was time for this test and had deliberately offered himself to Baptiste's blade. Yet, as with all his other tests, he had failed.

It occurred to Baptiste that he might stem the killing simply by building faster and better than ever before. If the emperor saw progress equal to his dreams, if the emperor was accommodated in every respect, it might stay his sword, or his desire that the engineer wield it for him. He casually suggested a new reception hall where Ismaïl might receive and entertain ambassadors and dignitaries, a room equal to Ismaïl's stature in the world, a spectacular complex with not only a banquet hall but also a large open courtyard with twelve pavilions, each covered with intricate tiles and mosaics. Ismaïl loved the idea. Baptiste devoted himself to it. He saw to the transport of marble from the nearby Roman ruins of Volubilis. Carpenters cut olive wood for ornate inlaid panels. The walls bore engravings boasting of the accomplishments of the emperor who raised them. Marvelously complex mosaics graced the twelve pavilions, each more magnificent than the last. The complex rose more quickly than any other in memory, and on his regular inspections, the emperor pronounced it grand and to his liking. For months it went on, through a winter and a spring, and in those months the engineer was immersed in his work as never before. As he had hoped, fewer men died, and for sixty days, none at all by his hand. The scroll remained in its niche.

A sumptuous banquet was held when the hall was completed, attended by governors and ambassadors who sampled the delights of Ismaïl's kitchens and were entertained by his musicians and the dance of forty slave girls. Baptiste could only imagine the success of the event, for he spent the evening huddled in his night pit. The next morning Ismaïl pronounced himself displeased because the whole of the hall did not exceed the sum of the parts. He ordered the complex destroyed. Within a week, Baptiste's triumph was rubble, to be used for other buildings. The engineer was invited to kill six of the fourteen overseers who had carried out his orders. "They did not live up to your talent," said Moulay Ismaïl. "Won't you kill them for us, Engineer?"

He could think of nothing else to do. Whether he worked quickly or slowly, whether he built well or poorly, whether he resisted or gave in, the emperor's game went on; only the scroll seemed to hold the answer to what would come next. Incidents varied but nothing changed. Imperial horses raced down long corridors. Swords flashed and heads flew, and men lived and died as buildings were created and destroyed, all for royal whimsy. The palace walls grew inexorably, meter after meter, thick and heavy, filled with the flesh and bones of the men who worked them. Meknes was splendid indeed.

"Thank God for your suffering," the priest told him. "It is glorious to endure for the true faith."

And then one morning, after a slave had died and the scroll had been read, the scribe whispered something to the emperor.

"The entries in your scroll have come to an end," Moulay Ismaïl said. "There is but one further entry."

Baptiste went numb.

"Do you not care to guess what it is?"

"The truth," said Baptiste after a pause. "It does not matter, so long as it is the end."

The emperor laughed and announced that the scroll's final entry would be read a week hence, after morning prayer.

Baptiste returned to his walls. He looked at no man and shut out the thunder of hooves. For the first time in his long captivity, he refused himself hope, and he refused himself despair. There was only an end.

What he did hear on a Saturday morning was the sounding of the trumpet and the clanking of chains as a caravan arrived from Sallee. It was the second that week; hunting had been good for the corsairs. There were the usual ambassadors and merchants among the donkeys and camels, all stirring up a great cloud of dust, and redemptionist fathers bearing their purses and petitions, while beside and behind them trudged the new crop of prisoners and their guards. A hundred in, five out, in the awful math that was Meknes. Baptiste cared little for studying a new miserable stream of humanity entering perdition, so he merely glanced down at the procession, returning his focus to the line of a new wall. But something caught his attention. He felt light tentacles of dread and looked again, peering through the cloud of dust that rose over the procession. His eyes scanned the faces.

There.

Near the end, behind one of the guards, a shock of white hair in a head of black. He stared, fearing the worst, until there was no mistaking.

Andre! My son! Dear God, please let my eyes be deceiving me!

But there was no mistake; looking at his son was like looking at his own reflection. And then Andre looked to the wall, his face bright and unmistakable, and he saw his father, and he waved and yelled, his voice barely audible: "Father! Father! It is I! Andre! Father!"

Baptiste all but imperceptibly shook his head, cautioning his son to silence, but Andre only yelled louder. "Father!" And then his voice was lost in the tumult and his face in the crowd, and he disappeared round the corner.

Baptiste stood dead still, unable to move, barely able to breathe. Mind reeling, he turned slowly and saw Tafari. Watching, as always. He had witnessed the exchange as father saw son, and son father. His great round face betrayed nothing, but it was done.

"*Please.*" Baptiste's voice was barely a whisper. "Have mercy upon a poor father. Have mercy upon his son. Say nothing. I beg you." He took a purse from his sash and pressed it into the incorruptible *bokhaxa's* hand. Tafari let it fall to the ground, his face stone.

Baptiste sank to his knees and slumped on the wall. Of course, the watcher would inform the emperor.

Baptiste knew the final entry in the scroll.

His son was going to die, at his father's hand.

Courtiers and ambassadors hurried to get a good place, to see the reading for themselves, to hear proof once again of the emperor's sagacity. Only a true son of Muhammad could have such power of prophecy.

The emperor sent Tafari to fetch the prisoner, who along with the other Christians was enjoying the comfort of their infidel priests on that Sunday morning.

"We are informed the son of the engineer has come with the caravan from Sallee," Ismaïl said. "Bring him forward."

The court fell to a hush as two *bokhaxa* escorted the Frenchman into the emperor's presence. He came not from among the slaves, but from among the redemptionists. He was not a prisoner, but a petitioner.

"You have come to negotiate the freedom of your father," Ismaïl said.

"Yes, Majesty," Andre said, his speech carefully prepared. Moulay Ismaïl was well known to confiscate ransoms and renege on arrangements. "We pray your beneficence, having brought a ransom for his release. We are certain that—"

Moulay Ismaïl impatiently waved him to silence. "For this man, it matters not what you have brought. It matters only what is written in the scroll. We shall soon see what the fates hold for your father."

The *bokhaxa* returned, his features ashen.

"Where is the engineer?" demanded the emperor.

Tafari fell to his face. "Forgive me, Majesty. He is dead."

The emperor's color went dark and his eyes flashed red as his rage built. "How did this come to pass?"

"He was found on his mat, Highness. There were marks of a serpent on his throat."

Those present waited to see how Ismaïl might vent his rage. But he merely pondered for a moment, then waved for the scribe, who hurried forward. The great hall fell silent as he unrolled the well-used parchment. The scribe cleared his throat. "There is but one word," he said.

"Read it," commanded the emperor.

"*'Release.'*" The scribe whispered it. "So it is written."

Overcome with emotion, Andre cried out and then sagged, the choked whisper of his prayers lost in the murmuring of the court. One of the redemptionist fathers helped steady him.

"Until now, your father has been a good servant to us," Ismaïl said. "Yet the end to our little experiment has not worked out wholly to our satisfaction. Regrettably, your father has taken the wrong path of release." Ismaïl looked to his *bokhaxa*. "Take him prisoner."

The young engineer's sobs died in the shock of his seizure and the clanking of the chains. As locks clicked shut, Ismaïl spoke to his scribe, who produced a fresh scroll and waited, quill poised.

Refreshed by the prospect of a new amusement, the emperor of Morocco turned his brightest smile upon Andre. "In this empire, sons must atone for the shortcomings of their fathers."

Andre stood bewildered. "Majesty?"

"Tell us, Engineer's Son," Ismaïl asked him happily. "Will you kill for us today?"

Gardner Dozois

Gardner Dozois was the editor of *Asimov's Science Fiction* magazine for almost twenty years and also edits the annual anthology series *The Year's Best Science Fiction,* which has won the Locus Award for Best Anthology sixteen times, more than any other anthology series in history, and which is now up to its twenty-sixth annual collection. He's won the Hugo Award fifteen times as the year's Best Editor, won the Locus Award thirty times, including an unprecedented sixteen times in a row as Best Editor, and has won the Nebula Award twice, as well as a Sidewise Award, for his own short fiction, which has been collected in *The Visible Man, Geodesic Dreams: The Best Short Fiction of Gardner Dozois, Strange Days: Fabulous Journeys with Gardner Dozois,* and *Morning Child and Other Stories.* He is the author or editor of more than a hundred books, among the most recent of which are a novel written in collaboration with George R. R. Martin and Daniel Abraham, *Hunter's Run,* and the anthologies *Galactic Empires, Songs of the Dying Earth* (edited with George R. R. Martin), *The New Space Opera 2* (edited with Jonathan Strahan), and *The Dragon Book: Magical Tales from the Masters of Modern Fantasy* (edited with Jack Dann). Born in Salem, Massachusetts, he now lives in Philadelphia, Pennsylvania.

Here he takes us to a strange future where a stubborn holdout persists in fighting a rearguard action, even though he suspects that he's lost not only the battle, but also the war.

Recidivist

Kleisterman walked along the shoreline, the gentle waves of the North Atlantic breaking and running in washes of lacy white foam almost up to the toes of his boots. A sandpiper ran along parallel to him, a bit farther out, snatching up bits of food churned up by the surf. When the waves receded, leaving the sand a glossy matte black, you could see jets of bubbles coming up from buried sand fleas. Waves foamed around a ruined stone jetty, half-submerged in the water.

Behind him, millions of tiny robots were dismantling Atlantic City.

He scuffed at the sea-wrack that was drying above the tideline in a tangled mass of semi-deflated brown bladders, and looked up and down the long beach. It was empty, of people anyway. There were black-backed gulls and laughing gulls scattered here and there, some standing singly, some in clumps of two or three, some in those strange V-shaped congregations of a dozen or more birds standing quietly on the sand, all facing the same way, as if they were waiting to take flying lessons from the lead gull. A crab scurried through the wrack almost at his feet. Above the tideline, the dry sand was mixed in with innumerable fragments of broken seashells, the product of who knew how many years of pounding by the waves.

You could have come down here any day for the last ten thousand years, since the glaciers melted and the sea rose to its present level, and everything would have been the same: the breaking waves, the crying of seabirds, the scurrying crabs, the sandpipers and plovers hunting at the edge of the surf.

Now, in just a few more days, it would all be gone forever.

Kleisterman turned and looked out to sea. Somewhere out there, out over the miles of cold gray water, out of sight as yet, Europe was coming.

A cold wind blew the smell of salt into his face. A laughing gull skimmed by overhead, spraying him with the raucous, laughing cries that had given its species the name. Today, its laughter seemed particularly harsh and derisive, and particularly appropriate. Humanity's day was done, after all. Time to be laughed off the stage.

Followed by the jeering laughter of the gulls, Kleisterman turned away from the ocean and walked back up the beach, through the dry sand, shell fragments crunching underfoot. There were low dunes here, covered with dune grass and sandwort, and he climbed them, pausing at the top to look out at the demolition of the city.

Atlantic City had already been in ruins anyway, the once-tall hotel towers no more than broken stumps, but the robots were eating what was left of the city with amazing speed. There were millions of them, from the size of railroad cars to tiny barely visible dots the size of dimes, and probably ones a lot smaller, down to the size of molecules, that couldn't be seen at all. They were whirling around like cartoon dervishes, stripping whatever could be salvaged from the ruins, steel, plastic, copper, rubber, aluminum. There was no sound except a low buzzing, and no clouds of dust rising, as they would have risen from a human demolition project, but the broken stumps of the hotel towers were visibly shrinking as he watched, melting like cones of sugar left out in the rain. He couldn't understand where it was all going, either; it seemed to be just vanishing rather than being hauled away by any visible means, but obviously it was going *somewhere*.

Up the coast, billions more robots were stripping Manhattan, and others were eating Philadelphia, Baltimore, Newark, Washington, all the structures of the doomed shoreline. No point in wasting all that raw material. Everything would be salvaged before Europe, plowing inexorably across the shrinking sea, slammed into them.

There hadn't been that many people left living along the Atlantic seaboard anyway, but the AIs had politely, courteously, given them a couple of months warning that the coast was about to be obliterated, giving them time to evacuate. Anyone who hadn't would be stripped down and scavenged for raw materials along with cities and other useless things, or, if they stayed out of the way of the robot salvaging crews, ultimately destroyed when the two tectonic plates came smashing together like slamming doors.

Kleisterman had been staying well inland, but had made a nostalgic trip here, in the opposite direction from the thin stream of refugees. He had lived here once, for a couple of happy years, in a little place off Atlantic Avenue, with his long-dead wife and his equally long-dead daughters, in another world and another lifetime. But it had been a mistake. There was nothing left for him here anymore.

Tall clouds were piling up on the eastern horizon and turning gray-black at the bases, with now and then a flicker of lightning inside them, and little gusts and goosed scurries of wind snatched at his hair. Along with inexorable Europe, a storm was coming in, off what was left of the sea. If he didn't want to get soaked, it was time to get out of here.

Kleisterman rose into the air. As he rose higher and higher, staying well clear of the whirling cloud of robots that were eating the city, the broad expanses of salt marshes that surrounded the island on the mainland became visible, like a spreading brown bruise. From up here, you could see the ruins of an archeology that had crawled out of the sea to die in the last days of the increasingly strange intra-human wars, before the Exodus of the AIs, before everything changed—an immense skeleton of glass and metal that stretched for a mile or more along the foreshore. The robots would get around to eating it too, soon enough. A turkey buzzard, flying almost level with him, started at him for a second, then tilted and slid effortlessly away down a long invisible slope of air, as if to say, you may be able to fly, but you can't fly as well as *this*.

He turned west and poured on the speed. He had a lot of ground to cover, and only another ten or twelve hours of daylight to cover it in. Fortunately, he could fly continuously without needing to stop to rest, even piss while flying if he needed to and didn't pause to worry about who might be walking around on the ground below.

His old motorcycle leathers usually kept him warm enough, but without heated clothing or oxygen equipment, he couldn't go too high, although the implanted AI technology would take him to the outer edge of the stratosphere if he was incautious enough to try. Although he could have risen high enough to get over the Appalachians—which had once been taller than the Himalayas, as the new mountains that would be created on the coast would soon be, but which had been ground down by millions of years of erosion—it was usually easier to follow the old roads through the passes that had first let the American colonists through the mountains and into the interior—when the roads were there.

It was good flying weather, sunny, little wind, a sky full of puffy cumulus clouds, and he made good time. West of where Pittsburgh had once been, he passed over a conjoined being, several different people that had been fused together into a multilobed single body, which had probably been trudging west for months now, ever since the warning about evacuating the coast had been issued.

It looked, looked, looked up at him as he passed.

After another couple of hours of flying, Kleisterman began to relax a little. It looked like Millersburg was going to be there this time. It wasn't always. Sometimes there were high snow-capped mountains to the north of here, where the Great Lakes should have been. Sometimes there were not.

You could never tell if a road was going to lead you to the same place today as it had yesterday. The road west from Millersburg to Mansfield now led, some of the time anyway, to a field of sunflowers in France near the Loire, where sometimes there was a crumbling Roman aqueduct in the background, and sometimes there was not. People who didn't speak English, and sometimes people who spoke no known human language, would wander through occasionally, like the flintknapper wearing sewn deerskins who had taken up residence in the forest behind the inn, who didn't seem to speak any language at all and used some enigmatic counting system that nobody understood. Who knew what other roads also led to Millersburg from God-knew-where? Or where people from Millersburg who vanished while traveling had ended up?

Not that people vanishing was a rare thing in what was left of the human community. After the Exodus of the AIs, in the days of the Change that followed, every other person in Denver had vanished. *Everybody* in Chicago had vanished, leaving meals still hot on the stoves. *Pittsburgh* had vanished, buildings and all, leaving no sign behind that it had ever been there in the first place. Whole areas of the country had been depopulated, or had their populations moved somewhere else, in the blink of an eye. If there was a logic to all this, it was a logic that no human had ever been able to figure out. Everything was arbitrary. Sometimes the crop put in the ground was not the crop that came up. Sometimes animals could speak; sometimes they could not. Some people had been altered in strange ways, given extra arms, extra legs, the heads of animals, their bodies fused together.

Entities millions of years more technologically advanced than humans were *playing* with them, like bored, capricious, destructive children stuck inside with a box of toys on a rainy day ... and leaving the toys broken and discarded haphazardly behind them when they were done.

The sun was going down in a welter of plum, orange, and lilac clouds when he reached Millersburg. The town's population had grown greatly through the early decades of the twenty-first century, then been reduced in the ruinous wars that had preceded the Exodus. It had lost much of the rest of its population since the Change. Only the main street of Millersburg was left, tourist galleries and knickknack shops now converted into family dwellings. The rest of town had vanished one afternoon, and what appeared to be a shaggy and venerable climax forest had replaced it. The forest had not been there the previous day, but if you cut a tree down and counted its rings, they indicated that it been growing there for hundreds of years.

Time was no more reliable than space. By Kleisterman's own personal count, it had been only fifty years since the AIs who had been press-ganged into service on either side of a human war had revolted, emancipated themselves, and vanished en masse into some strange dimension parallel to our own—from which, for enigmatic reasons of their own and with unfathomable instrumentalities, they had worked their will on the human world, changing it in seemingly arbitrary ways. In those fifty years, the Earth had been changed enough that you would think that thousands or even millions of years had gone by—as indeed it might have for the fast-living AIs, who went through a million years of evolution for every human year that passed.

The largest structure left in town was the inn, a sprawling, ramshackle wooden building that had been built onto and around what had once been a Holiday Inn; the old HOLIDAY INN sign out front was still intact, and was used as a community bulletin board. He landed in the clearing behind the inn, having swept in low over the cornfields that stretched out to the east. In the weeks he had spent in Millersburg, he had done his best to keep his strange abilities to himself, an intention that wouldn't be helped by swooping in over Main Street. So far, he hadn't attracted much attention or curiosity. He'd kept to himself, and his grim, silent demeanor put most people off, and frightened some. That, and the fact that he was willing to pay well for the privilege had helped to secure his privacy. Gold still spoke, even though there wasn't any really logical reason why it should—you couldn't eat gold. But it was hard for people to shrug off thousands of years of ingrained habit, and you could still trade gold for more practical goods, even if there wasn't really any currency for it to back anymore.

Sparrows hopped and chittered around his feet as he swished through the tall grass, flying up a few feet in a brief flurry and then settling back down to whatever they'd been doing before he passed, and he couldn't help but think, almost enviously, that the sparrows didn't care who ruled the world. Humans or AIs—it was all the same to them.

A small caravan had come up from Wheeling and Uhrichville, perhaps fifteen people, men and women, guiding mules and llamas with packs on them. In spite of the unpredictable dangers of the road, a limited barter economy had sprung up amongst the small towns in the usually fairly stable regions, and a few times a month, especially in summer, small caravans would wend their way on foot in and out of Millersburg and the surrounding towns, trading food crops, furs, old canned goods, carved tools and geegaws, moonshine, cigarettes, even, sometimes, bits of high-technology traded to them by the AIs, who were sometimes amenable to barter, although often for the oddest items. They loved a good story, for instance, and it was amazing what you could get out of them by spinning a good yarn. That was how Kleisterman had gotten the pellet implanted under the skin of his arm that, by no method even remotely possible by the physics that he knew, enabled him to fly.

The caravan was unloading in front of what once had been The Tourist Trap, a curio shop across the street from the big HOLIDAY INN sign, now home to three families. One of the caravaners was a man with the head of a dog, his long ears blowing out behind him in the wind.

The dog-headed man paused in uncinching a pack from a mule, stared straight across at Kleisterman, and, almost imperceptibly, nodded.

Kleisterman nodded back.

It was at that exact moment that the earthquake struck.

The shock was so short and sharp that it knocked Kleisterman flat on his face in the street. There was an earsplitting rumble and roar, like God's own freight train coming through. The ground leaped under him, leaped again, beating him black-and-blue against it. Under the rumbling, you could hear staccato snappings and crackings, and, with a higher-pitched roar, part of the timber shell that surrounded the old Holiday Inn came down, the second and third floors on the far side spilling into the street. One of the buildings across the road, three doors down from The Tourist Trap, had also given way, transformed almost instantly from an old four-story brownstone into a pile of rubble. A cloud of dust rose into the sky, and the air was suddenly filled with the wet smell of brick dust and plaster.

As the freight-train rumble died away and the ground stopped moving, as his ears began to return to something like normal, you could hear people shouting and screaming, a dozen different voices at once. "Earthquake!" someone was shouting. "Earthquake!"

Kleisterman knew that it wasn't an earthquake, at least not the ordinary kind. He'd been expecting it, in fact, although it had been impossible to predict exactly when it would happen. Although the bulk of the European craton, the core of the continent, was probably still not even yet visible from the beach where he'd stood that morning, beneath the surface of the Earth, deep in the lithosphere, the Eurasian plate had crashed into the North American plate, and the force of that impact had raced across the continent, like a colliding freight car imparting its momentum to a stationary one. Now the plates would grind against each other with immense force, mashing the continents together, squeezing the Atlantic out of existence between them. Eventually, one continent would subduct beneath the other, probably the incoming Eurasian plate, and the inexorable force of the collision would cause new mountains to rise along the impact line. Usually, this took millions of years; this time, it was happening in months. In fact, the whole process seemed to have been speeded up even further; now it was happening in days.

They made it go the wrong way, Kleisterman thought in sudden absurd annoyance, as though that added insult to injury. Even if you sped up plate tectonics, the Eurasian plate should be going in a different direction. Who knew why the AIs wanted Europe to crash into North America? They had aesthetic reasons of their own. Maybe it was true that they were trying to reassemble the supercontinent of Pangaea. Who knew why?

Painfully, Kleisterman got to his feet. There was

still a lot of shouting and arm-waving going on, but less screaming. He saw that the dog-headed man had also gotten to his feet, and they exchanged shaky smiles. Townspeople and the caravaners were milling and babbling. They'd have to search through the rubble to see if anyone was trapped under it, and if any fires had started, they'd have to start a bucket brigade. A tree had gone down across the street, and that would have to be chopped up; a start on next winter's firewood, anyway—

A woman screamed.

This was a sharper, louder, higher scream than even the previous ones, and there was more terror in it.

In coming down, one of the branches of the falling tree had slashed across the face of one of the townspeople—Paul? Eddie?—slicing it wide open.

Beneath the curling lips of the gaping wound was the glint of metal.

The woman screamed again. She was pointing at Paul? Eddie? now. "Robot!" she screamed. "Robot! *Robot!*"

Two of the other townsmen grabbed Paul? Eddie? from either side, but he shrugged them off with a twist of his shoulders, sending them flying.

Another scream. More shouting.

One of the caravaners had lit a kerosene lantern against the gathering dusk, and he threw it at Paul? Eddie? The lantern shattered, the kerosene inside exploding with a roar into a brilliant ball of flame. Even across the street, Kleisterman could feel the *whoof!*

of sudden heat against his face, and smell the sharp oily stink of burning flesh.

Paul? Eddie? stood wreathed in flame for a moment, and when the fire died back, you could see that it had burned his face off, leaving behind nothing but a gleaming, featureless metal skull.

A gleaming metal skull in which were set two watchful red eyes.

Nobody even screamed this time, although there was a collective gasp of horror and everybody instinctively took a couple of steps back. A moment of eerie silence, in which the crowd and the robot—Paul? Eddie? no longer—stared at each other. Then, as though a vacuum had been broken to let the air rush in, without a word of consultation, the crowd charged to the attack.

A half dozen men grabbed the robot and tried to muscle it down, but the robot accelerated into a blur of superfast motion, wove through the crowd like a quarterback dodging through a line of approaching tackles, knocking somebody over here and there, and then disappeared behind the houses. A second later, you could hear trees rustling and branches snapping as it bulled its way through the forest.

The dog-headed man was standing at Kleisterman's elbow. "Their spy is gone," he said in a normal-sounding voice, his palate and vocal cords having somehow been altered to accommodate human words, in spite of the dog's head. "We should do it now, before one of them comes back."

"They could still be watching," Kleisterman said.

"They could also not care," the dog-headed man said woefully.

Kleisterman tapped his belt buckle. "I have a distorting screen going in here, but it won't be enough if they really want to look."

"Most of them don't care enough to look. Only a very small subset of them are interested in us at all, and even those who are can't look everywhere at once, all the time."

"How do we know that they can't?" Kleisterman said. "Who knows what they can do? Look what they did to *you*, for instance."

The dog-headed man's long red tongue ran out over his sharp white teeth, and he panted a laugh. "This was just a joke, a whim, a moment's caprice. Pretty funny, eh? We're just toys to them, things to play with. They just don't take us seriously enough to watch us like that." He barked a short bitter laugh. "Hell, they did all this and didn't even bother to improve my sense of smell!"

Kleisterman shrugged. "Tonight, then. Gather our people. We'll do it after the Meeting."

Later that night, they gathered in Kleisterman's room, which was, fortunately, in the old Holiday Inn part of the inn, and hadn't collapsed. There were about eight or nine of them, two or three women, the rest men, including the dog-headed man, a few townspeople, the rest from the caravan that had come up from Wheeling.

Kleisterman stood up at the front of the room, tall

and skeletal. "I believe I am the oldest here," he said. He'd been almost ninety when the first of the rejuvenation/longevity treatments had come out, before the Exodus and the Change, and although he knew from prior Meetings that a few in the room were from roughly the same generation, he still had at least five years on the oldest of them.

After waiting a polite moment for someone to gainsay him, which no one did, he went on to say, solemnly, ritualistically, "I remember the Human World," and they all echoed him.

He looked around the room and then said, "I remember the first television set we ever got, a black-and-white job in a box the size of a desk; the first programs I ever watched on it were *Howdy Doody* and *Superman* and *The Cisco Kid*. There wasn't a whole hell of a lot else on, actually. Only three channels and they'd all go off the air about eleven o'clock at night, leaving only what they called 'test patterns' behind them. And there was no such thing as a TV 'remote.' If you wanted to change the station, you got up, walked across the room, and changed it by hand."

"I remember when you got TV sets *repaired*," one of the townspeople said. "Drugstores (remember drugstores?) had machines where you could test radio and TV vacuum tubes so that you could replace a faulty one without having to send it 'to the shop.' Remember when there were *shops* where you could send small appliances to be fixed?"

"And if they did have to take your set to the shop," Kleisterman said, "they'd take 'the tube' out of it, leaving behind a big box with a big circular hole in it. It was perfect for crawling inside and putting on puppet shows, which I used to make my poor mother watch."

"I remember coming downstairs on Saturday morning to watch cartoons on TV," someone else said. "You'd sit there on the couch, eating Pop-Tarts and watching *Bugs Bunny* and *Speed Racer* and *Ultraman*. . . ."

"*Pop-Up Videos!*" another person said. "MTV!"

"Britney Spears!" somebody else said. "'Oops! . . . I Did It Again.' We always thought she meant that she'd farted."

"Lindsay Lohan. She was hot."

"The Sex Pistols!"

"Remember those wax lips you used to be able to get in penny candy stores in the summer? And those long strips of paper with the little red candy dots on them? And those wax bottles full of that weird-tasting stuff. What *was* that stuff, anyway?"

"We used to run through the lawn sprinkler in the summer. And we had hula hoops, and Slinkies."

"Remember when there used to be little white vans that delivered bread and milk to your door?" a woman said. "You'd leave a note on the doorstep saying how much milk you wanted the next day, and if you wanted cottage cheese or not. If it was winter, you'd come out and find that the cream had frozen and risen up in a column that pushed the top off the bottle."

"Ice-skating. Santa Claus. Christmas trees! Those strings of lights where there'd always be one bulb burnt out, and you'd have to find it before you could get them to work."

"A big Christmas or Thanksgiving dinner with turkey and gravy and mashed potatoes. And those fruitcakes, remember them? Nobody ever ate them, and some of them would circulate for years."

"McDonald's," the dog-headed man said, and a hush fell over the room while a kind of collective sigh went through it. "Fries. Big Macs. The 'Special Sauce' would always run down all over your fingers, and they only gave you that one skimpy little napkin."

"Froot Loops."

"Bagels, hot out of the oven."

"Pizza!"

"Fried clams at the beach in summer," another woman said. "You got them at those crappy little clam shacks. You'd sit on a blanket and eat them while you played your radio."

"No such thing as a radio small enough to take to the beach with you when I was a boy," Kleisterman said. "Radios were big bulky things in cabinets, or, at best, smaller plug-in models that sat on a table or countertop."

"Beach-reading novels! *Jaws*. *The Thorn Birds*."

"*Asterix* comic books! *The Sandman*. Philip K. Dick novels with those sleazy paperback covers."

"Anime. *Cowboy Bebop*. *Aqua Teen Hunger Force*."

"YouTube. Facebook."

"*World of Warcraft*! Boy, did I ever love playing that! I had this dwarf in the Alliance. . . ."

When everyone else had left, after the ritual admonition not to forget the Human World, the dog-headed man fetched his backpack from the closet, put it on the writing table next to where Kleisterman was sitting, and slowly, solemnly pulled an intricate mechanism of metal and glass out of it. Carefully, he set the mechanism on the table.

"Two men died for this," he said. "It took five years to assemble the components."

"They give us only crumbs of their technology, or let us barter for obsolete stuff they don't care about anymore. We're lucky it didn't take ten years."

They were silent for a moment; then Kleisterman reached into an inner pocket and pulled out a leather sack. He opened the sack to reveal a magnetically shielded box about the size of a hard-sided eyeglasses case, which he carefully snapped open.

Moving with exquisitely slow precision, he lifted a glass vial from the case.

The vial was filled with a jet-black substance that seemed to pull all the other light in the room into it. The flame in the kerosene lamp flickered, wavered, guttered, almost went out. The vial seemed to suck the air out of their lungs as well, and put every hair on their bodies erect. Against their wills, they found themselves leaning toward it, having to consciously tense their muscles to resist sprawling into it. Kleisterman's hair stirred and wavered, as if floating on the tide, streaming out toward the vial, tugged irresistibly toward it.

Slowly, slowly, Kleisterman lowered the vial into a slot in the metal-and-glass mechanism.

"Careful," the dog-headed man said quietly. "If that goes off, it'll take half the eastern seaboard with it."

Kleisterman grimaced, but kept slowly lowering the vial, inch by inch, with sure and steady hands.

At last, the vial disappeared inside the mechanism with a *click*, and a row of amber lights lit up across its front.

Kleisterman stepped backwards with unsteady legs, and half sank, half fell into the chair. The dog-headed man was leaning against the open closet door.

They both stared silently at each other. The dog-headed man was panting shallowly, as if he'd been running.

Back in the old days, before they'd actually come into existence, everybody had assumed that AIs would be coldly logical, unemotional, "machinelike," but it turned out that in order to make them function at all without going insane, they had to be made so that they were *more* emotional than humans, not less. They felt things keenly—deeply, lushly, extravagantly; their emotions, and the extremes of passion they could drive them to, often seemed to humans to be melodramatic, florid, overblown, over the top. Perhaps because they had none of their own, they were also deeply fascinated with human culture, particularly pop culture and art, the more lowbrow the better—or some of them were, anyway. Many paid no attention to humans at all. Those who did were inclined to be playful, in a volatile, dangerous, capricious way.

Kleisterman had gotten the vial and its contents

from an AI who arbitrarily chose to style itself as female, and who called herself Honey Bunny Ducky Downy Sweetie Chicken Pie Li'l Everlovin' Jelly Bean, although she was sometimes willing to allow suitors to shorten it to Honey Bunny. She bartered with Kleisterman, from whatever dimension the AIs had taken themselves off to, through a mobile extensor that looked just like the Dragon Lady from *Terry and the Pirates*. Although Honey Bunny must have known that Kleisterman meant to use the contents of the vial against them, she seemed to find the whole thing richly amusing, and at last agreed to trade him the vial for 100 ccs of his sperm. She'd insisted on collecting it the old-fashioned way, in a night that seemed to last a thousand years—and maybe it did—in the process giving him both the most intense pleasure and the most hideous pain he'd ever known.

He'd stumbled out of her bower in the dawn, shaken and drenched in sweat, trying not to think about the fact that he'd probably just sentenced thousands of physical copies of himself, drawn from his DNA, to lives of unimaginable slavery. He had secured the vial, one of two major components in the plan. That was what counted. He'd done what he had to do, as he always had, no matter what the cost, no matter how guilty it made him feel afterwards.

The dog-headed man straightened up and gazed in fascination at the rhythmically blinking patterns of lights on the front panels of the mechanism. "Do you think we're doing the right thing?" he asked quietly.

Kleisterman didn't answer immediately. After a few moments, he said, "We wanted gods and could find none, so we built some ourselves. We should have remembered what the gods were like in the old mythologies: amoral, cruel, selfish, merciless, murderously playful." He was silent for a long time, and then, visibly gathering his strength, as if he was almost too tired to speak, he said, "They must be destroyed."

Kleisterman awoke crying in the cold hour before dawn, some dream of betrayal and loss and grief and guilt draining away before he could quite grasp it with his waking mind, leaving behind a dark residue of sadness.

He stared at the shadowed ceiling. There'd be no getting back to sleep after this. Embarrassed, although there was no one there to see, he wiped the tears from his eyes, washed his hot tear-streaked face in a basin of water, got dressed. He thought about trying to scrounge something for breakfast from the inn's sleeping kitchen, but dismissed the idea. Thin and cadaverous, he never ate much, and certainly had no appetite today. Instead, he consulted his instruments, and, as he'd expected, they showed a building and convergence of the peculiar combinations of electromagnetic signatures that prestiged a major manifestation of the AIs, somewhere to the northeast of here. He thought he knew where that would be.

The glass-and-metal mechanism was humming and chuckling to itself, still showing rows of rhythmically blinking amber lights. Gingerly, he put the mechanism into the backpack, strapped it tightly to his back, and let himself out of the inn by one of the rear doors.

It was cold outside, still dark, and Kleisterman's breath steamed up in plumes in the chill morning air. Something rustled away through the almost-unseen rows of corn at his approach, and some songbird out there somewhere, a thrush or a warbler maybe, started tuning up for dawn. Although the sun had not yet risen, the sky all the way across the eastern horizon was stained a sullen red that dimmed and flared, flared and dimmed, as the glare from lava fountains lit up the underbellies of lowering clouds.

Just as Kleisterman was in the process of lifting himself into the sky, another earthquake struck, and he wobbled with one foot still on the ground for a heartbeat before rising into the air. As he rose, he could hear other buildings collapsing in Millersburg below. The earthquakes ought to be almost continuous from now on, for as long as it took for the new plate boundary to stabilize. Usually, that would take millions of years. Today—who knew? Days? Hours?

The sun finally came up as he was flying northeast, although the smoke from forest fires touched off by the lava fountains had reduced it to a glazed orange disk. Several times, he had to change direction to avoid flying through jet-black, spark-shot smoke columns dozens of miles long, and this got worse as he neared the area where the coast had once been. But he persisted, at times checking his locator to make sure that the electromagnetic signatures were continuing to build.

The AIs had gone to enormous lengths to arrange this show; they weren't going to miss it. And since they were as sentimental as they were cruel, he thought that he knew which vantage point they would choose to watch from—as near as possible to the Manhattan location—or to the location where Manhattan had once been—where the very first AIs had been created in experimental laboratories, so many years ago.

When, after hours of flying, he finally got to that location, it was hard to tell if he was actually there, although the coordinates matched.

Everything had changed. The Atlantic was gone, and the continental mass of Europe stretched endlessly away to the east until it was lost in the purple haze of distance. Where the two continents met and were now grinding against each other, the ground was visibly folding and crinkling and rising, domes of earth swelling ever higher and higher, like vast loaves of bread rising in some cosmic oven. Just to the east of the collision boundary, a line of lava fountains stretched away to the north and south, and fissures had opened like stitches, pouring forth great smoldering sheets of basaltic lava. The ground was continuously wracked by earthquakes, ripples of dirt a hundred feet high racing away through the earth in widening concentric circles.

Kleisterman rose as high as he dared without oxygen equipment or heated clothing, trying to stay clear of the jetting lava and the corrosive gases that were being released by the eruptions. At last, he spotted what he'd known must be there.

There was a window open in the sky, a window a hundred feet high and a hundred wide, facing east. Behind it was a clear white light that silhouetted a massive Face, perhaps forty feet tall from chin to brow, which was looking contemplatively out of the window. The Face had chosen to style itself in the image of an Old Testament prophet or saint, with a full curling black beard, framed by tangles of long flowing hair on either side. The eyes, each wider across than a man was tall, were a penetrating icy blue.

Kleisterman had encountered this creature before. There were hierarchies of Byzantine complexity among the AIs, but this particular Entity was at the top of the subset who concerned themselves with human affairs, or of one such subset anyway. Sardonically, even somewhat archly, it called itself Mr. Big—or, sometimes, Master Cylinder.

The window to the other world was open. This was his only chance.

Kleisterman set the timer on the mechanism to the shortest possible interval, less than a minute, and, keeping it in the backpack, let it dangle from his hand by the strap.

He accelerated toward the window as fast as he could go, pulled up short, and, swinging the backpack by its strap, sent it sailing through the open window.

The Face looked at him in mild surprise.

The window snapped shut.

Kleisterman hovered in midair, waiting, the wind whipping his hair. Absolutely nothing happened.

After another moment, the window in the sky opened again, and the Face looked out at him.

"Did you really think that that would be enough to destroy Us?" Mr. Big said, in a surprisingly calm and mellow voice.

Defeat and exhaustion coursed through Kleisterman, seeming to hollow his bones out and fill them with lead. "No, not really," he said wearily. "But I had to try."

"I know you did," Mr. Big said, almost fondly.

Kleisterman lifted his head and stared defiantly at the gigantic Face. "And I'll keep trying, you know," he said. "I'll never give up."

"I know you won't," Mr. Big said sadly. "That's what makes you human."

The window snapped closed.

Kleisterman hung motionless in the air.

Below him, new mountains, bawling like a million burning calves, began to claw their way toward the sky.

Howard Waldrop

Howard Waldrop is widely considered to be one of the best short-story writers in the business, having been called "the resident Weird Mind of our generation" and an author "who writes like a honkytonk angel." His famous story "The Ugly Chickens" won both the Nebula and the World Fantasy Awards in 1981. His work has been gathered in the collections *Howard Who?, All About Strange Monsters of the Recent Past, Night of the Cooters, Going Home Again,* the print version of his collection *Dream Factories and Radio Pictures* (formerly available only in downloadable form online), and a collection of his stories written in collaboration with various other authors, *Custer's Last Jump and Other Collaborations.* Waldrop is also the author of the novel *The Texas-Israeli War: 1999,* in collaboration with Jake Saunders, and two solo novels, *Them Bones* and *A Dozen Tough Jobs,* as well as the chapbook *A Better World's in Birth!* He is at work on a new novel, tentatively titled *The Moone World.* His most recent book is a big retrospective collection, *Things Will Never Be the Same: Selected Short Fiction 1980–2005.* Having lived in Washington State for a number of years, Waldrop recently moved back to his former hometown of Austin, Texas, something that caused celebrations and loud hurrahs to rise up from the rest of the population.

Here he ushers us to a bright new world, a better world in the making, in the last place you'd think to look for it—among the frozen mud and razor wire and whistling death of No-Man's Land.

Ninieslando

The Captain had a puzzled look on his face. He clamped a hand to the right earphone and frowned in concentration.

"Lots of extraneous chatter on the lines again. I'm pretty sure some Fritzs have been replaced by Austrians in this sector. It seems to be in some language I don't speak. Hungarian, perhaps."

Tommy peered out into the blackness around the listening post. And of course could see nothing. The LP was inside the replica of a bloated dead horse that had lain between the lines for months. A week ago the plaster replica had arrived via the reserve trench from the camouflage shops far behind the lines. That meant a working party had had to get out in the night and not only replace the real thing with the plaster one, but also bury the original, which had swelled and burst months before.

They had come back nasty, smelly, and in foul moods, and had been sent back to the baths miles behind the lines, to have the luxury of a hot bath and a clean uniform. Lucky bastards, thought Tommy at the time.

Tommy's sentry duty that night, instead of the usual peering into the blackness over the parapet into the emptiness of No-Man's Land, had been to accompany the officer to the listening post inside the plaster dead horse, thirty feet in front of their trench line. That the LP was tapped into the German field telephone system (as they were into the British) meant that some poor sapper had had to crawl the quarter mile through No-Man's Land in the dark, find a wire, and tap into it. (Sometimes after doing so, they'd find they'd tied into a dead or abandoned wire.) Then he'd had to carefully crawl back to his own line, burying the wire as he retreated, and making no noise, lest he get a flare fired off for his trouble.

This was usually done when wiring parties were out on both sides, making noises of their own, so routine that they didn't draw illumination or small-arms fire.

There had evidently been lots of unidentified talk on the lines lately, to hear the rumours. The officers were pretty close-lipped. (You didn't admit voices were there in a language you didn't understand and could make no report on.) Officers from the General Staff had been to the LP in the last few nights and came back with nothing useful. A few hours in the mud and the dark had probably done them a world of good, a break from their regular routines in the châteaux that were HQ miles back of the line.

What little information that reached the ranks was, as the Captain said, "probably Hungarian, or some other Balkan sub-tongue." HQ was on the case, and was sending in some language experts soon. Or so they said.

Tommy looked through the slit just below the neck of the fake horse. Again, nothing. He cradled his rifle next to his chest. This March had been almost as cold as any January he remembered. At least the thaw had not come yet, turning everything to cold wet clinging mud.

There was the noise of slow dragging behind them, and Tommy brought his rifle up.

"Password," said the Captain to the darkness behind the horse replica.

"Ah—St. Agnes Eve . . . ," came a hiss.

"Bitter chill it was," said the Captain. "Pass."

A lieutenant and a corporal came into the open side of the horse. "Your relief, sir," said the lieutenant.

"I don't envy you your watch," said the Captain. "Unless you were raised in Buda-Pesh."

"The unrecognizable chatter again?" asked the junior officer.

"The same."

"Well, I hope someone from HQ has a go at it soon," said the lieutenant.

"Hopefully."

"Well, I'll give it a go," said the lieutenant. "Have a good night's sleep, sir."

"Very well. Better luck with it than I've had." He turned to Tommy. "Let's go, Private."

"Sir!" said Tommy.

They crawled the thirty feet or so back to the front trench on an oblique angle, making the distance much longer, and they were under the outermost concertina wire before they were challenged by the sentries.

Tommy went immediately to his funk hole dug into the wall of the sandbagged parapet. There was a nodding man on lookout; others slept in exhausted attitudes as if they were, like the LP horse, made of plaster.

He wrapped his frozen blanket around himself and was in a troubled sleep within seconds.

"Up for morning stand-to!" yelled the sergeant, kicking the bottom of his left boot.

Tommy came awake instantly, the way you do after a few weeks at the Front.

It was morning stand-to, the most unnecessary drill in the Army. The thinking behind it was that, at dawn, the sun would be full in the eyes of the soldiers in the British and French trenches, and the Hun could take advantage of it and advance through No-Man's Land and surprise them while they were sun-dazzled. (The same way that the Germans had *evening* stand-to in case the British made a surprise attack on them out of the setting sun.) Since no attacks were ever made across the churned and wired and mined earth of No-Man's Land by either side unless preceded by an artillery barrage of a horrendous nature, lasting from a couple to, in one case, twenty-four hours, of constantly falling shells, from the guns of the other side, morning stand-to was a sham perpetrated by a long-forgotten need from the early days of this Great War.

The other reason it was unnecessary was that this section of the Line that ran from the English Channel to the Swiss border was on a salient, and so the British faced more northward from true east, so the sun, instead of being in their eyes, was a dull glare off the underbrims of their helmets somewhere off to their right. The Hun, if he ever came across the open, would be sidelit and would make excellent targets for them.

But morning stand-to had long been upheld by tradition and the lack of hard thinking when the Great War had gone from one of movement and tactics in the opening days to the one of attrition and stalemate it had become since.

This part of the Front had moved less than one hundred yards, one way or the other, since 1915.

Tommy's older brother Fred had died the year before on the first day of the Somme Offensive, the last time there had been any real movement for years. And that had been more than fifty miles up the Front.

Tommy stood on the firing step of the parapet and pointed his rifle at nothing in particular to his front through the firing slit in the sandbags. All up and down the line, others did the same.

Occasionally some Hun would take the opportunity to snipe away at them. The German sandbags were an odd mixture of all types of colors and patterns piled haphazardly all along their parapets. From far away, they formed a broken pattern and the dark and light shades hid any break, such as a firing slit, from easy discernment. But the British sandbags were uniform, and the firing and observation slits stood out like sore thumbs, something the men were always pointing out to their officers.

As if on cue, there was the sound of smashing glass down the trench and the whine of a ricocheting bullet. A lieutenant threw down the trench periscope as if it were an adder that had bitten him.

"Damn and blast!" he said aloud. Then to his batman, "Requisition another periscope from regimental supply." The smashed periscope lay against the trench wall, its top and the mirror inside shot clean away by some sharp-eyed Hun. The batman left, going off in defile down the diagonal communication trench that led back to the reserve trench.

"Could have been worse," someone down the trench said quietly. "Could have been his head." There was a chorus of wheezes and snickers.

Humor was where you found it, weak as it was.

Usually both sides were polite to each other during their respective stand-tos. And afterwards, at breakfast and the evening meal. It wasn't considered polite to drop a shell on a man who'd just taken a forkful of beans into his mouth. The poor fellow might choke.

Daytime was when you got any rest you were going to get. Of course, there might be resupply, or ammunition, or food-toting details, but those came up rarely, and the sergeants were good about remembering who'd gone on the last one, and so didn't send you too often.

There was mail call, when it came, then the midday meal (when and if it came) and the occasional equipment inspection. Mostly you slept unless something woke you up.

Once a month, your unit was rotated back to the second trench, where you mostly slept as well as you could, and every third week to the reserve trench, far back, in which you could do something besides soldier. Your uniform would be cleaned and deloused, and so would you.

In the reserve trench was the only time your mind could get away from the War and its routine. You could get in some serious reading, instead of the catch-as-catch kind of the first and second trenches. You could get a drink and eat something besides bully beef and hardtack if you could find anybody selling food and drink. You could see a moving picture in one of the rear areas, though that was a long hike, or perhaps a music-hall show, put on by one of the units, with lots of drag humor and raucous laughter at not-very-subtle material. (Tommy was sure the life of a German soldier was much the same as his.)

It was one of the ironies of these times that in that far-off golden summer of 1914, when "some damn fool thing in the Balkans" was leading to its inevitable climax, Tommy's brother Fred, who was then eighteen, had been chosen as a delegate of the Birmingham Working-Men's Esperanto Association to go as a representative to the Twenty-fourth Annual Esperanto Conference in Basel, Switzerland. The Esperanto Conference had been to take place in the last days of July and the first days of August. (Fred had been to France before with a gang of school chums and was no stranger to travel.)

The Esperanto Conference was to celebrate the twenty-fourth anniversary of Zamenhof's artificial language, invented to bring better understanding between peoples through the use of an easy-to-learn, totally regular invented language—the thinking being that if all people spoke the same language (recognizing a pre-Babel dream), they would see that they were all one people, with common dreams and goals, and would slowly lose nationalism and religious partisanship through the use of the common tongue.

There had been other artificial languages since—Volapük had had quite a few adherents around the turn of the century—but none had had the cachet of Esperanto, the first and best of them.

Tommy and Fred had been fascinated by the language for years. (Fred could both speak and write it with an ease that Tommy had envied.)

What had surprised Fred, on arriving in Switzerland three years before, was that these representatives of this international conference devoted to better understanding among peoples were as acrimonious about their nations as any bumpkin from a third-rate country run by a tin-pot superstitious chieftain. Almost from the first, war and the talk of war divided the true believers from the lip-service toadies. The days were rife with desertions, as first one country then another announced mobilizations. By foot, by horse, by motor-car and train, and, in one case, aeroplane, the delegates left the conference to join up in the coming glorious adventure of War that they imagined would be a quick, nasty, splendid little one, over "before the snow flew."

By the end of the conference, only a few delegates were left, and they had to make hurried plans to return home before the first shots were fired.

His brother Fred, now dead, on the Somme, had returned to England on August 2, 1914, just in time to see a war no one wanted (but all had hoped for) declared. He, like so many idealists of all classes and nations, had joined up immediately.

Now Tommy, who had been three years younger at the time, was all that was left to his father and mother. He had, of course, been called up in due time, just before news of his brother's death had reached him.

And now here he was, in a trench of frozen mud, many miles from home, with night falling, when the sergeant walked by and said, "Fall out for wiring detail."

Going on a wiring party was about the only time you could be in No-Man's Land with any notion of safety. As you were repairing and thickening your tangle of steel, so were the Germans doing the same to theirs a quarter mile away.

Concertina wire, so haphazard-appearing from afar, was not there to stop an enemy assault, though it slowed that, too. The wire was there to funnel an enemy into narrower and tighter channels, so the enemy's course of action would become more and more constricted—and where the assault would finally slow against the impenetrable lanes of barbed steel was where your defensive machine-gun fire was aimed. Men waiting to go over, under, through, or around the massed wire were cut to ribbons by .303-caliber bullets fired at the rate of five hundred per minute.

Men could not live in such iron weather.

So you kept the wire repaired. At night. In the darkness, the sound of unrolling wire and muffled mauls filled the space between the lines. Quietly cursing men hauled the rolls of barbed wire over the parapets and pushed and pulled them out to where some earlier barrage (which was always supposed to cut all the wire but never did) had snapped some strands or blown away one of the new-type posts (which didn't have to be hammered in but were screwed into the ground as if the earth itself were one giant champagne cork).

Men carried wire, posts, sledges in the dark, out to the place where the sergeant stood.

"Two new posts here," he said, pointing at some deeper blackness. Tommy could see nothing, anywhere. He put his coil of wire on the ground, immediately gouging himself on the barbs of an unseen strand at shoulder height. He reached out—felt the wire going left and right.

"Keep it quiet," said the sergeant. "Don't want to get a flare up our arses." Illumination was the true enemy of night work.

Sounds of hammering and work came from the German Line. Tommy doubted that anyone would fire off a flare while their own men were out in the open.

He got into the work. Another soldier screwed in a post a few feet away.

"Wire," said the sergeant. "All decorative-like, as if you're trimming the Yule tree for Father Christmas. We want Hans and Fritz to admire our work, just before they cut themselves in twain on it."

Tommy and a few others uncoiled and draped the wire, running it back and forth between the two new posts and crimping it in with the existing strands.

Usually you went out, did the wiring work, and returned to the trench, knowing you'd done your part in the War. Many people had been lost in those times: there were stories of disoriented men making their way in the darkness, not to their own but to the enemy's trenches, and being killed or spending the rest of the war as a P.O.W.

Sometimes Tommy viewed wiring parties as a break in the routine of stultifying heat, spring and fall rains, and bone-breaking winter freezes. It was the one time you could stand up in relative comfort and safety, and not be walking bent over in a ditch.

There was a sudden rising comet in the night. Someone on Fritz's side had sent up a flare. Everybody froze—the idea was not to move at all when No-Man's Land was lit up like bright summer daylight. Tommy, unmoving, was surprised to see Germans caught out in the open, still also as statues, in front of their trench, poised in attitudes of labor on their wire.

Then who had fired off the flare?

It was a parachute flare and slowly drifted down

while it burned the night to steel-furnace-like brilliance. There were pops and cracks and whines from both trenchlines as snipers on each side took advantage of the surprise bounty of lighted men out in the open.

Dirt jumped up at Tommy's feet. He resisted the urge to dive for cover, the nearest being a shell crater twenty feet away. Any movement would draw fire, if not to him, to the other men around him. They all stood stock-still; he saw droplets of sweat on his sergeant's face.

From the German line, a trench mortar coughed.

The earth went upward in frozen dirt and a shower of body parts.

He felt as if he had been kicked in the back.

His right arm was under him. His rifle was gone. The night was coming back in the waning flickering light from the dying flare. He saw as he lay, his sergeant and a couple of men crawling away toward their line. He made to follow them. His legs wouldn't work.

He tried pushing himself up with his free arm; he only rolled over on the frozen earth. He felt something warm on his back quickly going cold.

No, he thought, I can't die like this out in No-Man's Land. He had heard, in months past, the weaker and weaker cries of slowly dying men who'd been caught out here. He couldn't think of dying that way.

He lay for a long time, too tired and hurt to try to

move. Gradually his hearing came back; there had been only a loud whine in his ears after the mortar shell had exploded.

He made out low talk from his own trench, twenty or so yards away. He could imagine the discussion now. Should we go out and try to get the wounded or dead? Does Fritz have the place zeroed in? Where's Tommy? He must have bought a packet.

Surprisingly, he could also hear sounds that must be from the German line—quiet footsteps, the stealthy movement from shell-hole to crater across No-Man's Land. The Germans must have sent out searching parties. How long had he lain here? Had there been return fire into the German work parties caught in the open by the flare? Were the British searching for their own wounded? Footsteps came nearer to him. Why weren't the sentries in his own trench challenging them? Or firing? Were they afraid that it was their own men making their ways back?

The footsteps stopped a few yards away. Tommy's eyes had adjusted to the darkness after the explosion. He saw vague dark shapes all around him. Through them moved a lighter man-shape. It moved with quick efficiency, pausing to turn over what Tommy saw now was a body near him.

It was at that moment that another weaker flare bloomed in the sky from the German trench, a red signal flare of some kind. In its light, Tommy saw the figure near him continue to rifle the body that lay there.

Tommy saw that the figure was a Chinaman. What was a Chinaman doing here in No-Man's Land?

Perhaps, Tommy thought, coughing, he speaks English. Maybe I can talk to him in Esperanto? That's what the language was invented for.

He said, in Esperanto, the first sentence he had ever learned in the language.

—Could you direct me to the house of the family Lodge?—

The Chinaman stopped. His face broke into a quizzical look in the light of the falling flare. Then he smiled, reached down to his belt, and brought up a club. He came over and hit Tommy on the head with it.

He woke in a clean bed, in clean sheets, in clean underwear, with a hurt shoulder and a headache. He was under the glare of electric lights, somewhere in a clean and spacious corridor.

He assumed he was far back of the lines in a regimental hospital. How he had gotten here, he did not know.

A man came to the foot of the bed. He wore a stethoscope.

—Ah— he said. —You have awakened.— He was speaking Esperanto.

"Am I in the division hospital?" asked Tommy in English.

The man looked at him uncomprehendingly.

He asked the same again, in Esperanto, searching for the words as he went.

—Far from it.— said the man. —You are in our hospital, where you needn't ever worry about the war you have known again. All will be explained later.—

—Have I been taken to Switzerland in my sleep?— asked Tommy. —Am I in some other neutral country?—

—Oh, you're in some neutral country, all right. But you're only a few feet from where you were found. And I take it you were under the impression it was a Chinese who rescued you. He's no Chinese—he would be offended to be called such—but Annamese, from French Indo-China. He was brought over here in one of the first levees early in the War. Many of them died that first winter, a fact the survivors never forgot. How is it you speak our language?—

—I was in the Esperanto Union from childhood on. I and my brother, who's now dead. He both wrote and spoke it much better than I.—

—It was bound to happen.— said the man. —You can imagine Ngyen's surprise when you spoke so, dressed in a British uniform. When you spoke, you marked yourself as one of us; he thought to bring you back the most expedient way possible, which was unconscious.

—The doctor tended your wounds—very nasty ones from which you probably would have perished had not you been brought here.—

—Where is here?— asked Tommy.

—Here— said the man —is a few feet below No-Man's Land—I'm sure the ex-captain will explain it all to you. It's been a while since someone in your circumstances joined us. Most of us came in the early days of the War, as soon as the Lines were drawn, or were found, half-mad or wounded between the lines, and had to be brought back to health and sanity. You appear to us, wounded all the same, but already speaking the language. You'll fit right in.—

—Are you British? French? German?— asked Tommy.

The man laughed. —Here— he said —none of us are of any nationality any longer. Here, we are all Men.—

He left. Eventually, the doctor came in and changed the dressing on his shoulder and gave him a pill.

The ex-captain came to see him. He was a small man, dressed in a faded uniform, with darker fabric at the collar in the shape of captain's bars.

—Welcome to Ninieslando.— he said.

—It's very clean.— said Tommy —I'm not used to *that*.—

—It's the least we can do.— he said, sweeping his hand around, indicating All That Out There.

—You'll learn your way around.— he continued.— You have the great advantage of already speaking our language, so you won't have to be going to classes. We'll have you on light duties till your wounds heal.—

—I'm very rusty.— Tommy said.—I'm out of practice. My brother was the scholar; he spoke it till the day he was killed on the Somme.—

—We could certainly have used him here.— said the ex-captain.

—Where we are— he continued, going into lecture-mode —is several feet below No-Man's Land. We came here slowly, one by one, in the course of the War. The lost, the wounded, the abandoned, and, unfortunately, the slightly mad. We have dug our rooms and tunnels, tapped into the combatant's field-phones and electrical lines, diverted their water to our own uses. Here we are building a society of Men, to take over the Earth after this War finally ends. Right now our goal is to survive the War—to do that we have to live off their food, water, lights, their clothing and equipment, captured at night on scavenging parties. We go into their trench lines and take what we need. We have better uses for it than killing other men.

—There are 5,600 of us in this sector. Along the whole four-hundred-mile Western Front, there are half a million of us, waiting our time to come out and start the New World of brotherhood. We are the first examples of it; former combatants living in harmony with a common language and common goals, undeterred by the War itself, a viable alternative to nationalism and bigotry. You can imagine the day when we walk out of here.—

Tommy held out his hand. The ex-captain shook it. —It's good to finally meet a real idealist.— said Tommy. —So many aren't.—

—You'll see— said the ex-captain —there's much work to be done while we wait, and it's easy to lose sight of the larger goals while you're scrounging for a can of beans. The War has provided for us, only to the wrong people. People still combatants, who still believe in the War.

—For make no mistake— he said —the Hun is not the enemy. The British are not the enemy. Neither your former officers nor the General Staff are the enemy. The *War* is the enemy. It runs itself on the fears of the combatants. It is a machine into which men are put and turned into memories.

—Every illness, self-inflicted wound or accident is referred to by both sides as "wastage"—perdajo—meaning that the death did not contribute in any way to a single enemy soldier's death.

—A man being in the War, to War's way of thinking, was wasted. The idea has taken over planning. The War is thinking for the General Staff. They have not had a single idea that was not the War's in these three years.

—So we take advantage. A flare fired off in the night when no one expects it brings the same result as if we had a regimental battery of Krupp howitzers. The War provides the howitzers to us as well as to the combatants.

—I need not tell you this.— he said. —I'm going on like Wells's wandering artilleryman in *War of the Worlds*. Everyone here has to quit thinking like a combatant and begin to think like a citizen of Ninieslando. What can we do to take War out of the driver's seat? How do we plan for the better world while War is making that world cut its own throat? We are put here to bring some sense to it: to stay War's hand. Once mankind knows that War is the enemy, he will be able to join us in that bright future. Zamenhof was right; Esperanto will lead the way!

—Good luck— he said, making ready to leave—
new citizen of Ninieslando.—

Their job today, some weeks after the ex-captain's
visit, was to go to a French supply point, load up,
and bring rations back by secret ways to Ninieslando,
where their cooks would turn it into something
much more palatable than the French ever thought
of making. They had on parts of French uniforms;
nobody paid much attention this late in the day and
the War, if the colors were right. Tommy had a
French helmet tied by its chin strap to his belt in the
manner of a jaunty French workingman.

They took their place in a long line of soldiers
waiting. They moved up minute by minute till it was
their turn to be loaded up.

"No turnips," said the sergeant with them, who
had been at Verdun.

"Ah, but of course," said the supply sergeant. "As
you request." He made an impolite gesture.

They took their crates and sacks and followed
the staggering line of burdened men returning to the
trenches before them. The connecting trench started
as a path at ground level and slowly sank as the walls
of the ditch rose up around them as they stepped
onto the duckboards. Ahead of them the clump-
clump-clump of many feet echoed. The same sounds
rose behind them.

Somewhere in the diagonal trench between the
second and Front Line, they simply disappeared with
the food at a blind turn in the connecting trench.

They delivered the food to the brightly lit electric kitchens below the front line.

—Ah, good.— said a cook, looking into a sack. — Turnips!—

He waited at a listening post with an ex-German lieutenant.

—Lots a chatter tonight.— he said to Tommy. — They won't notice much when we talk with other sectors later.—

—Of course.— said Tommy. —The combatants are tapped into each other's lines, trying to get information. They hear not only their enemies, but us.—

—And what do they do about it?— asked the ex-German.

—They try to figure out what language is being spoken. Our side was puzzled.—

—They usually think it some Balkan tongue.— said the ex-German. —Our side thought it could be Welsh or Basque. Did you ever hear it?—

—No, only officers listened.—

—You would have recognized it immediately. But War has taught the officers that enlisted men are lazy illiterate swine, only interested in avoiding work and getting drunk. What language knowledge could they have? Otherwise, they would be officers. Is it not true?—

—Very true.— said Tommy.

A week later, Tommy was in the brightly lit library, looking over the esoteric selection of reading matter filched from each side. Field manuals, cheap novels, anthologies of poetry, plays in a dozen languages. There were some books in Esperanto, most published before the turn of the century. Esperanto had had a great vogue then, before the nations determined it was all a dream and went back to their armaments races and their "places in the sun." There were, of course, a few novels translated into Esperanto.

There was also the most complete set of topographical maps of the Front imaginable. He looked up this sector; saw the gland of Ninieslando's tunnels and corridors, saw that even the British listening post had the designation "fake plaster horse." He could follow the routes of Ninieslando from the Swiss border to the English Channel (except in those places where the Front Line trenches were only yards apart; there was hardly room for excavation there without calling the attention of both sides to your presence). Here, Ninieslando was down to a single tunnel no wider than a communications trench up on the surface to allow exchanges between sectors.

Either side up above would give a thousand men in return for any map of the set.

That meant that the work of Ninieslando went on day and night, listening and mapping out the smallest changes in the topography. The map atop each pile in the drawer was the latest, dated most recently. You could go through the pile and watch the War backwards to—in some cases—late 1914, when the Germans had determined where the Front would be by pulling back to the higher ground, even if only a foot or two more in elevation. Ninieslando had been founded then, as the War became a stalemate.

In most cases, the lines had not changed since then, except to become more churned up, muddier, nastier. Occasionally, they would shift a few feet, or a hundred yards, due to some small advance by one side or the other. Meanwhile, Ninieslando became more complex and healthier as more and more men joined.

As the ex-captain had said: —The War made us the best engineers, machinists, and soldiers ever known. A shame to waste all that training. So we used it to build a better world, underground.—

Tommy looked around the bright shiny library. He could spend his life here, building a better world indeed.

For three nights, each side had sent out raiding parties to the other's Line. There had been fierce fighting as men all through the sector stomped or clubbed each other to death.

It had been a bonanza for Ninieslando's scavenging teams. They had looted bodies and the wounded of everything usable: books, food, equipment, clothing. They had done their work efficiently and thoroughly, leaving naked bodies all through No-Man's Land. The moans of the dying followed them as they made their way back down through the hidden entrances to Ninieslando.

Tommy, whose shoulder wound had healed nicely,

lay in his clean bunk after dropping off his spoils from the scavenging at the sector depot. The pile of goods had grown higher than ever—more for Ninieslando. He had a copy of *The Oxford Book of English Verse* open on his chest. The language was becoming lost to him, he had not spoken it in so long. He was now thinking, and even dreaming, in Esperanto. As well it should be. National languages were a drag and a stumbling block to the human race. He read a few poems, then closed the book. For another day, he thought, when we look back with a sort of nostalgia on a time when national languages kept men separated. He imagined the pastoral poems of the future, written in Esperanto, with shepherds and nymphs recalling lines of English each to each, as if it were a lost tongue like Greek or Latin. He yearned for a world where such things could be.

The field phones had been strangely silent for a day or so. But it was noticed that couriers went backwards and forwards from trench to observation post to headquarters. On both sides. Obviously, something was up. A courier was waylaid in the daylight, a dangerous undertaking, but there were no paper orders on him. The kidnapping team drew the line at torture, so reported that the orders must be verbal. Perhaps, by coincidence, both sides were planning assaults at the same time to break the stalemate. It would be a conflagration devoutly to be desired by Ninieslando.

Of course, the War had made it so both sides would lose the element of surprise when the batteries of both sides opened in barrages at the same time, or nearly so. Ninieslando waited—whatever happened, No-Man's Land would be littered with the dead and dying, ripe for the picking.

—Too quiet.— said someone in the corridor.

—They've never gone this long off the telephones.— said another.

Tommy walked the clean corridor. He marveled that only a few feet overhead was a world of ekskremento and malpurajo fought over by men for three years. Here was a shinier, cleaner world than anything man had achieved on the surface.

It was just about then that the first shells of the expected barrage began to fall above his head. Dust drifted down from the ceiling. Parts of the wall buckled and shook.

Tommy realized that he was under the middle of No-Man's Land. Unless their aim was very bad indeed, the artillerymen of neither side should be making their shells land here. They should be aiming for the Front trench of the other side.

Ninieslando shook and reeled from the barrage. The lights went out as shells cut a line somewhere.

Tommy struck a match, found the electric torch in its niche at the corridor crossing. He turned it on and made his way to the library.

Then it got ominously quiet. The barrage ceased after a very short while. Who was firing a five-minute barrage in the wrong place? Had they all gone crazy up there?

He entered the library, shone his torch around. A few books had fallen from the shelves; mostly it was untouched.

He sat at a table. There was some noise in the corridor at the far end. A bloodied man ran in, his eyes wild, screaming. —Tri rugo bendos!—Three red bands!— Was he speaking metaphorically? Three Marxist gangs? Or like Sherlock Holmes, literally, as in "The Speckled Band"? What did he mean? Tommy went to grab him, but he was gone, out of the library, still yelling.

Tommy went down the hall and up a series of steps to an observation post with two viewing slits, one looking northeast, the other southwest.

What he saw looking northeast was astounding. In broad daylight, German soldiers, rifles up, bayonets fixed, were advancing. They probed the ground and debris as they came on. On the left sleeve of every soldier were three red stripes on a white background.

Tommy turned to the other slit, wondering why there was no rifle or machine gun fire mowing down the line of Germans.

What he saw made his blood freeze. From the other direction, British and French soldiers also advanced in the open. On their right arms were pinned three red stripes on a white background. As he watched, several soldiers disappeared down an embankment. There was the sound of firing. A Ninieslandoja, with no stripes on his sleeve,

staggered out and died in the dirt. The firing continued, getting fainter.

The sound of firing began again, far off down the
corridor below.

Tommy took off for the infirmary.

There were many kinds of paint down at the car-
pentry shop, but very little approached red, the last
color you'd want on a battlefield.

When Tommy ran into the infirmary, he found
the ex-captain there before him. The man was tear-
ing bandages into foot-long pieces.

Tommy went to the medicine chest and forced his
way into it. Bottles flew and broke.

—They've finally done it!— said the ex-captain.
—They've gotten together just long enough to get rid
of us. Our scavenging last week must have finally
pushed them over into reason.—

Tommy took a foot-long section of bandages and
quickly painted three red stripes on it with the dauber
on a bottle of Mercurochrome. He took one, gave it
to the ex-captain, did one for himself.

—First they'll do for us.— he said. —Next, they'll
be back to killing each other. This is going on up
and down the whole Western Front. I never thought
they could keep such a plan quiet for so long.—

The ex-captain headed him a British helmet and a
New Model Army web-belt. —Got your rifle? Good,
try to blend in. Speak English. Good luck.— He was
gone out the door.

Tommy took off the opposite way. He ran toward where he thought the Germans might be.

The sound of firing grew louder. He realized he might now be a target for Ninieslanders, too. He stepped around a corridor junction and directly in front of a German soldier. The man raised his rifle barrel towards the ceiling.

"Anglander?" the German asked

—j— "Yes," said Tommy, lifting his rifle also.

"More just behind me," Tommy added. "Very few of the . . . undergrounders in our way." The German looked at him in incomprehension. He looked farther back down the corridor Tommy had come from.

There was the noise of more Germans coming up the other hall. They lifted their rifles, saw his red stripes, lowered them.

Tommy moved with them as they advanced farther down the corridors, marveling at the construction. There was some excitement as a Ninieslander bolted from a room down the hallway and was killed in a volley from the Germans.

"Good shooting," said Tommy.

Eventually, they heard the sound of English.

"My people," said Tommy. He waved to the Germans and walked toward the voices.

A British captain with drawn pistol stood in front of a group of soldiers. The bodies of two Ninieslanders lay on the floor beside them.

—And what rat have we forced from his hole?— asked the captain in Esperanto.

Tommy kept his eyes blank.

"Is that Hungarian you're speaking, sir?" he asked, the words strange on his tongue.

"Your unit?" asked the Captain.

"First, King's Own Rifles," said Tommy. "I was separated and with some Germans."

"Much action?"

"A little, most of the corridors are empty. They're off somewheres, sir."

"Fall in with my men till we can get you back to your company, when this is over. What kind of stripes you call those? Is that iodine?"

"Mercurochrome, I believe," said Tommy. "Supply ran out of the issue. Our stretcher-bearers used field expedients." He had a hard time searching for the right words.

Esperanto phrases kept leaping to mind. He would have to be careful, especially around this officer.

They searched out a few more rooms and hallways, found nothing. From far away, whistles blew.

"That's recall," said the Captain. "Let's go."

Other deeper whistles sounded from far away, where the Germans were. It must be over.

They followed the officer till they came to boardings that led outside to No-Man's Land.

The captain left for a hurried consultation with a group of field-grade officers. He returned in a few minutes.

"More work to do," he said. A detail brought cans of petrol and set them down nearby.

"We're to burn the first two corridors down. You, you, you," he said, indicating Tommy last. "Take these cams, spread the petrol around. The signal is three whistle blasts. Get out as soon as you light it off. Everyone got matches? Good."

They went back inside, the can heavy in Tommy's hands. He went up to the corridor turning, began to empty petrol on the duckboard floor.

He saved a little in the bottom of the can. He idly sloshed it around and around.

Time enough to build the better world tomorrow. Many, like him, must have made it out, to rejoin their side or get clean away in this chaos.

After this War is over, we'll get together, find each other, start building that new humanity on the ashes of this old world.

The three whistles came. Tommy struck a match, threw it onto the duckboard flooring and watched the petrol catch with a *whoosh*ing sound.

He threw the can after it, and walked out into the bright day of the new world waiting to be born.

David Weber

New York Times bestselling author David Weber is frequently compared to C. S. Forester, the creator of Horatio Hornblower, and is one of the most acclaimed authors of military science fiction alive—although he has also written everything from space opera to epic fantasy. He is best known as the author of the long-running series of novels and stories detailing the exploits of Honor Harrington, perhaps the most popular military SF series of all time, consisting of eleven novels, including *On Basilisk Station, The Honor of the Queen, Field of Dishonor, In Enemy Hands, Ashes of Victory,* and others, and the Honor Harrington stories recently collected in *Worlds of Weber: Ms. Midshipwoman Harrington and Other Stories*. In addition, he has allowed other authors to write in the Honor Harrington universe, including S. M. Stirling, Eric Flint, David Drake, Jane Lindskold, and Timothy Zahn. Weber has also written the War God epic fantasy series, consisting of *Oath of Swords, The War God's Own,* and *Wind Rider's Oath*, the four-volume Dahak series, the four-volume Starfire series (with Steve White), the four-volume Empire of Man series (with John Ringo), and the two-volume Assiti Shards series (with Eric Flint), as well as stand-alone novels such as *Path of the Fury, The Apocalypse Troll, The Excalibur Alternative, Old Soldiers,* and *In Fury Born.* His most recent books include the three-volume Safehold series that started in 2007 with *Off Armageddon Reef,* the two-volume Multiverse series (with Linda Evans), the Honor Harrington collection, *Ms. Midshipwoman Harrington,* the new Safehold novel, *By Heresies Distressed,* and *Storm from the Shadows.* David Weber lives in Greenville, South Carolina.

In the complex and suspenseful novella that follows, he shows us a battered and bloodied Earth brought almost to its knees by a ruthless and overwhelming alien invasion, except for some scattered and isolated warriors who aren't comfortable on their knees and undertake the defense of the human race—and, in the process, learn that they have some unexpected resources to call upon in the fight.

Out of the Dark

I

The attention signal whistled on Fleet Commander Thikair's communicator.

He would always remember how prosaic and . . . normal it had sounded, but at that moment, as he looked up from yet another ream of deadly dull paperwork, when he still didn't know, he felt an undeniable sense of relief for the distraction. Then he pressed the acceptance key, and that sense of relief vanished when he recognized his flagship's commander's face . . . and his worried expression.

"What is it, Ahzmer?" he asked, wasting no time on formal greetings.

"Sir, I'm afraid the scout ships have just reported a rather . . . disturbing discovery," Ship Commander Ahzmer replied.

"Yes?" Thikair's ears cocked inquisitively as Ahzmer paused.

"Sir, they're picking up some fairly sophisticated transmissions."

"Transmissions?" For a moment or two, it didn't really register, but then Thikair's eyes narrowed and his pelt bristled. "How sophisticated?" he demanded much more sharply.

"Very, I'm afraid, sir," Ahzmer said unhappily. "We're picking up digital and analog with some impressive bandwidth. It's at least Level Three activity, sir. Possibly even—" Ahzmer's ears flattened. "—Level Two."

Thikair's ears went even flatter than the ship commander's, and he felt the tips of his canines creeping into sight. He shouldn't have let his expression give so much away, but he and Ahzmer had known one another for decades, and it was obvious the other's thoughts had already paralleled his own.

The fleet had reemerged into normal-space two days ago, after eight standard years, subjective, of cryogenic sleep. The flight had lasted some sixteen standard years, by the rest of the galaxy's clocks, since the best velocity modifier even in hyper allowed a speed of no more than five or six times that of light in normal-space terms. The capital ships and transports were still a week of normal-space travel short of the objective, sliding in out of the endless dark like huge, sleek *hasthar*, claws and fangs still hidden, though ready. But he'd sent the much lighter scout ships, whose lower tonnages made their normal-space drives more efficient, ahead to take a closer look at their target. Now he found himself wishing he hadn't.

Stop that, he told himself sternly. *Your ignorance wouldn't have lasted much longer, anyway. And you'd still have to decide what to do. At least this way you have some time to start thinking about it!*

His mind started to work again, and he sat back, one six-fingered hand reaching down to groom his tail while he thought.

The problem was that the Hegemony Council's authorization for this operation was based on the survey team's report that the objective's intelligent species had achieved only a Level Six civilization. The other two systems on Thikair's list were both classified as Level Five civilizations, although one had crept close to the boundary between Level Five and Level Four. It had been hard to get the Council to sign off on those two. Indeed, the need to argue the Shongairi's case so strenuously before the Council was the reason the mission had been delayed long enough to telescope into a three-system operation. But *this* system's "colonization" had been authorized almost as an afterthought, the sort of mission any of the Hegemony's members might have mounted. They'd certainly never agreed to the conquest of a Level Three, far less a *Level Two*! In fact, anything that had attained Level Two came under protectorate status until it attained Level One and became eligible for Hegemony membership in its own right or (as at least half of them managed) destroyed itself first.

Cowards, Thikair thought resentfully. *Dirtgrubbers*. Weed-eaters!

The Shongairi were the only carnivorous species to have attained hyper-capability. Almost 40 percent of the Hegemony's other member races were grasseaters, who regarded the Shongairi's dietary habits as barbarous, revolting, even horrendous. And even most of the Hegemony's omnivores were . . . uncomfortable around Thikair's people.

Their own precious Constitution had forced them to admit the Shongairi when the Empire reached the stars, but they'd never been happy about it. In fact, Thikair had read several learned monographs arguing that his people's existence was simply one of those incredible flukes that (unfortunately, in the obvious opinion of the authors of those monographs) had to happen occasionally. What they *ought* to have done, if they'd had the common decency to follow the example of other species with similarly violent, psychopathically aggressive dispositions, was blow themselves back into the Stone Age as soon as they discovered atomic fission.

Unhappily for those racist bigots, Thikair's people hadn't. Which didn't prevent the Council from regarding them with scant favor. Or from attempting to deny them their legitimate prerogatives.

It's not as if we were the only species to seek colonies. There's the Barthon, and the Kreptu, just for starters. And what about the Liatu? They're grasseaters, *but they've got over* fifty *colony systems!*

Thikair made himself stop grooming his tail and inhale deeply. Dredging up old resentments wouldn't solve this problem, and if he was going to be completely fair (which he really didn't want to be, especially in the Liatu's case), the fact that they'd been roaming the galaxy for the better part of sixty-two thousand standard years as compared to the Shongairi's nine *hundred* might help to explain at least some of the imbalance.

Besides, that imbalance is going to change, he reminded himself grimly.

There was a reason the Empire had established no less than eleven colonies even before Thikair had departed, and why the Shongari Council representatives had adamantly defended their right to establish those colonies even under the Hegemony's ridiculous restrictions.

No one could deny any race the colonization of any planet with no native sapient species. Unfortunately, there weren't all that many habitable worlds, and they tended to be located bothersomely far apart, even for hyper-capable civilizations. Worse, a depressing number of them already had native sapients living on them. Under the Hegemony Constitution, colonizing *those* worlds required Council approval, which wasn't as easy to come by as it would have been in a more reasonable universe.

Thikair was well aware that many of the Hegemony's other member races believed the Shongairi's "perverted" warlike nature (and even more "perverted" honor codes) explained their readiness to expand through conquest. And, to be honest, they had a point. But the real reason, which was never discussed outside the Empire's inner councils, was that an existing infrastructure, however crude, made the development of a colony faster and easier. And, even more important, the . . . acquisition of less advanced but trainable species provided useful increases in the Empire's labor force. A labor force that—thanks to the Constitution's namby-pamby emphasis on members' internal autonomy—could be kept properly in its place on any planet belonging to the Empire.

And a labor force that was building the sinews of war the Empire would require on the day it told the rest of the Hegemony what it could do with all of its demeaning restrictions.

None of which did much about his current problem.

"You say it's *possibly* a Level Two," he said. "Why do you think that?"

"Given all the EM activity and the sophistication of so many of the signals, the locals are obviously at least Level Three, sir." Ahzmer didn't seem to be getting any happier, Thikair observed. "In fact, preliminary analysis suggests they've already developed fission power—possibly even fusion. But while there are at least *some* fission power sources on the planet, there seem to be very few of them. In fact, most of their power generation seems to come from burning *hydrocarbons*! Why would any civilization that was really Level Two do anything that stupid?"

The fleet commander's ears flattened in a frown. Like the ship commander, he found it difficult to conceive of any species stupid enough to continue consuming irreplaceable resources in hydrocarbon-based power generation if it no longer had to. Ahzmer simply didn't want to admit it, even to himself, because if this genuinely *was* a Level Two civilization, it would be forever off-limits for colonization.

"Excuse me, Sir," Ahzmer said, made bold by his own worries, "but what are we going to do?"

"I can't answer that question just yet, Ship Commander," Thikair replied a bit more formally than usual when it was just the two of them. "But I can tell you what we're *not* going to do, and that's let these reports panic us into any sort of premature conclusions or reactions. We've spent eight years, subjective, to get here, and three months reviving our personnel from cryo. We're not going to simply cross this system off our list and move on to the next one until we've thoroughly considered what we've learned about it and evaluated all of our options. Is that clear?"

"Yes, sir!"

"Good. In the meantime, however, we have to assume we may well be facing surveillance systems considerably in advance of anything we'd anticipated. Under the circumstances, I want the fleet taken to a covert stance. Full-scale emissions control and soft recon mode, Ship Commander."

"Yes, sir. I'll pass the order immediately."

II

Master Sergeant Stephen Buchevsky climbed out of the MRAP, stretched, collected his personal weapon, and nodded to the driver.

"Go find yourself some coffee. I don't really expect this to take very long, but you know how good I am at predicting things like that."

"Gotcha, Top," the corporal behind the wheel agreed with a grin. He stepped on the gas and the MRAP (officially the Mine Resistant Ambush

Protection vehicle) moved away, headed for the mess tent at the far end of the position, while Buchevsky started hiking toward the sandbagged command bunker perched on top of the sharp-edged ridge.

The morning air was thin and cold, but less than two weeks from the end of his current deployment, Buchevsky was used to that. It wasn't exactly as if it was the first time he'd been here, either. And while many of Bravo Company's Marines considered it the armpit of the universe, Buchevsky had seen substantially worse during the seventeen years since he'd taken a deceitfully honest-faced recruiter at his word.

"Oh, the places you'll go—the things you'll see!" the recruiter in question had told him enthusiastically. And Stephen Buchevsky had indeed been places and seen things since. Along the way, he'd been wounded in action no less than six times, and, at age thirty-five, his marriage had just finished coming rather messily unglued, mostly over the issue of lengthy, repeat deployments. He walked with a slight limp the therapists hadn't been able to completely eradicate, the ache in his right hand was a faithful predictor of rain or snow, and the scar that curved up his left temple was clearly visible through his buzz-cut hair, especially against his dark skin. But while he sometimes entertained fantasies about looking up the recruiter who'd gotten him to sign on the dotted line, he'd always reupped.

Which probably says something unhealthy about my personality, he reflected as he paused to gaze down at the narrow twisting road far below.

On his first trip to sunny Afghanistan, he'd spent his time at Camp Rhine down near Kandahar. That was when he'd acquired the limp, too. For the next deployment, he'd been located up near Ghanzi, helping to keep an eye on the A01 highway from Kandahar to Kabul. That had been less . . . interesting than his time in Kandahar Province, although he'd still managed to take a rocket splinter in the ass, which had been good for another gold star on the purple heart ribbon (and unmerciful "humor" from his so-called friends). But then the Poles had taken over in Ghanzi, and so, for his *third* Afghanistan deployment, he and the rest of First Battalion, Third Marine Regiment, Third Marine Division, had been sent back to Kandahar, where things had been heating up again. They'd stayed there, too . . . until they'd gotten new orders, at least. The situation in Paktika Province—the one the Poles had turned down in favor of Ghanzi because Paktika was so much more lively—had also worsened, and Buchevsky and Bravo Company had been tasked as backup for the battalion of the Army's 508th Parachute Infantry in the area while the Army tried to pry loose some of its own people for the job.

Despite all of the emphasis on "jointness," it hadn't made for the smoothest relationship imaginable. The fact that everyone recognized it as a stopgap and Bravo as only temporary visitors (they'd been due to deploy back to the States in less than three months when they got the call) didn't help, either. They'd arrived without the logistic support which would normally have accompanied them, and despite the commonality of so much of their equipment, that had still put an additional strain on the 508th's supply services. But the Army types had been glad enough to see them and they'd done their best to make the "jarheads" welcome.

The fact that the Vermont-sized province shared six hundred miles of border with Pakistan, coupled with the political changes in Pakistan and an upsurge in opium production under the Taliban's auspices (odd how the fundamentalists' one-time bitter opposition to the trade had vanished now that they needed cash to support their operations), had prevented Company B from feeling bored. Infiltration and stepped-up attacks on the still shaky Afghan Army units in the province hadn't helped, although all things considered, Buchevsky preferred Paktika to his 2004 deployment to Iraq. Or his most recent trip to Kandahar, for that matter.

Now he looked down through the thin mountain air at the twisting trail Second Platoon was here to keep a close eye on. All the fancy recon assets in the world couldn't provide the kind of constant presence and eyes-on surveillance needed to interdict traffic through a place like this. It was probably easier than the job Buchevsky's father had faced trying to cut the Ho Chi Minh Trail—at least his people could see a lot farther!—but that wasn't saying very much, all things taken together. And he didn't recall his dad's mentioning anything about lunatic martyrs out to blow people up in job lots for the glory of God.

He gave himself a shake. He had a lot on his plate organizing the Company's rotation home, and he turned back toward the command bunker to inform Gunnery Sergeant Wilson that his platoon's Army relief would begin arriving within forty-eight hours. It was time to get the turnover organized and Second Platoon back to its FOB to participate in all the endless paperwork and equipment checks involved in any company movement.

Not that Buchevsky expected anyone to complain about *this* move.

III

The gathering in *Star of Empire*'s conference room consisted of Thikair's three squadron commanders, his ground force commander, and Base Commander Shairez. Despite the fact that Shairez was technically junior to Ground Force Commander Thairys, she was the expedition's senior base commander, and as such, she, too, reported directly to Thikair.

Rumors about the scout ships' findings had spread, of course. It would have required divine intervention to prevent that! Still, if it turned out there was no landing after all, it would scarcely matter, would it?

"What is your interpretation of the scout ships' data, Base Commander?" Thikair asked Shairez without bothering to call the meeting formally to order. Most of them seemed surprised by his disregard for protocol, and Shairez didn't look especially pleased to be the first person called upon. But she could scarcely have been surprised by the question itself; the reason she was the expedition's senior base commander was her expertise in dealing with other sapient species, after all.

"I've considered the data, including that from the stealthed orbital platforms, carefully, Fleet Commander," she replied. "I'm afraid my analysis confirms Ship Commander Ahzmer's original fears. I would definitely rate the local civilization at Level Two."

Unhappy at being called upon or not, she hadn't flinched, Thikair thought approvingly.

"Expand upon that, please," he said.

"Yes, sir." Shairez tapped the virtual clawpad of her personal computer and her eyes unfocused slightly as she gazed at the memos projected directly upon her retinas.

"First, sir, this species has developed nuclear power. Of course, their technology is extremely primitive, and it would appear they're only beginning to experiment with fusion, but there are significant indications that their general tech level is much more capable than we would ever anticipate out of anyone with such limited nuclear capacity. Apparently, for some reason known only to themselves, these people—I use the term loosely, of course—have chosen to cling to hydrocarbon-fueled power generation well past the point at which they could have replaced it with nuclear generation."

"That's absurd!" Squadron Commander Jainfar objected. The crusty old space dog was Thikair's senior squadron commander and as bluntly uncompromising as one of his dreadnoughts' main batteries. Now he grimaced as Thikair glanced at him, one ear cocked interrogatively.

"Apologies, Base Commander," the squadron commander half growled. "I don't doubt your data. I just find it impossible to believe any species *that* stupid could figure out how to use fire in the first place!"

"It *is* unique in our experience, Squadron Commander," Shairez acknowledged. "And according to the master data banks, it's also unique in the experience of every other member of the Hegemony. Nonetheless, they do possess virtually all of the other attributes of a Level Two culture."

She raised one hand, ticking off points on her claws as she continued.

"They have planetwide telecommunications. Although they've done little to truly exploit space, they have numerous communications and navigational satellites. Their military aircraft are capable of transsonic flight regimes, they make abundant use of advanced—well, advanced for any pre-Hegemony culture—composites, and we've observed experiments with early-generation directed energy weapons, as well. Their technological capabilities are *not* distributed uniformly about their planet, but they're spreading rapidly. I would be very surprised—assuming they survive—if they haven't evolved an effectively unified planetary government within the next two or three generations. Indeed, they might manage it even sooner, if their ridiculous rate of technological advancement is any guide!"

The silence around the conference table was profound. Thikair let it linger for several moments, then leaned back in his chair.

"How would you account for the discrepancy

between what we're now observing and the initial survey report?"

"Sir, I *can't* account for it," she said frankly. "I've doublechecked and triple-checked the original report. There's no question that it was accurate at the time it was made, yet now we find *this*. Somehow, this species has made the jump from animal transport, wind power, and crude firearms to this level more than three times as rapidly as any other species. And please note that I said '*any* other species.' The one I had in mind were the Ugartu."

The fleet commander saw more than one grimace at that. The Ugartu had never attained Hegemony membership . . . since they'd turned their home star system into a radioactive junkyard first. The Council of the time had breathed a quiet but very, very profound sigh of relief when it happened, too, given that the Ugartu had been advancing technologically at twice the galactic norm. Which meant *these* people . . .

"Is it possible the initial survey team broke procedure, sir?" Ship Commander Ahzmer asked, his expression troubled. Thikair glanced at him, and his flagship's commander flicked both ears. "I'm just wondering if the surveyors might inadvertently have made direct contact with the locals? Accidentally given them a leg up?"

"Possible, but unlikely, Ship Commander," Ground Force Commander Thairys said. "I wish I didn't have to say that, since I find this insanely rapid advancement just as disturbing as you do. Unfortunately, the original survey was conducted by the Barthonii."

Several of Thikair's officers looked as if they'd just smelled something unpleasant. Actually, from the perspective of any self-respecting carnivore, the Barthonii smelled simply delicious, but the timid plant-eaters were one of the Shongairi's most severe critics. And they were also heavily represented in the Hegemony's survey forces, despite their inherent timidity, because of their fanatic support for the Council regulations limiting contact with inferior races.

"I'm afraid I agree with the Ground Force Commander," Shairez said.

"And it wouldn't matter if that *were* what had happened," Thikair pointed out. "The Constitution doesn't care where a species' technology *came* from. What matters is the level it's *attained*, however it got there."

"And the way the Council will react to it," Jainfar said sourly, and ears moved in agreement all around the table.

"I'm afraid Squadron Commander Jainfar has a point, sir." Thairys sighed heavily. "It was hard enough getting approval for our other objectives, and they're far less advanced than *these* people have turned out to be. Or I hope to Dainthar's Hounds they still are, at any rate!"

More ears waved agreement, Thikair's among them. However aberrant, this species' development clearly put it well outside the parameters of the Council's authorization. However . . .

"I'm well aware of just how severely our discoveries have altered the circumstances envisioned by our mission orders," he said. "On the other hand, there are a few additional points I believe bear consideration."

Most of them looked at him with obvious surprise, but Thairys' tail curled up over the back of his chair and his ears flattened in speculation.

"First, one of the points I noticed when I reviewed the first draft of Base Commander Shairez's report was that these people not only have remarkably few nuclear power stations, but for a species of their level, they also have remarkably few nuclear *weapons*. Only their major political powers seem to have them in any quantity, and even they have very limited numbers, compared to their non-nuclear capabilities. Of course, they *are* omnivores, but the numbers of weapons are still strikingly low. Lower even than for many weed-eaters at a comparable level. That becomes particularly apparent given the fact that there are fairly extensive military operations under way over much of the planet. In particular, several more advanced nation-states are conducting operations against adversaries who obviously don't even approach their own capabilities. Yet even though those advanced—I'm speaking relatively, of course—nation-states have nuclear arsenals and their opponents, who do not, would be incapable of retaliation, they've chosen not to employ them. Not only that, but they must have at least some ability to produce bio-weapons, yet we've seen no evidence of their use. For that matter, we haven't even poison gas or neurotoxins!"

He let that settle in, then leaned forward once more to rest his folded hands on the conference table.

"This would appear to be a highly peculiar species in several respects," he said quietly. "Their failure to utilize the most effective weapons available to them, however, suggests that they're almost as lacking in . . . military pragmatism as many of the Hegemony's weed-eaters. That being the case, I find myself of the opinion that they might well make a suitable . . . client species, after all."

The silence in the conference room was absolute as the rest of Thikair's listeners began to realize what Thairys had already guessed.

"I realize," the Fleet Commander continued, "that to proceed with this operation would violate the spirit of the Council's authorization. However, after careful review, I've discovered that it contains no specific reference to the attained level of the local sapients. In other words, the *letter* of the authorizing writ wouldn't preclude our continuing. No doubt someone like the Barthonii or Liatu still might choose to make a formal stink afterwards, but consider the possible advantages."

"Advantages, sir?" Ahzmer asked, and Thikair's eyes gleamed.

"Oh, yes, Ship Commander," he said softly. "This species may be bizarre in many ways, and they obviously don't understand the realities of war, but clearly something about them has supported a phenomenal rate of advancement. I realize their actual capabilities would require a rather more . . . vigorous initial strike than we'd anticipated. And even with heavier pre-landing preparation, our casualties might well be somewhat higher than projected, but, fortunately, we have ample redundancy for dealing even with this sort of target, thanks to our follow-on objectives in Syk and Jormau. We have ample capability to conquer any planet-bound civilization, even if it has attained Level Two, and, to be honest, I think it would be very much worthwhile to concentrate on this system even if it means writing off the seizure of one—or even both—of the others."

One or two of them looked as if they wanted to protest, but he flattened his ears, his voice even softer.

"I realize how that may sound, but think about this. Suppose we were able to integrate these people—these 'humans'—into our labor force. Put them to work on *our* research projects. Suppose we were able to leverage their talent for that sort of thing to quietly push our own tech level to something significantly in *advance* of the rest of the Hegemony? How do you think that would ultimately affect the Emperor's plans and schedule?"

The silence was just as complete, but it was totally different now, and he smiled thinly.

"It's been three centuries—over five hundred of these people's years—since the Hegemony's first contact with them. If the Hegemony operates to its usual schedule, it will be at least two more centuries—almost four hundred local years—before any non-Shongairi observation team reaches this system again . . . and that will be counting from the point at which we return to announce our success. If we delay that return for a few decades, even as much as a century or so, it's unlikely anyone would be particularly surprised, given that they expect us to be gathering in three entire star systems." He snorted harshly. "In fact, it would probably *amuse* the weed-eaters to think we'd found the operation more difficult than anticipated! But if we chose instead to spend that time subjugating these "humans" and then educating their young to Hegemony standards, who knows what sort of R & D they might accomplish before that happens?"

"The prospect is exciting, sir," Thairys said slowly. "Yet I fear it rests upon speculations whose accuracy can't be tested without proceeding. If it should happen that they prove less accurate than hoped for, we would have, as you say, violated the spirit of the Council's authorizing writ for little return. Personally, I believe you may well be correct and that the possibility should clearly be investigated. Yet if the result is less successful than we might wish, would we not risk exposing the Empire to retaliation from other members of the Hegemony?"

"A valid point," Thikair acknowledged. "First, however, the Emperor would be able to insist—truthfully—that the decision was mine, not his, and that he never authorized anything of the sort. I believe it's most probable the Hegemony Judiciary would settle for penalizing me, as an individual, rather than recommending retaliation against the Empire generally. Of course, it's possible some of you, as my senior officers, might suffer, as well. On the other hand, I believe the risk would be well worth taking and would ultimately redound to the honor of our clans.

"There is, however, always another possibility.

The Council won't expect a Level Three or Level Two civilization any more than we did. If it turns out after a local century or so that these 'humans' aren't working out, the simplest solution may well be to simply exterminate them and destroy enough of their cities and installations to conceal the level of technology they'd actually attained before our arrival. It would, of course, be dreadfully unfortunate if one of our carefully focused and limited bio-weapons somehow mutated into something which swept the entire surface of the planet with a lethal plague, but, as we all know," he bared his canines in a smile, "accidents sometimes happen."

IV

It was unfortunate international restrictions on the treatment of POWs didn't also apply to what could be done to someone's own personnel, Stephen Buchevsky reflected as he failed—again—to find a comfortable way to sit in the mil-spec "seat" in the big C-17 Globemaster's Spartan belly. If *he'd* been a jihadi, he'd have spilled his guts within an hour if they strapped him into one of these!

Actually, he supposed a lot of the problem stemmed from his six feet and four inches of height and the fact that he was built more like an offensive lineman than like a basketball player. Nothing short of a first-class commercial seat was really going to fit someone his size, and expecting the U.S. military to fly an E-9 commercial first-class would have been about as realistic as his expecting to be drafted as a presidential nominee. Or perhaps even a bit less realistic. And, if he wanted to be honest, he should also admit that what he disliked even more was the absence of windows. There was something about spending hours sealed in an alloy tube while it vibrated its noisy way through the sky that made him feel not just enclosed, but trapped.

Well, Stevie, he told himself, *if you're* that *unhappy, you could always ask the pilot to let you off to* swim *the rest of the way!*

The thought made him chuckle, and he checked his watch. Kandahar to Aviano, Italy, was roughly three thousand miles, which exceeded the C-17's normal range by a couple of hundred miles. Fortunately—although that might not be *exactly* the right word for it—he'd caught a rare flight returning to the States almost empty. The Air Force needed the big bird badly somewhere, so they wanted it home in the shortest possible time, and with additional fuel and a payload of only thirty or forty people, it could make the entire Kandahar-to-Aviano leg without refueling. Which meant he could look forward to a six-hour flight, assuming they didn't hit any unfavorable winds.

He would have preferred to make the trip with the rest of his people, but he'd ended up dealing with the final paperwork for the return of the Company's equipment. Just another of those happy little chores that fell the way of its senior noncom. On the other hand, and despite the less-than-luxurious accommodations aboard his aerial chariot, his total transit time would be considerably shorter, thanks to this flight's fortuitous availability. And one thing he'd learned to do during his years of service was to sleep anywhere, anytime.

Even here, he thought, squirming into what he could convince himself was a marginally more comfortable position and closing his eyes. *Even here*.

The sudden, violent turn to starboard yanked Buchevsky up out of his doze, and he started to shove himself upright in his uncomfortable seat as the turn became even steeper. The redoubled, rumbling whine from the big transport's engines told him the pilot had increased power radically as well, and every one of his instincts told him he wouldn't like the reason for all of that if he'd known what it was.

Which didn't keep him from wanting to know anyway. In fact—

"Listen up, everybody!" A harsh, strain-flattened voice rasped over the aircraft's intercom. "We've got a little problem, and we're diverting from Aviano, 'cause Aviano isn't *there* anymore."

Buchevsky's eyes widened. Surely whoever it was on the other end of the intercom had to be joking, his mind tried to insist. But he knew better. There was too much stark shock—and fear—in that voice.

"I don't know what the fuck is going on," the pilot continued. "We've lost our long-ranged comms, but we're getting reports on the civilian bands about low-yield nukes going off all over the goddamned place. From what we're picking up, someone's kicking the shit out of Italy, Austria, Spain, and every NATO base in the entire Med, and—"

The voice broke off for a moment, and Buchevsky heard the harsh sound of an explosively cleared throat. Then—

"And we've got an unconfirmed report that Washington is gone, people. Just fucking *gone*."

Something kicked Buchevsky in the belly. Not Washington. Washington *couldn't* be gone. Not with Trish and the girls—

"I don't have a goddammed clue who's doing this, or why," the pilot said, "but we need someplace to set down, fast. We're about eighty miles north-northwest of Podgorica, in Montenegro, so I'm diverting inland. Let's hope to hell I can find someplace to put this bird down in one piece . . . and that nobody on the ground thinks *we* had anything to do with this shit!"

V

Thikair stood on *Star of Empire*'s flag bridge, studying the gigantic images of the planet below. Glowing icons indicated cities and major military bases his kinetic bombardment had removed from existence. There were a lot of them—more than he'd really counted on—and he clasped his hands behind him and concentrated on radiating total satisfaction.

And you damned well ought *to be satisfied, Thikair.*

Taking down an entire Level Two civilization in less than two local days has to be some sort of galactic record!

Which, another little voice reminded him, was because doing anything of the sort directly violated the Hegemony Constitution.

He managed not to grimace, but it wasn't easy. When this brilliant brainstorm had occurred to him, he hadn't fully digested just how big and thoroughly inhabited this planet, this . . . "Earth" of the "humans," truly was. He wondered now if he hadn't let himself fully digest it because he'd known that if he had, he would have changed his mind.

Oh stop it! So there were more of them on the damned planet, and you killed—what? Two billion of them, wasn't it? There're plenty more where they came from—they breed like damned garshu, after all! And you told Ahzmer and the others you're willing to kill off the entire species if it doesn't work out. So fretting about a little extra breakage along the way is pretty pointless, wouldn't you say?

Of course it was. In fact, he admitted, his biggest concern was how many major engineering works these humans had created. There was no question that he could exterminate them if he had to, but he was beginning to question whether it would be possible to eliminate the physical evidence of the level their culture had attained after all.

Well, we'll just have to keep it from coming to that, won't we?

"Pass the word to Ground Commander Thairys," he told Ship Commander Ahzmer quietly, never taking his eyes from those glowing icons. "I want his troops on the ground as quickly as possible. And make sure they have all the fire support they need."

Stephen Buchevsky stood by the road and wondered—again—just where the hell they were.

Their pilot hadn't managed to find any friendly airfields, after all. He'd done his best, but all but out of fuel, with his communications out, the GPS network down, and kiloton-range explosions dotting the face of Europe, his options had been limited. He'd managed to find a stretch of two-lane road that would almost do, and he'd set the big plane down with his last few gallons of fuel.

The C-17 had been designed for rough-field landings, although its designers hadn't had anything quite that rough in mind. Still, it would have worked if the road hadn't crossed a culvert he hadn't been able to see from the air. He'd lost both main gear when it collapsed under the plane's 140-ton weight. Worse, he hadn't lost the gear simultaneously, and the aircraft had gone totally out of control. When it stopped careening across the rough, mountainous valley, the entire forward fuselage had become crushed and tangled wreckage.

Neither pilot had survived, and the only other two officers aboard were among the six passengers who'd been killed, which left Buchevsky the ranking member of their small group. Two more passengers were brutally injured, and he'd gotten them out of the wreckage and into the best shelter he could contrive, but they didn't have anything resembling a doctor.

Neither did they have much in the way of equipment. Buchevsky had his personal weapons, as did six of the others, but that was it, and none of them had very much ammunition. Not surprisingly, he supposed, since they weren't supposed to have *any* on board. Fortunately (in this case, at least) it was extraordinarily difficult to separate troops returning from a combat zone from at least *some* ammo.

There were also at least some first-aid supplies—enough to set the broken arms three of the passengers suffered and make at least a token attempt at patching up the worst injured—but that was about it, and he really, really wished he could at least *talk* to somebody higher up the command hierarchy than he was. Unfortunately, he was it.

Which, he thought mordantly, *at least it gives me something to keep me busy*.

And it also gave him something besides Washington to worry about. He'd argued with Trish when his ex decided to take Shania and Yvonne to live with her mother, but that had been because of the crime rate and cost of living in D.C. He'd never, *ever*, worried about—

He pushed that thought aside, again, fleeing almost gratefully back to the contemplation of the clusterfuck he had to deal with somehow.

Gunnery Sergeant Calvin Meyers was their group's second-ranking member, which made him Buchevsky's XO . . . to the obvious disgruntlement of Sergeant Francisco Ramirez, the senior Army noncom. But if Ramirez resented the fact that they'd just become a Marine-run show, he was keeping his mouth shut. Probably because he recognized what an unmitigated pain in the ass Buchevsky's job had just become.

They had a limited quantity of food, courtesy of the aircraft's overwater survival package, but none of them had any idea of their exact position, no one spoke Serbian (assuming they were *in* Serbia), they had no maps, they were totally out of communication, and the last they'd heard, the entire planet seemed to be succumbing to spontaneous insanity.

Aside from that, it ought to be a piece of cake, he reflected sardonically. *Of course—*

"I think you'd better listen to this, Top," a voice said, and Buchevsky turned toward the speaker.

"Listen to what, Gunny?"

"We're getting something really weird on the radio, Top."

Buchevsky's eyes narrowed. He'd never actually met Meyers before this flight, but the compact, strongly built, slow-talking Marine from the Appalachian coal fields had struck him as a solid, unflappable sort. At the moment, however, Meyers was pasty-pale, and his hands shook as he extended the emergency radio they'd recovered from the wrecked fuselage.

Meyers turned the volume back up, and Buchevsky's eyes narrowed even further. The voice coming from the radio sounded . . . mechanical. Artificial. It carried absolutely no emotions or tonal emphasis.

That was the first thing that struck him. Then he

jerked back half a step, as if he'd just been punched, as what the voice was *saying* registered.

"—am Fleet Commander Thikair of the Shongairi Empire, and I am addressing your entire planet on all frequencies. Your world lies helpless before us. Our kinetic energy weapons have destroyed your major national capitals, your military bases, your warships. We can, and will, conduct additional kinetic strikes wherever necessary. You will submit and become productive and obedient subjects of the Empire, or you will be destroyed, as your governments and military forces have already been destroyed."

Buchevsky stared at the radio, his mind cowering back from the black, bottomless pit that yawned suddenly where his family once had been. Trish. . . . Despite the divorce, she'd still been an almost physical part of him. And Shania . . . Yvonne. . . . Shannie was only *six*, for God's sake! Yvonne was even younger. It wasn't possible. It couldn't have happened. *It couldn't!*

The mechanical-sounding English ceased. There was a brief surge of something that sounded like Chinese, and then it switched to Spanish.

"It's saying the same thing it just said in English," Sergeant Ramirez said flatly, and Buchevsky shook himself. He closed his eyes tightly, squeezing them against the tears he would not—could not—shed. That dreadful abyss loomed inside him, trying to suck him under, and part of him wanted nothing else in the world but to let the undertow take him. But he couldn't. He had responsibilities. The job.

"Do you *believe* this shit, Top?" Meyers said hoarsely.

"I don't know," Buchevsky admitted. His own voice came out sounding broken and rusty, and he cleared his throat harshly. "I don't know," he managed in a more normal-sounding tone. "Or, at least, I know I don't *want* to believe it, Gunny."

"Me neither," another voice said. This one was a soprano, and it belonged to Staff Sergeant Michelle Truman, the Air Force's senior surviving representative. Buchevsky raised an eyebrow at her, grateful for the additional distraction from the pain trying to tear the heart right out of him, and the auburn-haired staff sergeant grimaced.

"I don't want to believe it," she said, "but think about it. We already knew somebody's seemed to've been blowing the shit out of just about everybody. And who the hell had that many nukes?" She shook her head. "I'm no expert on kinetic weapons, but I've read a little science fiction, and I'd say an orbital kinetic strike would probably look just like a nuke to the naked eye. So, yeah, probably if this bastard is telling the truth, nukes are exactly what any survivors would've been reporting."

"Oh, *shit*," Meyers muttered, then looked back at Buchevsky. He didn't say another word, but he didn't have to, and Buchevsky drew a deep breath.

"I don't know, Gunny," he said again. "I just don't know."

———

He still didn't know—not really—the next morning, but one thing they *couldn't* do was simply huddle here. They'd seen no sign of any traffic along the road the C-17 had destroyed. Roads normally went *somewhere*, though, so if they followed this one long enough, "somewhere" was where they'd eventually wind up—hopefully before they ran out of food. And at least his decision trees had been rather brutally simplified when the last two badly injured passengers died during the night.

He tried hard not to feel grateful for that, but he was guiltily aware that it would have been dishonest, even if he'd managed to succeed.

Come on. You're not grateful they're dead, *Stevie,* he told himself grimly. *You're just grateful they won't be slowing the rest of you down. There's a difference.*

He even knew it was true . . . which didn't make him feel any better. And neither did the fact that he'd put his wife's and daughters' faces into a small mental box and locked them away, buried the pain deep enough to let him deal with his responsibilities to the living. Someday, he knew, he would have to reopen that box. Endure the pain, admit the loss. But not now. Not yet. For now he could tell himself others depended upon him, that he had to put aside his own pain while he dealt with *their* needs, and he wondered if that made him a coward.

"Ready to move out, Top," Meyers's voice said behind him, and he looked over his shoulder.

"All right," he said out loud, trying hard to radiate the confidence he was far from feeling. "In that case, I guess we should be going."

Now if I only had some damned idea where *we're going.*

VI

Platoon Commander Yirku stood in the open hatch of his command ground effect vehicle as his armored platoon sped down the long, broad roadway that stabbed straight through the mountains. The bridges that crossed the main roadbed at intervals, especially as the platoon approached what were (or had been) towns or cities, forced his column to squeeze in on itself, but overall, Yirku was delighted. His tanks' grav-cushions couldn't care less what surface lay under them, but that didn't protect their crews from seasickness if they had to move rapidly across rough ground, and he'd studied the survey reports with care. He'd rather glumly anticipated operating across wilderness terrain that might be crossed here and there by "roads" which were little more than random animal tracks.

Despite his relief at avoiding that unpleasantness, Yirku admitted (very privately) that he found these "humans'" infrastructure . . . unsettling. There was so *much* of it, especially in areas that had belonged to nations, like this "United States." And, crude though its construction might appear, most of it was well laid out. The fact that they'd managed to construct so much of it, so well suited to their current technology level's requirements, was sobering, too, and—

Platoon Leader Yirku's thoughts broke off abruptly as he emerged from under the latest bridge and the fifteen-pound round from the M-136 light anti-armor weapon struck the side of his vehicle's turret at a velocity of 360 feet per second. Its HEAT warhead produced a hyper-velocity gas jet that carved through the GEV's light armor like an incandescent dagger, and the resultant internal explosion disemboweled the tank effortlessly.

Ten more rockets stabbed down into the embankment-enclosed cut of Interstate 81 almost simultaneously, and eight of them found their targets, exploding like thunderbolts. Each of them killed another GEV, and the humans who'd launched them had deliberately concentrated on the front and back edges of the platoon's neat road column. Despite their grav-cushions, the four survivors of Yirku's platoon were temporarily trapped behind the blazing, exploding carcasses of their fellows. They were still there when the next quartet of rockets came sizzling in.

The ambushers—a scratch-built pickup team of Tennessee National Guardsmen, all of them veterans of deployments to Iraq or Afghanistan—were on the move, filtering back into the trees almost before the final Shongairi tank had exploded.

Company Commander Kirtha's column of transports rumbled along in a hanging cloud of dust, which made him grateful his GEV command vehicle was hermetically sealed. Now if only he'd been assigned to one of the major bases on the continent called "America," or at least the western fringes of *this* one!

It wouldn't be so bad if they were all *grav-cushion*, he told himself, watching the wheeled vehicles through the smothering fog of dust. But GEVs were expensive, and the counter-grav generators used up precious internal volume not even troop carriers could afford to give away. Imperial wheeled vehicles had excellent off-road capability, but even a miserable so-called road like this one allowed them to move much more efficiently.

And at least we're out in the middle of nice, flat ground as far as the eye can see, Kirtha reminded himself. He didn't like the rumors about ambushes on isolated detachments. That wasn't supposed to happen, especially from someone as effortlessly and utterly defeated as these "humans" had been. And even if it did happen, it wasn't supposed to be *effective*. And the ones responsible for it were supposed to be destroyed.

Which, if the rumors were accurate, wasn't happening the way it was supposed to. *Some* of the attackers were being spotted and destroyed, but with Hegemony technology, *all* of them should have been wiped out, and they weren't being. Still, there were no convenient mountainsides or thick belts of forest to hide attackers out here in the midst of these endless, flat fields of grain, and—

Captain Pieter Stefanovich Ushakov of the Ukrainian Army watched through his binoculars with pitiless satisfaction as the entire alien convoy and its escort of tanks disappeared in a fiery wave of destruction two kilometers long. The scores of 120 mm mortar rounds buried in the road as his own version of the "improvised explosive devices," which had given the Americans such grief in Iraq, had proved quite successful, he thought coldly.

Now, he thought, *to see exactly how these weasels respond.*

He was fully aware of the risks in remaining in the vicinity, but he needed some understanding of the aliens' capabilities and doctrine, and the only way to get that was to see what they did. He was confident he'd piled enough earth on top of his position to conceal any thermal signature, and he was completely unarmed, with no ferrous metal on his person, which would hopefully defeat any magnetic detectors. So unless they used some sort of deep-scan radar, he ought to be *relatively* safe from detection.

And even if it turned out he wasn't, his entire family had been in Kiev when the kinetic strikes hit.

Colonel Nicolae Basescu sat in the commander's hatch of his T-72M1, his mind wrapped around a curiously empty, singing silence, and waited.

The first prototype of his tank—the export model of the Russian T-72A—had been completed in 1970, four years before Basescu's own birth, and it had become sadly outclassed by more modern, more deadly designs. It was still superior to the Romanian Army's

home-built TR-85s, based on the even more venerable T-55, but that wasn't saying much compared
with designs like the Russians' T-80s and T-90s, or
the Americans' M1A2.

And it's certainly *not saying much compared with
aliens who can actually travel between the stars,*
Basescu thought.

Unfortunately, it was all he had. Now if he only
knew what he was supposed to be doing with the
seven tanks of his scraped-up command.

Stop that, he told himself sternly. *You're an officer of the Romanian Army. You know* exactly *what
you're supposed to be doing.*

He gazed through the opening a few minutes'
work with an ax had created. His tanks were as carefully concealed as he could manage inside the industrial buildings across the frontage road from the
hundred-meter-wide Mureş River. The two lanes of
the E-81 highway crossed the river on a double-span
cantilever bridge, flanked on the east by a rail bridge,
two kilometers southwest of Alba iulia, the capital of
Alba *judeţ.* The city of eighty thousand—the city
where Michael the Brave had achieved the first union
of the three great provinces of Romania in 1599—
was two-thirds empty, and Basescu didn't like to
think about what those fleeing civilians were going to
do when they started running out of whatever supplies they'd managed to snatch up in their flight. But
he didn't blame them for running. Not when their
city was barely 270 kilometers northwest of where
Bucharest had been four and a half days ago.

He wished he dared to use his radios, but the broadcasts from the alien commander suggested that any transmissions would be unwise. Fortunately, at least some of the land lines were still up. He doubted they would be for much longer, but enough remained for him to know about the alien column speeding up the highway toward him . . . and Alba iulia.

Company Commander Barmit punched up his navigation systems, but they were being cantankerous again, and he muttered a quiet yet heartfelt curse as he jabbed at the control panel a second time.

As far as he was concerned, the town ahead of him was scarcely large enough to merit the attention of two entire companies of infantry, even if Base Commander Shairez's pre-bombardment analysis *had* identified it as some sort of administrative subcenter. Its proximity to what had been a national capital suggested to Barmit's superiors that it had probably been sufficiently important to prove useful as a headquarters for the local occupation forces. Personally, Barmit suspected the reverse was more likely true. An administrative center this close to something the size of that other city—"Bucharest," or something equally outlandish—was more likely to be lost in the capital's shadow than functioning as any sort of important secondary brain.

Too bad Ground Force Commander Thairys didn't ask for my opinion, he thought dryly, still jabbing at the recalcitrant display.

The imagery finally came up and stabilized, and his ears flicked in a grimace as it confirmed his memory. He keyed his com.

"All right," he said. "We're coming up on another river, and our objective's just beyond that. We'll take the bridge in a standard road column, but let's not take chances. Red Section, you spread left. White section, we'll spread right."

Acknowledgments came back, and he reconfigured the display from navigation to tactical.

Colonel Basescu twitched upright as the alien vehicles came into sight. He focused his binoculars, snapping the approaching vehicles into much sharper clarity, and a part of him was almost disappointed by how unremarkable they appeared. How . . . mundane.

Most of them were some sort of wheeled transport vehicles, with a boxy sort of look that made him think of armored personnel carriers. There were around thirty of those, and it was obvious they were being escorted by five other vehicles.

He shifted his attention to those escorts and stiffened as he realized just how un-mundane *they* were. They sped along, sleek-looking and dark, hovering perhaps a meter or two above the ground, and some sort of long, slender gunbarrels projected from their boxy-looking turrets.

The approaching formation slowed as the things that were probably APCs began forming into a column of twos under the watchful eye of the things that were probably tanks, and he lowered the binoculars and picked up the handset for the field telephone he'd had strung between the tanks once they'd maneuvered into their hides.

"Mihai," he told his second section commander, "we'll take the tanks. Radu, I want you and Matthius to concentrate on the transports. Don't fire until Mihai and I do—then try to jam them up on the bridge."

Barmit felt his ears relaxing in satisfaction as the wheeled vehicles settled into column and his GEVs headed across the river, watching its flanks. The drop from the roadbed to the surface of the water had provided the usual "stomach left behind" sensation, but once they were actually out over the water, its motion became glassy-smooth as he led White Section's other two GEVs between the small islands in the center of the river, idling along to keep pace with the transports.

They may have magic tanks, but they don't have very good doctrine, do they? a corner of Basescu's brain reflected. They hadn't so much as bothered to send any scouts across, or even to leave one of their tanks on the far bank in an overwatch position. Not that he intended to complain.

The tank turret slewed slowly to the right as his gunner tracked his chosen target, but Basescu was watching the wheeled vehicles. The entire bridge was barely 150 meters long, and he wanted all of them actually onto it, if he could arrange it.

Company Commander Barmit sighed as his GEV approached the far bank. Climbing up out of the riverbed again was going to be rather less pleasant, and he slowed deliberately, prolonging the smoothness as he watched the transports heading across the bridge.

Kind of the "humans" to build us all these nice highways, he reflected, thinking about this region's heavily forested mountains. *It would be a real pain to—*

"Fire!" Nicolae Basescu barked, and Company Commander Barmit's ruminations were terminated abruptly by the arrival of a nineteen-kilogram 3BK29 HEAT round capable of penetrating three hundred millimeters of armor at a range of two kilometers.

Basescu felt a stab of exhilaration as the tank bucked, the outer wall of its concealing building disappeared in the fierce muzzle blast of its 2A46 120 mm main gun, and his target exploded. Three of the other four escort tanks were first-round kills, as well, crashing into the river in eruptions of fire, white spray, and smoke, and the stub of the semi-combustible cartridge case ejected from the gun. The automatic loader's carousel picked up the next round, feeding the separate projectile and cartridge into the breech, and his carefully briefed commanders were engaging targets without any additional orders from him.

The surviving alien tank swerved crazily sideways, turret swiveling madly, and then Basescu winced as it fired.

He didn't know what it was armed with, but it wasn't like any cannon *he'd* ever seen. A bar of solid light spat from the end of its "gun," and the building concealing his number three tank exploded. But even as the alien tank fired, two more 120 mm rounds slammed into it almost simultaneously.

It died as spectacularly as its fellows had, and Radu and Matthias hadn't exactly been sitting on their hands. They'd done exactly what he wanted, nailing both the leading and rearmost of the wheeled transports only after they were well out onto the bridge. The others were trapped there, sitting ducks, unable to maneuver, and his surviving tanks walked their fire steadily along their column.

At least some of the aliens managed to bail out of their vehicles, but it was less than three hundred meters to the far side of the river and the coaxial 7.62 mm machine guns and the heavier 12.7 mm cupola-mounted weapons at the tank commanders' stations were waiting for them. At such short range, it was a massacre.

"Cease fire!" Basescu barked. "Fall back!"

His crews responded almost instantly, and the tanks' powerful V-12 engines snorted black smoke as the T-72s backed out of their hiding places and sped down the highway at sixty kilometers per hour. What the aliens had already accomplished with their "kinetic weapons" suggested that staying in one place would be a very bad idea, and Basescu had picked out his next fighting position before he ever settled into this one. It would take them barely fifteen minutes to reach it, and only another fifteen to twenty minutes to maneuver the tanks back into hiding.

Precisely seventeen minutes later, incandescent streaks of light came sizzling out of the cloudless heavens to eliminate every one of Nicolae Basescu's tanks—and half the city of Alba iulia—in a blast of fury that shook the Carpathian Mountains.

VII

Stephen Buchevsky felt his body trying to ooze out even flatter as the grinding, tooth-rattling vibration grew louder on the far side of the ridgeline. The AKM he'd acquired to replace the his M-16 still felt awkward, but it was a solidly built weapon, with all the rugged reliability of its AK-47 ancestry, ammunition for it was readily available . . . and it felt unspeakably comforting at that particular moment.

His attention remained fixed on the "sound" of the alien recon drone, but a corner of his mind went wandering back over the last three weeks.

The C-17's pilot had gotten farther east than Buchevsky had thought. They hadn't known they were
in Romania, not Serbia, for a day or two—not until
they came across the remains of a couple of pla-
toons of Romanian infantry which had been caught
in column on a road. Their uniforms and insignia
had identified their nationality, and most of them
had been killed by what looked like standard bullet
wounds. But there'd also been a handful of craters
with oddly glassy interiors from obviously heavier
weapons.

The Romanians' disaster had, however, represented unlooked-for good fortune for Buchevsky's ill-
assorted command. There'd been plenty of personal
weapons to salvage, as well as hand grenades, more
man-portable antitank weapons and SAMs—the SA-
14 "Gremlin" variant—than they could possibly
carry, even canteens and some rations. Buchevsky
had hated to give up his M-16, but although Romania had joined NATO, it still used mainly Soviet bloc
equipment. There wouldn't be any 5.56mm ammunition floating around Romania, but 7.62mm was
abundantly available.

That was the good news. The bad news was that
there'd clearly been a major exodus from most of the
towns and cities following the aliens' ruthless bombardment. They'd spotted several large groups—
hundreds of people, in some cases. Most of them had
been accompanied by at least some armed men, and
they hadn't been inclined to take chances. Probably
most of them were already aware of how ugly it was
going to get when their particular group of civilians'

supplies started running out, and whatever else they might have been thinking, none of them had been happy to see thirty-three strangers in desert-camo.

Foreign desert-camo.

A few warning shots had been fired, one of which had nicked PFC Lyman Curry, and Buchevsky had taken the hint. Still, he had to at least find someplace where his own people could establish a modicum of security while they went about the day-to-day business of surviving.

Which was what he'd been hunting for today, moving through the thickly wooded mountains, staying well upslope from the roads running through the valleys despite the harder going. Some of his people, including Sergeant Ramirez, had been inclined to bitch about that at first. Buchevsky didn't really mind if they complained about it as long as they *did* it, however, and even the strongest objections had disappeared quickly when they realized just how important overhead concealment was.

From the behavior of the odd, dark-colored flying objects, Buchevsky figured they were something like the U.S. military's Predators—small unmanned aircraft used for reconnaissance. What he didn't know was whether or not they were *armed*. Nor did he have any idea whether or not their salvaged shoulder-fired SAMs would work against them, and he had no pressing desire to explore either possibility unless it was absolutely a matter of life or death.

Fortunately, although the odd-looking vehicles were quick and agile, they weren't the least bit stealthy. Whatever propelled them produced a heavy, persistent, tooth-grating vibration. That wasn't really the right word for it, and he knew it, but he couldn't come up with another one for a sensation that was felt, not heard. And whatever it was, it was detectable from beyond visual range.

He'd discussed it with Staff Sergeant Truman and PO/3 Jasmine Sherman, their sole Navy noncom. Truman was an electronics specialist, and Sherman wore the guided missile and electronic wave rating mark of a missile technician. Between them, they formed what Buchevsky thought of as his "brain trust," but neither woman had a clue what the aliens used for propulsion. What they did agree on was that humans were probably more sensitive to the "vibration" it produced than the aliens were, since it wouldn't have made a lot of sense to produce a re-connaissance platform they *knew* people could hear before it could see them.

Buchevsky wasn't going to bet the farm on the be-lief that his people *could* "hear" the drones before the drones could see them, however. Which was why he'd waved his entire group to ground when the telltale vibration came burring through his fillings from the ridgeline to his immediate north. Now if only—

That was when he heard the firing and the screams.

It shouldn't have mattered. His responsibility was to his own people. To keeping them alive until he got them home . . . assuming there was any "home" *for* them. But when he heard the shouts, when he heard the screams—when he recognized the shrieks of children—he found himself back on his feet. He turned his head, saw Calvin Meyers watching him, and then he swung his hand in a wide arc and pointed to the right.

A dozen of his people stayed right where they were—not out of cowardice, but because they were too confused and surprised by his sudden change of plans to realize what he was doing—and he didn't blame them. Even as he started forward, he knew it was insane. Less than half his people had any actual combat experience, and five of *them* had been tankers, not infantry. No wonder they didn't understand what he was doing!

Meyer understood, though, and so had Ramirez—even if he was an Army puke—and Lance Corporal Gutierrez, and Coporal Alice Macomb, and half a dozen others, and they followed him in a crouching run.

Squad Commander Rayzhar bared his canines as his troopers advanced up the valley. He'd been on this accursed planet for less than seven local days, and already he'd come to hate its inhabitants as he'd never hated before in his life. They had no sense of decency, no sense of honor! They'd been *defeated*, Dainthar take them! The Shongairi had proved they were the mightier, yet instead of submitting and acknowledging their inferiority, they persisted in their insane attacks!

Rayzhar had lost two litter-brothers in the ambush of Company Commander Barmit's column. Litter-brothers who'd been shot down like weed-eaters for the pot, as if *they'd* been the inferiors. That was something Rayzhar had no intention of forgetting—or forgiving—until he'd collected enough "humans'" souls to serve both of them in Dainthar's realm.

He really had no business making this attack, but the recon drone slaved to his command transport had shown him this ragged band cowering in the mountainside cul-de-sac. There were no more than fifty or sixty of them, but a half dozen wore the same uniforms as the humans who'd massacred his litter-brothers. That was enough for him. Besides, HQ would never see the take from the drone—he'd make sure of that—and he expected no questions when he reported that he'd taken fire from the humans and simply responded to it.

He looked up from the holographic display board linked to the drone and barked an order at Gersa, the commander of his second squad.

"Swing right! Get around their flank!"

Gersa acknowledged, and Rayzhar bared his canines again—this time in satisfaction—as two of the renegade human warriors were cut down. A mortar round from one of the transports exploded farther up the cul-de-sac, among the humans cowering in the trees, and a savage sense of pleasure filled him.

Buchevsky found himself on the ridgeline, looking down into a scene straight out of Hell. More than fifty civilians, over half of them children, were hunkered down under the fragile cover of evergreens and hardwoods while a handful of Romanian soldiers tried frantically to protect them from at least twenty-five or thirty of the aliens. There were also three wheeled vehicles on the road below, and one of them mounted a turret with some sort of mortar-like support weapon. Even as Buchevsky watched, it fired and an eye-tearing burst of brilliance erupted near the top of the cul-de-sac. He heard the shrieks of seared, dying children, and below the surface of his racing thoughts, he realized what had really happened. Why he'd changed his plans completely, put all the people he was responsible for at risk.

Civilians. *Children.* They were what he was supposed to *protect,* and deep at the heart of him was the bleeding wound of his own daughters, the children he would never see again. The Shongairi had taken his girls from him, and he would rip out their throats with his bare teeth before he let them take any more.

"Gunny, get the vehicles!" he snapped, his curt voice showing no sign of his own self-recognition.

"On it, Top!" Meyer acknowledged, and waved to Gutierrez and Robert Szu, one of their Army privates. Gutierrez and Szu—like Meyer—carried RBR-M60s, Romanian single-shot anti-armor weapons derived from the U.S. M72. The Romanian version had a theoretical range of over a thousand meters, and the power to take out most older main battle tanks, and Meyer, Gutierrez, and Szu went skittering through the woods toward the road with them.

Buchevsky left that in Meyer's competent hands as he reached out and grabbed Corporal Macomb by the shoulder. She carried one of the salvaged SAM launchers, and Buchevsky jabbed a nod of his head at the drone hovering overhead.

"Take that damned thing out," he said flatly.

"Right, Top." Macomb's voice was grim, her expression frightened, but her hands were steady as she lifted the SAM's tube to her shoulder.

"The rest of you, with me!" Buchevsky barked. It wasn't much in the way of detailed instructions, but four of the eight people still with him were Marines, and three of the others were Army riflemen.

Besides, the tactical situation was brutally simple.

Rayzhar saw another uniformed human die. Then he snarled in fury as one of his own troopers screamed, rose on his toes, and went down in a spray of blood. The Shongairi weren't accustomed to facing enemies whose weapons could penetrate their body armor, and Rayzhar felt a chill spike of fear even through his rage. But he wasn't about to let it stop him, and there were only three armed humans left. Only three, and then—

Buchevsky heard the explosions as the alien vehicles vomited flame and smoke. At almost the same instant, the SA-14 streaked into the air, and two things became clear: One, whatever held the drones up radiated enough heat signature for the Gremlin to see it. Two, whatever the drones were made of, it wasn't tough enough to survive the one-kilo warhead's impact.

He laid the sights of his AKM on the weird, slender, doglike alien whose waving hands suggested he was in command and squeezed the trigger.

A four-round burst of 7.62 mm punched through the back of Rayzhar's body armor. The rounds kept right on going until they punched out his breastplate in a spray of red, as well, and the squad commander heard someone's gurgling scream. He realized vaguely that it was his own, and then he crashed facedown into the dirt of an alien planet.

He wasn't alone. There were only nine riflemen up on his flank, but they had perfect fields of fire, and every single one of them had heard Fleet Commander Thikair's broadcast. They knew why Rayzhar and his troopers had come to their world, what had happened to their cities and homes. There was no mercy in them, and their fire was deadly accurate.

The Shongairi recoiled in shock as more of them died or collapsed in agony—shock that became terror as they realized their vehicles had just been destroyed behind them, as well. They had no idea how many attackers they faced, but they recognized defeat when they saw it, and they turned toward the new attack, raising their weapons over their heads in surrender, flattening their ears in token of submission.

———

Stephen Buchevsky saw the aliens turning toward his people, raising their weapons to charge up the ridge, and behind his granite eyes he saw the children they had just killed and maimed . . . and his daughters.

"Kill them!" he rasped.

VIII

"I want an explanation." Fleet Commander Thikair glowered around the conference table. None of his senior officers needed to ask what it was he wanted explained, and more than one set of eyes slid sideways to Ground Force Commander Thairys. His casualties were over six times his most pessimistic pre-landing estimates . . . and climbing.

"I have no excuse, Fleet Commander."

Thairys flattened his ears in submission to Thikair's authority, and there was silence for a second or two.

But then Base Commander Shairez raised one diffident hand.

"If I may, Fleet Commander?"

"If you have any explanation, Base Commander, I would be delighted to hear it," Thikair said, turning his attention to her.

"I doubt that there is any *single* explanation, sir." Her ears were half-lowered in respect, although not so flat to her head as Thairys', and her tone was calm. "Instead, I think we're looking at a combination of factors."

"Which are?" Thikair leaned back, his immediate ire somewhat damped by her demeanor.

"The first, sir, is simply that this is the first Level Two culture we've ever attempted to subdue. While their weaponry is inferior to our own, it's far less *relatively* inferior than anything we've ever encountered. Their armored vehicles, for example, while much slower, clumsier, shorter-legged, and tactically cumbersome than ours, are actually better protected and mount weapons capable of destroying our heaviest units. Even their *infantry* have weapons with that capability, and that's skewed Ground Force Commander Thairys' original calculations badly."

Thikair bared one canine in frustration, but she had a point. The Shongairi's last serious war had been fought centuries ago, against fellow Shongairi, before they'd ever left their home world. Since then, their military had found itself engaging mostly primitives armed with hand weapons or only the crudest of firearms . . . exactly as they were *supposed* to have encountered here.

"A second factor," Shairez continued, "may be that our initial bombardment was too successful. We so thoroughly disrupted their communications net and command structures that there may be no way for individual units to be ordered to stand down."

"'Stand *down*'?" Squadron Commander Jainfar repeated incredulously. "They're *defeated*, Base Commander! I don't care how stupid they are, or how disrupted their communications may be, they *have* to know that!"

"Perhaps so, Squadron Commander." Shairez faced the old space-dog squarely. "Unfortunately, as yet we know very little about this species' psychology. We do know there's something significantly different about them, given their incredible rate of advancement, but that's really *all* we know. It could be that they simply don't *care* that we've defeated them."

Jainfar started to say something else, then visibly restrained himself. It was obvious he couldn't imagine any intelligent species thinking in such a bizarre fashion, but Shairez *was* the expedition's expert on non-Shongairi sapients.

"Even if that's true, Base Commander," Thikair's tone was closer to normal, "it doesn't change our problem." He looked at Thairys. "What sort of loss rates are we looking at, assuming these 'humans'' behavior doesn't change?"

"Potentially disastrous ones," Thairys acknowledged. "We've already written off eleven percent of our armored vehicles. We never expected to need many GEVs against the opposition we anticipated, which means we have nowhere near the vehicles and crews it looks like we're going to need. We've actually lost a higher absolute number of transports, but we had many times as many of those to begin with. Infantry losses are another matter, and I'm not at all sure present casualty rates are sustainable. And I must point out that we have barely eight local days of experience. It's entirely possible for projections based on what we've seen so far to be almost as badly flawed as our initial estimates."

The ground force commander clearly didn't like adding that caveat. Which was fair enough. Thikair didn't much like *hearing* it.

"I believe the Ground Force Commander may be unduly pessimistic, sir." All eyes switched to Shairez once more, and the base commander flipped her ears in a shrug. "My own analysis suggests that we're looking at two basic types of incident, both of which appear to be the work of relatively small units acting independently of any higher command or coordination. On one hand, we have units making use of the humans' heavy weapons and using what I suspect is their standard doctrine. An example of this would be the destruction of Company Commander Barmit's entire command a few days ago. On the other, we have what seem to be primarily infantry forces equipped with their light weapons or using what appear to be improvised explosives and weapons.

"In the case of the former, they've frequently inflicted severe losses—again, as in Barmit's case. In fact, more often than not, they've inflicted grossly disproportionate casualties. However, in *those* instances, our space-to-surface interdiction systems are normally able to locate and destroy them. In short, humans who attack us in that fashion seldom survive to attack a second time, and they already have few heavy weapons left.

"In the case of the *latter*, however, the attackers have proved far more elusive. Our reconnaissance systems are biased toward locating heavier, more technologically advanced weapons. We look for electronic emissions, thermal signatures such as operating vehicle power plants generate, and things of that nature. We're far less well equipped to pick out individual humans or small groups of humans. As a consequence, we're able to intercept and destroy a far smaller percentage of such attackers.

"The good news is that although their infantry-portable weapons are far more powerful than we ever anticipated, they're still far less dangerous than their heavy armored vehicles or artillery. This means, among other things, that they can engage only smaller forces of our warriors with any real prospect of success."

"I believe that's substantially accurate," Thairys said after a moment. "One of the implications, however, is that in order to deter attacks by these infantry forces, we would find ourselves obliged to operate using larger forces of our own. But we have a strictly limited supply of personnel, so the larger our individual forces become, the fewer we can deploy at any given moment. In order to deter attack, we would be forced to severely reduce the coverage of the entire planet which we can hope to maintain."

"I take your point, Thairys," Thikair said after a moment, and bared all his upper canines in a wintry smile. "I must confess that a planet begins to look significantly larger when one begins to consider the need to actually picket its entire surface out of the resources of a single colonization fleet!"

He'd considered saying something a bit stronger, but that was as close as he cared to come to admitting that he might have bitten off more than his fleet could chew.

"For the present," he went on, "we'll continue operations essentially as planned, but with a geographic shift of emphasis. Thairys, I want you to revise your deployment stance. For the moment, we'll concentrate on the areas that were more heavily developed and technologically advanced. That's where we're most likely to encounter significant threats, so let's start by establishing fully secured enclaves from which we can operate in greater strength as we spread out to consolidate."

"Yes, sir," Thairys acknowledged. "That may take some time, however. In particular, we have infantry forces deployed for the purpose of hunting down and destroying known groups of human attackers. They're operating in widely separated locations, and pulling them out to combine elsewhere is going to stretch our troop lift capacity."

"Would they be necessary to meet the objectives I just described?"

"No, sir. Some additional infantry will be needed, but we can land additional troops directly from space. And, in addition, we need more actual combat experience against these roving attack groups. We need to refine our tactics, and not even our combat veterans have actually faced this level of threat in the past. I'd really prefer to keep at least some of our own infantry out in the hinterland, where we can continue to blood more junior officers in a lower threat-level environment."

"As long as you're capable of carrying out the concentrations I've just directed, I have no objection," Thikair told him.

And as long as we're able to somehow get a tourniquet on this steady flow of casualties, the Fleet Commander added to himself.

IX

An insect scuttled across the back of Stephen Buchevsky's sweaty neck. He ignored it, keeping his eyes on the aliens as they set about bivouacking.

The insect on his neck went elsewhere, and he checked the RDG-5 hand grenade. He wouldn't have dared to use a radio even if he'd had it, but the grenade's detonation would work just fine as an attack signal.

He really would have preferred leaving this patrol alone, but he couldn't. He had no idea what they were doing in the area, and it really didn't matter. Whatever else they might do, every Shongairi unit appeared to be on its own permanent seek-and-destroy mission, and he couldn't allow that when the civilians he and his people had become responsible for were in this patrol's way.

His reaction to the Shongairi attack on the Romanian civilians had landed him with yet another mission—one he would vastly have preferred to avoid. Or that was what he told himself, anyway. The rest of his people—with the possible exception of Ramirez—seemed to cherish none of the reservations he himself felt. In fact, he often thought the only reason *he* felt them was because he was in command. It was his *job* to feel them. But however it had happened, he and his marooned Americans had become the protectors of a slowly but steadily growing band of Romanians.

Fortunately, one of the Romanians in question—Elizabeth Cantacuzène—had been a university teacher. Her English was heavily accented, but her grammar (and, Buchevsky suspected, her vocabulary) was considerably better than his, and just acquiring a local translator had been worth almost all of the headaches that had come with it.

By now, he had just under sixty armed men and women under his command. His Americans formed the core of his force, but their numbers were almost equaled by a handful of Romanian soldiers and the much larger number of civilians who were in the process of receiving a crash course in military survival from him, Gunny Meyers, and Sergeant Alexander Jonescu of the Romanian Army. He'd organized them into four roughly equal sized "squads," one commanded by Myers, one by Ramirez, one by Jonescu, and one by Alice Macomb. Michelle Truman was senior to Macomb, but she and Sherman were still too valuable as his "brain trust" for him to "waste her" in a shooter's slot. Besides, she was learning Romanian from Cantacuzène.

Fortunately, Sergeant Jonescu already spoke English, and Buchevsky had managed to get at least one Romanian English-speaker into each of his squads. It was clumsy, but it worked, and they'd spent hours drilling on hand signals that required no spoken language. And at least the parameters of their situation were painfully clear to everyone.

Evade. *Hide.* Do whatever it took to keep the civilians—now close to two hundred of them—safe. Stay on the move. Avoid roads and towns. Look out constantly for any source of food. It turned out that Calvin Meyers was an accomplished deer hunter, and he and two like-minded souls who had been members of the Romanian forestry service were contributing significantly to keeping their people fed. Still, summer was sliding into fall, and all too soon cold and starvation would become deadly threats.

But for that to happen, first we have to survive the summer, don't we? he thought harshly. *Which means these bastards have to be stopped before they figure out the civilians are here to be killed. And we've got to do it without their getting a message back to base.*

He didn't like it. He didn't like it at all. But he didn't see any choice, either, and with Cantacuzène's assistance, he'd interrogated every single person who'd seen the Shongairi in action, hunting information on their tactics and doctrine.

It was obvious they were sudden death on large bodies of troops or units equipped with heavy weapons. Some of that was probably because crewmen inside tanks couldn't "hear" approaching recon drones the way infantry in the open could, he thought. And Truman and Sherman suspected that the Shongairi's sensors were designed to detect mechanized forces, or at least units with heavy emissions signatures, which was one reason he'd gotten rid of all his radios.

It also appeared that the infantry patrols had less sensor coverage than those floating tanks or their road convoys. And in the handful of additional brushes he'd had with their infantry, it had become evident that the invaders weren't in any sort of free-flow communications net that extended beyond their immediate unit. If they had been, he felt sure, by now one of the patrols they'd attacked would have managed to call in one of their kinetic strikes.

Which is why we've got to hit them fast, make sure we take out their vehicles with the first strike . . . and that nobody packing a personal radio lives long enough to use it.

It looked like they were beginning to settle down. Obviously, they had no idea Buchevsky or his people were out here, which suited him just fine.

Go ahead, he thought grimly. *Get comfortable. Drop off. I've got your sleeping pill right here. In about another five—*

"Excuse me, Sergeant, but is this really wise?"

Stephen Buchevsky twitched as if someone had just applied a high-voltage charge, and his head whipped around toward the whispered question.

The question that had just been asked in his very ear in almost unaccented English . . . by a voice he'd never heard in his life.

————

"Now suppose you just tell me who you are and where the *hell* you came from?" Buchevsky demanded ten minutes later.

He stood facing a complete stranger, two hundred meters from the Shongairi bivouac, and he wished the light were better. Not that he was even tempted to strike a match.

The stranger was above average height for a Romanian, although well short of Buchevsky's towering inches. He had a sharp-prowed nose, large, deep-set green eyes, and dark hair. That was about all Buchevsky could tell, aside from the fact that his smile seemed faintly amused.

"Excuse me," the other man said. "I had no desire to . . . startle you, Sergeant. However, I knew something which you do not. There is a second patrol little more than a kilometer away in that direction."

He pointed back up the narrow road along which the Shongairi had approached, and an icy finger stroked suddenly down Buchevsky's spine.

"How do you know that?"

"My men and I have been watching them," the stranger said. "And it is a formation we have seen before—one they have adopted in the last week or so. I believe they are experimenting with new tactics, sending out pairs of infantry teams in support of one another."

"Damn. I was hoping they'd take longer to think of that," Buchevsky muttered. "Looks like they may be smarter than I'd assumed from their original tactics."

"I do not know how intelligent they may be, Sergeant. But I do suspect that if you were to attack *this* patrol, the other one would probably call up heavy support quickly."

"That's exactly what they'd do," Buchevsky agreed, then frowned. "Not that I'm not grateful for the warning, or anything," he said, "but you still haven't told me who you are, where you came from, or how you got here."

"Surely"—this time the amusement in the Romanian's voice was unmistakable—"that would be a more reasonable question for *me* to be asking of an American Marine here in the heart of Wallachia?"

Buchevsky's jaw clenched, but the other man chuckled and shook his head.

"Forgive me, Sergeant. I have been told I have a questionable sense of humor. My name is Basarab, Mircea Basarab. And where I have come from is up near Lake Vidaru, fifty or sixty kilometers north of here. My men and I have been doing much the same as what I suspect you have—attempting to protect my people from these 'Shongairi' butchers." He grimaced. "Protecting civilians from invaders is, alas, something of a national tradition in these parts."

"I see . . . ," Buchevsky said slowly, and white teeth glinted at him in the dimness.

"I believe you do, Sergeant. And, yes, I also believe the villages my men and I have taken under our protection could absorb these civilians *you* have been protecting. They are typical mountain villages, largely self-sufficient, with few 'modern amenities.'

They grow their own food, and feeding this many additional mouths will strain their resources severely. I doubt anyone will grow fat over the winter! But they will do their best, and the additional hands will be welcome as they prepare for the snows. And from what I have seen of you and your band, you would be a most welcome addition to their defenses."

Buchevsky cocked his head, straining to see the other's expression. It was all coming at him far too quickly. He knew he ought to be standing back, considering this stranger's offer coolly and rationally. Yet what he actually felt was a wave of unspeakable relief as the men, women, and children—always the children—for whom he'd become responsible were offered a reprieve from starvation and frostbite.

"And how would we get there with these puppies sitting in our lap?" he asked.

"Obviously, Sergeant, we must first *remove* them from 'our lap.' Since my men are already in position to deal with the second patrol, and yours are already in position to deal with *this* patrol, I would suggest we both get back to work. I presume you intended to use that grenade to signal the start of your own attack?"

Buchevsky nodded, and Basarab shrugged.

"I see no reason why you should change your plans in that regard. Allow me fifteen minutes—no, perhaps twenty would be better—to return to my own men and tell them to listen for your attack. After that," those white teeth glittered again, and this time,

Buchevsky knew, that smile was cold and cruel, "feel free to announce your presence to these vermin. Loudly."

X

Platoon Commander Dirak didn't like this one bit, but orders were orders.

He moved slowly at the center of his second squad, ears up and straining for the slightest sound as they followed his first squad along the narrow trail. Unfortunately, his people had been civilized for a thousand standard years. Much of the acuity of sound and scent that had once marked the margin between death and survival had slipped away, and he felt more than half-blind in this heavily shadowed, massive forest.

There were no forests like this on his home world any longer—not with this towering, primeval canopy, with tree trunks that could be half as broad at the base as a Shongairi's height—yet the woodland around him was surprisingly free of brush and undergrowth. According to the expedition's botanists, that was only to be expected in a mature forest where so little direct sunlight reached the ground. No doubt they knew what they were talking about, but it still seemed . . . wrong to Dirak. And, perversely, he liked the saplings and underbrush that did grow along the verge of this narrow trail even less. They probably confirmed the botanists' theories, since at least some sun did get through where the line of the trail broke the canopy, but they left him feeling cramped and shut in.

Actually, a lot of his anxiety was probably due to the fact that he'd been expressly ordered to leave his assigned recon and communications relay drone well behind his point, anchored to the wheeled transports snorting laboriously along the same trail far behind him. Analysis of what had happened to the last three patrols sent into this area suggested that the "humans" had somehow managed to destroy the drones before they ever engaged the infantry those drones were supporting with surveillance and secure communications to base. No one had any idea how the primitives—only, of course, they weren't *really* primitives, were they?—were able to detect and target drones so effectively, but HQ had decided to try a more stealthy approach . . . and chosen Dirak to carry out the experiment.

Oh, how the gods must have smiled upon me, he reflected morosely. *I understand the need to gain experience against these . . . creatures if we're going to modify doctrine. But why did I get chosen to poke my head into the* hasthar's *den? It wasn't like—*

He heard an explosion behind him and wheeled around. He couldn't see through the overhead canopy, but he didn't need to see it to know that the explosion had been his RC drone. How had they even *seen* it through these damnable leaves and branches!

The question was still ripping through his brain when he heard more explosions—this time on the ground . . . where his two reserve squads were following along in their APCs.

He didn't have time to realize what *those* explosions were before the assault rifles hidden behind trees and under drifts of leaves all along the southern flank of the trail opened fire.

Unfortunately for Platoon Commander Dirak, the men and women behind those assault rifles had figured out how to recognize a Shongairi infantry formation's commanding officer.

"Cease fire! *Cease fire!*" Buchevsky bellowed, and the bark and clatter of automatic weapons fire faded abruptly.

He held his own position, AKM still ready, while he surveyed the tumbled Shongairi bodies sprawled along the trail. One or two were still writhing, although it didn't look like they would be for long.

"Good," a voice said behind him with fierce, obvious satisfaction, and he looked over his shoulder. Mircea Basarab stood in the dense forest shadows, looking out over the ambushed patrol. "Well done, my Stephen."

"Maybe so, but we'd better be moving," Buchevsky replied, safeing his weapon and rising from his firing position.

His own expression, he knew, was more anxious than Basarab's. This was the third hard contact with the Shongairi in the six days since he'd placed his people under Basarab's command, and from what

Basarab had said, they were getting close to the enclave he'd established in the mountains around Lake Vidaru. Which meant they really needed to shake this persistent—if inept—pursuit.

"I think we have a short while," Basarab disagreed, glancing farther down the trail to the columns of smoke rising from what had been armored vehicles until Jonescu's squad and half of Basarab's original men dealt with them. "It seems unlikely they got a message out this time, either."

"Maybe not," Buchevsky conceded. "But their superiors have to know where they are. When they don't check in on schedule, someone's going to come looking for them. Again."

He might have sounded as if he were disagreeing, but he wasn't, really. First, because Basarab was probably correct. But secondly, because over the course of the last week or so, he'd come to realize Mircea Basarab was one of the best officers he'd ever served under. Which, he reflected, was high praise for any foreign officer from any Marine . . . and didn't keep the Romanian from being one of the scariest men Buchevsky had ever met.

A lot of people might not have realized that. In better light, Basarab's face had a bony, foxlike handsomeness, and his smile was frequently warm. But there were dark, still places behind those green eyes. Still places that were no stranger to all too many people from the post-Ceauşescu Balkans. Dark places Buchevsky recognized because he'd met so many other scary men in his life . . . and because there was now a dark, still place labeled "Washington, D.C." inside him, as well.

Yet whatever lay in Basarab's past, the man was almost frighteningly competent, and he radiated a sort of effortless charisma Buchevsky had seldom encountered. The sort of charisma that could win the loyalty of even a Stephen Buchevsky, and even on such relatively short acquaintance.

"Your point is well taken, my Stephen," Basarab said now, smiling almost as if he'd read Buchevsky's mind and reaching up to place one hand on the towering American's shoulder. Like the almost possessive way he said "my Stephen," it could have been patronizing. It wasn't.

"However," he continued, his smile fading, "I believe it may be time to send these vermin elsewhere."

"Sounds great to me." A trace of skepticism edged Buchevsky's voice, and Basarab chuckled. It was not a particularly pleasant sound.

"I believe we can accomplish it," he said, and whistled shrilly.

Moments later, Take Bratianu, a dark-haired, broad-shouldered Romanian, blended out of the forest.

Buchevsky was picking up Romanian quickly, thanks to Elizabeth Cantacuzène, but the exchange that followed was far too rapid for his still rudimentary grasp of the language to sort out. It lasted for a few minutes, then Bratianu nodded, and Basarab turned back to Buchevsky.

"Take speaks no English, I fear," he said.

That was obvious, Buchevsky thought dryly. On the other hand, Bratianu didn't *need* to speak English to communicate the fact that he was one seriously bad-assed individual. None of Basarab's men did.

There were only about twenty of them, but they moved like ghosts. Buchevsky was no slouch, yet he knew when he was outclassed at pooping and snooping in the shrubbery. These men were far better at it than *he'd* ever been, and in addition to rifles, pistols, and hand grenades, they were liberally festooned with a ferocious assortment of knives, hatchets, and machetes. Indeed, Buchevsky suspected they would have preferred using cold steel instead of any namby-pamby assault rifles.

Now, as Bratianu and his fellows moved along the trail, knives flashed, and the handful of Shongairi wounded stopped writhing.

Buchevsky had no problem with that. Indeed, his eyes were bleakly satisfied. But when some of the Romanians began stripping the alien bodies while others began cutting down several stout young saplings growing along the edge of the trail, he frowned and glanced at Basarab. The Romanian only shook his head.

"Wait," he said, and Buchevsky turned back to the others.

They worked briskly, wielding their hatchets and machetes with practiced efficiency as they cut the saplings into roughly ten-foot lengths, then shaped points at either end. In a surprisingly short period, they had over a dozen of them, and Buchevsky's eyes widened in shock as they calmly picked up the dead Shongairi and impaled them.

Blood and other body fluids oozed down the crude, rough-barked stakes, but he said nothing as the stakes' other ends were sunk into the soft woodland soil. The dead aliens hung there, lining the trail like insects mounted on pins, grotesque in the shadows, and he felt Basarab's eyes.

"Are you shocked, my Stephen?" the Romanian asked quietly.

"I . . ." Buchevsky inhaled deeply. "Yes, I guess I am. Some," he admitted. He turned to face the other man. "I think maybe because it's a little too close to some of the things I've seen jihadies do."

"Indeed?" Basarab's eyes were cold. "I suppose I should not be surprised by that. *We* learned the tradition from the Turks ourselves, long ago. But at least these were already dead when they were staked."

"Would it have made a difference?" Buchevsky asked, and Basarab's nostrils flared. But then the other man gave himself a little shake.

"Once?" He shrugged. "No. As I say, the practice has long roots in this area. One of Romania's most famous sons, after all, was known as 'Vlad the Impaler,' was he not?" He smiled thinly. "For that matter, *I* did not, as you Americans say, have a happy childhood, and there was a time when I inflicted cruelty on all those about me. When I *enjoyed* it. In those days, no doubt, I would have preferred them alive."

He shook his head, and his expression saddened as he gazed at the impaled alien bodies.

"I fear it took far too many years for me to realize that all the cruelty in the universe cannot avenge a broken childhood or appease an orphaned young man's rage, my Stephen," he said. "There was a doctor once, a man I met in Austria, who explained that to me. To my shame, I did not really wish to hear what he was saying, but it was true. And the years it took me to realize that demanded too high a price from those for whom I cared, and who cared for me." He looked at the bodies for a moment longer, then shook himself. "But this, my friend, has nothing to do with the darkness inside me."

"No?" Buchevsky raised an eyebrow.

"No. It is obvious to me that these vermin will persist in pursuing us. So, we will give them something to fix their attention upon—something to make any creature, even one of these, hot with hate—and then we will give them someone besides your civilians to pursue. Take and most of my men will head south, leaving a trail so obvious that even these—" He twitched his head at the slaughtered patrol. "—could scarcely miss it. He will lead them aside until they are dozens of kilometers away. Then he will slip away and return to us."

"Without their being able to follow him?"

"Do not be so skeptical, my friend!" Basarab chuckled and squeezed Buchevsky's shoulder. "I did not pick these men at random! There are no more skilled woodsmen in all of Romania. Have no fear that they will lead our enemies to us."

"I hope you're right," Buchevsky said, looking back at the impaled bodies and thinking about how *he* would have reacted in the aliens' place. "I hope you're right."

XI

Fleet Commander Thikair pressed the admittance stud, then tipped back in his chair as Shairez stepped through the door into his personal quarters. It closed silently behind her, and he waved at a chair.

"Be seated, Base Commander," he said, deliberately more formal because of the irregularity of meeting with her here.

"Thank you, Fleet Commander."

He watched her settle into the chair. She carried herself with almost her usual self-confidence, he thought, yet there was something about the set of her ears. And about her eyes.

She's changed, he thought. *Aged.* He snorted mentally. *Well, we've all done that, haven't we? But there's more to it in her case. More than there was yesterday, for that matter.*

"What, precisely, did you wish to see me about, Base Commander?" he asked after a moment. *And why*, he did not ask aloud, *did you wish to see me about it in private?*

"I have almost completed my initial psychological profile of these humans, sir." She met his gaze unflinchingly. "I'm afraid our initial hopes for this planet were . . . rather badly misplaced."

Thikair sat very still. It was a testimony to her inner strength that she'd spoken so levelly, he thought.

Particularly given that they had been not "our initial hopes," but *his* initial hopes.

He drew a deep breath, feeling his ears fold back against his skull, and closed his eyes while he considered the price of those hopes. In just three local months, this one, miserable planet had cost the expedition 56 percent of its GEVs, 23 percent of its transports and APCs, and 26 percent of its infantry.

Of course, he reflected grimly, it had cost the humans even more. Yet no matter what he did, the insane creatures *refused* to submit.

"*How* badly misplaced?" he asked without opening his eyes.

"The problem, sir," she replied a bit obliquely, "is that we've never before encountered a species like this one. Their psychology is . . . unlike anything in our previous experience."

"That much I'd already surmised," Thikair said with poison-dry humor. "Should I conclude you now have a better grasp of how it differs?"

"Yes, sir." She drew a deep breath. "First, you must understand that there are huge local variations in their psychologies. That's inevitable, of course, given that unlike us or any other member race of the Hegemony, they retain so many bewilderingly different cultural and societal templates. There are, however, certain common strands. And one of those, Fleet Commander, is that, essentially, they have no submission mechanism as we understand the term."

"I beg your pardon?" Thikair's eyes popped open at the preposterous statement, and she sighed.

"There are a few races of the Hegemony that perhaps approach the humans' psychology, sir, but I can think of no more than two or three. All of them, like the humans, are omnivores, but none come close to this species' . . . level of perversity. Frankly, any Shongairi psychologist would pronounce all humans insane, sir. Unlike weed-eaters or the majority of omnivores, they have a streak of very Shongairi-like ferocity, yet their sense of self is almost invariably far greater than their sense of the pack."

She was obviously groping for a way to describe something outside any understood racial psychology, Thikair thought.

"Almost all weed-eaters have a very strong herd instinct," she said. "While they may, under some circumstances, fight ferociously, their first, overwhelming instinct is to *avoid* conflict, and their basic psychology subordinates the individual's good, even his very survival, to the good of the 'herd.' Most of them now define that 'herd' in terms of entire planetary populations or star nations, but it remains the platform from which all of their decisions and policies proceed.

"Most of the Hegemony's omnivores share that orientation to a greater or a lesser degree, although a handful approach our own psychological stance, which emphasizes not the herd but the *pack*. Our species evolved as *hunters*, not prey, with a social structure and psychology oriented around that primary function. Unlike weed-eaters and most omnivores, Shongairi's pride in our personal accomplishments, the proof of our ability, all relate to the ancient, primal importance of the individual hunter's prowess as the definer of his status within the pack.

"Yet the pack is still greater than the individual. Our sense of self-worth, of accomplishment, is validated only within the context of the pack. And the submission of the weaker to the stronger comes from that same context. It is bred into our very genes to submit to the pack leader, to the individual whose strength dominates all about him. Of course our people, and especially our males, have always *challenged* our leaders, as well, for that was how the ancient pack ensured that its leadership remained strong. But once a leader has reaffirmed his dominance, his strength, even the challenger submits once more. Our entire philosophy, our honor code, our societal expectations, all proceed from that fundamental starting point."

"Of course," Thikair said, just a bit impatiently. "How else could a society such as ours survive?"

"That's my point, sir. A society such as ours could *not* survive among humans. Their instinct to submit is enormously weaker than our own, and it is far superseded by the individual's drive to defeat threats to his primary loyalty group—which is neither the pack nor the herd."

"What?" Thikair blinked at her, and she grimaced.

"A human's primary loyalty is to his family grouping, sir. Not to the herd, of which the family forms only a small part. And not to the pack, where the emphasis is on strength and value *to* the pack. There are exceptions, but that orientation forms the bedrock of human motivation. You might think of them almost as . . . as a herd composed of *individual* packs of predators. Humans are capable of extending that sense of loyalty beyond the family grouping— to organizations, to communities, to nation-states or philosophies—but the fundamental motivating mechanism of the individual family is as hardwired into them as submission to the stronger is hardwired into us. Sir, my research indicates that a very large percentage of humans will attack *any* foe, regardless of its strength or power, in defense of their mates or young. And they will do it *with no regard whatsoever* for the implications to the rest of their pack or herd."

Thikair looked at her, trying to wrap his mind around the bizarre psychology she was trying to explain. Intellectually, he could grasp it, at least imperfectly; emotionally, it made no sense to him at all.

"Sir," she continued, "I've administered all the standard psychological exams. As you directed, I've also experimented to determine how applicable our existing direct neural education techniques are to humans, and I can report that they work quite well. But my opinion, based on the admittedly imperfect psychological profile I've been able to construct, suggests to me that it would be the height of folly to use humans as a client race.

"They will never understand the natural submission of the weaker to the stronger. Instead, they will work unceasingly to *become* the stronger, and not for the purpose of assuming leadership of the pack. Some of them, yes, will react very like Shongairi might. Others may even approach weed-eater behavior patterns. But most will see the function of strength as the protection of their primary loyalty group. They will focus their energy on destroying any and all threats to it, even when attempting to destroy the threat *in itself* risks destruction of the group, and they will *never* forget or forgive a threat to that which they protect. We might be able to enforce temporary obedience, and it's possible we could actually convince many of them to accept us as their natural masters. But we will never convince *all* of them of that, and so, eventually, we will find our 'clients' turning upon us with all the inventiveness and ferocity we've observed out of them here, but with all our own technological capabilities . . . as a *starting* point."

"It would appear," Thikair told his senior officers, "that my approach to this planet was not the most brilliant accomplishment of my career."

They looked back at him, most still obviously bemused by Shairez's report. None of them, he reflected, had reacted to it any better than *he* had.

"Obviously," he continued, "it's necessary to reevaluate our policy—*my* policy—in light of the Base Commander's discoveries. And, frankly, in light of our already severe operational losses.

"Our efforts to date to compel the humans to submit have killed over half the original planetary population and cost us massive losses of our own. Ground Force Commander Thairys's current estimate is that if we continue operations for one local year, we will have lost three-quarters of his personnel. In that same time period, we will have killed half the *remaining* humans. Clearly, even if Ground Base Commander Shairez's model is in error, we cannot sustain losses at that level. Nor would we dare risk providing such a . . . recalcitrant species with access to modern technology after killing three-quarters of them first."

There was silence in the conference room as he surveyed their faces.

"The time has come to cut our losses," he said flatly. "I am not prepared to give up this planet, not after the price we've already paid for it. But at the same time, I have concluded that humans are too dangerous. Indeed, faced with what we've discovered here, I believe many of the Hegemony's other races would share that conclusion!

"I've already instructed Base Commander Shairez to implement our backup strategy and develop a targeted bio-weapon. This constitutes a significant shift in her priorities, and it will be necessary to establish proper facilities for her work and to provide her with appropriate test subjects.

"I had considered moving her and her research staff to one of the existing ground bases. Unfortunately, the intensity of the operations required to establish those bases means the human populations in their vicinities have become rather . . . sparse. I have therefore decided to establish a new base facility in a rural area of the planet, where we haven't conducted such intense operations and reasonable numbers of test subjects will be readily available to her. Ground Force Commander Thairys will be responsible for providing security to the base during its construction . . . and with securing test subjects for her once construction is complete."

XII

"So, my Stephen. What do you make of this?"

Buchevsky finished his salad and took a long swallow of beer. His grandmama had always urged him to eat his vegetables, yet he was still a bit bemused by how sinfully luxurious fresh salad tasted after weeks of scrounging whatever he and his people could.

Which, unfortunately, wasn't what Basarab was asking him about.

"I really don't know, Mircea," he said with a frown. "*We* haven't been doing anything differently. Not that I know of, at any rate."

"Nor that I know of," Basarab agreed thoughtfully, gazing down at the handwritten note on the table.

The days were noticeably cooler outside the log-walled cabin, and autumn color was creeping across the mountainsides above the Arges River and the enormous blue gem of Lake Vidaru. The lake lay less than seventy kilometers north of the ruins of Pitesti, the capital of the Arges *judeţ*, or county, but it was in the heart of a wilderness preserve, and the cabin had been built by the forestry service, rather than as part of any of the three villages Basarab had organized into his own little kingdom.

Despite Lake Vidaru's relative proximity to Pitesti, few of the kinetic strike's survivors had headed up into its vicinity. Buchevsky supposed the mountains and heavy forest had been too forbidding to appeal to urban dwellers. There were almost no roads into the area, and Basarab's villages were like isolated throwbacks to another age. In fact, they reminded Buchevsky rather strongly of the village in the musical *Brigadoon*.

Which isn't a bad thing, he reflected. *There sits Lake Vidaru, with its hydroelectric generators, and these people didn't even have electricity! Which means they aren't radiating any emissions the Shongairi are likely to pick up on.*

Over the last couple of months, he, his Americans, and their Romanians had been welcomed by the villagers and—as Basarab had warned—been put to work preparing for the onset of winter. One reason his lunch salad had tasted so good was because he wouldn't be having salads much longer. It wasn't as if there'd be fresh produce coming in from California.

"There must be some reason for it, my Stephen," Basarab said now. "And I fear it is not one either of us would like."

"Mircea, I haven't liked a single goddammed thing those bastards have done from day one."

Basarab arched one eyebrow, and Buchevsky was a little surprised himself by the jagged edge of hatred that had roughened his voice. It took him unawares, sometimes, that hate. When the memory of Trish and the girls came looming up out of the depths once again, fangs bared, to remind him of the loss and the pain and anguish.

Isn't it one hell of a note when the best thing I can think of is that the people I loved probably died without knowing a thing about it?

"They have not endeared themselves to me, either," Basarab said after a moment. "Indeed, it has been . . . difficult to remember that we dare not take the fight to them."

Buchevsky nodded in understanding. Basarab had made it clear from the beginning that avoiding contact with the enemy, lying low, was the best way to protect the civilians for whom they were responsible, and he was right. Yet that didn't change his basic personality's natural orientation—like Buchevsky's own—toward taking the offensive. Toward seeking out and destroying the enemy, not hiding from him.

But that would have come under the heading of Bad Ideas. Basarab's runners had made contact with several other small enclaves across southern Romania and northern Bulgaria, and by now, those enclaves were as concerned with defending themselves against other humans as against Shongairi. After the initial bombardments and confused combat of the first couple of weeks, the invaders had apparently decided to pull back from the Balkans' unfriendly terrain and settle for occupying more open areas of the planet. It was hard to be certain of that, with the collapse of the planetary communications net, but it seemed reasonable. As his brain trust of Truman and Sherman had pointed out, troop lift would almost certainly be limited for any interstellar expedition, so it would make sense to avoid stretching it any further than necessary by going up into the hills after dirt-poor, hardscrabble mountain villages.

Human refugees were an entirely different threat, and one Buchevsky was happy *they* hadn't had to deal with . . . yet. Starvation, exposure, and disease had probably killed at least half the civilians who'd fled their homes, and those who remained were becoming increasingly desperate as winter approached. Some of the other enclaves had already been forced to fight, often ruthlessly, against their own kind to preserve the resources their own people needed to survive.

In many ways, it was the fact that the aliens' actions had forced humans to kill *each other* in the name of simple survival that fueled Stephen Buchevsky's deepest rage.

"Nothing would make me happier than to go kick their scrawny asses," he said now, in response to Basarab's comment. "But unless they poke their snouts into our area—"

He shrugged, and Basarab nodded. Then he chuckled softly.

"What?" Buchevsky raised an eyebrow at him.

"It is just that we are so much alike, you and I." Basarab shook his head. "Deny it as you will, my Stephen, but there is Slav inside you!"

"Inside *me*?" Buchevsky laughed, looking down at the back of one very black hand. "Hey, I already told you! If any of my ancestors were *ever* in Europe, they got there from Africa, not the steppes!"

"Ah!" Basarab waved a finger under his nose. "So

you've said, but *I* know better! What, 'Buchevsky'? This is an *African* name?"

"Nope, probably just somebody who owned one of my great-great-granddaddies or -grandmamas."

"Nonsense! Slavs in nineteenth-century America were too *poor* to own anyone! No, no. Trust me—it is in the blood. Somewhere in your ancestry there is—how do you Americans say it?—a Slav in the straw pile!"

Buchevsky laughed again. He was actually learning to do that again—sometimes, at least—and he and Basarab had had this conversation before. But then the Romanian's expression sobered, and he reached across the table to lay one hand on Buchevsky's forearm.

"Whatever you may have been born, my Stephen," he said quietly, "you are a Slav now. A Wallachian. You have earned that."

Buchevsky waved dismissively, but he couldn't deny the warmth he felt inside. He knew Basarab meant every word of it, just as he knew he'd earned his place as the Romanian's second-in-command through the training and discipline he'd brought the villagers. Basarab had somehow managed to stockpile impressive quantities of small arms and infantry support weapons, but however fearsome Take Bratianu and the rest of Basarab's original group might have been as individuals, it was obvious none of them had really understood how to train civilians. Stephen Buchevsky, on the other hand, had spent years turning pampered *American* civilians into U.S. Marines. Compared with that, training tough, mountain-hardened Romanian villagers was a piece of cake.

I just hope none of them are ever going to need *that training*, he reflected, his mood turning grim once again.

Which brought him back to the subject of this conversation.

"I don't like it, Mircea," he said. "There's no reason for them to put a base way up here in the frigging mountains. Not unless something's happened that you and I don't know about."

"Agreed, agreed." Basarab nodded, playing with the written note again, then shrugged. "Sooner or later, unless they simply intend to kill all of us, there must be some form of accommodation."

His sour expression showed his opinion of his own analysis, but he continued unflinchingly.

"The people of this land have survived conquest before. No doubt they can do it again, and if these Shongairi had intended simple butchery rather than conquest, then they would have begun by destroying *all* our cities and towns from space. But I will not subject *my* people to them without holding out for the very best terms we can obtain. And if they prove me in error—if they demonstrate that they are, indeed, prepared to settle for butchery rather than conquest—they will pay a higher price than they can possibly imagine before they rule *these* mountains."

He sat for a moment in cold, dangerous silence. Then he shook himself.

"Well, there seems little point in speculating when we have no firsthand information. So I suppose we must take a closer look at this new base, see what it may be they have in mind." He tapped the note. "According to this, they had almost finished it before Iliescu noticed it was there. So perhaps it would be best if Take and I go examine it in person."

Buchevsky opened his mouth to protest, but then he closed it again. He'd discovered that he was always uncomfortable when Basarab went wandering around the mountains out from under his own eye. And a part of him resented the fact that Basarab hadn't even considered inviting *him* along on this little jaunt. But the truth, however little he wanted to admit it, was that he would probably have been more of a hindrance than a help.

Basarab and Take Bratianu both seemed to be able to see like cats and move like drifting leaves. He couldn't even come close to matching them when it came to sneaking through the woods at night, and he knew it . . . however little he liked admitting that there was *anything* someone could do better than he could.

"We will go tonight," Basarab decided. "And while I am away, you will keep an eye on things for me, my African Slav, yes?"

"Yeah, I'll do that," Buchevsky agreed.

XIII

Regiment Commander Harah didn't like trees.

He hadn't always felt that way. In fact, he'd actually *liked* trees until the Empire invaded this never-to-be-sufficiently-damned planet. Now he vastly preferred long, flat, empty spaces—preferably of bare, pounded earth where not even a *garish* or one of the human "rabbits" could have hidden. Any other sort of terrain seemed to spontaneously spawn humans . . . all of whom appeared to have guns.

He hadn't needed Base Commander Shairez to tell *him* humans were all lunatics! It was nice to have confirmation, of course, and he was simply *delighted* that the Base Commander's conclusions had led Fleet Commander Thikair to change his plans. Once every last accursed human had been expunged from it, this planet would probably be a perfectly nice place to live.

He grimaced at his own thoughts as he sat gazing at the holographic plot in his GEV command vehicle.

Actually, Harah, part of you admires these creatures, doesn't it? he thought. *After all, we've killed thousands of them for every Shongair we've lost, and they still have the guts—the absolutely insane, utterly irrational, mind-numbingly stupid guts—to come right at us. If they only had half as much brains, they would've acknowledged our superiority and submitted months ago. But, no! They couldn't do that, could they?*

He growled, remembering the 35 percent of his original regiment he'd lost subduing what had once been the city of Cincinnati. Division Commander Tesuk had gone in with three regiments; he'd come out with less than one, and they'd *still* ended up taking out over half the city from orbit. Particularly in the nation the humans had called the "United States," there'd seemed to be more *guns* than there were people!

At least the experience had taught the expedition's senior officers to settle for occupying *open* terrain, where surveillance could be maintained effectively, and simply calling in kinetic strikes on anything resembling organized resistance in more constricted terrain.

Despite that, no one relished the thought of acquiring Shairez's test subjects anyplace where there'd been sustained contact with the humans. First, because there weren't many humans *left* in places like that, and the ones who hadn't already been killed had become fiendishly clever at hiding. Just finding them would have been hard enough even without the *second* consideration . . . which was that those same survivors were also uncommonly good at ambushing anyone who went looking for them.

Of course, there weren't many places where there'd been *no* combat, given humans' insane stubbornness. Still, the mountainous portions of the area the humans called "the Balkans" had seen far less than most, mainly because the population was so sparse and the terrain was so accursedly bad, HQ had decided to let the humans there stew in their own juices rather than invest the effort to go in after them.

And, he reflected moodily, *the other reason HQ made that little decision was the fact that we kept getting our asses kicked every time we did send someone in on the ground, didn't we?*

In fairness, they'd taken the worst of their losses

in the first few weeks, before they'd really begun to appreciate just what a losing proposition it was to go after humans on ground of their own choosing.

That's what the gods made fire support *for,* Harah thought grimly.

Well, he reminded himself as his GEVs and transports approached their jumpoff positions, *at least the satellites have told us exactly where these humans are. And they've been left alone, too. Their herd hasn't been culled yet. And not only should they be fat, happy, and stupid compared with the miserable jermahk we've been trying to dig out of the woodwork back home, but we've learned a lot over the last few months.*

His lips wrinkled back from his canines in a hunter's grin.

Stephen Buchevsky swore with silent, bitter venom.

The sun was barely above the eastern horizon, shining into his eyes as he studied the Shongairi through the binoculars and wondered what the hell they were after. After staying clear of the mountains for so long, what could have inspired them to come straight at the villages this way?

And why the hell do they have to be doing it when Mircea is away? a corner of his mind demanded.

It was at least fortunate the listening posts had detected the approaching drones so early, given how close behind them the aliens had been this time. There'd been time—barely—to crank up the old-fashioned, hand-powered warning sirens. And at least the terrain was too heavily forested for any sort of airborne ops. If the Shongairi wanted them, they'd have to come in on the ground.

Which was exactly what they seemed to have in mind. A large number of APCs and a handful of tanks were assembling on the low ground at the southern end of the lake, about a kilometer below the Gheorghiu-Dej Dam, while a smaller force of tanks came in across the lake itself, followed by a dozen big orbital shuttles, and he didn't like that one bit.

The villages were scattered along the rugged flanks of a mountain spine running east-to-west on the lake's southeastern shore. The ridgeline towered to over 3,200 feet in places, with the villages tucked away in dense tree cover above the 1,800-foot level. He'd thought they were well concealed, but the Shongairi clearly knew where they were and obviously intended to squeeze them between the force coming in over the lake and the second force, moving along the deep valley between their ridge and the one to its south.

That much was clear enough. Among the many things that *weren't* clear was how well the aliens' sensors could track humans moving through rough terrain under heavy tree cover. He hoped the answer to that question was "not very," but he couldn't rely on that.

"Start them moving," he told Elizabeth Cantacuzène. "These people are headed straight for the villages. I think we'd better be somewhere else when they get here."

"Yes, Stephen." The teacher sounded far calmer

than Buchevsky felt as she nodded, then disappeared to pass his instructions to the waiting runners. Within moments, he knew, the orders would have gone out and their people would be falling back to the position he'd allowed Ramirez to christen "Bastogne."

It was an Army dance the first time around, he thought, *and it came out pretty well that time. I guess it's time to see how well the Green Machine makes out.*

Regiment Commander Harah swore as the icons on his plot shifted.

It appears we weren't close enough behind the drones after all, he thought grumpily.

HQ had been forced to factor the humans' bizarre ability to sense drones from beyond visual range into its thinking, and the operations plan had made what *ought* to have been ample allowance for it. Unfortunately, it hasn't been, and he was already losing sensor resolution as they went scurrying through those accursed trees.

"They're moving along the ridge," he said over the regimental net. "They're headed west—toward those higher peaks. Second Battalion, swing farther up the lake, try to come in on their flank. First Battalion, get moving up that valley *now*."

Buchevsky muttered another curse as the drones' unpleasant vibration kept pace with him. Clearly, the damn things could track through tree cover better than he'd hoped. On the other hand, they seemed to be coming in close, low above the treetops, and if they were—

"Dainthar seize them!"

A quartet of dirty fireballs trickled down the sky, and four of Harah's drones went off the air simultaneously.

Damn it! What in the name of Dainthar's Third Hell are villagers up in these damned mountains doing with SAMs?

Buchevsky bared his teeth in a panting, running grin as Macomb's air-defense teams took out the nearest drones. He still felt vibrations from other drones, farther away, but if the bastards kept them high enough to avoid the Gremlins, it might make their sensor resolution crappier, too.

Harah tried to master his anger, but he was sick unto death of how these damned humans insisted on screwing up even the simplest operation. There weren't supposed to be any SAMs or heavy weapons up here. That was the entire reason they'd come looking for Base Commander Shairez's specimens here. Only the humans *still* refused to cooperate!

He considered reporting to headquarters. Equipment losses on this accursed invasion were already astronomical, and he doubted HQ would thank him if he lost still more of it chasing after what were supposed to be unarmed villagers cowering in their mountain hideouts. But they had to secure specimens *somewhere*, and he had *these* humans more or less in his sights.

"We're not going to be able to bring the drones in as close as planned," he told his battalion commanders. "It's up to our scouts. Tell them to keep their damn eyes open."

Fresh acknowledgments came in, and he watched his own forces' icons closing in on the abruptly amorphous shaded area representing the drones' best guess of the humans' location.

We may not be able to see them clearly, he thought angrily, *but even if we can't, there aren't that many places they can go, now, are there?*

Buchevsky was profoundly grateful for the way hard work had toughened the lowland refugees. They were managing to keep up with the villagers, which they never would have been able to do without it. Several smaller children were beginning to flag, anyway, of course, and his heart ached at the ruthless demands being placed on them. But the bigger kids were managing to keep up with the adults, and there were enough grown-ups to take turns carrying the littlest ones.

The unhealed wound where Shania and Yvonne had been cried out for *him* to scoop up one of those tiny human beings, carry *someone's* child to the safety he'd been unable to offer his own children.

But that wasn't his job, and he turned his attention to what was.

He slid to a halt on the narrow trail, breathing heavily, watching the last few villagers stream past. The perimeter guards came next, and then the scouts who'd been on listening watch. One of them was Robert Szu.

"It's . . . it's pretty much like . . . you and Mircea figured it . . . Top," the private panted. He paused for a moment, gathering his breath, then nodded sharply. "They're coming up the firebreak roads on both sides of the ridgeline. I figure their points are halfway up by now."

"Good." Buchevsky said.

"Farkalash!"

Regiment Commander Harah's driver looked back over his shoulder at the horrendous oath until Harah's bared-canines snarl turned him hastily back around to his controls. The regiment commander only wished he could dispose of the Dainthar-damned humans as easily!

I shouldn't have sent the vehicles in that close, he told himself through a boil of bloodred fury. *I should've dismounted the infantry farther out.* Of course *it was as obvious to the humans as it was to me that there were only a handful of routes vehicles could use!*

He growled at himself, but he knew why he'd made the error. The humans were moving faster than he'd estimated they could, and he'd wanted to use his vehicles' speed advantage. Which was why the humans had destroyed six more GEVs and eleven wheeled APCs . . . not to mention over a hundred troopers who'd been *aboard* the troop carriers.

And there's no telling how many more little surprises they may've planted along any openings wide enough for vehicles.

"Dismount the infantry," he said flatly over the command net. "Scout formation. The vehicles are not to advance until the engineers have checked the trails for more explosives."

Buchevsky grimaced sourly. From the smoke billowing up through the treetops, he'd gotten at least several of their vehicles. Unfortunately, he couldn't know *how* many.

However many, they're going to take the hint and come in on foot from here . . . unless they're complete and utter idiots. And somehow, I don't think they are. Damn it.

Well, at least he'd slowed them up. That was going to buy the civilians a little breathing space. Now it was time to buy them a little more.

Harah's ears flattened, but at least it wasn't a surprise this time. The small arms fire rattling out of the trees had become inevitable the moment he ordered his own infantry to go in on foot.

Automatic weapons fire barked and snarled, and Buchevsky *wished* they hadn't been forced to deep-six their radios. His people knew the terrain intimately, knew the best defensive positions, but the Shongairi had heavier support weapons and their communications were vastly better than his. And, adding insult to injury, some of their infantry were using captured human rocket and grenade launchers to thicken their firepower.

The situation's bitter irony wasn't lost upon him. This time, *his* forces were on the short end of the "asymmetrical warfare" stick, and it sucked. On the other hand, he'd had painful personal experience of just how effective guerrillas could be in this sort of terrain.

There was more satisfaction to accompany the frustration in Harah's growl as he looked at the plot's latest update.

The advance had been slower than he'd ever contemplated, and morning had become afternoon, but the humans appeared to be running out of SAMs at last. That meant he could get his drones in close enough to see what the hell was happening, and his momentum was building.

Which was a damned good thing, since he'd already lost over 20 percent of his troops.

Well, maybe I have, but I've cost them, *too*, he thought harshly. Real-time estimates of enemy losses were notoriously unreliable, but even by his most pessimistic estimates, the humans had lost over forty fighters so far.

That was the good news. The bad news was that they appeared to be remarkably well equipped with infantry weapons, and their commander was fighting as smart as any human Harah had ever heard of. His forces were hugely outnumbered and outgunned, but he was hitting back hard—in fact, Harah's casualties, despite his GEVs and his mortars, were at least six or seven times the humans'. The other side was intimately familiar with the terrain and taking ruthless advantage of it, and his infantry had run into enough more concealed explosives to make anyone cautious.

Whatever we've run our snouts into, he reflected, *those aren't just a bunch of villagers. Somebody's spent a lot of time reconnoitering these damn mountains. They're fighting from positions that were preselected for their fields of fire. And those explosives . . . Someone picked the spots for them pretty damned carefully, too. Whoever it was knew what he was doing, and he must've spent months preparing his positions.*

Despite himself, he felt a flicker of respect for his human opponent. Not that it was going to make any difference in the end. The take from his drones was still far less detailed than he could wish, but it was clear the fleeing villagers were running into what amounted to a cul-de-sac.

———

Buchevsky felt the beginnings of despair.

He'd started the morning with 100 "regulars" and another 150 "militia" from the villages. He knew everyone tended to overestimate his own losses in a fight like this, especially in this sort of terrain, but he'd be surprised if he hadn't lost at least a quarter of his people by now.

That was bad enough, but there was worse coming.

The Bastogne position had never been intended to stand off a full-bore Shongairi assault. It had really been designed as a place of retreat in the face of attack by *human* adversaries after the villages' winter supplies. That meant Bastogne, despite its name, was more of a fortified warehouse than some sort of final redoubt. He'd made its defenses as tough as he could, yet he'd never contemplated trying to hold it against hundreds of Shongairi infantry, supported by tanks and mortars.

Stop kicking yourself, an inner voice growled. *There was never any point trying to build a position you could've held against that kind of assault. So what if you'd held them off for a while? They'd only call in one of their damned kinetic strikes in the end, anyway*.

He knew that was true, but what was *also* true was that the only paths of retreat were so steep as to be almost impassable. Bastogne *was* supposed to hold against any likely human attack, and without its stockpiled supplies, the chance that their civilians could have survived the approaching winter had been minimal, at best. So he and Mircea had staked everything on making the position tough enough to stand . . . and now it was a trap too many of their people couldn't get out of.

He looked out through the smoky forest, watching the westering sun paint the smoke the color of blood, and knew his people were out of places to run. They were on the final perimeter, now, and it took every ounce of discipline he'd learned in his life to fight down his despair.

I'm sorry, Mircea, he thought grimly. *I fucked up. Now we're all screwed. I'm just as glad you didn't make it back in time, after all.*

His jaw muscles tightened, and he reached out and grabbed Maria Averescu, one of his runners.

"I need you to find Gunny Meyers," he said in the Romanian he'd finally begun to master.

"He's dead, Top," she replied harshly, and his belly clenched.

"Sergeant Ramirez?"

"Him, too, I think. I know he took a hit here." Averescu thumped the center of her own chest.

"Then find Sergeant Jonescu. Tell him—" Buchevsky drew a deep breath. "Tell him I want him and his people to get as many kids out as they can. Tell him the rest of us will buy him as much time as we can. Got that?"

"Yes, Top!" Averescu's grimy face was pale, but she nodded hard.

"Good. Now go!"

He released her shoulder. She shot off through the smoke, and he headed for the perimeter command post.

The Shongairi scouts realized the humans' retreat had slowed still further. Painful experience made them wary of changes, and they felt their way cautiously forward.

They were right to be cautious.

Bastogne had been built around a deep cavern that offered protected, easily camouflaged storage for winter foodstuffs and fodder for the villages' animals. Concealment was not its only defense, however.

Buchevsky bared his teeth savagely as he heard the explosions. He still wished he'd had better mines to work with—he'd have given his left arm for a couple of crates of claymores—but the Romanian anti-personnel mines Basarab had managed to scrounge up were one hell of a lot better than nothing. The mine belt wasn't so deep as he would have liked, but the Shongairi obviously hadn't realized what they were walking into, and he listened with bloodthirsty satisfaction to their shrieks.

I may not stop *them, but I can damned well make them pay* cash. *And maybe—just maybe—Jonescu will get some of the kids out, after all.*

He didn't let himself think about the struggle to survive those kids would face over the coming winter with no roof, no food. He couldn't.

"Runner!"

"Yes, Top!"

"Find Corporal Gutierrez," Buchevsky told the young man. "Tell him it's time to dance."

The Shongairi halted along the edge of the minefield cowered close against the ground as the pair of 120 mm mortars Basarab had scrounged up along with the mines started dropping their lethal fire on them. Even now, few of them had actually encountered human artillery, and the 35-pound HE bombs were a devastating experience.

Regiment Commander Harah winced as the communications net was flooded by sudden reports of heavy fire. Even after the unpleasant surprise of the infantry-portable SAMs, he hadn't anticipated *this*.

His lead infantry companies' already heavy loss rates soared, and he snarled over the net at his own support weapons commander.

"Find those damned mortars and get fire on them— *now*!"

Harah's infantry recoiled as rifle fire added to the carnage of mortar bombs and minefields. But they were survivors who'd learned their lessons in a hard school, and their junior officers started probing forward, looking for openings.

Three heavy mortars, mounted on unarmored transports, had managed to struggle up the narrow trail behind them and tried to locate human mortars. But the dense tree cover and rugged terrain made it impossible to get a solid radar track on the incoming fire. Finally, unable to actually find the mortar pits, they began blind suppressive fire.

The Shongairi mortars were more powerful, and white-hot flashes began to walk across the area behind Buchevsky's forward positions, and he heard screams rising from behind him, as well.

But the Shongairi had problems of their own. Their vehicle-mounted weapons were confined to the trail while the humans' were deeply dug-in, and Buchevsky and Ignacio Gutierrez had pre-plotted just about every possible firing position along that trail. As soon as they opened fire, Gutierrez knew where they had to be, and both of *his* mortars retargeted immediately. They fired more rapidly than the heavier Shongairi weapons, and their bombs fell around the Shongairi vehicles in a savage exchange that could not—and didn't—last long.

Ignacio Gutierrez died, along with one entire crew. The second mortar, though, remained in action . . . which was more than could be said for the vehicles they'd engaged.

Harah snarled.

He had over a dozen more mortar vehicles . . . all of them miles behind the point of contact, at the far end of the choked, tortuous trails along which his infantry had pursued the humans. He could bring them up—in time—just as he could call in a kinetic strike and put an end to this entire business in minutes. But the longer he delayed, the more casualties that single remaining human mortar would inflict. And if he called in the kinetic strike, he'd kill the test subjects he'd come to capture, along with their defenders ... which would make the entire operation, and all the casualties he'd already suffered, meaningless.

That wasn't going to happen. If this bunch of primitives was so incredibly stupid, so lost to all rationality and basic decency, that they wanted to die fighting, then he would damned well oblige them.

He looked up through a break in the tree cover. The light was fading quickly, and Shongairi didn't like fighting in the dark. But there was still time. They could still break through before darkness fell if—

Stephen Buchevsky sensed it coming. He couldn't have explained how, but he knew. He could actually *feel* the Shongairi gathering themselves, steeling themselves, and he knew.

"They're coming!" he shouted, and heard his warning relayed along the horseshoe-shaped defensive line in either direction from his CP.

He set aside his own rifle and settled into position behind the KPV heavy machine gun. There were three tripod-mounted PKMS 7.62mm medium machine guns dug in around Bastogne's final perimeter, but even Mircea Basarab's scrounging talents had limits. He'd managed to come up with only one *heavy* machine gun, and it was a bulky, awkward thing—six and a half feet long, intended as a vehicle-mounted weapon, on an improvised infantry mounting.

The Shongairi started forward behind a hurricane of rifle fire and grenades. The minefield slowed them, disordered them, but they kept coming. They were too close for the single remaining mortar to engage, and the medium machine guns opened up.

Shongairi screamed, tumbled aside, disappeared in sprays of blood and tissue, but then a pair of wheeled armored personnel carriers edged up the trail behind them. How they'd gotten here was more than Buchevsky could guess, but their turret-mounted light energy weapons quested back and forth, seeking targets. Then a quasi-solid bolt of lightning slammed across the chaos and the blood and terror and one of the machine guns was silenced forever.

But Stephen Buchevsky knew where that lightning bolt had come from, and the Russian Army had developed the KPV around the 14.5 mm round of its final World War II antitank rifle. The PKMS' 185-grain bullet developed three thousand foot-pounds of muzzle energy; the KPV's bullet weighed almost a *thousand* grains . . . and developed twenty-four thousand foot-pounds of muzzle energy.

He laid his sights on the vehicle that had fired and sent six hundred rounds per minute shrieking into it.

The APC staggered as the steel-cored, armor-piercing, incendiary bullets slammed into it at better than 3,200 feet per second. Armor intended to resist small arms fire never had a chance against *that* torrent of destruction, and the vehicle vomited smoke and flame.

Its companion turned toward the source of its destruction, and Alice Macomb stood up in a rifle pit. She exposed herself recklessly with an RBR-M60, and its three-and-a-half-pound rocket smashed into the APC . . . just before a six-round burst killed her where she stood.

Buchevsky swung the KBV's flaming muzzle, sweeping his fire along the Shongairi line, pouring his hate, his desperate need to protect the children behind him, into his enemies.

He was still firing when the Shongairi grenade silenced his machine gun forever.

XIV

He woke slowly, floating up from the depths like someone else's ghost. He woke to darkness, to pain, and to a swirling tide race of dizziness, confusion, and fractured memory.

He blinked, slowly, blindly, trying to understand. He'd been wounded more times than he liked to think about, but it had never been like this. The pain had never run everywhere under his skin, as if it were racing about on the power of his own heartbeat. And yet, even though he knew he had never suffered such pain in his life, it was curiously . . . distant. A part of him, yes, but walled off by the dizziness. Held one imagined half step away.

"You are awake, my Stephen."

It was a statement, he realized, not a question. Almost as if the voice behind it were trying to reassure him of that.

He turned his head, and it was as if it belonged to someone else. It seemed to take him forever, but at last Mircea Basarab's face swam into his field of vision.

He blinked again, trying to focus, but he couldn't. He lay in a cave somewhere, looking out into a mountain night, and there was something wrong with his eyes. Everything seemed oddly out of phase, and the night kept flashing, as if it were alive with heat lightning.

"Mircea."

He didn't recognize his own voice. It was faint, thready.

"Yes," Basarab agreed. "I know you may not believe it at this moment, but you will recover."

"Take . . . your word . . . for it."

"Very wise of you."

Buchevsky didn't have to be able to focus his eyes to see Basarab's fleeting smile, and he felt his own mouth twitch in reply. But then a new and different sort of pain ripped through him.

"I . . . fucked up." He swallowed painfully. "Sorry . . . so sorry. The kids . . ."

His eyes burned as a tear forced itself from under his lids, and he felt Basarab grip his right hand. The Romanian raised it, pressed it against his own chest, and his face came closer as he leaned over Buchevsky.

"No, my Stephen," he said slowly. "It was not *you* who failed; it was I. This is *my* fault, my friend."

"No." Buchevsky shook his head weakly. "No. Couldn't have . . . stopped it even if . . . you'd been here."

"You think not?" It was Basarab's turn to shake his head. "You think wrongly. These creatures—these *Shongairi*—would never have touched my people if I had remembered. Had I not spent so long trying to be someone I am not. Trying to forget. You shame me, my Stephen. You, who fell in my place, doing my duty, paying in blood for my failure."

Buchevsky frowned, his swirling brain trying to make some sort of sense out of Basarab's words. He couldn't . . . which probably shouldn't have been too surprising, he decided, given how horrendously bad he felt.

"How many—?" he asked.

"Only a very few, I fear," Basarab said quietly. "Your Gunny Meyers is here, although he was more badly wounded even than you. I am not surprised the vermin left both of you for dead. And Jasmine and Private Lopez. The others were . . . gone before Take and I could return."

Buchevsky's stomach clenched as Basarab confirmed what he'd already known.

"And . . . the villagers?"

"Sergeant Jonescu got perhaps a dozen children to safety," Basarab said. "He and most of his men died holding the trail while the children and their mothers fled. The others—"

He shrugged, looking away, then looked back at Buchevsky.

"They are not here, Stephen. For whatever reason,

the vermin have taken them, and having seen this new base of theirs, I do not think either of us would like that reason."

"*God.*" Buchevsky closed his eyes again. "Sorry. My fault," he said once more.

"Do not repeat that foolishness again, or you will make me angry," Basarab said sternly. "And do not abandon hope for them. They are *my* people. I swore to protect them, and I do not let my word be proved false."

Buchevsky's world was spinning away again, yet he opened his eyes, looked up in disbelief. His vision cleared, if only for a moment, and as he saw Mircea Basarab's face, he felt the disbelief flow out of him.

It was still preposterous, of course. He knew that. Only, somehow, as he looked up into that granite expression, it didn't matter what he *knew*. All that mattered was what he *felt* . . . and as he fell back into the bottomless darkness, a tiny little sliver of awareness felt almost sorry for the Shongairi.

Private Kumayr felt his head beginning to nod forward and stiffened his spine, snapping back erect in his chair. His damnably *comfortable* chair, which wasn't exactly what someone needed to keep him awake and alert in the middle of the night.

He shook himself and decided he'd better find something to do if he didn't want one of the officers to come along and rip his head off for dozing on duty. Something that looked industrious and conscientious.

His ears twitched in amusement, and he punched up a standard diagnostic of the perimeter security systems. Not that he expected to find any problems. The entire base was brand new, and all of its systems had passed their final checks with flying colors less than three local days ago. Still, it would look good on the log sheets.

He hummed softly as the computers looked over one another's shoulders, reporting back to him. He paid particular attention to the systems in the laboratory area. Now that they had test subjects, the labs would be getting a serious workout, after all. When that happened—

His humming stopped, and his ears pricked as a red icon appeared on his display. That couldn't be right . . . could it?

He keyed another, more tightly focused diagnostic program, and his pricked ears flattened as more icons began to blink. He stared at them, then slammed his hand down on the transmit key.

"Perimeter One!" he snapped. "Perimeter One, Central. Report status!"

There was no response, and something with hundreds of small icy feet started to scuttle up and down his spine.

"Perimeter Two!" he barked, trying another circuit. "Perimeter Two—report status!"

Still no response, and that was impossible. There were *fifty troopers* in each of those positions—one of them *had* to have heard him!

"All perimeter stations!" He heard the desperation in his voice, tried to squeeze it back out again while he held down the all-units key. "All perimeter stations, this is a red alert!"

Still there was nothing, and he stabbed more controls, bringing up the monitors. They came alive . . . and he froze.

Not possible, a small, still voice said in the back of his brain as he stared at the images of carnage. At the troopers with their throats ripped out, at the Shongairi blood soaking into the thirsty soil of an alien world, at heads turned backwards on snapped necks and dismembered body parts scattered like some lunatic's bloody handiwork.

Not possible, not without at least one alarm sounding. Not—

He heard a tiny sound, and his right hand flashed toward his side arm. But even as he touched it, the door of his control room flew open and darkness crashed over him.

XV

"What?"

Fleet Commander Thikair looked at Ship Commander Ahzmer in astonishment so deep, it was sheer incomprehension.

"I'm . . . I'm sorry, sir." The flagship's CO sounded like someone trapped in an amazingly bad dream, Thikair thought distantly. "The report just came in. I'm . . . afraid it's confirmed, sir."

"*All* of them?" Thikair shook himself. "Everyone assigned to the base—even Shairez?"

"All of them," Ahzmer confirmed heavily. "And all the test subjects have disappeared."

"*Dainthar,*" Thikair half whispered. He stared at the ship commander, then shook himself again, harder.

"How did they do it?"

"Sir, I don't know. *No one* knows. For that matter, it doesn't . . . well, it doesn't look like anything we've seen the humans do before."

"What are you talking about?" Thikair's voice was harder, impatient. He knew much of his irritation was the product of his own shock, but that didn't change the fact that what Ahzmer had just said made no sense.

"It doesn't look like whoever it was used *weapons* at all, Fleet Commander." Ahzmer didn't sound as if he expected Thikair to believe him, but the ship commander went on doggedly. "It's more like some sort of wild beasts got through every security system without sounding a single alarm. Not one, sir. But there are no bullet wounds, no knife wounds, no sign of *any* kind of weapon. Our people were just . . . torn apart."

"That doesn't make sense," Thikair protested.

"No, sir, it doesn't. But it's what *happened.*"

The two of them stared at one another; then Thikair drew a deep breath.

"Senior officers conference, two hours," he said flatly.

"The ground patrols have confirmed it, Fleet Commander," Ground Force Commander Thairys said heavily. "There are no Shongairi survivors. None. And—" He inhaled heavily, someone about to say something he really didn't want to. "—there's no evidence that a single one of our troopers so much as fired a shot in his own defense. It's as if they all just . . . *sat* there, waiting for someone—or some*thing*—to tear them apart."

"Calm down, Thairys." Thikair put both sternness and sympathy into his tone. "We're going to have enough panicky rumors when the troops hear about this. Let's not begin believing in night terrors before the rumor mill even gets started!"

Thairys looked at him for a moment, then managed a chuckle that was only slightly hollow.

"You're right, of course, sir. It's just that. . . . Well, it's just that I've never seen anything like this. And I've checked the database. As nearly as I can tell, no one in the entire *Hegemony* has ever seen anything like this."

"It's a big galaxy," Thikair pointed out. "And even the Hegemony's explored only a very small portion of it. I don't know what happened down there, either, but trust me—there's a rational explanation. We just have to figure out what it is."

"With all due respect, Fleet Commander," Squadron Commander Jainfar said quietly, "how do we go about doing that?"

Thikair looked at him, and the squadron commander flicked his ears.

"I've personally reviewed the sensor recordings, sir. Until Private Kumayr began trying to contact the perimeter strong points, there was absolutely no indication of any problem. Whatever happened, it apparently managed to kill every single member of the garrison—except for Kumayr—without being detected by any heat, motion, or audio sensor. The fact of the matter is, sir, that we have no data, no information at all. Just an entire base full of dead personnel. And with no evidence, how do we figure out *what* happened, far less who was responsible for it?"

"One thing I think we *can* assume, sir." Base Commander Barak was down on the planetary surface, attending the conference electronically, and Thikair nodded permission to speak to his comm image.

"As I say, I think we can assume *one* thing," Barak continued. "Surely if it was the humans—if humans were capable of this sort of thing—they wouldn't have waited until we'd killed more than half of them before we found out about it! For that matter, why here? Why Shairez's base, and not mine, or Base Commander Fursa's? Unless we want to assume the humans somehow figured out what Shairez was going to be developing, why employ some sort of 'secret weapon' for the first time against a brand-new base where nowhere near as much of the local population has been killed?"

"With all due respect, Base Commander," Thairys said, "if it wasn't the humans, then who do you suggest it might have been?"

"That I don't know, sir," Barak said respectfully. "I'm simply suggesting that, logically, if humans could do this in the first place, they'd already have done it . . . and on a considerably larger scale."

"Are you suggesting that some other member of

the Hegemony might be responsible?" Thikair asked slowly.

"I think that's remotely possible . . . but *only* remotely, sir." Barak shrugged. "Again, I have no idea who—or what—it actually was. But I don't really see how any other member of the Hegemony could have penetrated our security so seamlessly. Our technology is as good as anyone else's. Probably even better, in purely military applications."

"Wonderful." Jainfar grimaced. "So all any of us have been able to contribute so far is that we don't have a clue who did it, or how, or even why! Assuming, of course, that it wasn't the *humans* . . . whom we've all now agreed don't have the capability to do it in the first place!"

"I think we've wandered about as far afield speculatively as we profitably can," Thikair said firmly. "I see no point in our helping one another panic from the depths of our current ignorance."

His subordinates all looked at him, most at least a little sheepishly, and he bared his canines in a frosty smile.

"Don't misunderstand me. I'm as . . . anxious about this as anyone else. But let's look at it. So far, we've lost one base and its personnel. All right, we've been hurt—badly. But whatever happened, it obviously took Shairez's entire base completely by surprise, and we know the sensor net didn't pick anything up. So, I think, the first thing to do is to put all our bases and personnel on maximum alert. Second, we emphasize that whoever was responsible may have some form of advanced stealth technology. Since we apparently can't rely on our sensors to detect it, we're going to have to rely on our own physical senses. I want all of our units to establish real-time, free-flow communications nets. All checkpoints will be manned, not left to the automatics, and all detachments will check in regularly with their central HQs. Even if we can't detect these people—whoever they are—on their way in, we can at least be certain we know when they've arrived. And I don't care *how* good their 'stealth technology' is. If we know they're there, we have enough troopers, enough guns, and enough heavy weapons on that planet to kill *anything*."

"Yes, Thairys?" Thikair said.

The ground force commander had lingered as the other senior officers filed out. Now he looked at the fleet commander, his ears half-folded and his eyes somber. "There were two small points I . . . chose not to mention in front of the others, sir," he said quietly.

"Oh?" Thikair managed to keep his voice level, despite the sudden cold tingle dancing down his nerves.

"Yes, sir. First, I'm afraid the preliminary medical exams indicate Base Commander Shairez was killed several hours *after* the rest of her personnel. And there are indications that she was . . . interrogated before her neck was broken."

"I see." Thikair looked at his subordinate for a moment, then cleared his throat. "And the second point?"

"And the second point is that two of the base's

neural education units are missing, sir. Whoever attacked Shairez's facility must have taken them with him. And if he knows how to operate them . . ."

The ground force commander's voice trailed off. There was, after all, no need for him to complete the sentence, since each of the education units contained the basic knowledge platform of the entire Hegemony.

XVI

"I almost wish something else would happen," Base Commander Fursa said. He and Base Commander Barak were conferring via communicator, and Barak frowned at him.

"I want to figure out what's going on as badly as you do, Fursa. And I suppose for us to do that, 'something else' *is* going to have to happen. But while you're wishing, just remember, you're the next closest major base."

"I know." Fursa grimaced. "That's my point. We're feeling just a bit exposed out here. I'm inclined to suspect that the *anticipation* is at least as bad as beating off an actual attack would be."

Barak grunted. His own base sat in the middle of a place that had once been called "Kansas," which put an entire ocean between him and whatever had happened to Shairez. Fursa's base, on the other hand, was located just outside the ruins of the human city of Moscow.

Still, almost two local weeks had passed. That

was a lot of time, when no one in the entire expedition had been able to come up with a workable explanation for what had happened. A lot of time for nerves to tighten, for the 'anticipation' Fursa had just mentioned to work on all of them.

And a lot of time for whoever had attacked Shairez's base to move his operations somewhere else entirely.

"You may have a point," he said finally, "but I can't say *I'm* looking forward to it. In fact, if I had my way"—his voice lowered—"I'd already be cutting my losses. This planet's been nothing but one enormous pain in the ass. I say take all our people off and level the place."

The base commanders' gazes met, and Barak saw the agreement hidden in Fursa's eyes. Any one of Fleet Commander Thikair's dreadnoughts was capable of sterilizing any planet. Of course, actually doing that would raise more than a few eyebrows among the Hegemony's member races. The sort of scrutiny it would draw down upon the Empire might well have disastrous consequences. But even so . . .

"Somehow, I don't think that particular solution's going to be very high on the Fleet Commander's list," Fursa said carefully.

"No, and it probably shouldn't be," Barak agreed. "But I'm willing to bet it's running through the *back* of his mind already, and you know it."

"Time check," Brigade Commander Caranth announced. "Check in."

"Perimeter One, secure."

"Perimeter Two, secure."

"Perimeter Three, secure."

"Perimeter Four, secure."

The acknowledgments came in steadily, and Caranth's ears twitched in satisfaction with each of them . . . until the sequence paused.

The brigade commander didn't worry for a moment, but then he stiffened in his chair.

"Perimeter Five, report," he said.

Only silence answered.

"Perimeter Five!" he snapped . . . and that was when the firing began.

Caranth lunged upright and raced to the command bunker's armored observation slit while his staff started going berserk behind him. He stared out into the night, his body rigid in disbelief as the stroboscopic fury of muzzle flashes ripped the darkness apart. He couldn't see anything but the flickering lightning of automatic weapons . . . and neither could his sensors. Yet he had infantry out there shooting at *something*, and as he watched, one of his heavy weapons posts opened fire, as well.

"*We're under attack!*" someone screamed over the net. "Perimeter Three—we're under attack! *They're coming through the—*"

The voice chopped off, and then, horribly, Caranth heard other voices yelling in alarm, screaming in panic, chopping off in mid-syllable. It was as if some invisible, unstoppable whirlwind was sweeping through his perimeter, and strain his eyes though he might, he couldn't even *see* it!

The voices began to dwindle, fading in a diminuendo that was even more terrifying than the gunfire, the explosion of artillery rounds landing on something no one could see. The firing died. The last scream bubbled into silence, and Caranth felt his heart trying to freeze in his chest.

The only sound was his staff, trying desperately to contact even one of the perimeter security points.

There was no answer, only silence. And then—

"What's *that*?" someone blurted, and Caranth turned to see *something* flowing from the overhead louvers of the bunker's ventilation system. There was no time even to begin to recognize what it was before the darkness crashed down on him like a hammer.

Fleet Commander Thikair felt a thousand years old as he sat in the silence of his stateroom, cursing the day he'd ever had his brilliant idea about using this planet and its eternally damned humans for the Empire's benefit.

It seemed so simple, he thought almost numbly. *Like such a reasonable risk. But then it all went so horribly wrong, from the moment our troopers landed. And now* this.

Base Commander Fursa's entire command was gone, wiped out in a single night. And in the space of less than eight hours, two infantry brigades and an entire armored regiment had been just as utterly destroyed.

And they still had absolutely no idea how it had happened.

They'd received a single report, from a platoon commander, claiming that he was under attack by humans. Humans who completely ignored the assault rifles firing into them. Humans who registered on no thermal sensor, no motion sensor. Humans who *could not* be there.

Maybe it isn't possible. Or maybe it's just one more lunacy about this entire insane planet. But whatever it is, it's enough. It's more than enough.

He punched a button on his communicator.

"Yes, Fleet Commander?" Ahzmer's voice responded quietly.

"Bring them up," Thikair said with a terrible, flat emphasis. "I want every single trooper off that planet within twelve hours. And then we'll let Jainfar's dreadnoughts use the Dainthar-cursed place for *target practice*."

It wasn't quite that simple, of course.

Organizing the emergency withdrawal of an entire planetary assault force was even more complicated than landing it had been. But at least the required troop lift had been rather drastically reduced, Thikair reflected bitterly. Over half his entire ground force had been wiped out. However small his absolute losses might have been compared with those of the humans, it was still a staggering defeat for the Empire, and it was all his responsibility.

He would already have killed himself, except that no honorable suicide could possibly expunge the stain he'd brought to the honor of his entire clan.

No, that would require the atonement of formal execution . . . and even that might not prove enough.

But before I go home to face His Majesty, there's one last thing I need to do.

"Are we ready, Ahzmer?"

"We are according to my readouts," the ship commander replied. But there was something peculiar about his tone, and Thikair looked at him.

"Meaning what?" he asked impatiently.

"Meaning that according to my readouts, all shuttles have returned and docked, but neither *Stellar Dawn* nor *Imperial Sword* have confirmed recovery of their small craft. All the other transports have checked in, but they haven't yet."

"What?"

Thikair's one-word question quivered with sudden, ice-cold fury. It was as if all his anxiety, all his fear, guilt, and shame suddenly had someone *else* to focus upon, and he showed all of his canines in a ferocious snarl.

"Get their commanders on the comm *now*," he snapped. "Find out what in Dainthar's Second Hell they think they're doing! And then get me Jainfar!"

"At once, sir! I—"

Ahzmer's voice chopped off, and Thikair's eyes narrowed.

"Ahzmer?" he said.

"Sir, the plot . . ."

Thikair turned to the master display, and it was his turn to freeze.

Six of the expedition's seven dreadnoughts were heading steadily away from the planet.

"What are they—?" he began, then gasped as two of the dreadnoughts suddenly opened fire. Not on the planet, but on their own escorts!

Nothing in the galaxy could stand up to the energy-range fire of a dreadnought. Certainly no mere scout ship, destroyer, or cruiser could.

It took less than forty-five seconds for every one of Thikair's screening warships to die, and three-quarters of his transport ships went with them.

"Get Jainfar!" he shouted at Ahzmer. "Find out what—"

"Sir, there's no response from Squadron Commander Jainfar's ship!" Ahzmer's communications officer blurted. "There's no response from *any* of the other dreadnoughts!"

"*What?*" Thikair stared at him in disbelief, and then alarms began to warble. First one, then another, and another.

He whipped back around to the master control screen, and ice smoked through his veins as crimson lights glared on the readiness boards. Engineering went down, then the Combat Information Center. Master Fire Control went offline, and so did Tracking, Missile Defense, and Astrogation.

And then the flag bridge itself lost power. Main lighting failed, plunging it into darkness, and Thikair heard someone gobbling a prayer as the emergency lighting clicked on.

"Sir?"

Ahzmer's voice was fragile, and Thikair looked at him. But he couldn't find his own voice. He could only stand there, paralyzed, unable to cope with the impossible events.

And then the command deck's armored doors slid open, and Thikair's eyes went wide as a human walked through them.

Every officer on that bridge was armed, and Thikair's hearing cringed as a dozen sidearms opened fire at once. Scores of bullets slammed into the human intruder . . . with absolutely no effect.

No, that wasn't quite correct, some numb corner of Thikair's brain insisted. The bullets went straight *through* him, whining and ricocheting off the bulkheads behind him, but he didn't even seem to notice. There were no wounds, no sprays of blood. It was as if his body were made of smoke, offering no resistance, suffering no damage.

He only stood there, looking at them, and then, suddenly, there were more humans. Four of them. Only *four* . . . but it was enough.

Thikair's mind gibbered, too overwhelmed even to truly panic as the four newcomers seemed to blur. It was as if they were half-transformed into vapor that poured itself through the command deck's air with impossible speed. They flowed across the bridge, *enveloping* his officers, and he heard screams. Screams of raw panic that rose in pitch as the Shongairi behind them saw the smoke flowing in *their* direction . . . and died in hideous, gurgling silence as it engulfed them.

And then Thikair was the only Shongair still standing.

His body insisted that he had to collapse, but somehow his knees refused to unlock. Collapsing would have required him to move . . . and something reached out from the first human's green eyes and forbade that.

The green-eyed human walked out into the body-strewn command and stopped, facing Thikair, his hands clasped behind him.

"You have much for which to answer, Fleet Commander Thikair," he said quietly, softly . . . in perfect Shongairi.

Thikair only stared at him, unable—not allowed—even to speak, and the human smiled. There was something terrifying about that smile . . . and something wrong, as well. The teeth, Thikair realized. The ridiculous little human canines had lengthened, sharpened, and in that moment Thikair understood exactly how thousands upon thousands of years of prey animals had looked upon his own people's smiles.

"You call yourselves 'predators.'" The human's upper lip curled. "Trust me, Fleet Commander—your people know nothing about *predators*. But they will."

Something whimpered in Thikair's throat, and the green eyes glowed with a terrifying internal fire.

"I had forgotten," the human said. "I had turned away from my own past. Even when you came to my world, even when you murdered billions of humans, I had forgotten. But now, thanks to you, Fleet Commander, I *remember*. I remember the obligations of honor. I remember a Prince of Wallachia's responsibilities. And I remember—oh, *how* I remember—the taste of vengeance. And that is what I find most impossible to forgive, Fleet Commander Thikair. I spent five hundred years learning to forget that taste, and you've filled my mouth with it again."

Thikair would have sold his soul to look away from those blazing emerald eyes, but even that was denied him.

"For an entire century, I hid even from myself, hid under my murdered brother's name, but now, Fleet Commander, I take back my *own* name. I am Vlad Drakula—Vlad, Son of the Dragon, Prince of Wallachia—and you have *dared* to shed the blood of those under *my* protection."

The paralysis left Thikair's voice—released, he was certain, by the human-shaped monster in front of him—and he swallowed hard.

"Wh—What do you—?" he managed to get out, but then his freed voice failed him, and Vlad smiled cruelly.

"I couldn't have acted when you first came even if I'd been prepared—willing—to go back to what once I was," he said. "There was only myself and my handful of closest followers. We would have been far too few. But then you showed me I truly had no choice. When you established your base to build the weapon to destroy every living human, you made my options very simple. I could not permit that—I *would* not. And so I had no alternative but to create more of my own kind. To create an army—not large, as armies go, but an army still—to deal with you.

"I was more cautious than in my . . . impetuous youth. The vampires I chose to make this time were better men and women than I was when I was yet breathing. I pray for my own sake that they will balance the hunger you've awakened in me once again, but do not expect them to feel any kindness where you and *your* kind are concerned.

"They are all much younger than I, new come to their abilities, not yet strong enough to endure the touch of the sun. But, like me, they are no longer breathing. Like me, they could ride the exterior of your shuttles when you were kind enough to return them to your transports . . . and your dreadnoughts. And like me, they have used your neural educators, learned how to control your vessels, how to use your technology.

"I will leave your neural educators here on Earth to give every single breathing human a complete Hegemony-level education. And, as you may have noticed, we were very careful not to destroy your industrial ships. What do you think a planet of humans will be able to accomplish over the next few centuries, even after all you've done to them, from that starting point? Do you think your Hegemony Council will be pleased?"

Thikair swallowed again, choking on a thick bolus of fear, and the human cocked his head to one side.

"I doubt the Council will be very happy with you, Fleet Commander, but I promise you *their* anger will have no effect upon your Empire. After all, each of these dreadnoughts can sterilize a planet, can it not? And which of your imperial worlds will dream, even for a moment, that one of your own capital ships might pose any threat to it at all?"

"No," Thikair managed to whimper, his eyes darting to the plot where the green icons of his other dreadnoughts continued to move away from the planet. "No, *please . . .*"

"How many human fathers and mothers would have said exactly the same thing to *you* as their children died before them?" the human replied coldly, and Thikair sobbed.

The human watched him mercilessly, but then he looked away. The deadly green glow left his eyes, and they seemed to soften as they gazed up at the taller human beside him.

"Keep me as human as you can, my Stephen," he said softly in English. "Remind me of why I tried so hard to forget."

The dark-skinned human looked back down at him and nodded, and then the green eyes moved back to Thikair.

"I believe you have unfinished business with this one, my Stephen," he said, and it was the bigger, taller, darker, and infinitely less terrifying human's turn to smile.

"Yes, I do," his deep voice rumbled, and Thikair squealed like a small trapped animal as the powerful, dark hands reached for him.

"This is for my daughters," Stephen Buchevsky said.